"Stop trying t[o] [change the]
subject, Jacob[.]"

Ann fairly shouted.

"I'm cold and I'm wet from this storm we're stuck in, and I'm not in the mood to spar with you anymore. Why won't you tell me what's wrong?"

With an abrupt twist, Jacob stalked angrily to the driftwood pile, hefted a few more pieces, then stalked back and laid them in the fire. Sparks and hisses sounded in the room. Startled, Ann stepped back. Then he stopped and removed his parka, his boots and his down overalls.

When he reached for his sweater, Ann exclaimed, "What are you doing?"

"Opening up. That's what you wanted, isn't it?" He whipped off his sweater and his turtleneck.

"Yes, but . . . you're undressing?" Her voice rose an octave or two.

His eyes darkened. "So should you."

Ann's mouth worked, but no sound came out.

"Did you hear me, Ann? I told you to take off your clothes."

Dear Reader,

Welcome to Silhouette **Special Edition** . . . welcome to romance. Each month, Silhouette **Special Edition** publishes six novels with you in mind—stories of love and life, tales that you can identify with—romance with that little "something special" added in.

This month is packed full of goodies in celebration of Halloween! Don't miss the continuation of Nora Roberts's magical new series, THE DONOVAN LEGACY. This month we're proud to present *Entranced*—Sebastian Donovan's story. And in November, don't miss the third of this enchanting series—*Charmed*.

October also launches a new series from Sherryl Woods—VOWS. These warm, tender tales will light up the autumn and winter nights with love. Don't miss *Love*—Jason Halloran's story in October, *Honor*—Kevin Halloran's story in November or *Cherish*—Brandon Halloran's story in December.

We're also pleased to introduce new author Sierra Rydell. Her first Silhouette **Special Edition** will be published this month as a PREMIERE title. It's called *On Middle Ground* and is set in Alaska—the author's home state. This month, watch for the debut of a new writer in each of Silhouette Books's four lines: Silhouette **Special Edition**, Silhouette Romance, Silhouette Desire and Silhouette Intimate Moments. Each book will have the special PREMIERE banner on it.

Rounding out this exciting month are books from other favorite writers: Andrea Edwards and Maggi Charles. And meet Patt Bucheister—her first **Special Edition**, *Tilt at Windmills*, debuts this month! Her work has been much celebrated, and we're delighted she's joined us with this wonderful book.

I hope you enjoy this book and all of the stories to come.

Sincerely,

Tara Gavin
Senior Editor
Silhouette Books

SIERRA RYDELL

ON MIDDLE GROUND

Silhouette®

SPECIAL EDITION®

Published by Silhouette Books New York

America's Publisher of Contemporary Romance

To Renee: As always, your insight sharpens my own.
To Brad: May your red pen never run out of ink.
To Tom: Thanks for keeping all those back issues of
National Geographic.

SILHOUETTE BOOKS
300 East 42nd St., New York, N.Y. 10017

ON MIDDLE GROUND

Copyright © 1992 by Ramona Rolle-Berg

ISBN: 0-373-09772-7

First Silhouette Books printing October 1992

All the characters in this book have no existence outside the imagination of the author and have no relation whatsoever to anyone bearing the same name or names. They are not even distantly inspired by any individual known or unknown to the author, and all incidents are pure invention.

Printed in the U.S.A.

SIERRA RYDELL's

first novel for Silhouette Books—*On Middle Ground*—was a finalist in the 1991 Romance Writers of America Golden Heart contest.

She has traveled extensively, even managing to see such exotic locales as Crete and Egypt with her twin sister during their college years. Her hobbies include everything from singing to ballroom dancing—she taught classes at Stanford University—to Kenpo Karate—"I'm thinking of writing a romance called *Ninja's Passion*. Just kidding!"

She lives in Anchorage, Alaska, with her husband and her recently born baby, Forrest. And although she's been writing full-time since 1986, she's also an actress and model, *and* runs a talent agency.

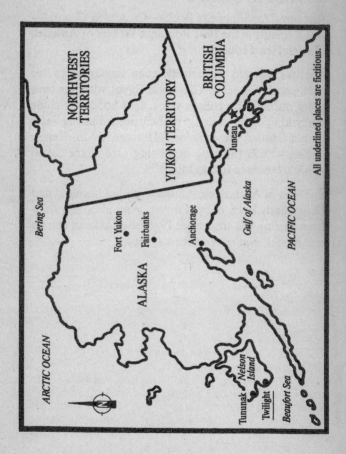

All underlined places are fictitious.

Chapter One

The warmth was spreading quickly now, pulling at him, urging him to give in, to surrender. He wanted to. God, how he wanted to. But he couldn't. He had to get up, keep walking. Warmth was his enemy; pain his only salvation. Oh God, Jonathan was gone. He had to stay awake, he had to. For Lia.

Slowly, painfully, he turned his head, seeking the comfort of her presence. But she was no longer beside him. Fear knotted his gut as he scanned the bleak landscape behind him for the motionless figure curled upon the frozen ocean of ice.

I'm coming, Lia! Don't give in. I can't lose you, too!

Bathed in sweat, he saw himself stand on feet long since numbed; saw himself stumble to retrace each hard-won step forward; saw himself reach out and gather the woman into his arms. Time held no meaning in this icy realm. Only cold and numbness and the terrifying temptation of sleep—and death.

Her body was stiff and unyielding; her beautiful black eyes closed and lifeless. Panic pumped hot blood into cold hands.

Lia! Wake up and look at me. Lia!

There was a tiny, fluttered movement. Through a blinding white tunnel he viewed the scene, husband and wife staring at each other across an ever-deepening chasm of life and death, an ocean frozen deeper and wider than the one on which they lay huddled.

The silence was white and absolute.

She blinked once, her eyes peaceful, accepting, begging him to let her go.

He felt a helpless rage. *No! We can make it! I know we can...Lia! Try, please, try. We've come so far. Don't give up now.*

He shook her again, refusing to believe, but she was already gone. He'd seen her pain. Now, in silence, he felt her loss.

And he couldn't bear it.

"No!" Jacob Toovak awoke suddenly, the remains of a loud silence ringing in his mind. Blood surged through his heart. He was hot. So hot! He covered his ears with his fists, desperately trying to blot out the sound; to stop the memory. But it was frozen in time.

His eyes squeezed shut in anguish. Would it ever stop? He threw back the covers to his bed, his feet hitting the bare floor with a cold slap. The one-room house was chilly but Jacob's nude body felt scorched. Burned from the inside out by a memory that seared his soul.

The nightmare was frighteningly real and horrifyingly familiar. The visions had returned every night for the past week. They came with the change in season and the merging of land and sea. They came with the certainty of unfinished business.

Swiftly he crossed the room to the window, one powerful arm carelessly thrusting aside a silver-haired, wolf-pelt curtain. No, it wasn't cold that he feared. Jacob scowled as he stared out the frost-laden window. Cold held no terror. He understood it as few men did.

It was the heat—the heat that seared him.

With hands that still shook from the aftereffects of his nightmare, he unlatched the window, allowing the Arctic breeze to cool the sweat on his body. The Alaskan landscape was a reassuring familiar gray. It was early, six-thirty, maybe seven. The sun wouldn't rise for several hours yet. Pale clouds hung low on a practically featureless horizon of low bluffs and rolling hills. There were no trees on Nelson Island, no trees anywhere within a hundred mile radius of Twilight, his village. Only flat land, a pale moon and a merciless sea.

The Bering Sea. Just looking at the pallid expanse of frozen ocean caused Jacob pain. For generations long forgotten, the Yup'ik Eskimo had subsisted from its treasures: salmon, herring, seal and walrus. He, too, had fished with joy and pride of kinship, heeding the old ways that respected the sea and the life-sustaining bounty it provided. But with Lia's death, joy had ended. As had so many other things.

Jacob inhaled deeply, willing the wind to cool his blood and slow his heart. He knew it would do both if he stood there long enough. His left hand gripped the wolf pelt. Would he ever forget?

He stared out at the landscape, where sky and land and sea were practically indistinguishable. Then he focused closer in, on the thermometer he'd nailed to the post outside the door. Twenty-five degrees. His hand dropped and he turned away, dispirited. No wonder he was burning up. The wolf pelt muffled the hollow sound of the wind as it settled back into place. Once again, silence surrounded him.

His glance avoided the double bed and landed instead on the green Formica countertop in the part of the room he called the kitchen. The tools beckoned him, as did the carvings of walrus ivory in various stages of completion. From past failed attempts, Jacob knew that more sleep was out of the question. Might as well do something productive.

He crossed to the foot of the bed and pulled on the clothes he'd worn the day before, leaving his feet bare. Then he moved to the table, sat down and picked up his tools. He began working, but for some reason, the work didn't provide the distraction it usually did. This morning the nightmare refused to release him; and he couldn't let it go.

After that last fateful hunt on the Bering Sea, the nightmare started. The months he'd spent in the hospital recuperating from severe malnutrition and frostbite, too weak to fight the threatening images, had allowed it to take a firm foothold in his mind. Only after returning to Twilight this summer and facing some of his subconscious demons had the nightmare eased.

But he had yet to hunt in the spring. And he still hated the silence of the Bering Sea.

Callused fingers closed around the cool pale ivory carving, his thumb smoothing down along the emerging curve of the Eskimo hunter's arm, as he forced his mind to respond to his will.

But it was no use. Since last week, he'd felt on edge and strangely expectant. Last night, when his father had gathered the men in the village and announced that two hunters from Toksook Bay, their nearest neighbor, hadn't returned from a hunt, Jacob thought he'd finally uncovered the cause of his sleepless nights. Thankfully the men had been found. Yet the feelings remained, eerie, persistent, stronger tonight than any previous night.

He'd learned to trust his instincts. Without them he would never have made it back to Twilight in the first place, back from the journey on the frozen Bering Sea. Jonathan hadn't believed they'd make it back, and in the end, neither had Lia. Jacob had been the only one, the only believer.

And for that belief he would pay the price of remembrance.

The delicate carving slipped from his fingers and fragmented on impact with the countertop. Jacob inhaled sharply. One small foot had broken away.

Slowly he expelled the pent-up breath. Days had gone into that portion of the carving. Hiding the flaw would not be easy—perhaps impossible. He reached for the broken limb, remembering a time when nothing had seemed impossible. Back then, he had been a brash young hunter and, like all providers, he'd longed to pit his skill and his strength against the awesome challenge of an ocean frozen deeper than a man was tall.

But he was no longer young. And he'd learned that not all things were possible.

"What you need, Jacob Toovak," he said aloud, "is a swift kick in the pants."

He said the words jokingly, as if levity would brighten his mood and erase the idea of his returning to the Bering Sea in spring. Just then, a familiar steady droning sound pierced the cold silence. An airplane. Swallowing hard against the sudden spurt of anxiety twisting his stomach, Jacob laid the ivory carving on the counter and grabbed his boots and parka.

He'd learned to trust his instincts. And right now, they were telling him the answer to his nightmares was on that plane.

* * *

"Hey, Mom, hurry up! You won't *belieeeve* this place!"

An almost forgotten sense of excitement stole over Ann Elliot as she heard the happiness in her son Patrick's voice. Everything had happened so fast these last two weeks: the job offer and her acceptance, the seemingly endless packing, and finally, the move itself. Why, to think that just last month, she'd been at her wits end . . .

"Holy sh—"

"Mom! Sharon said—"

"I heard what she said, Patrick, so there's no need to repeat it. And stay inside. It's got to be ten below out here."

Hefting a suitcase in each hand, she paused to both apologize and thank the two stern-faced men whose snowmobiles had ferried the three of them the short distance from the airstrip to the house. Great, she thought as she trudged along the snow-trodden path to their new home. Within the hour, every living person in the tiny Yup'ik Eskimo community of Twilight, Alaska, would know that the new high school math and science teacher couldn't properly control her own children. She could already hear them whispering and wondering how she would manage to control theirs.

Resigned, she hurried inside, dropping the cases in the tiny entryway. "This is the last time I'll say it, Sharon. I won't have you swearing, got that?" Angrily she pushed the hood of her down jacket off her head. "From now on..." Her voice wavered, then died as the impact of her surroundings sank into her consciousness. "Oh, my God," she whispered, stepping into the room.

"Totally rad, eh, Mom?"

"You're nuts, Patrick Elliot," the teenage girl responded in disgust. "This isn't a house, it's a shack. Mom, you can't seriously expect us to *live* here? It's freezing! There's no heat, no electricity!"

Patrick's response was a loud whoop of delight. "Yeah, Mom! It'll be just like the olden times—we were learning about them in school. People used to cut their own wood and cook over an open fire. Neat!"

Ann drew in a deep breath, let it out again and stepped back to shut the door with deliberate calm. "'Neat' is not the word I would have chosen," she told her son dryly, shooting a warning glance at her daughter's explosive expression.

"So where's the phone?" Sharon asked, her head swiveling about in disbelief. "Can anybody make out a phone?"

Silence met her question as all three pairs of eyes searched the dark rectangular room. Ann was still in shock. She'd been warned that the living arrangements were basic, but this...this was a far cry from what she'd imagined.

Sharon wailed, "I knew moving out to the boondocks was a crazy idea. What are we going to do without a phone?"

"We'll manage, I suppose," Ann said, wondering herself how they were going to accomplish that. "But first we need some light."

"You realize my friends won't even be able to reach me."

"Yeah, and all I can say is good riddance," mumbled Patrick, just loud enough to be heard. He'd moved into the room and was looking around. "Hey, over here! A couple of lamps."

"It's not my fault nobody likes you," Sharon shot back, making no move to join her mother and Patrick as they converged on the objects. "At least in Anchorage we had a real apartment. Not as good as Dad's house used to be, but—"

"That's enough, Sharon," Ann snapped. "We're not going back to Anchorage—not until next spring, anyway. So start making the best of it, okay?"

With that, Ann picked up the book of matches that someone had laid out and lit the two kerosene lamps. Immediately the room became cheerier. But not much.

The word "rustic" took on a whole new meaning as she surveyed what appeared to be the kitchen/dining/living room. When she'd agreed to teach the high school students in this tiny, out-of-the-way community nestled on the edge of Nelson Island, she hadn't cared how remote the place was. She'd been desperate for money and the job offer couldn't have come at a better time.

Now she wasn't so sure. Maybe she *had* made a mistake.

The soft light bathed the stacks of boxes she'd mailed last week. *At least we won't be without clothes,* she thought, looking around. Unlike their Anchorage apartment, which she'd decorated with the few remaining furnishings left over after selling their "nice" things to pay off her husband's debts, this place was...well, tiny. The kitchen, which occupied one corner of the room, had a royal blue countertop, with three doorless shelves suspended over it. The rickety dinette chairs would never fit a man's build, Ann guessed, thanking God that wouldn't be a problem.

And then there was the living room. It contained an old sofa that had likely started out white before Alaska's statehood in '59 but was definitely dark brown now, one coffee table, two mismatched end tables, one brownish-tweed recliner that looked as if it was reclining in its upright position, and an ancient-looking cook stove with controls that Ann couldn't even begin to decipher. On the floor was the only other colorful item besides the royal blue countertop—a huge bright orange oval rug that Ann supposed had been added to create some semblance of a "country hearth" atmosphere. Well, she decided as her stunned gaze settled on one of the kerosene lamps glowing softly against what she now noticed were pale green walls, "country" would definitely describe the living room, but which country? She doubted very much if the decorator was a subscriber to *Southern Living*.

"I've got dibs on this room," Patrick's voice, only slightly muffled through the walls, came from somewhere to her right. Why, thought Ann as she picked up one of the lamps and followed her daughter's stampede down the short hallway, why were life's ups and downs so much harder to bear when children were involved? Before entering the room, Ann sent up a silent prayer.

She was disappointed.

Unlike the pale green paint covering the walls of the living room, the walls here were of raw wood. In the dim arc of light thrown by the lamp, two single beds, covered by handmade beige spreads, were revealed. The single square window was draped by a brightly patterned length of material. Opposite the window stood a six-shelf chest of drawers. Two weathered nightstands and another bright oval rug—pink, this time—completed the ensemble.

For once, Patrick was speechless.

Again, the school superintendent had said it was "basic," but Ann had taken that to mean no automatic dishwasher, no microwave, no wall-to-wall carpeting. Now, though, she could tell that her idea of roughing it was a far cry from the reality. Just what had she gotten them into? She surveyed the tear in the makeshift curtain and the dirty, unswept floor. How was she going to get the guts to tell the children they would obviously be sharing it?

Oh, Lord! Ann squeezed her eyes shut, then opened them wide as an awful thought occurred to her. *What if there's no bathroom!*

Telling herself to calm down, that surely things weren't *that* bad, she smiled brightly at her two kids and announced, "This is charming."

Sharon rolled her eyes. "Sure, Mom. If you're a homeless person."

Patrick was suspiciously silent; he seemed to be considering that as an option.

"Oh come on, you two," she cajoled, offering a silent prayer that they need never know just how close they had come to being homeless. "All it needs is a little elbow grease. Why, I can already imagine how nice it will be with your Batman poster on the wall over there, Patrick, and your knick-knacks on the dresser, Sharon. It might be a little rustic, but it's got lots of potential."

"For disaster," Sharon mumbled, going to sit on one of the beds. The expression on her face was slightly nauseous.

Apparently the gist of her mother's comment hadn't sunk in yet. Ann decided not to wait for the inevitable explosion. Spinning on her heel, she made her way down the rest of the hallway. She felt like Jacques Cousteau in a dark, cold underwater cave, except that she was *In Search Of The Commode.* Was she getting hysterical? Had these last two weeks finally cracked the control that had frozen her emotions for so many years? Opening the first door she spotted, Ann peered inside. There wasn't much to look at: a crude chest of drawers, a double bed and another oval rug—red. Retreating, she reached for the only other door, praying for success.

And there it was. Small to be sure, but at this point it amounted to a very big luxury. With a relieved sigh, Ann leaned her forehead against the wall and closed her eyes. How this place was going to come anywhere near cozy she had no idea.

Suddenly a hoarse cry of rage rent the air. Ann raised her head. Apparently Sharon had figured it out.

"Mom...Mom!"

"Down here, honey," she responded, straightening and closing the bathroom door.

Two pairs of very agitated feet dashed up to her.

"Mom!" Patrick said again, rushing up to Ann, his eyes filled with worry. "Sharon said that you said we have to share a room."

She nodded. "I'm afraid so."

"Aw, Mom!"

"See, I told you so," Sharon announced in disgust, flipping her long spiral curls over her shoulder. Opening the bathroom door, she peeked inside.

"Hey!" Patrick sputtered, slapping his sister's hair out of his face. "You mean I really gotta share with spiral gyra over there?"

"It's no picnic living with you, either, bat breath," Sharon wailed, and slammed the door. "Oh, yuck!" She turned to her mother. "I can't shower in there. There's hardly any room."

"If you cut that mane, there'll be plenty of space," Patrick shot back.

"Look, this is never gonna work. Why did you take this job anyway? Dad would never have let us live like this."

Ann bit back her reply that he wouldn't have cared. There was so much her daughter didn't know. Two years had passed since she and Richard had separated; but only one year since his untimely death. Now was not the time to disillusion her daughter about her father. Sharon wasn't ready for the truth, and perhaps never would be. "Sharon—"

"I mean, I'm fifteen years old, practically a woman! I shouldn't have to sleep in the same room with *him.*"

Ann took several deep breaths. "Let's just cease and desist, okay? We're here and you're going to have to get used to a lot more than just sharing a room, so you both might as well look on the bright side."

The moment the words were out of her mouth, a gust of wind shook the entire house. A loud crash reverberated through the walls.

"What was that?" asked Patrick.

"I don't know," she said, holding out her arm to stop him from barreling back into the living room. "But I want the both of you to go back to your room and decide who's going to sleep where. Here—" she handed Patrick the lamp "—be careful, and wait until I call you before you come out."

"But, Mom," Patrick objected, "shouldn't I be with you?"

Ever since his father's death, Patrick had taken it upon himself to be the man of the house. It was all Ann could do not to reach out and give him a fierce hug. A familiar ache rose in her throat. She wanted her kids to have so much. But the odds were against a thirty-three-year-old widow with two growing kids marrying again. Even if she did want to, another marriage was highly unlikely. Richard had told her often enough how plain she was.

"I'll be all right, sweetheart." She put her hand on his shoulder. "Now please, do as I say."

Ann waited until they were in their room, then made her way down the hallway. She paused at the entrance to the dimly lighted living area. Snow-covered boxes covered the floor space. The front door stood wide open, allowing cold wind and snow to swirl into the room. Shivering, her eyes caught a movement off to her left. She blinked.

What in the world?

Chapter Two

Two figures stood there, shrouded in shadows and covered with snow. For a moment she thought they were the two men who had ferried the three of them from the airstrip. But the sizes were all wrong, and so were their clothes. Where one was lean and tall—six feet, she estimated—the other was big and broad, filling the small room with the force of his presence. This second man was bareheaded and bent over the boxes, mumbling to his taller companion in a language she didn't understand. He was wearing a fur parka and jeans. Calf-high fur boots covered his feet; well-worn gloves, his hands. His voice and the sheer physical strength he portrayed as he picked up three of her larger moving boxes indicated that this stranger—whoever he was—was in charge.

"Here, better let me give you a hand with those," she spoke, hurrying forward. But at that precise moment, her foot slid on something slick and her feet shot out from under her.

"Watch out!"

"What the—"

The oath was cut short as she careened into and knocked the legs out from under both men. Ann cried out, alarmed as boxes flew in all directions. Her hands rose instinctively, the

sudden impact with the floor taking the air from her lungs.
The heavy crush of a body a scant second later almost finished her off.

Stunned and breathless, she lay pinned beneath the massive chest. Ann inhaled, taking quick shallow little gasps.
Every part of her body felt battered.

As if from far off, she heard the quick shuffle of footsteps.

"Jacob. Billy. You all right?"

Beneath the crush of fur, Ann recognized the concerned
voice. It was Ben Toovak, Twilight's mayor and the man who
had hired her. She tried groaning, but it came out more like a
squeak. Somehow she'd hoped to make a better first impression.

"Yeah, Ben, I'm fine," came from somewhere off to her
left. The youthful voice sounded amused. "But I'm not too
sure about Mrs. Elliot."

"Jacob, son, get up before you kill Mrs. Elliot."

After what seemed like an eternity, "Jacob" rolled off her
and sat up—all two tons of him. But Ann wasn't certain she
could take a deep breath even if she wanted to. Squished did
not adequately describe her present physical condition.

"Are you all right?"

The Crusher's voice was deep-timbered. Her eyelids flickered twice, then opened.

"I—yes, I think so," she squeaked.

He was leaning over her. Black hair hung in a single straight
sheet to his collar. His features were distinctly Native, broad
and round and open, with high cheekbones and a wide full
mouth. But it was his eyes that caught and held her attention. They were midnight-black and angry. And they were
unflinchingly direct, despite the muted light.

"You sure you're okay, Mrs. Elliot?" asked Billy.

Ann resisted the impulse to say no. The dark eyes continued their silent perusal. He made her self-conscious of her
prone position.

"I'm fine," she said, breaking the contact.

"Don't just stand there, Billy, help her up," said the Mayor.

"If you ask me, she don't look so hot. Maybe we ought to
let her cool out some more."

The boy looked to be about seventeen, with short straight
black hair and wide-set eyes. At six feet, he was tall for a Na-

tive. Biting down on her lip, Ann managed a weak smile at the youth and sat up. "Really, I'm fine. I don't suppose you'd look too hot, either, if you'd just survived a head-on collision with an iceberg," she said, motioning toward a silent Jacob.

From the front doorway, a muffled laugh joined those of Billy's and Ben's. To Ann, the new visitor looked like a walking snowman. A blanket of white crystals covered the girl's knee-length dresslike parka and jeans. In her arms, she carried another of Ann's moving boxes.

"Where do you want this, Mrs. Elliot?" asked the girl.

Did everyone know who she was? Obviously, Ann thought, tossing a bemused glance around the cluttered room. With just under three-hundred people, Twilight was more village than town. A new face was likely a big event.

"For now, anywhere you can find space. As you can see, it's going to take me a while to organize everything."

"I'll help you, if you want." The teenage girl smiled shyly. "It would be fun. Like Christmas when you get to open presents and you don't know what you'll find."

"Right," Billy teased, tugging on one of the girl's waist-long black braids. "Next she'll tell us she still believes in Santa Claus."

She glared up at him. "I do not."

"Sure you don't." He turned to Ann. "This is Siksik and I'm Billy Muktoyuk, Twilight's basketball pro." He mimed shooting a free throw. "The old guy's Ben Toovak, our esteemed leader, and you've already run into Jacob, the resident iceberg."

Ann winced and shot a quick look sideways. No change. Those angry black eyes were still trained on her. Unnerved, she looked away and encountered Siksik's pained expression.

"Billy. . ." Ben was trying to hide his smile behind a frown of disapproval, but Ann suspected they all knew he was a softy. "If you've finished the introductions, there are a few more boxes outside."

Hoping to ease Siksik's embarrassment at Billy's teasing, Ann remarked, "Thanks for volunteering, Siksik. If the kids and I need help, I'll be sure to call you."

Siksik threw her a grateful glance and Ann watched her exit with Ben, who shut the door behind them.

The silence was as loud as it was abrupt. Ann glanced sideways again, baffled by Jacob Toovak's continued scrutiny. Was he that upset because she'd knocked him down? She definitely shouldn't have called him an iceberg. What if this incident became a village joke? A sense of humor didn't seem to be one of the man's outstanding character traits.

Suddenly Jacob Toovak jerked to his feet, pulled off his gloves and shoved them deep into his pockets, giving his back to Ann. Startled, her eyes followed the stilted movements. There wasn't a hint of pliancy in the forceful body his profile presented. He stood with his back straight, his shoulders stiff, his mouth unyielding. Several moments ticked by. Ann got the impression he was steeling himself against something. Her? She cleared her throat. It was time to make amends.

At the sound, Jacob Toovak turned. Their gazes met and again Ann was struck by the expression in his eyes, only it was different now. Haunted. Not angry as he'd been at first.

"Can you stand?"

She'd been so absorbed with the man, she'd completely forgotten she was still sprawled on the floor. Ann looked up at the hand he'd extended, almost afraid to take it. Her hands moved to wipe themselves on her down jacket, and she realized she was garnering her defenses.

"Thank you. I'd like to apologize for running into you like that. I should have realized when we tracked our boots in here that the floor would be slippery." She placed her hand in his. He helped her up. "Ann Elliot."

"Jacob Toovak."

A tiny ripple of unease shivered up her arm as her cold fingers vanished in his grasp. His hand, like everything else about him, was massive. She noted he hadn't offered any of the conventional "that's okay" or "never mind, forget it" responses people uttered when faced with an apology. "So," Ann paused, searching for something to say. "You're Ben's son, Mr. Toovak?"

"Jacob. Unlike those of the *kass'aq* culture, we Yup'ik aren't a formal people."

Am I supposed to call him Jacob? Ann wasn't sure. Especially considering the past few minutes. She decided to play it safe.

"*Kass'aq.* That sounds Russian."

He nodded. "It's our word for the white man."

Having grown up in Anchorage, Ann was familiar with the names of the various Native peoples. But as she looked at Jacob Toovak's handmade clothes, she realized how sparse her knowledge really was.

"The Yup'ik are an open, giving people, Mrs. Elliot. You need only ask and they will gladly tell you all about themselves."

Startled, her eyes flew up to his. "I—I suppose I won't have much choice, really. I mean, it's rather like learning a language, isn't it? If you really want to become fluent, the best course of action is to live someplace where the language is spoken."

Dark eyebrows raised a fraction. "And that's why you're here? You want to learn about the Yup'ik?"

He pronounced it "u-pick," which was different from the "yup-ick" sounding adaptation she'd been using.

"It's part of the reason I'm here." Her gaze dropped to examine the dark spots on the silvery parka he wore. She wondered what kind of fur it was. "I'm fairly certain many of my impressions of Native life and people will undergo changes in the next few months."

"This should do it, Mrs. Elliot," Billy said as the door burst open. His arms were loaded with two boxes. Siksik and Ben followed, each carrying one. At their entrance, Jacob's gaze veered to the kitchen, his attention once again absorbed, concentrated. Ann didn't know what to make of him.

"Thank you. I really appreciate your help." She smiled at the trio, then spoke directly to Billy and Siksik. "I guess I'll see you two in class tomorrow, right?"

A chorus of groans followed their footsteps outside. Ben turned to her with a knowing smile.

"Children never change, do they?" He crossed the room to where she stood next to his son. "Although it's late in coming, welcome to Twilight."

Ann smiled and shook the hand he'd extended. She'd developed an instinctive liking for the man during their few telephone conversations. Meeting him, seeing the kind expression on his broad, weathered face, only confirmed her impression.

"Thank you. I'm really glad to be here. We all are."

Ben glanced at Jacob, an odd expression in his eyes, then back at her. "Has my son been telling you about our village?"

There was a small silence. "Well, actually, you weren't gone very long," she offered finally. "I was just going to ask him to tell me about the school." The statement was a blatant fib. She hadn't been about to ask him anything. And judging from Jacob's absorbed expression as he looked around the house, he wasn't interested in playing tour guide. Ann wasn't even sure he was listening.

Ben hesitated, his glance settling briefly on his son. "Jacob can give you a good idea of what you'll be up against. He's been teaching your classes."

Ann just managed to contain a groan. Though they hadn't exchanged more than a few words, she already knew she wasn't going to be at ease with this man. Ben was fine, he was easy to talk to. And the kids—no problem. But there was something about Jacob Toovak that set her on edge. She pasted a smile on her face.

"I see."

"My son agreed to do so until the school superintendent could hire a substitute."

Ann was watching Jacob when he turned to Ben.

"I don't recall 'agreeing' to anything, Father."

His tone was even, yet judging from Ben's obvious discomfiture, Ann sensed undercurrents of friction.

"No, I guess you didn't, son." Ben spoke a few rapid words of Yup'ik, then glanced at Ann. "Mr. Card—he was the last teacher—left shortly after the term started in August. Under the circumstances, the village council decided that Jacob was the most qualified to fill in."

Ann wanted to ask exactly what circumstances, but just then Jacob pulled off his parka and laid it over one of the end tables. Was he planning on staying awhile? The thought filled her with dismay.

"I hope you enjoy your stay here. This home needs the laughter of children." Ben looked over at Jacob, his dark eyes seemingly troubled, then turned to Ann. "Mrs. Elliot—"

"Please, call me Ann."

His soft black eyes left her face to glance around the room. "Is something wrong with the electricity? The generator should be working. I had Billy test it last week."

"There's electricity?" Relief flooded her senses. The kids would be ecstatic.

Jacob shot her a penetrating look. "We may be basic, but we're not primitive."

Ann blushed, embarrassed. Ben threw Jacob a look of annoyance as he crossed the room, sidestepping the boxes to the kitchen. Reaching behind the cook stove, he flicked a switch. Nothing happened.

"I'll be right back. It's probably something simple." Ben shuffled outside, throwing Jacob a warning glance before the door slammed shut behind him.

Jacob bent and hefted the two boxes closest to his feet. "Where do you want these?"

"Mr. Toovak, you don't have to do that. We can take care of it from here."

"You're determined to begin classes tomorrow?"

She nodded. She didn't know what to make of the quizzical look he gave her. "Then I'll need to bring you up to date on what the students have accomplished so far this term. And I might as well move boxes while I'm doing it."

He did have a point, Ann conceded. She'd need his input if she wanted to be prepared tomorrow. Only, she had the impression he was forcing himself into helping her, and that made her uncomfortable. Squinting in the dim light, she studied the coding she'd used on each box. "That top one stays here," she replied, looking up at Jacob, gray eyes riveted on the broad expanse of chest outlined by a cream-colored, cable-knit sweater. She blinked, disturbed by her behavior. "The bottom one belongs in my bedroom. I'll take care of it."

Ann could swear a look of panic crossed his face, but it was gone so quickly, and he turned away so abruptly, that she decided she must have imagined it.

His movements were precise and economical. So were the words he used to describe his students' lower level of achievement in math and science. Watching him walking the few steps into the living area, she somehow felt certain the control he exhibited was an intricate part of who he was. What was odd about her certainty—and what she couldn't explain—was the feeling that, somehow, that control was being severely tested.

"What level would you say they're at?"

"Except for Siksik and Billy and maybe one or two others, higher mathematics is a foreign concept. You'll have your work cut out for you just to get them used to algebra."

Ann watched Jacob as he stacked. His face was expressionless, yet the tension in the air was palpable. "So the test results we get in Anchorage are pretty much on target?"

"If by that you mean the remote villages test lower on aptitude exams, then yes. But that doesn't mean the children here are backward or incapable of learning. They have a different life-style and consequently study the aspects of that way of life. Most of them attend school because the state forces the villages to educate their young in *kass'aq* ways."

"I see."

Jacob's face tightened. "Do you? I doubt it. You have a lot to learn about the Yup'ik, Mrs. Elliot."

"That's why I'm here, Mr. Toovak." Apparently he could no more call her Ann than she could use his first name.

"To teach."

"Yes, of course."

He bent and picked up two more boxes. "You could do that in Anchorage."

"True, but not full time, and that's what I wanted." *More like needed,* Ann thought as she picked up a box and carried it into the kitchen. She had other reasons, but they were not open for casual discussion—even if such were possible with this man, which she seriously doubted. "Teachers in Anchorage are lucky. They may be underpaid and overworked for Anchorage—and having substituted for them, I know they are—but they do earn some of the highest teaching salaries in the nation. And that translates into fewer vacancies. If you like teaching, you just don't get up and walk out of a job like that. Not in today's economy."

And not if you needed to feed a family. Ben's offer had been a godsend. Until spring she'd have no monthly rent to worry about, no utility bills to cry over and no car expenses to pay. There were no cars on Nelson Island. Everyone used snowmobiles and three and four-wheelers. Foodstuffs not provided by nature were brought in by plane.

"Why did the last teacher leave?"

He looked around, his gaze lingering on one object and then another. He almost seemed to be testing himself. "Twilight turned out to be too remote."

There was a long brittle silence.

"Well, that won't happen with me." She tried sounding confident, but it was obvious he didn't believe her.

"The walls are thin. By your standards, I suppose this *is* a shack," Jacob replied, repeating Sharon's earlier description of the cabin.

A sharp gasp escaped her. "What...I mean, how...?"

"Your daughter's not very impressed with the accommodations."

Mortified, Ann winced. "Sharon's young. All she needs is a little time to adjust."

"And if she doesn't, what then?" Jacob paused, a definite challenge in his eyes. "Do you just pack up your boxes and leave on the next available flight?"

Now she thought she understood the reason for the intense scrutiny he'd subjected her to. He expected her to leave, just as the other teacher had.

"No, I told you, she'll adjust. We all will."

"Even now that you've seen how primitive the conditions are compared to what you're used to?"

Ann didn't hesitate. "Of course, that goes without saying." She decided to ignore the knowledge that he had somehow overheard Sharon's remarks. "I signed a contract and I intend to fulfill it. My family and I will remain in Twilight until spring."

"Forceful words, Mrs. Elliot. What will you say when it's forty below outside and your daughter complains that her eyelashes are frozen? Or when a fifty-mile-an-hour wind blows up so much snow that you can't find your way to the school building? What then?"

She looked up, beginning to get angry. This man had no concept of what she was and wasn't used to.

"It's obvious to me that your people survive this weather generation after generation. So why shouldn't we?" Though she was unaware of it, her words rang true to her feelings, showing Jacob that this was something she believed in. "I admit, my children are used to a different standard of living, but so what? That doesn't mean we can't adapt and learn new things."

Suddenly the room was flooded with light as the generator kicked on. They blinked and stared at each other, a weighing, evaluating sort of we-know-where-we-stand look. She swallowed, distinctly uncomfortable with her reaction to this man.

A sound made her glance away. Patrick was walking toward them, having traversed about half the distance across the room from the hallway. He was alone.

"Mom, are you all right? We heard a big crash and people talking . . . and then when the lights came on out here . . ."

"Patrick—" She started to send him back—to admonish him for disobeying her orders—but he had to have been worried. Considering the situation, she really couldn't blame him.

But where was Sharon? Her daughter was usually the first to answer the door, the first to pick up the phone. Was her absence just another subtle dig, intended to demonstrate her lack of interest in her new surroundings? Or had she for once decided to obey instructions and stay put?

Patrick hurried to her side, all the while staring up at the stranger. Ann brushed back his light brown curls and looked at Jacob.

"Mr. Toovak, this is Patrick," she said, her voice filled with pride.

He was gazing intently at her son, his eyes gentle and welcoming, the smile on his face genuine. Ann was shocked at the change in him, especially considering the antagonism she'd felt emanating from him earlier. Nevertheless, she was grateful for his attempt to lighten the atmosphere in the room.

"Hello, Patrick," Jacob said.

Ann felt her son squirm. He looked up at her. "Is he a real live Eskimo?"

Jacob chuckled and Ann felt herself smile, too, despite the embarrassment that flushed her cheeks at her son's innocent remark.

"I'm about as real and as alive an Eskimo as you're ever likely to meet," Jacob said.

"So that's why you're wearing those funny-looking boots, right, Mr. Toovak?"

"Patrick! Of all the—"

"That's all right, Mrs. Elliot." Ann was amazed at the change in him. He turned back to the young boy. "You can call me Jacob, and these—" he pointed to his feet "—are mukluks. They're made from seal skin and caribou hide."

"Neat!" Patrick looked up at her for permission and she nodded. "Jacob sure doesn't sound like an Eskimo name. I

had a friend at my old school whose name was Jacob and I
know for sure *he* wasn't an Eskimo."

Jacob's lips quirked at the child's obvious displeasure.
"Believe it or not, Patrick, I'd use Toovak instead of Jacob,
if I could. But Toovak's a pretty common name around here."

"Oh." He thought about it for a moment. "Like Smith,
you mean?"

"Right."

Ann tried to keep a straight face, but it wasn't easy, especially when she saw Jacob holding back a laugh of his own as
he turned away to pick up his parka. It was then that she noticed his limp.

It was slight, but not so slight that it wasn't noticeable when
he walked even the few steps across the room. The muted light
from the kerosene lamp must have obscured it. Had she hurt
him earlier? The thought disturbed her, but shared laughter
stopped her from delving deeper into why. Patrick had asked
Jacob something about igloos.

"Yes, it's cold in an igloo, but it's colder outside. And no,
you can't see mine, because the Yup'ik don't live in igloos."

"You don't?" His voice registered all the disgust and disappointment a ten-year-old could mount. "I thought all real
Eskimos lived in igloos."

Jacob slipped the parka on, then zipped it closed. "Do your
friends all live in apartments?"

"Heck no!" the boy exclaimed, moving closer to the older
man. "You sure do have a lot to learn about us, Jacob," he
said in all seriousness. "If you have any questions, just ask
me, okay?"

Ann watched the interplay between Jacob and her son, a
bemused expression on her face. Patrick looked so serious.
For an instant her mind's eye perceived him as the adult he
was destined to be. She sighed, wondering as she blinked away
the image, if she was up to the challenge it would represent.
Especially since Patrick was getting to the age where he'd begun shying away from the typically "female" activities she
tended to be better at.

She walked over and put her hand on his small shoulder,
squeezing it tightly. He looked up into her eyes. "Take one of
your boxes and go start unpacking, will you, Patrick? I'd like
a word with Mr. Toovak."

"Jacob, Mom."

Her gaze flickered to the man, then back to the boy.

"Jacob." She forced a smile and watched her son walk over to one of the smaller boxes and pick it up.

"See ya, Jacob."

"Tonight, actually," Jacob said, surprising them both. "The mayor has invited the three of you to dinner. Since I'll be there, I'll see you then."

"Totally rad! Wait till I tell Sharon!" Patrick said, rushing from the room.

Without him, the room again fell silent. "It would seem you've made a conquest," Ann said, and shivered against the chill in the air, hugging herself, rubbing her arms. "About this dinner—"

"It's customary," he interrupted abruptly, making his way over to the black stove. "This is your heating system."

Disliking his preemptory attitude, Ann nevertheless followed behind him, observing wordlessly as he reached down to grab what looked like a long hook fashioned from cast iron. "Now watch," he said, and proceeded to explain to her how to light the stove to heat the house.

Ben returned as they were finishing up. "Sorry about the delay." His gaze darted from Ann's strained features to his son's uncompromising face. "Jenna called from Providence Hospital. Hanna's doing fine, but they can't fly home. The Anchorage airport's closed due to bad weather."

"But it was clear this morning," Ann commented.

Ben shrugged. "Apparently a heavy fog drifted in mid-morning. You were lucky to get here."

Was she? Ann took a look at Jacob's closed expression, fairly certain he was wondering the same thing.

Chapter Three

"Do you remember your first Emperor Goose?"

Siksik looked up from her position on Jacob's polar bear rug, her long legs stretched comfortably straight out in front of her. In her lap lay the beginnings of a dried grass basket. "Who could forget? The fog was so dense. It seemed like we walked a long way that morning, you and Jonathan with your fishing gear and me with that little bow and arrow you'd made for me. Mom said it was the best goose we ever ate. And you were so mad because everyone was making a fuss over my puny little bird when you two had caught a fat seal." She laughed, a soft, lighthearted sound, her fingers manipulating the long grass blades into a tight circular coil.

"Yeah," Jacob chuckled, remembering his father's praise later that day. "It *was* the first thing you ever caught, so I forgave you for taking the glory."

His eyes warmed as he looked down at his sister's gleaming black head. Though they were seventeen years apart, they were very close. She was a big girl, strong and athletic, but while the description fit Jacob, he knew it bothered his sister. The village children often teased her because of her height. All except Billy Muktoyuk, who topped six feet.

"Don't forget that all three of us had the honor of sharing with the main families," Jacob added. In Twilight, as in most Yup'ik villages where subsistence was the way of life, the sharing of food was customary. The main families received the offerings and, in turn, shared their gifts with their relatives. Nothing was ever wasted.

"I'm supposed to remind you to pick up Mrs. Elliot and to bring your plate with you for dinner. Mom doesn't have enough to go around."

Jacob grunted, his own hands busy with the ivory carving. He didn't want to think about this evening's dinner.

As if she'd somehow discerned his thoughts, Siksik remarked, "What do you think of the new teacher? She seems real nice."

"I'm waiting until after the first *beckcheektook*. If she survives the blizzard, ask me again."

Siksik nodded as if this were perfectly acceptable, her gaze focused on her work.

As he watched his sister, his thoughts sped back to that morning. He'd arrived at the shoreline just as the Twin Otter landed. Practically the whole village had turned out, everyone eager to watch or to help unload the cargo bay of mail and supplies. Jacob's curiosity would have pulled him to the frozen landing strip even if his instincts hadn't insisted.

A woman, a young boy and a teenage girl had deplaned. At first he'd been surprised. Normally he arranged housing for incoming visitors. Twilight was small enough that lodging was scarce and visitors usually ended up staying in private homes. However, no one had told him about their arrival. He'd watched the villagers welcome her as the new teacher. That had been his second surprise. Remaining aloof, he'd watched the older woman greet the villagers, all the while wondering why he hadn't been told. Then he'd followed behind Billy's snowmobile, his own loaded with their belongings. Billy hadn't stopped at the usual teacher's lodging, a small one-room house much like Jacob's. Instead he'd passed by that house, driving farther through the village until it became obvious to Jacob where Billy was going.

He was headed for Jacob's old house. The house that he hadn't set foot in since Lia's death. That was when Jacob knew that this woman was the cause of his sleepless nights.

He looked up from the Eskimo hunter carving. "Why didn't Dad tell me about the new teacher? And why is she moving into my old house? Is there something wrong with the place Mr. Card stayed in?"

"Not that I know of, except that maybe it was too small for her and her children. Besides, your old place has been empty for three years." She grunted over a particularly stubborn blade, then continued in Yup'ik. "I think you were away at the Gathering of the Clans when she was hired. Probably the village council decided and Dad forgot to tell you when you got back." She looked up, a question in her eyes. "You don't mind, do you?"

Brother and sister looked at each other. Jacob didn't bother hiding the confusion he was feeling, the emotions that had seized hold of his mind when he'd entered the house. Stepping into that room, he'd been overcome with the same violent emotions he'd felt when he'd first set foot on the tundra after three years away at college in Fairbanks. Part of him had wanted to leave immediately, had wanted to return to his one-room house and forget the presence of the new teacher. He'd felt afraid and confused, caught like a fish in a complex net of choices, only one of which led to freedom and understanding. So he'd endured the house, the memories and the pain.

"I know you feel horrible about what happened." Siksik's voice was soft, hesitant. "But it wasn't your fault, Jacob. Each of you had an equal chance to make it back home."

"Did we?"

"Yes, you did. All three of you knew what to do to survive. We're taught that from early on. Only Jonathan wasn't strong like you. And Lia…" She shrugged, then added, "It's part of our way, Jacob."

"Siksik…" he began, but she dropped her work and held up her hand.

"I know, you loved them both. So did I, but Jonathan—he was always doing something he shouldn't. He would have gone alone that day if you hadn't agreed to go with him."

"And Lia?" Jacob heard the bitterness in his voice.

"Listen, brother, I may be fifteen, but I know something about love. For Lia it was 'Where you go, I go,'" she murmured.

Jacob looked at her sharply for a long moment, but her head had dropped over her work again. "When did you get to be so smart?"

"Listening to Mom," she replied matter-of-factly, giving Jacob the impression that, for the moment, she was the elder of the two. "I asked her why no one talks about Lia anymore and she told me because it would hurt you."

Jacob smiled wryly. "So why are we talking about her?" His hands stilled, wrapped around the ivory carving.

"Because of great-grandma Siksik. When she died, I didn't want to talk about her, either. But after a while, I discovered that it was nice remembering the things we used to do together. And every time I tell one of her stories, I can't help but remember her, too." She looked up, her black eyes reflecting certainty. "It's been three years since Lia died. Lots has happened to you since then. I figured it was time."

He looked down at the carving that was missing a foot, then down to his own sock-clad feet. He'd lost more than the toes on his right foot as a result of that fateful hunt. To him, it was a constant reminder of his failure.

"By the way, did you get to meet Mrs. Elliot's kids after we left? Her daughter's supposed to be my age."

Jacob resumed carving, grateful for the distraction. Though Siksik would find out for herself tonight, he had the feeling that Sharon Elliot wasn't going to like her classmates any more than she liked her new home. "I met her son. He seems like a good kid." He wondered what had happened to Mr. Elliot, then decided Mrs. Elliot's ringless left hand was none of his business. He looked down at the coil forming in his sister's capable hands. "So, what's this basket going to be used for?"

"Mom said she needed a new one for the *mat-chew* potatoes. But if it's good enough, she might want to sell it."

Jacob had been reared eating the vegetable raw or in stews his mother cooked. The potato part actually resembled a scrubbed dandelion root. "You do good work," he praised, happy to see her smile.

An hour later, Siksik left to help their mother with dinner. After Jacob closed the door behind his sister, he went to the kitchen to prepare some tea, his mind replaying Siksik's surprising words. So, his family wasn't talking about Lia because they thought it would hurt him. Well, in a way they were right, but not for the reasons they probably thought. He would always love Lia, but he'd learned to live without her. What he hadn't reconciled was his part in her death. Every time he walked outside, every time he saw that pale expanse of featureless ocean and heard that singular silence, he remembered.

He'd tried running away. Three years he'd spent in Fairbanks, earning his degrees and creating a westernized life-style for himself. A life-style away from the Bering Sea, away from his land and its seasons. He'd learned the *kass'aq* ways and had eaten the *kass'aq* foods, but he hadn't been able to adapt or to escape. The nightmares had returned, bringing with them a yearning pain. They'd reminded him of who and what he was.

So he'd come home to Twilight, and he'd found a small measure of peace.

Until last week.

Reaching up, he opened the cabinet and took down a mug. Seeing the dishes there reminded him of his mother's request. He didn't want to attend the dinner. And he most certainly didn't feel like picking up Mrs. Elliot and her children.

All afternoon he'd been rehashing their conversation, trying to decide whether his unusual aversion to the woman was due to the strain he'd felt about the surroundings he'd found himself in, or something else entirely. He'd been angry when he'd entered his and Lia's home. Angry and upset. But when Mrs. Elliot—what was her first name, Ann?—skidded into him, he'd been snatched out of the past into the present.

She'd been so shocked. As he pictured her sprawled on the floor beside him, he remembered how small she'd felt beneath him. Her heart had tripped like the fast beating of a ceremonial drum and, even in the shadowy light of the kerosene lamp, he'd reacted to the wild splay of her curly hair. He hadn't been able to discern its color, but the knot in his stomach had continued to tighten until he'd rolled off her.

He remembered clearly the moment he'd extended his hand to help her up. She'd swallowed hard and had taken a moment to wipe her hand along the material of her coat. The unconscious gesture had angered him. He didn't want himself aware of her vulnerability. He didn't want himself aware of anything about her.

Scowling, Jacob took a sip of the tea. As he reached up and transferred his dishes to the countertop, he wondered what his mother intended cooking and how Mrs. Elliot would react to the Native foods.

Ann was trying to decide what to wear when a knock reverberated through the house.

"Mom! Hey, guess what? Jacob's here!" yelled Patrick. A scant second later the door slammed back against its hinges. "Hi, Jacob. You taking us to dinner? Come on in. Mom's not ready yet."

In her bedroom, Ann stiffened. When Mr. Toovak had issued his "invitation," he hadn't indicated that he'd be picking them up. For a moment she stood listening to Patrick's excited chatter as he described her earlier difficulty in getting the shower head to work. She reddened, annoyed. Sometimes she wished her kids had inherited just a little of their father's innate tactfulness. Richard had never uttered an out-of-place comment in public.

No, Ann's practical side answered, he'd saved all of those for their bedroom. She shook her head, determined not to go into one of her if-things-had-been-different moods. Two years ago she'd finally mustered the courage to break off the thirteen-year-old marriage. Since then she'd been working hard as a substitute teacher to reestablish a measure of financial control over her life. This steady job would ease the burden, and no one, not even Jacob Toovak and his brooding objections, would make her give it up. Now that they were here, her goal was to rekindle the love and companionship her family used to share for and with each other. Richard was dead, his emotional abuse a thing of the past. It was time they moved forward.

"So, get the lead out," she muttered, peering into several of the ten or so boxes strewn about the room in various stages of unpacking. Quickly she searched for the pants and sweater boxes, one ear on the muffled conversation in the living room. Finding them, she reached in and pulled out a pair of gray brushed cords, a matching turtleneck and a green musk-ox sweater that always made her feel good because of its softer-than-cashmere feel. Though she knew she wasn't beautiful, she did know the combination always made her look neatly presentable. And since there would be no avoiding Mr. Toovak's mocking gaze, either tonight or in the future, she might as well give herself a much needed booster shot.

Scowling, she pulled the turtleneck over her head, then freed her hair with a flick of her hands. She wished he hadn't been the substitute teacher. Melding herself and her children into this admittedly foreign society with its new customs and unusual language wasn't going to be easy. And having Jacob Toovak looking over her shoulder at every turn was going to make things doubly difficult. He didn't think she could cut it in Twilight. Well, he was in for a shocker.

She was here to stay.

Quickly she finished dressing and entered the living area. The sight of him stopped her in her tracks.

"Good evening, Mr. Toovak."

"Jacob, Mom," Patrick reminded her from where he sat on the sofa next to their guest.

Ann took in the sealskin parka and mukluks that he'd worn earlier this morning. The outfit suited him, emphasizing his Eskimo ancestry. She crossed the small room at a consciously sedate pace, quelling the niggling urge to stand back and away. Dressed like that, he was intimidating. His size didn't help matters, either. Far away or close up—he was solid. And shockingly attractive. Ann swallowed, her throat dry.

"I didn't realize...uh...you would be bringing us to your father's home."

He stood, thick black lashes veiling his eyes as he looked down at her. "Someone came by and told you where to go, then?"

Was there a subtle dig in that comment, as if he would be oh so glad if she went back to Anchorage? Her lips tightened as she gazed into his impassive features. "Twilight *is* small. I figured we could ask someone to point out the way."

Jacob's eyes were shuttered, giving nothing away. "My father sent me to ensure you didn't injure yourself on the way to his home. Given this morning's warm temperatures, it will be slick out tonight."

Ann received the distinct impression he didn't particularly care whether she injured herself or not. "How thoughtful. He's very kind...." Her voice trailed off as she felt the touch of his gaze on her body. The dark eyes were swift and impersonal in their perusal, yet a tingling reaction fluttered in her stomach. She shifted from one tennis shoe clad foot to the other, willing herself to maintain her calm beneath his gaze.

"I'd suggest you carry those shoes in a paper bag and wear boots and coveralls to the house. The temperature's dropping."

"Coveralls? I'm afraid we don't have—" Ann broke off at his abruptly narrowed gaze. She knew what that look meant. Thinking quickly, she improvised. "The kids and I have ski bibs that we normally wear under our jackets."

"I'm not sure mine will still fit," Patrick interjected innocently.

Ann groaned, color flooding her cheeks. Thankfully, the familiar smell of her daughter's hair spray diverted everyone's attention. She turned and just managed to stifle a groan at her daughter's outlandish appearance.

"Where are you going, the circus?" asked Patrick.

Sharon's pale skin flushed bright red and she threw her brother a hate-filled glance.

"Patrick," Ann intervened, hoping to avoid a fight. Quickly she urged Sharon forward. Now was definitely not the time to admonish her. From experience, Ann knew it would take her daughter twenty minutes to remove all that makeup and twenty minutes more to redo the damage to her hair. "Jacob Toovak, my daughter, Sharon."

The two eyed each other. Sharon appeared red-faced and defensive about Patrick's remark. Jacob's obvious wait-and-see attitude wasn't exactly promising, either. *Great,* Ann thought, *maybe I ought to tell Patrick to go find the bibs.* But he wouldn't know where to look and, judging by Sharon's expression, her daughter's embarrassment wasn't putting her in a sociable mood. Patrick would at least keep the conversation flowing. She started for her bedroom.

"Sharon, sweetheart, please offer Jacob a drink while—"

"Wait a minute," Jacob interrupted her, his voice resonating in the small room. Ann stopped midstride and turned around.

"You've brought *alcohol* with you?" Jacob stepped forward.

Ann blinked, confused. He made it sound like she'd offered him poison. Which, considering how she felt about him, wasn't a bad idea.

"Actually, I was offering you a glass of juice or water." Patrick stepped close to her, his gray eyes wide and questioning. She noted Jacob observed the movement and backed down. "We haven't unpacked the wine yet."

"So you did bring alcohol?"

"Yes, I did." Hard as she tried preventing it, her voice wavered slightly. "Occasionally, I like a glass."

"In all the conversations you've had with my father, with the school superintendent—with everybody—about your coming here, no one mentioned that Twilight is a dry village?"

Dry? Ann's eyes widened. "I didn't know."

"Major attitude problem," Ann heard Sharon mutter.

"You'll have to get rid of it."

"Yes, of...of course. Now that I know," she added defensively. "I'll send them back to a friend in Anchorage."

She released Patrick, refusing to back down under Jacob's obvious disbelief at her statement. She thanked the heavens for the saving anger that flowed into her, washing away the last of her habitual defensiveness. It was a trait she'd come to hate, her tendency to take the blame for everything that went wrong in her life. It had started way back as a teen, and her unhappy marriage to Richard had only increased the tendency. There was no reason for her to assume guilt just because she had two measly bottles of white wine in her packing boxes. She was as close to a teetotaler as anyone could get. That no one had taken the time to inform her about the ban wasn't her fault. Her chin lifted. And she had no intention of pouring out two perfectly good bottles of wine. No matter what his eyes were saying.

"What's dry?"

Ann gazed down at her son, grateful for his insatiable curiosity. The tension between her and Jacob was broken. "Dry means without alcohol. Like a desert is dry because it's without water." Her gaze returned to Jacob. She was relieved to see that he'd relaxed. "Would you still like something to drink? I think Sharon made some orange juice earlier, so there's that, or water."

He nodded. She gazed at her daughter. "Sharon?"

"Sure, Mom."

With a last worried frown, Ann hurried into her bedroom.

"What do you want?" Sharon asked, making her way to the refrigerator. "Water or juice? There's milk, too, if you want."

Preoccupied, Jacob missed Sharon's question, his attention captured by Ann Elliot's retreating backside. He hadn't handled that very well, hadn't handled the shock of her appearance well, either. He'd already been floored once today, but when she'd emerged wearing that green qiviut sweater, he'd known he was in serious trouble. In truth, a woman hadn't affected him so swiftly and deeply since Lia.

She'd walked into the room, her hair a riotous tangle of shoulder-length curls, light brown, like her son's. She was small-boned, with rounded hips emphasized by the soft lines of the gray cords. Fragile had been his first thought. Too breakable to survive the icy cold of a Twilight winter. And yet, the sight of her in that sweater was enough to make him want to—

His thoughts came to a blinding halt when he remembered how she'd offered him alcohol. Of all the irresponsible actions! Just thinking about it rekindled his anger, the careless offer making him more certain than ever that she didn't belong here.

"Hey, Mr. Toovak, what would you like? Water or juice?"

He'd been staring at nothing in particular. Now he focused on Sharon and realized she was watching him curiously, waiting for a reply. "Juice, please."

Unsettled, Jacob sat back down on his old couch and unzipped his parka. Deliberately he looked around, forcing himself to look past the painful memories to the house itself. Had the furniture always been this old? This run-down? He noted several items that needed attention.

"Here you go."

"Thanks." He accepted the glass and took a healthy swallow, savoring the treat. Orange juice was a luxury in Twilight. At five dollars for a small can of frozen concentrate, he'd bet that she wouldn't be restocking her shelves very often. He looked across at Sharon Elliot, uncertain what to make of her.

She was a walking advertisement for everything that was a current fad in western society: neon-colored unisex clothes that were two sizes too big, a wild tangle of curls that stuck out stiffly in all directions, makeup that was too heavy and too dark. She was as different from Twilight teenagers as a caterpillar was from a butterfly.

"Jacob?"

"Hmm?" He looked across at the boy and felt a tinge of discomfort. He hadn't meant to scare the child. He summoned a smile. Patrick smiled back.

"On the plane up here, the pilot was talkin' to this other guy, and he was makin' all these weirdo sounds and I couldn't understand anything they said."

Jacob's smile widened. "They were speaking Yup'ik. That's our language."

"Are they gonna talk . . . Yu—" he stumbled over the unfamiliar word.

"Yup'ik," Jacob repeated gently.

"Are they gonna talk Yup'ik at school?"

"Probably some, but I wouldn't worry about it. All the kids speak English and the teachers teach in English, too." Jacob watched the relief spread across Patrick's earnest face. He glanced across at Sharon, knowing she had to have questions about her classes, but she'd picked up a fashion magazine from the end table and was leafing through it.

"Jacob?"

"Yes?"

"How can Twilight be dry with all this ice around?"

Jacob chuckled and stretched forward, setting his empty glass on the table.

Sharon looked up. "Want some more?"

"No, but thanks," he replied, then turned and answered Patrick's question. "Dry is another way of saying that it's illegal to sell or drink alcohol in Twilight. The law's there for everyone's protection."

"You gotta be kidding," Sharon muttered.

"Cut it out, Sharon. No one asked you to butt in." Patrick turned to Jacob. "Don't mind her, she's just mad because there's no phone."

Jacob nodded as if he understood that piece of reasoning. "There's a telephone at the grocery store."

The magazine was lowered and a pair of dark brown eyes gazed at him curiously. "Can anybody use it?"

He nodded. "But it's expensive."

The girl shrugged and ducked behind the magazine again.

"You've never *ever* seen anybody drunk?"

"I have, Patrick, but the smaller kids around here haven't. And they never will so long as they stay in Twilight."

"I've seen drunk people on TV," Patrick offered after a moment. "And I saw Jimmy, Sharon's *ex*-boyfriend, too," Patrick dared in a whisper, but Sharon heard.

"Jimmy is not my ex-boyfriend."

"Oh yes he is," Ann said as she emerged from the bedrooms, her arms loaded with three ski bibs. Thanks goodness she hadn't had to overturn every box. "You promised me that you'd settled that business once and for all. Right?" She stopped by the lounger and gazed pointedly down at her daughter.

"Yeah, right," the girl mumbled.

Jacob noted Sharon's pale skin and wondered if her mother knew she'd just lied.

"Put these on and then we'll go," Ann instructed, handing Patrick and Sharon the clothing. Sharon's speaking glance in Patrick's direction and the ensuing silence didn't bode well. Obviously they'd been squabbling again. Ann sighed, upset. Her kids used to be so close. As she donned her own bib, her gaze fell on Jacob's suddenly stern features. Now what?

"You need to put on boots, Sharon. And socks."

"What for?" Sharon peered down at her bare ankles and leather flats, dismissing his objection. "I'll be fine. We do this all the time at school."

Would the day never end? Ann shot a quick glance at Jacob, whose eyes mirrored a mocking contempt she had no trouble discerning. Her fingers clenched into small, frustrated fists. "Sweetheart, go put on some socks and change your shoes, okay?"

"But, Mom. It's really no big deal. I do this all the time back home."

"I know, and I told you I didn't like it then, didn't I?"

For an instant rebellion flared hot in Sharon's eyes. Then, abruptly, her shoulders sagged, her eyes dulled and she shrugged, as if she didn't care one way or the other. Turning, she headed silently to her room.

While they waited, Ann could almost feel Jacob's certainty that Sharon's attitude only further exemplified their overall unsuitability. But he kept his expression neutral and, after Sharon's reappearance, held open the door.

"Ready?" he requested curtly. "Mother will probably have dinner on the table already."

Chapter Four

Ann shut the door behind her, surprised to discover the wind had died down some during the day. Patrick had already run on ahead, with Sharon slow but not too far behind. As she moved into step beside a silent Jacob, Ann peered out into the partially moonlit night, trying to gain some image of Twilight.

The landscape looked flat and bluish-gray, with an occasional icy knoll disturbing the horizon. The only discernable relief was the houses themselves. They jutted up from the frozen ground in a haphazard array devoid of any rhyme or reason. As they walked, Ann's annoyance with Jacob's attitude increased. Common courtesy demanded he point out buildings of interest—the local church, most certainly the school. But he didn't, and after a few more minutes of listening to the crunch of snow beneath their steps, Ann realized he wasn't going to. Resigned, she returned her full attention to her surroundings.

Their own house, which she'd thought was small, was situated away from the main village and was actually one of the larger resident dwellings. A scattered few off in the distance appeared larger, but she couldn't see them clearly. Most of those backlit by moonlight were smaller one-room houses. And most, regardless of size, were nuzzled into the snow and surrounded by three- and four-wheelers, snowmobiles and parts of all three.

The snow-covered church was easily recognized by the cross on the roof. The large rectangular building to the left of it she imagined might be the high school. She heard a steady droning sound, but couldn't locate the source. Some of the homes had electricity, for she could see lights shining through the cracks in various curtains. Others were totally dark and still others would flicker occasionally, indicating lamplight of some sort. Surprisingly there were few dogs—Ann automatically cautioned Patrick as he called ahead to his sister, then ran back toward one house to play with a frisky husky.

"Does he bite?" she finally ventured the question, nodding toward the dog. Her eyes she kept steady on her children, but the rest of her body was keenly aware of the looming male presence beside her. An awareness she didn't like at all. His attractiveness made her far too uncomfortable and sensitive of her own shortcomings as a woman.

"All dogs bite."

She glanced at him sharply, but he kept walking, either refusing to look her way or just not caring to do so. Quelling the urge to yell, she asked, "Are you this charmingly polite and gracious with every visitor, Mr. Toovak? Or is it just me?"

"Just you."

Ann swallowed hard. She should have expected his blunt response. Everything about him was clipped and cold. Everything, that is, except his eyes. They were bleak. "Mind telling me why? Other than the fact that you don't believe the children and I belong here, of course."

"That's reason enough."

"No, it isn't," she shot back, unsure just why she was bothering to try to change his mind. It was obvious he didn't intend to. "We haven't even been here twenty-four hours yet. How can you make such a rash judgment about someone you don't even know and still call yourself qualified to teach?"

Beneath dense brows, his black eyes regarded her coolly. They moved from the top of her hatless head to the tips of her moon boots and back up again. It took all Ann's willpower not to squirm.

"You're questioning my credentials?"

"Why not?" she muttered. "You're questioning mine. How does it feel?"

She watched his eyes for signs of reaction but there were none. Just then the husky's excited barking brought a man out of the house. Ann recognized the young basketball player, Billy Muktoyuk. The teen waved a greeting, then uttered a sharp Yup'ik command. Immediately the dog quieted. She listened as Patrick politely introduced himself, then forgot all about his sister until Ann called out and pointedly reminded him.

Jacob cut his gaze from the trio to the woman beside him. Moonlight created shadows along her cheekbones, shadows that made her gray eyes larger and more luminous. She was angry with him and rightfully so. He was being rude and bullheaded. But his instincts had warned him that Ann Elliot spelled trouble. For a week of sleepless nights he'd endured the nightmare, aware on a subconscious level that soon his well-ordered, emotionally isolated life would change.

And change it had. In the space of one single day he'd experienced shock and disbelief, anger and astonishment. Most disturbing was the unexpected physical awareness of her as a woman. Walking beside her now, he couldn't control his heart's tripping cadence. He didn't like that. He didn't like anything that made him feel.

"Go home," he spoke out abruptly.

Startled, Ann's head swung around. "Wh-what about dinner? Ben's expecting us?"

He regarded her coldly. "I mean, go back to the home you came from. Your home in Anchorage."

Frustrated anger flushed her cheeks. "You're beginning to sound like a broken record, Mr. Toovak. Like it or not, we're staying. I gave up our apartment when I signed the contract. There's no home to go home to."

He stared at her, suspicious. "You could find another apartment."

She sighed. Would he never quit? "We're staying, okay? That's all there is to it."

"The last teacher had little tolerance for our culture and knew nothing of who we are as a people. The student's background already serves well enough as a liability."

"I know that," she replied impatiently. "But I—"

"Then why insist on remaining here?" Jacob interrupted. "You must realize you won't survive our winter, that you're not suited for this job. Exactly what do you know about our people?"

He seemed very large and very close as they stood facing each other. Recalling the solid press of muscles on top of her this morning, Ann's toes curled inside her boots. The sheer width of his chest had blocked her view of the rest of the room. When compared to Richard's slender frame and flabby sedentary body, this man's strength was intimidating.

But she wouldn't let that or his attitude deter her. Her failed marriage had taught her many things, but one lesson in particular stood out from the rest: giving in meant giving up. She wouldn't let this man malign her qualifications without putting up a fight.

"What I don't know, I'll learn. I assure you, Ben was sufficiently concerned in his own right to brief me on the possible hardships I'd encounter if I accepted the position. But I did accept the job and I'm eager to get started. Why can't you just let me get on with it?"

"The students, Mrs. Elliot. That's why. They deserve more. Much more than a gray-eyed she-wolf looking for easy money and temporary shelter for her young."

She gasped. "How dare you?"

Jacob looked over at her children playing with the husky, then back at the woman. "I dare because I'm right. Why else would you move your children away from their friends and everything they find familiar? It's obvious your daughter doesn't want to be here. You're alone, no marriage band encircles your finger. All the evidence points to my conclusion. You're not here because you wish to teach Native teenagers, you're here because you needed the job."

Ann's gloved hands clenched into fists. Her first impulse was to cower and retreat, just like she used to do whenever Richard yelled at her for any number of transgressions. But that was the old Ann. The new Ann wasn't about to endure this man's cold shot-in-the-dark accusation—even if it was right. And what was wrong with needing the job, anyway?

"I'm a darned good teacher, Mr. Toovak, and regardless of why you imagine I'm here—and I do mean, imagine—understand that I am here to stay. Your father offered me a contract and I signed it! Legally, that gives me certain guarantees.'' He muttered a word that she didn't understand. "I seem to remember your saying just this morning, and I quote, 'The Yup'ik are an open, giving people.' Did I *imagine* that, or were you lying?''

The question hung heavily in the Arctic air. But before Jacob could reply, Patrick ran back to them.

"Mom, mom! Do you think I could have a dog? Please? It would be so radical—''

Not now! she wanted to scream. Instead she pulled her glance from Jacob's stunned features. "Patrick, honey, no. We just got here—''

"Aw, Mom!" He kicked at a pile of snow, then glanced warily from his mother to his new friend. "You guys fighting?''

Abruptly all the hostility drained out of Ann. Her kids had endured enough adult strife in their lives. She'd moved them to Twilight to heal, not to hurt.

"Of course not, honey. Mr. Toovak—I mean, Jacob—and I were just having a difference of opinion. But we worked it out. Didn't we, Jacob?''

Her eyes locked with his, warning him to agree although they both knew he had no compunction to do so. Her courage and her protective instincts intrigued him. She was a fighter all right, Jacob acknowledged sourly as he reached out and tugged playfully on her son's worn woolen cap. Yet even as he reassured Patrick, he was thinking how well his description of a she-wolf fit.

"Are we almost there?" Patrick asked, a smile back on his face as he gazed up at him.

Jacob nodded. "See the church over there?" He pointed off to his left. "My father's home is the house just to the right.''

Ann watched Patrick run off, calling to his sister. When they were sufficiently out of hearing distance, she ventured softly, "Thank you. I appreciate your keeping our...uh... discussion private, and I apologize for my rudeness. That comment was uncalled for.''

"But valid, right?" She merely regarded him with frosty gray eyes. "Nothing you've said has changed my mind. I still believe you should leave.''

"Then we know where we stand, don't we, *Jacob?*'' Ann replied evenly, though inside she was shaking with a combination of outrage at his high-handedness and a relief that it couldn't go on much longer. The man was impossibly arrogant and too attractive for his own good! Deliberately she turned away and gazed ahead to where Ben had come out of the house to greet them, a welcoming smile on his craggy features.

Jacob reached out, his gloved hand encircling her upper arm. She refused to face him. "I'll be watching you, *Ann.* Don't mess up."

Angry, her eyes locked with his and for a brief second, a different emotion seared between them. Then she yanked her arm free. "I don't take kindly to threats, Jacob. But just for your information, you may watch all you wish. Maybe you'll even learn something. Like manners," she muttered, then gave a sharp cry as she felt her feet slip out from beneath her.

Jacob reacted swiftly. His arm snaked out, catching her about the waist and lifting her away from the slick spot. In the instant her body contacted his, senses long buried clamored to life. Abruptly he set her down.

"Do you make a habit of this?"

"Of course not," Ann managed stiffly, too aware of the arm curved tightly around her waist. Even through layers of down, his strength was evident. He'd lifted her without any strain whatsoever. "Thank you. You can release me now."

Jacob let her go. In silence, they stepped away from each other. Ann pasted a smile on her face and crossed the remaining few yards, shaking Ben's hand and allowing him to pull her into the warmth of his home. Three others gathered around the doorway, welcoming smiles on their faces. "Yes, I'm all right," Ann replied in response to Ben's concern. "I hope we haven't kept you waiting too long."

"No, not at all," Ben replied. "Come in, please. Ann, I'd like you to meet my wife, Oopick, and my other son, Mark. You already know my daughter Siksik."

"Your daughter?" Ann smiled, surprised by the news. She looked from Siksik to her two older brothers. The family resemblance was there, she could see that now. Her arms reached out and curved around the shoulders of each of her children. "This is Sharon and this is Patrick," she introduced them proudly. "Thank you for inviting us this evening. To be honest, I don't know if we would have eaten tonight if you hadn't. I still need to figure out how to use that cook stove.''

Everyone laughed. "If you want, I'll show you," Oopick Toovak volunteered shyly before returning to the portion of the big room that was the kitchen. Mark Toovak helped them remove their jackets, ski bibs and boots. Then they all wandered into the main room. Ann looked around her with interest, noting the mixture of Yup'ik and *kass'aq* fixtures. An aged brown couch and a couple of faded recliners were grouped together around a small TV with a VCR connected to it. There was a dining table, a kitchen counter and cabinets. All very familiar and western.

But the floor was uncarpeted and laid with linoleum. There were no throw rugs. Suspended on one wall was a rack that held an unfamiliar assortment of what looked to Ann like fishing gear, clothes and boots. There were baskets of various sizes sitting out on the floor against the walls, obviously handmade, each holding a particular dried food. One larger basket held a variety of animal skin swatches, which Ann guessed Oopick used to sew their Native clothing.

And then there were some pale brown shapes that looked like miniatures of the huge Walt Disney character balloons often seen in holiday parades. Ann had no idea what they were, but since each was tied off at the throat, she assumed they were containers of some sort.

"Any questions?" a deep voice spoke from behind her.

She turned and found Mark Toovak. "A lot, actually." Mark was younger than his brother, with the same jet-black hair and broad open features. But whereas Jacob's eyes were intense, even somber, Mark's danced mischievously, full of light and merriment. Physically he was leaner than his brother, but not by much. Both men had inherited their father's broad build and strong arms. "I look around at your parents' home and I realize how much I have to learn about your people."

"Just ask," he replied, his smile open and clearly appreciative. Ann found herself relaxing. "We're easygoing as a rule. Otherwise we couldn't live in such close quarters."

"Your brother said pretty much the same thing." She still found it difficult to call him Jacob.

Mark scowled across the room at his brother, who had been shanghaied by Patrick again. "Like I said, we're pretty easygoing, as a rule. Our Fearless Fighter over there tends to be the exception.''

"Fearless Fighter? Is that a Yup'ik title?''

Mark threw his head back and laughed, a loud infectious sound that had everyone turning their heads to find out what was so funny. He told them what she'd said, while Ann swallowed against a rising tide of embarrassment. Jacob's expression was easily read. To him, her blunder was another sign of her ignorance. Dismayed, her cheeks flushed even more.

"Sorry about that,'' Mark said after he'd settled down. "But it's not often I get a good laugh at big brother's expense. He takes life way too seriously.'' Chuckling, he leaned forward and whispered in her ear, "Siksik told me about the iceberg remark. If you want my advice, I'd say, stay away from him. On the other hand, don't apply that to me.''

Ann blinked and digested the implication. Had he implied that he found her attractive? No, of course not. Who was she kidding? She must have misunderstood. "I could use a few friends.''

"Good. I missed my opportunity to be a teacher's pet while I was in school.''

Ann laughed, a bit unsure once again, and moved forward to a shelf, studying a U-shaped blade with an intricately carved bone handle. Ben joined her and Mark left to see to an errand his father wanted done.

"Please, pick it up. That's an *ulu*.'' Ben pronounced it "oo-loo.'' "The women use them mostly for skinning and slicing salmon. Or anything else that requires a sharp blade. This one is an heirloom. It belonged to Siksik's namesake, her great-grandma Siksik. Oopick and I plan to give it to her when she marries and starts her own family.''

Ann gazed across the room at Siksik, who was just then pointing at a silver glitter star on Sharon's phosphorescent pink T-shirt. "They're so different,'' she said to Ben, referring to their daughters. "It's hard to believe they're the same age.'' When he didn't comment, Ann turned and found him observing her instead.

"You are ready for classes tomorrow? I'm sure Jacob would agree to teach a few more days if you need time to settle in.''

The idea was preposterous. No way would she hand him any more ammunition against her. No, she'd have to teach tomorrow. Ready or not, prepared or not.

As if he'd heard his name spoken, Jacob looked up from the hides he was showing Patrick and encountered Ann's gaze. She tried her best not to let her eyes linger over the cream cable-knit sweater and jeans, tried not to let herself think of the attractive picture he made sitting next to her son. She'd told Mark she needed a few friends. Jacob Toovak wasn't likely to be one of them.

"No, I'll do just fine, thanks," she commented, then moved on to draw Ben out regarding village activities. For a while they talked, getting acquainted, exchanging ideas. Ann found herself relaxing and smiling frequently. After Ben had excused himself to help his wife, she picked up and began examining a hand-crafted doll. Absorbed, she missed Mark's approach until his voice sounded in her ear.

"So, tell me, what do you think of your new home away from home?"

Startled, she turned and faced him. He'd been outside apparently, and the cold night air still clung to his clothes. She shivered. "Actually, I really haven't had a chance to see Twilight properly. It was dark when we flew in and now it's dark again. I'm getting the distinct impression that whoever named Twilight definitely knew what he was doing."

"Well, at the very least we know he arrived in winter. Darkness doesn't exist here during the summer unless a thunderstorm threatens."

"You get many of those?"

"A few, but don't worry, I'll protect you."

This time Ann laughed freely at his audacity. "You remind me of my son. Are you always this persistent?"

Though he chuckled, his eyes remained somber. "You didn't answer my question. The house working out all right?"

"We're doing just fine," she replied diplomatically. "Of course we haven't unpacked everything yet, but—"

"It's hard to put things in their place when there's no place to put them, right?"

Ann blushed.

"Don't worry, I sometimes feel that way about the whole village. As if it should be in a museum that you visit occasionally. Only, after closing time, you get to go back to a nice three-bedroom apartment with wall-to-wall carpeting." He laughed at her shocked expression. "We're not all died-in-the-wool traditionalists, you know, despite what my elder brother may have led you to believe."

"Then...then what are you doing here? Why not just move to Anchorage or something?"

"I guess because we can't all do what we want to do in this life," he replied, a cloud settling over his features. He nodded down at the doll in her hand. "*Aanaq*—that's Yup'ik slang for mom—makes those. Brings in extra income during the winter months."

He showed her other Yup'ik implements. The miniature parade balloons turned out to be seal stomachs scraped and dried for use as containers. She was just adjusting to the shock of that when Oopick called out that dinner was ready. Looking around for Sharon and Patrick, Ann found them with Siksik, the three of them off in a corner, sitting on a fur rug of some type. Above their heads was a gun rack, with ten or more rifles secured on it. Patrick was pointing at the guns and Siksik was doing most of the talking. Ann smiled. She'd hoped that meeting a girl her own age would be a positive step toward changing Sharon's moodiness of late. While her daughter wasn't talking, she was at least listening. One step at a time, Ann told herself.

Dinner was surprisingly good, and different enough to be interesting yet not overwhelming. They ate seal that Oopick had prepared. To Ann, and luckily to Sharon, it tasted something like beef. With it Oopick served, of all things, Rice-A-Roni and canned corn.

"I expected to see more dogs in the village," Ann ventured the half statement, half question.

"Times change," Jacob muttered darkly, drawing a sympathetic gaze from his mother.

"Yeah, and usually for the better," Mark added with a pointed look at his brother.

"In my grandmother Siksik's time, the village was very isolated," Ben recalled, the slow, deep cadence of his words evoking a vivid image in Ann's mind as she listened. "Tradition was our way of life. There were no snowmobiles and three-wheelers, no shortwave radios and prefabricated housing. We lived in sod houses, and there were dogs everywhere."

"But Billy still has a pet," Ann remarked when he'd finished. "At least that tradition hasn't completely died out."

"Billy's dog isn't really a pet," Siksik corrected her gently. "Most everyone here couldn't afford to keep a pet just for the fun of it. Billy's dog earns his keep just like every other member of the Muktoyuk family."

"He does?" Patrick asked. "How?"

"By working to contribute to the family's subsistence food supply," Jacob answered, drawn into the conversation despite himself.

"What's sus—"

"Subsistence," Jacob repeated the word slowly, aware of another pair of gray eyes that were listening and watching. Inside he felt as tightly stretched as a ceremonial walrus drum. That bothered him considerably. He didn't want to feel anything. "That means surviving off the food supply provided by nature."

"So you hunt moose and bear, huh? Do you use those guns over there? Can I go with you sometime maybe?"

"Patrick," Ann admonished.

"How gross," commented Sharon, shooting her mother a concerned glance. "You're not going to cook that kind of stuff, are you? I'll be sick."

"Sharon!"

"You keep saying you need to lose weight, Sharon, so now's your big chance," Patrick said.

Sharon's face flushed bright red. Ben and Oopick and Mark and Siksik were all laughing, clearly not offended. Ann was mortified.

"Can I, Jacob? Can I?"

Jacob sidestepped a direct reply, knowing with certainty that his own reluctance about a hunt on the Bering Sea eliminated any hopes the boy harbored of accompanying him. "There are no moose on Nelson Island. Nor are there any bear."

"Too bad," Sharon muttered sarcastically. Ann sent her daughter a warning glance.

"Aw, jeez. Then what do you guys hunt?"

"Jacob doesn't hunt anything," Mark joined in, ignoring his brother's black look. "But when *we* hunt, it's walrus in late spring, duck and geese in summer. In the fall, we harvest the plants and berries on land and trap fox and hare for pelts. We have one rule, though.''

"What's that?" Patrick asked.

"Never take more than you need, and use everything you take," Siksik replied softly, a sweet smile on her face.

"Everything?" Patrick asked. "Even the guts?"

"Patrick!" Ann gasped.

"Especially the guts," Mark answered, and chuckled.

"Yuck!" said Sharon, a distinctly queasy expression on her face.

Ann shot a quick glance at Jacob, wondering why he didn't hunt. Most of all, though, she realized that the woman in her was responding to his voice. She found she liked the low gravelly sound, and the Yup'ik inflections when he spoke English were different, interesting.

"Food is very expensive here," Oopick commented from her end of the table. "I pay four dollars for a box of soap powder."

"And six for a half gallon of ice cream," Siksik volunteered.

"Six dollars!" gulped out Patrick.

Apparently even her son could relate to that, thought Ann, amused. She again glanced at Oopick, taking a closer look at the woman who had so warmly welcomed relative strangers into her home. Like her daughter, the woman was open and gracious. She wore her salt and pepper hair split down the middle of her forehead and braided, just as Siksik's was, with a beaded clasp tying the ends together. The wrinkles in her plump face were deeply etched, but when she smiled, her black eyes reflected the satisfaction of living a good life surrounded by her children.

"I guess we won't be eating a whole lot of ice cream," Ann commented.

"You could always try *Akutaq*," Mark said, a very definite gleam in his eyes.

That gleam made Ann suspicious. She'd already made one embarrassing comment and she was loath to make another. Her gaze swung to Jacob. "What's *Akutaq?*"

If he was surprised that she'd asked him and not his brother, he didn't show it. "Eskimo ice cream. A traditional dish that's often made and eaten at celebrations."

"Good. Let's make some, Mom," Patrick said.

Ben smiled. "And what are you celebrating?"

Patrick thought for a moment, then his eyes lit up. "We could celebrate getting here, couldn't we?"

Everyone except Sharon laughed. The evening passed quickly as the two families sat in the living area and became better acquainted. Jacob's occasional hooded glances continued to unnerve Ann, but she somehow found the aplomb to pretend she didn't notice. Then it was time to leave. While Ann helped Patrick and Sharon into their ski bibs and coats, her musings about the success of the evening were interrupted by sharp words between Jacob and his brother, obviously in the midst of a long-standing argument.

"We discussed it at the Gathering of the Clans and I'm going to bring it up at the next village meeting," Jacob said. "The threat's real. We may not survive without the priority. Think about it."

Mark sighed. "I have. And I don't see it as a threat. Just because you're scared of progress doesn't mean the rest of us are. If you ask me, it's time for us to move forward, not back."

"And lose our rights? Maybe even everything that we are?" Jacob asked.

"You're exaggerating. It wouldn't come to that."

"Don't bet on it."

Ann felt as if she were eavesdropping and dragged the kids to say goodbye to Ben and Oopick and Siksik. By the time they'd finished, Mark had left.

"You needn't accompany us," Ann murmured to Jacob once they were outside. Again, the kids had run ahead of them.

"I insist," he commented curtly, her earlier accusation still fresh on his mind. The Yup'ik *were* open and giving. He just didn't feel particularly open or giving toward her, not in the way he should for his village's new school teacher, anyway. What he did feel . . . He shook his head violently, missing Ann's startled sideways glance.

She picked up the pace, stepping carefully but quickly, wanting to rid herself of Jacob's disturbing presence. She didn't like being made to feel a burden. She'd endured that for thirteen years.

They walked along, the windless night broken by a low level droning. Ann looked around for the source.

"That's the power plant," Jacob replied, noting her pre-occupation.

"Oh." She nodded, her gaze on her children. After a few more minutes of silence she felt impelled to say, "Thank you for indulging Patrick's questions. I enjoyed meeting your family. Siksik, in particular, will make a nice friend for Sharon."

He looked at her intently. "And what about Mark? Will he make a nice friend for you?"

Ann reached up and repositioned the hood of her jacket, the gesture rearranging the springy curls lying against her shoulders. Jacob's lips tightened as they followed the unconscious movement. "I hope so," she replied, oblivious to Jacob's hidden meaning. "He's nice. Very outgoing, it seemed to me. I'm sorry I didn't get a chance to say good-night."

"He was angry."

"Because you didn't agree with him on the subsistence controversy?"

He glanced her way, surprise crossing his otherwise stoic features.

A definite feeling of satisfaction settled within Ann. While saying her goodbyes to his family, her mind had hit on the topic causing their dispute. She sensed his curiosity but felt no compunction to explain that, before the separation, she had spent many evenings accompanying Richard to dinners with his political friends. In recent years, the subsistence issue had been a frequent topic of conversation.

"It's a confusing issue but, if I understand it correctly, the Alaska Supreme Court ruled that providing a subsistence priority to Natives violates our state constitution because all Alaskans must be treated equally."

"That's right, only we're not treated equally. That's the problem and Mark knows it. And so does the Federal government, otherwise it wouldn't have sanctioned the Alaska National Interest Lands Conservation Act in the first place. That law ensures that we do have priority on federal lands."

"But what about state lands? Can the state be split into pieces like that?"

"No, it can't. Not and still provide good management of resources."

"So you've got the state constitution which mandates one thing and federal law which mandates another."

"Right."

"What's the solution?"

"There isn't one, yet. That's what all the fighting is about. Supposedly, the state legislators have six months to remove the rural priority provision."

"And if they don't?"

"Then the feds will come in and take over the management of all hunting and fishing in the state."

"And that's what you want? For them to come in and take over? Tell us what to do?"

He shrugged. "What I want is for the *kass'aqs* to leave us alone," Jacob muttered, frustration thickening his accent. As always, talking about it filled him with dread, pushing all other concerns to the background. "The *kass'aqs* are banding together against us. Why does Mark fail to understand? He would have us just give up our preferential hunting and fishing rights. And in return for what? Progress?" He shook his head. "We can't eat progress. It won't keep us fed during the winter. No, I don't believe a recreational sportsman should be considered equal to a subsistence hunter."

Ann hadn't bargained for such a fervent response. But it was better than having him take potshots at her. And it was better than the silence.

"What about a compromise?"

"History has shown us what form the *kass'aq* compromise takes. They will legislate what they want and give back nothing but empty words and promises no better than the paper on which they're written."

Ann swallowed, trying hard not to take offense. She had a feeling he wasn't talking about her in particular, but the system as a whole. "The governor's probably doing all he can given the volatility of the issue. After all, everyone will be affected by the ruling, right? Not just the Native community."

Again, Jacob looked at her, surprised.

"Just because I'm not Yup'ik, doesn't mean I'm oblivious to what's affecting Native communities. Maybe Mark sees the state already taking advantage of the Yup'ik. Maybe that's what he doesn't like, the idea of *not* being treated the same as everyone else."

Jacob was intrigued in spite of himself. Her knowledgeable responses were unusual. Then he scowled. "How would you know?"

This time she did take offense. Her chin lifted. "I'm a single woman bringing up two children. I know how hard it is to make ends meet. I know about discrimination."

Ann watched Jacob's face as he bit back a retort. She sensed he might be struggling with some deep-rooted emotions, but she couldn't be certain.

"To compromise might end our way of life."

They were a few feet from the house, Patrick and Sharon had already gone inside. "I hardly think that's what Mark wants," she said, turning to face him. "He seems as proud of his heritage as you are. Are you sure you two are really on different sides?"

For a long moment Jacob looked anguished, then he nodded. "Yes. We've never been on the same side about anything." His face was tight, pained; it was a look Ann recognized. Mark had it, too. "Good night. I'll tell Mark that he's got another ally."

"Jacob—" she called out, but he'd already turned and walked off. Ann closed the door, carefully making her way around scattered boxes to her children's bedroom. Quietly she reminded them not to wait until morning to find out which boxes held what they intended wearing on their first day. Then she kissed them good-night and returned to her room. As she rummaged through her own boxes, she thought about the evening, about the people she'd met, about Jacob. Laying out her clothing, she undressed and climbed into bed. After revising her first day's lesson plan to better reflect Jacob's comments, she turned off the light and slid beneath the covers. She lay there, her mind filled with impressions, most of which centered around one individual.

Jacob Toovak.

She had a gut instinct that there was more to him than met the eye. The brooding anger, haunting quiet and rude comments were facades. She didn't know how she knew this. She just knew. His passionate defense of Yup'ik rights pointed to a man with deep feelings. Once again she wondered about Mark's comment that Jacob didn't hunt. Why? she wondered. What event had caused him to give up something so essential to the Yup'ik life-style? And why, when she'd known him barely twenty-four hours, was he occupying most of her thoughts?

She turned over, punching her pillow before settling down again. Never had she met a man who so instantly set her on edge. Hopefully she wouldn't have to spend too much time with him.

Chapter Five

"Ann!" Surprise laced the gentle voice of Mary Opik, the Native arts and crafts teacher who had befriended her these last two weeks. "You're here! Jacob didn't think you'd be in today because of the storm."

"Oh he didn't, did he?" Her voice was faint from the grueling walk through the windstorm. Hurrying past the older woman, she sped down the hallway of the administration portion of the high school building to her office. The morning had started off badly enough without Jacob adding his two cents' worth. She shoved the hood of her down jacket off her light brown curls.

"Well, I may be late, but at least I made it." With a relieved sigh, Ann plopped her briefcase on top of her desk and turned to greet her friend, who was leaning against the doorjamb of the office, teacup in hand. She groaned at the sight as she pulled off her gloves, then bent and removed her boots. "What I wouldn't give for a cup of something hot right now."

"Want me to get you some tea?"

"No, no thanks. I can't afford to waste any more time than I already have. I really do need to get upstairs. God only knows what's going on in that classroom of mine."

"I imagine math is going on, so quit worrying and slow down. Jacob's up there subbing for you right now. Lucky you, huh?"

Lucky? For a moment Ann saw red. Then she sighed, knowing that mere verbal assurances wouldn't alter Jacob's opinion of her. He still believed that, when things like the weather got really rough, she'd be the first passenger on the next plane out. Damn him! He might be one of the most intriguing men she'd ever met, but he ranked right up there with the most irritating, too. And to top it all off, he'd probably expect a thank-you for filling in!

"I swear, Mary, Rudolph couldn't find his own nose in this storm." Her friend laughed while she quickly removed her jacket and ski bib, then overturned the paper bag carrying her indoor shoes and slipped them on.

"Yeah, it's a nice one. Third storm in two weeks. More snow than we've had in a long time this early in the season." She held out her hand. Ann passed her the garments.

"The kids and I stepped out of the house and we could hardly see two feet in front of our faces! Naturally, Patrick thought it was 'really rad,' but I, on the other hand, had visions of him getting blown halfway to Siberia."

"I have relatives there, you know," Mary said, then chuckled. Seeing Ann's sober expression, she sighed. "Quit worrying. Ben isn't the type to hold a few late minutes against you."

"I know," Ann said, her voice flustered. *But Jacob certainly is.* And no matter how much she might tell herself his opinion didn't matter, it did. Hastily she picked up her lesson plan and her math books. "Gotta go. I'll see you later, okay?"

Ann hurried down the hallway, rushing through the double doors that led to the stairs dividing administration from the rest of the school. She took the steps at a run, then turned right, into the corridor that led to her classroom. Her pulse quickened over the coming confrontation with Jacob. She didn't fool herself into thinking it would be a pleasant interlude. He would expect that thank-you and she would have to give it to him. And nicely, too, considering the twelve pairs of eyes that would be watching the two of them.

For two weeks now she'd been on her best behavior, trying her darnedest to meld into the small teaching community with as little upheaval as possible. But from the onset, nothing had progressed as planned. First she'd discovered that the office Ben had assigned her was directly across the narrow hallway from Jacob's, where he conducted the day-to-day business affairs of the people of Twilight. She'd been immediately tempted to ask Ben to reassign her, but for one thing, there wasn't another office available, and for the other, what excuse could she have given?

Ben, your son makes me nervous. I don't want him watching me all the time.

Right. And then what? Ben would want to know why, only Ann was no more prepared to be honest with him about the feelings his son generated within her than she was prepared to lie to him that nothing at all was occurring. Sure, she could easily have solved her dilemma by shutting her office door. But she'd quickly discovered that such an action would make her appear unsociable in the eyes of the other teachers. And from the four or five times they'd connected, she'd garnered the distinct impression that Jacob was well aware of just what she'd like to do and why she wasn't doing it. Frustrated, she'd eventually resigned herself to mentally blocking him out. Still, with that broad frame and those dark serious eyes, his presence seemed always to be hovering over her. And not once in the last fourteen days had he walked across the hallway to chat as the other teachers had done.

Not once.

But several times after she'd completed a private student conference, she'd found him watching her, his eyes somber, contemplative. He hadn't said anything, merely stared at her a few endless moments while she'd stared back in equally silent contemplation. Then he'd calmly returned to his work, while she'd pretended to return her concentration to her self-imposed task of familiarizing herself with the mathematic abilities of each of her students.

"Pretended is right," Ann mumbled as she continued down the hallway to her classroom. She'd wasted a lot of valuable time trying to unscramble her thoughts about a man that just wouldn't be unscrambled.

But he'd been right on the money about her students. Mathematically, at least, they were less advanced than those she'd taught in Anchorage. And they functioned at a variety of levels, levels that had no correlation with age. Most of the seniors were just learning the rudiments of algebra, while others, like Siksik, were already more advanced.

But unlike the city kids, these teens didn't really hate math. From all indications, their enthusiasm for learning was real. As long as there wasn't a more important task to do like going hunting for seal, or any of a variety of chores that supported their subsistence life-styles. Yes, her students were all perfectly willing to study and to learn. Unfortunately her daughter wasn't one of them. Ann had privately hoped that having Sharon as a student in her class would give them some common ground. But if anything, her moodiness had increased.

Ann paused and looked down at her watch. Fifteen minutes late. As she reached for the door, it opened. Startled, she stepped back.

"Oh, good, there you are," Ben Toovak said as he stepped into the hallway.

Ann grimaced. "I'm sorry I was late, but you see—"

"The storm, I know," he interrupted her, an understanding smile on his face. Ann relaxed. "Can you come to my office after class? And bring Jacob?"

Bring Jacob? Ann groaned. "All right, but what's up?"

"The Alaska state aptitude test arrived yesterday. There are one or two things we need to work out."

Ann nodded and watched him leave before turning and glancing nervously through the small square viewing window. What did Jacob have to do with the aptitude test?

"All right, everyone. Time's up. Hand in your quizzes, please."

Amid groans and not a few protests in Yup'ik, Ann passed smilingly down the aisles between the rows of desks and collected papers. Absently she listened to the low-level bilingual chatter and last-minute pleas for more time. She'd been pleased and not a little embarrassed by their enthusiastic reception twenty minutes earlier. Except for Jacob, who had left after her entrance, the twelve students that had turned so expectantly and greeted her so warmly as she'd entered the classroom seemed to genuinely like her.

She wished she knew more about the Yup'ik and their language. Already she was becoming attached to these kids. And along with that attachment came a sense of responsibility for their futures. Most would remain to live out their lives in Twilight, but some, like Billy and Siksik, wanted more. As she accepted Siksik's quiz and watched the young girl's open friendliness as she made her way to the rear of the class to sit beside Sharon, Ann renewed her commitment to learn their language. Patrick was already picking up selected words from his new friends.

She only wished Sharon would do the same. But despite Siksik's shy overtures of friendship, her daughter continued to show no signs that she was even interested in befriending the teenage girl. Ann sighed, reminding herself that they'd only been in Twilight two weeks. Hardly enough time to settle in, much less to effect a shifting of her daughter's recent apathy. Ann only hoped Sharon soon snapped out of whatever was bothering her. The three of them would remain in Twilight until spring, and nothing, not even Sharon's protestations, would change that.

As she stopped to converse with the boys whose quizzes she was collecting, Sharon's and Siksik's two higher-pitched voices were easily discernable.

"Why not come sit up front with me and my friends? Dorothy and Alice have been dying to meet you, only they're even shier than me. We've all been wanting to ask you questions about what it's like living in Anchorage and where you get your clothes and stuff. Why don't you come on? I'll introduce you."

"Not right now, okay?" The quick glance she gave Siksik was uneasy, preoccupied. "Maybe later."

Ann, who was keeping one eye on the two girls, thought that if her daughter slid any farther down in her seat she'd be on the floor. All that makeup. And that hair! She fit in with her classmates about as well as a square peg in a round hole.

"Are you all right?" Siksik asked gently.

"Are you still here?" Sharon shot back sarcastically. When Siksik made no move to return to her seat, Sharon glanced up, a curiously vulnerable expression on her face. "Aren't you going to leave?"

Siksik shook her head and sat down.

Ann, who was watching and listening, marveled at Siksik's persistence.

"What's wrong?" Siksik asked. Sharon didn't answer. "You don't like it here very much, do you?"

Sharon slumped back in her seat, her concentration fixed on smoothing the imaginary wrinkles out of her New Kids On The Block T-shirt.

"Maybe if you came and sat up front with us, things wouldn't seem so bad."

"I'm fine right here."

"But this is where the boys sit."

"So? Is there some other weird law—besides the one about alcohol—that says girls can't sit in the back of the class?"

Siksik shook her head, her usually gentle features confused. Ann pretended to be shuffling papers but the overheard conversation had a worried frown tugging at her forehead.

"No, there's no law against it. I guess we just think it's nicer to sit with our friends. You'll have more fun if you come up," Siksik's soft voice cajoled. "Not that the guys aren't fun. They are. I've known most of them since I was born. But well . . . you know what I mean . . . they're different. Guys."

"Yeah, total dwebes. Not a stud muffin among 'em," Sharon agreed, flicking a stray curl behind her shoulder. The movement drew Siksik's attention to the wild arrangement of her hair.

"Could I do my hair like yours?"

Sharon looked up from picking the lint off her black-and-white striped crop pants to glance sideways at Siksik's neatly plaited waist-long braids. "Get real. You see a beauty salon around here?"

Sensing her daughter had spotted her, Ann slowly began inching her way up front again. But she could still hear everything being said and the lingering bitterness in Sharon's voice worried her.

"So, you want to come sit up with us?"

"Like I said, no thanks. The last thing I need is to sit up front and have everyone think I'm sucking up."

Again, Siksik frowned. "You know, you sure talk funny. I thought I understood English pretty well, but I guess I was wrong. What's sucking up mean? And dwebes and what was the other one? Stud—"

Sharon groaned. "Don't you know anything?! Stud muffin! That means sexy, born to kill, you know, hot stuff."

"Oh, I get it!" Siksik's face lit up. "Like Billy, right?"

"Billy?" Sharon eyed her, plainly disgusted. "At the school I used to go to there were lots of guys better than him. Lots."

Siksik looked skeptical. "Well, I think he's great. A—a real stud muffin." She seemed pleased with herself. Sharon just rolled her eyes, waiting for the girl to leave. But she didn't.

"You sure you don't want to come up front? I always sit up there whenever Jacob teaches. And he's my brother."

"Goody for you," she mumbled in a low whisper. "Just go away, okay? I've got stuff on my mind and I need to be alone."

"But maybe I can help."

"Jeez, and maybe you can't, all right?" Sharon looked up, blinking furiously.

Tears? Was Sharon crying? Hearing the suspiciously wobbly voice, all of Ann's maternal instincts urged her to turn around and talk with her daughter. But she couldn't. Not now and not even later, perhaps. Unless she was willing to admit to eavesdropping.

"Well, if you want to talk or have any questions, just come and ask me," Siksik volunteered softly, then rose and walked away.

"Hey, wait!"

Siksik paused, her glance hopeful as she retraced the few steps she'd taken.

Sharon motioned for her to sit down, and when she had, Sharon leaned forward and whispered, "Where can I get a cigarette?"

Siksik looked skeptical. "You smoke?"

"Didn't I just say so?" Sharon hissed, and cast a furtive look around. "Besides, practically everyone around here does it, so what's the big deal? Just yesterday I saw a little boy puffin' away, so don't tell me there's some rule against it."

"No, there's no rule, but smoking will kill you."

"Yeah, well, it's not the worst thing that can happen to you," Sharon mumbled. "Just forget I asked, all right? And don't worry about me. I can take care of myself."

Returning to the front of the classroom, Ann laid the quizzes on her desktop still upset at what she'd heard. Not the least of which was the sudden knowledge that Sharon smoked. Ann had also noticed how everyone in the village smoked. Well, no more, at least no more for Sharon. And she'd have to watch Patrick, too. She felt certain Sharon's ex-boyfriend, Jimmy, was to blame for getting her started. She breathed a silent prayer of thanks that he was out of her daughter's life. Turning, she surveyed the class.

"Who wants to go to the board and work through the first problem?"

As with most classrooms, volunteers weren't exactly a dime a dozen. Ann glanced around the modern well-equipped classroom, her gaze drifting from the bright-eyed girls who sat in the front rows to the hunched-up boys slouched way down in the back.

"Billy, how about you?"

"How about not me?" Billy mumbled, shooting an obvious wink at her daughter.

Ann's finely arched eyebrows raised a fraction. Was Billy attracted to Sharon? Ann watched him closely as he stood amid his cheering friends and sauntered self-importantly toward the front. He picked up a piece of white chalk and tossed it up and down like a basketball several times before turning to the blackboard.

"Hell, I don't know why I should do this stuff," he commented, disgusted. "It's not like I'll need it to get into the pros. A few good seasons at U.C.L.A. and Boston Celtics here I come."

Titters of laughter skipped through the group. Unlike her former students, these Yup'ik teens were never blatantly rude, but they weren't above a little ruckus now and then. Ann decided this might be a good time to discuss what she saw as a big motivation problem. And Billy, with his high hopes for a career in the pros, would be the perfect example.

"You know, Billy, it's a long way from Twilight to the Boston Celtics. I'm not saying you won't succeed, because if you want it enough I believe you will. But getting there will require a great deal of careful planning and a lot of hard work. It's not all fun and games, Billy. And it's not as easy as you might think." She glanced around the room at her students. "Can anybody tell me what Billy will need to do to get from here to there?"

"He'll need to get at least twenty good huskies and a lot of dog food," Ann heard Paul Ayac respond. His classmates, who all knew of Paul's desire to be a world class, long-distance musher and run the Iditarod, laughed.

"First, Billy will have to graduate high school," Siksik volunteered, her shy eyes admiringly fixed on the young man. He seemed not to notice.

"No prob," Billy confidently replied.

Ann let that pass for now. She pointed to another student. "Ed, what else will Billy need to do if he wants a career in the pros?"

"College?"

"That's right. He'll have to get accepted into a college or a university. And not just any college, right, Billy?"

"You got that right, Mrs. Elliot. If we keep winning like we have this season, I ought to get some good offers."

"Offers?" asked Ann.

"From scouts, Mrs. Elliot," Siksik volunteered the information. "Billy has lots of videotapes from all the college and pro-basketball games on TV. That's how he learned to play so well."

"I'm impressed." Ann watched Billy's head drop with embarrassment, but he couldn't hide the small smile of pride. Obviously Billy thought that all he needed was for a scout to make an offer and everything else would take care of itself. She shook her head. He had a lot to learn. And he might as well start now.

"Does anyone know what it takes to get into a good college?"

"A brain," Ann heard another student say.

"Yeah, too bad he doesn't have one."

Everyone laughed. Everyone except Billy, who was becoming more uncomfortable by the minute. "You want me to do this problem or what, Mrs. Elliot?"

Ann nodded. "But let's finish up this discussion first. Sharon, what else will Billy need?"

Her daughter didn't answer. "Sharon?" Ann repeated. Finally her daughter looked up. The expression on her face was withdrawn. "What do you think?"

"He'll need bucks to get outta here," she answered, throwing Ann a resentful look for drawing attention to her.

Ann nodded, inwardly worried at Sharon's continued behavior. "That's right. He'll need money to pay for classes and books and things. Unless, of course, he wins a full scholarship or obtains financial aid. But there's one thing no one's mentioned yet." The students gazed at her expectantly. "Billy will need to take the S.A.T."

Silence filled the room at her announcement. Ann gazed at the confused faces, a little perplexed herself. Hadn't anyone, Jacob at the very least, told them about this mandatory test?

"What's that?" Billy finally braved the question.

Apparently not. Ann shelved the disturbing revelation and answered Billy's question. "It stands for Scholastic Aptitude Test, and it's one of the tools university admissions people use to decide whether they want you attending their college or not."

"You mean you can't go to any school you want to go to?" a student asked. "Even if you can afford it?"

"That's right. Colleges only have spaces for a specific number of new full time students each year. So they're forced to set certain minimum academic standards for admission. Grade Point Average, GPA is one of them. The S.A.T. is another. As a high school graduate, Billy will have to meet and beat U.C.L.A.'s standards if he wants a good chance to go there."

His youthful face lit up. "Yeah, man! U.C.L.A., here I come!" His gaze landed on Sharon. "Awesome."

Her daughter glanced away, embarrassed. Billy's outlandishness made Ann smile. For all of his cockiness, he really was a good kid. She was honestly happy for him, too few of the students she taught had any goals at all beyond graduation. She supposed a farfetched dream was better than no dream at all.

"Well then, Billy, if you want to go to U.C.L.A., you'll have to take the S.A.T. And it's only given twice a year, once in the spring and then again in the fall."

"Forget it, Billy," came a remark from the rear.

"Yeah, give it up, Billy. It's not worth all the hassle. Your dad won't let you go anyway. Not when you can make good money at the cannery."

Ann let the comments slide, knowing that if Billy wanted it badly enough, nothing she or his friends could say would change his mind. "Half of the test evaluates verbal skills, like reading comprehension and vocabulary."

Billy groaned. "And the other half?"

"You guessed it. Math. You can finish up that problem now."

The remaining few minutes of class were productive if not a little short due to the time they'd spent discussing college. But as Ann watched them exit the classroom, she knew she'd made the right decision. The students had been a lot more attentive to the quiz answers now that they understood that it did have a place in society. And even if they only thought of it as a tool to gain entrance into college, at least they understood it was good for something.

Content, she picked up her stuff and headed toward Jacob's office. Out of the corner of her eye she spotted Sharon and Siksik together. Apparently Siksik was saying something Sharon didn't like because she saw her daughter vehemently shake her long curls, then turn and push her way into the girl's bathroom. Ann frowned, her gray eyes encountering Siksik's sad features across the hallway. When she started toward the young girl, Siksik turned and walked off. Ann sighed, aware that she would definitely have to talk with her daughter soon. But before that, she needed to pick up Jacob.

Neither task was one she particularly relished.

In the bathroom, Sharon huddled over the single toilet. Sweat beaded on her forehead. Her lungs screamed for air. Her stomach clenched tight. *No!* she wailed inwardly. *No! I can't be pregnant! Please, dear God, I know I haven't been the best lately, but please, don't let it be true. Please.*

Silence reigned in the small stall. Silence, save for the labored sound of her distress. No longer could she deny the clues her own body was broadcasting. No longer could she continue telling herself she was imagining symptoms that simply weren't there.

Because they were there. Oh, God, they were there. Everything she'd ever heard of: no appetite, throwing up all the time, moody. And the worst one of all, a missed period. Three weeks late.

Oh, God! What am I going to do?

Trembling, Sharon flushed the toilet, then turned and slumped down on the seat. If only there was someone to talk to! Not Mom, certainly. Fresh tears started down her face as she imagined her mother's reaction. She'd have a heart attack, probably. And then, if she survived that, she'd probably kill Jimmy.

She sniffed, then wiped dejectedly at the tears. Somehow she had to find a way to contact him. He had to know. Jimmy would stand by her. Jimmy wouldn't let something like Mom's disapproval keep him from helping her. Her head dropped into her hands. She remembered the look on his face when she'd told him her mother was forcing her to move away. He'd been really cut up. They'd even cried and he'd held her really tight, vowing there'd never be another for him. They'd gotten very close that night, though she'd been certain they hadn't actually gone all the way. But apparently it had been enough.

And now they were having a baby. Only she couldn't reach him because there wasn't even a private phone anywhere in the whole village! Was there anyone who could help her?

Suddenly she thought of Siksik. The girl was certainly friendly. If you liked geeks, that is. Frustration churned her stomach, making her moan nauseously. Quickly she stood and bent over the toilet again, retching dry heaves that left her drained and exhausted. Afterward, she leaned her forehead against the stall, absorbing the cool comfort of its surface.

Her shoulders drooped. How was she going to keep everyone from finding out? She already stuck out like a sore thumb. She dreaded the way the kids always stared at her and whispered whenever she walked down the hallway. Back home, she'd never had that problem. Back home, all her friends were just like her. Here, she was the outsider. And everything around her was strange, different. Half the time she couldn't even understand what they were saying.

Sharon rubbed her stomach, feeling it settle. She had to find a way to tell Jimmy, she decided as she left the stall, checking her makeup in the mirror, then exiting the bathroom for her next class. And she had to do it soon.

Chapter Six

"Ben, you wanted to talk to me?"

"To you and Jacob. Please, come in." He passed her a sheaf of papers, then waved them both to the seats placed in front of his desk. "You've administered the Alaska state aptitude test before?" he asked, looking at Ann.

"Yes, I have." She accepted the packet and began leafing through the pages. "I wish, though, that they would improve the format. Unofficially, I've been lobbying a long time for an updated design. Not enough children understand the test the way the questions are presently formulated."

Ben's weathered face creased into a sudden smile. "Jacob said as much to me last year when the fifth, sixth and eighth graders took their test. Perhaps you could work with him—improve the design. With your contacts and his understanding of our culture, you two could devise an exam much more suitable for our children."

Silence greeted his suggestion.

Work with Jacob? No way, thought Ann. Patrick and Sharon, especially Sharon, needed her right now. A relationship—even a working one—was out of the question. As for Jacob, he was just too dangerous to her peace of mind, and was definitely the last person she'd consider working with closely!

She shot a quick glance at him. The sardonic glint in his eye was indication enough of his opinion of Ben's suggestion. She sighed. What had she been worried about? He no more wanted to establish a relationship with her than she did with him.

"Let me get more comfortable with my schedule first," Ann replied awkwardly, loathe to disappoint Ben. To change the subject she nodded toward the selection of Native crafts displayed on the wall behind him. "Your artwork is beautiful."

Ben spun around in his chair and glanced up. "Oopick made the beaded headdress. She spent an entire winter softening the skins and sewing on the wolf fur and beads. Unfortunately I do not use it often enough. We have few occasions to perform the old ceremonial dances anymore."

"What about the fans? That's polar bear hair isn't it?"

"It is," Ben answered. "My grandmother Siksik made those for Oopick when she was chosen to perform the Woman Of The Sea Dance at the annual Christmas potlatch. It's a great honor. We hope Siksik will dance it someday."

To Ann, it seemed that every answer created more questions. There was so much to learn. On the wall beside the headdress hung a breathtaking spirit mask. The carver had used driftwood to fashion and connect the two thin concentric circles Mary had explained represented the Earth and Universe. Intricate ivory carvings of a seal, a walrus, a wolf and a fish graced the axis points of each circle. There were small feathers, too, though Ann couldn't remember their significance. She wondered who had created the piece. "Ben, the spirit mask? Who—"

"We're getting off the subject, Father," Jacob interrupted gruffly. He didn't want Ann knowing he'd carved the mask. It would lead to questions he didn't want to answer. She thought him tough and uncompromising and he wanted to keep it that way. Without her wariness around him, he very much doubted he would have any success in keeping her at arm's length.

For days he'd sat watching her from his office, listening to her soft voice and gentle promptings as she talked with each of her students. Her concern for them was genuine. Her smiles ready and open.

But not for him. And he needed to keep it that way, too. Whenever he looked at her, he thought of fire light and fur rugs, man-woman intimacies he'd long denied himself. The risk of involvement—the pain of emotions like love and death—was too great a price for him to ever pay again.

Ben paused, a probing look in his wise old eyes. Jacob didn't flinch. If anyone could read his unease, it was his father. After a two-second eternity, Ben spoke.

"We spoke last week about your traveling to Tununak to talk to the mayor about the subsistence issue. Did you set it up?"

"Yes. But twice I had to cancel because of the weather. For now, my meeting is set for Saturday. This storm should have passed far enough inland by then."

"Good. I want you to take Ann with you. While you're with the mayor, she can administer the test."

"Me?" Ann wrenched her gaze from the beauty of the spirit mask carving. Her breath caught. "With Jacob? No, I—"

"I don't think that's a good idea, Father—" Jacob began, but Ben cut them both off.

"Ann, the district superintendent has assigned you as control person for the test. Did you see his letter? It's on top."

Alarmed, Ann scanned the typewritten request. There it was all right. As control person, it would be her job to explain the testing procedure to the students, to keep track of time, to establish comfortable conditions and answer their questions. She groaned, anxiety knotting tightly in her stomach. Travel to Tununak? Just the two of them?

She looked up. "Why did he assign me? I would think one of the other teachers . . . someone familiar with Tununak . . . familiar with the students there . . ." Her voice trailed off under Ben's speculative gaze. It wouldn't do to have him think she was shirking her duties. "But when do I give our own children the test?"

"You have two weeks. I know I need not remind you how important the tests are to our villages. The results will be used to justify our tax base. If we don't get them in by the end of October, we chance losing funding for books, computers and lab experiments, all the educational supplies that our children need if they intend to interact with the *kass'aq* culture successfully. Because of the unpredictability of the weather, I strongly suggest you accompany Jacob on Saturday."

"That's only three days from now, Ben. What about Patrick and Sharon? I can't just leave them alone."

"The test is only three hours' long, Ann. You can complete the task in a half day if you two leave early in the morning and head straight across the bay."

Jacob stiffened. Head straight across the bay? What was he thinking? "Father—"

"Just a moment, Jacob," Ben forestalled him. "Ann, I will ask Siksik to invite your daughter to our home on Saturday. Patrick will no doubt enjoy some time with his new friend, Paul."

Ann blinked. He'd certainly kept tabs on them. With all the adjustments she'd been undergoing, she tended to forget how small Twilight was. Her eyes shifted from Ben to his son and she was startled by the hot intensity of his gaze. Then abruptly it changed. Jacob didn't want to go. No, that wasn't quite right. He wanted to go, but he didn't want her along.

So, what else was new? Her chin lifted, a motion Jacob observed with a mocking lift of one eyebrow as he met her determined gaze. But inside he was shaking, as much from disbelief at his father's suggestion as from anticipation of Ann's company.

"You wanted to say something, son?"

Jacob broke the electric contact with Ann. "I'm not going to cross the bay. It's too early in the season."

Jacob held still beneath his father's gaze. They both knew his excuse to be a lie. And they both knew why.

Ben sighed, his expression sad.

Ann looked from one to the other, trying but failing to comprehend the obvious undercurrents.

"Fine, son, but if you follow the shoreline, the trip will take longer and you'll have to leave that much earlier on Saturday."

Jacob said nothing. Again, Ben sighed.

"Just make certain that before you two speed off on that snowmobile Ann has everything she needs to make the trip safely."

* * *

They met at seven on Saturday morning, Jacob's snowmobile already packed with his few belongings and her test materials. It was still dark, but the half moon in the sky lighted the terrain with blue-black rays. As she walked toward Jacob, she eyed the tract vehicle warily. Although she'd been around a snowmobile or two in the past, she'd never had the desire to ride one. And looking at its motorcycle handlebars, front skis and narrow bench seat, she didn't now, either.

"Mom, why can't I go, huh? Why can't I?" Patrick whispered sleepily, stamping his feet to keep warm. "I could even drive. Paul showed me how last week."

"He did? I don't remember your asking me—"

"It's not that dangerous, Mom," Patrick interjected quickly. "Otherwise all the kids wouldn't be doing it. You've seen 'em. Besides, we wore helmets and couldn't go really fast because we were in town." He yawned, then continued. "That's what I want to do, though. Go really fast, you know? Zoom! Boy that would be—"

"Rad, I know," Ann broke in, hard put to keep a stern expression on her face. "But you should have asked me, young man. You know I always like to know where you are, Patrick."

He hung his head and mumbled, "Sorry, Mom," then looked up again. "Can I come?"

"No, sweetheart. Believe me, if this wasn't work related I wouldn't even think of going without you, okay?" *Liar,* she admonished herself. She wouldn't even be *going* if this weren't work related. Reaching out, she tugged up the zipper on her son's jacket. "Just wait until you get to Paul's. I'll bet you'll be so busy you won't even realize how fast the time's going."

"Yes, I will," he said, then kicked at some snow. "You'll be back by noon?"

"Noon," Ann promised, giving him a quick hug. She'd said her goodbyes to Sharon inside the house. "Now, go back inside. It's too cold out here. And tell your sister to fix you some breakfast when you wake up again."

Patrick shot Jacob an embarrassed look. "I'm not a baby, Mom. Besides, Sharon makes yuckie breakfasts. Lately all she wants is crackers."

"Right. Just tell Sharon that Siksik's expecting her at nine. Paul's mom is expecting you then, too."

Patrick turned and ran back up the stairs. "Hey, Jacob. Will you take me snowmobiling sometime? Paul said you're almost as fast as his dad."

Jacob chuckled, recognizing the ploy. "Paul said that, did he?" Patrick nodded. "Well, Paul was wrong." Patrick looked crestfallen. "I'm faster."

His face lit up. "Really? Awesome! Will you take me sometime?"

Jacob's gaze swung to Ann, who shrugged as if to say "It's up to you."

"Sure, Patrick. We'll do it sometime soon."

"All right!" Patrick yelled, then turned and disappeared inside.

Quiet surrounded them. Feeling her nervousness returning, Ann awkwardly hefted the helmet Jacob had handed her when he'd arrived. "Thanks for indulging Patrick," Ann whispered, though in the silence, her voice carried easily to the man silhouetted in the moonlight.

"He's a good boy."

"Yes. Yes, he is."

They stood facing one another. Then Jacob turned away, donned his helmet and mounted the machine. "Let's go."

Ann didn't move. "I suppose . . . I suppose this is a good time to let you know that I've never ridden a snowmobile before."

Jacob turned, paused, then dismounted. He walked over to where she stood, impatience clear in every step. He took the helmet from her nerveless fingers. "Pull your hair back from your face, then look up," he ordered. Ann complied and felt him fit the helmet over her head. "Okay?" She swallowed hard, then nodded. He reached and flipped down the visor. "Now, straddle the back seat."

She did, looking around. "No seat belt?"

"I'm your seat belt," Jacob mumbled and with that, he moved forward and mounted the machine, efficiently redonning his helmet. "Put your arms around me, Ann," he instructed, hoping his voice wouldn't betray him. When she tentatively slid her arms around his waist, he almost groaned, then purposefully twisted full right. Immediately, her arms fell to their sides.

"I didn't ask you to put your arms around me for the fun of it," he growled. "You'll fall off if you don't hold me tight. Now do it right," he ordered brusquely, wanting to kill his father for suggesting this trip. This time when he tried twisting left, her arms retained their hold on him. "Better. Remember, don't let go."

And with that last order, Jacob gunned the engine and they were off.

The yellow and white snowmobile sped through land that appeared never to have known the touch of man. Jacob said nothing and Ann thanked God for small favors. He'd said quite enough for now.

When she felt more comfortable with the motion of the snowmobile, Ann relaxed and looked around her. Photographs of Alaska usually depicted the famous Mount Denali, a Kodiak bear or the flat Arctic slope with its oil development facilities. Seldom had she seen western Alaska, the land of the Yup'ik. She was grateful for the visor of the helmet Jacob had provided. Its clear acrylic design blocked out the snow and wind that was kicked up as they sped through drifts of newly fallen snow. It was then that she realized that the terrain wasn't quite so flat and featureless as she'd been led to believe.

In fact, the shifting blizzard winds had created a sort of icy desert landscape, complete with dunes. Every so often they'd ride to the top of one and Ann had to swallow the feeling of exhilaration she felt as they sped down into the ravines. Once she spotted a series of oddly shaped dunes and discovered only when they sped by that they weren't dunes at all, but cabins. She couldn't think why abandoned cabins would be located here in the middle of nowhere, but then, she wasn't Yup'ik. She was fairly certain there was an explanation.

They'd been following the shoreline for forty minutes when Tununak came into view. Ann was surprised at how quickly they'd arrived. Within minutes, they were roaring into a town that closely resembled Twilight. When Jacob turned off the snowmobile, she immediately let go and jumped off. Spending even forty minutes pressed up against his broad back was frustratingly pleasurable. Against her will, she was already thinking of the ride back.

"Try not to trip, okay? We're not late," Jacob remarked as he whipped off his helmet, then swung his leg around and stood.

He watched Ann busy herself by removing her helmet and self-consciously shaking out her matted hair.

He liked its springy wildness. Seeing it jump to life beneath her probing fingers brought on thoughts that shocked him with their intensity. Would she react to his caress with the same wild readiness?

Ann purposefully kept quiet. She didn't want to look at him. The scent of his body still clung to her clothes and she knew he'd likely notice her awareness if she didn't adequately control herself before encountering those midnight-black eyes again. She didn't understand the way he looked at her sometimes. Resentment was there in the coldness of his eyes and anger in the tight line of his lips. But every so often she glimpsed another emotion entirely. An emotion that made her far more uncomfortable than his anger. This emotion was hot. It seethed like the sizzling lava of a volcano. Her heart pumped madly whenever she encountered that gaze.

The sound of Yup'ik voices made her look up. Though a bit far off, the villagers were excitedly exiting their homes and coming forward to greet them.

Jacob gazed about him at the poverty and run-down condition of the village. He frowned, unconsciously clenching and unclenching his gloved hands.

Ann mistook the gesture. "I understand that you'd scheduled this as a solo trip, Jacob, but it's not my fault, okay? I would appreciate it if you would lighten up. You look like a hungry wolf getting ready for a meal."

"I am hungry."

The look in Jacob's eyes as he answered her made her pulse jump erratically. But then he shrugged and turned away, making her think she'd imagined the heat in his gaze.

"You're beautiful, but you're not always on my mind."

Stunned, she stepped back. He couldn't have shocked her more if he'd told her to strip. "I'm..."

"Don't tell me you don't know it," he said roughly. "Everyone in Twilight has fallen under your spell."

"They h-have?" Ann stammered, still shocked by his first revelation. He thought her beautiful? *Beautiful?* Heat flushed her cheeks. Then, abruptly, she sobered. When would she ever learn? "You don't have to insult my intelligence, Jacob. I know what I am and what I'm not, and beautiful has never been it."

Jacob turned and regarded her intently. She meant what she'd said. She really didn't consider herself beautiful. He wondered why, then angrily shoved the thought aside. He didn't want to know more about her. The more he knew, the more he wanted to know. He resented that. He flicked his head toward the village.

"That's the reason I'm angry and upset. The state spends five hundred million each year to educate only one hundred thousand students statewide. I know the majority are in Anchorage and Fairbanks, but why is it we receive so little aid when we need it the most? Native communities rank lowest in income per capita and highest in unemployment. Our families live in poverty, our children go uneducated." Disgust tinged his voice. "How are we to provide for our families if we lose the subsistence priority? And why do we have to force our children to take tests that target *kass'aq* ideals and situations?"

"Because to do nothing would cause even greater harm for your children," she replied hesitantly, unsure of his mood. "If you've had second thoughts, Jacob, and want my help redesigning the tests, just ask. I don't need false compliments. The project is something I believe in, anyway."

He faced her, his expression dark with an unreadable emotion. "What makes you think we can work together? You've been here more than two weeks already and we haven't exactly hit it off."

"And whose fault is that?" Ann said defensively.

"Mine, I suppose."

"You've got that right."

The tension between them was palpable. Jacob stood still, surprised by the hurt shadowing her eyes. "Ann—"

"No, don't." The flattened palm of her hand encountered his chest. She pulled back as if burned. "Just leave it alone, okay, Jacob? It's not necessary for us to like each other. I can do my job without it. I've *been* doing my job without it. If you don't like me, then you don't. Believe me, it's no skin off my back."

She was lying and they both knew it.

Jacob's eyes narrowed as he held her gaze. It was time to set the record straight. Though her presence made him acutely uncomfortable, he knew that the discomfort had more to do with her slender body and wide vulnerable eyes than with her commitment to her students.

"Ann, I—"

"They're here," she said, turning away to greet the villagers.

The morning sped by as Ann met the mayor and other village elders, who drew her out about a variety of concerns they had regarding the education of their children. She also talked with the teachers and finally, after a late lunch, she administered the test to the twenty-five students assembled in one of the classrooms. Afterward, as she zipped up her jacket and pulled on her gloves, she was glad that she'd asked one of the teachers to contact Ben and tell him of their delay. She'd taken more time than had originally been planned, and this way at least the kids wouldn't worry. She exited the school building, hoping Jacob's meeting, which had also run late, was now finished.

Jacob. Just the thought of him made her heart race. He was such a cool man, yet he created such a hot reaction within her. She shook her head, confused. Since before her separation, she'd been convinced her emotions were so deeply buried, so inaccessible, that no stranger could crack the wall of her reserve. But she'd been wrong. Jacob Toovak could. In fact, Jacob Toovak already had. And within him lay the power to widen that crack into a cavern. Every time he came near, Ann knew her emotions poured closer and closer to the surface.

"Ready?"

Ann jumped, then blushed when she realized it was Jacob. Beside him stood the mayor. She said a warm goodbye, thanked him for his hospitality, then turned and stored her materials inside the hollow compartment under the snowmobile's seat. Straddling the vehicle, she sternly told herself not to make a big deal out of a quick ride home. Taking a deep breath, she waited for Jacob to mount, then slid her arms around his waist.

"Ready."

Jacob nodded and gunned the engine and, in a repeat of the morning, they sped off. Ten minutes into the trip Jacob abruptly increased his speed.

"What are you doing?" she called out, uncertain he would even hear her above the loud roar of the snowmobile's powerful engine.

Without slowing, he pointed back and to their right, out toward the sea. A dark swirling mass of dense, leaden clouds marred the horizon. The late afternoon sun disappeared behind a rent in the clouds. Puffs of ice vapor twisted in the distance. A storm was rapidly approaching.

"Can we make it home?" Ann shouted worriedly.

Jacob shook his head. He'd experienced these Arctic windstorms many times. They had but a few minutes and then it would be upon them. Concentrating, his eyes squinted into the distance. A fish camp, long ago abandoned, lay close to the shoreline. If they could make it there before the storm hit, they'd be safe. His fingers tightened about the handlebars.

"Hold on!" he yelled.

Ann clenched her arms tighter around his waist as Jacob, demonstrating a daredevil mastery over the vehicle, drove the snowmobile up along braided ice streams and across miles of frozen unmarked tundra. He didn't look back and he didn't slow down, even when they rocketed off the crests of ice ridges to land with neck-breaking jolts in deep ravines of ice and snow. Ann somehow managed to hang on.

The rising wind warned Ann of the storm's rapid approach. She'd lost track of how far they'd traveled. Her reality was the sight of a broad back and the steady roar of the engine. Outside of that, there was only the wind, the cold and the punishing snow that whipped against her helmet and body, threatening to suffocate her.

Where were they going? Did Jacob have a plan? In the dwindling daylight, everything was beginning to look shadowy and featureless. Time sped by as they raced ahead of the storm. She knew Jacob had to be tiring. It was his arms and legs that kept the snowmobile balanced and upright amid the constant bombardment of the jolting terrain, but he never stopped or complained. And when an eerie twilight swallowed them up, he merely flicked on the snowmobile's headlight and raced on.

"Jacob!" Ann called out, intent on making him stop before he lost the reserves of energy he would need to shelter from the storm.

"A bit farther...wait...over there!"

Ann hunched forward over Jacob's left shoulder to see, her eyes squinting through the darkness beyond the headlight's illuminated path. Suddenly the storm surrounded them. At the same time, the ground broke away from under them.

Ann screamed Jacob's name, choked by the swirling snow and sudden weightlessness. Frantically she tried to hang onto him. Her fingers grabbed for his parka but the momentum of the heavy machine carried him away. She flew through the air, then hit the ground, ice chips and blowing wind whipping at her tumbling body and knocking the breath from her lungs.

The wind's force was so hard, the blowing ice chips so vicious, that Jacob could barely see. He slipped and slid, attempting to ride the machine down the crumpled dune, anything to maintain control. But its weight was too great. Finally he hurled himself away, afraid if he didn't, he might be crushed. Arms flung wide, he hit the ground rolling, snow surrounding him and filling his clothes. It seemed an eternity until he rolled to a stop.

Dazed, he lay face-down in the snow as painful memories warred against the need to jump up and find Ann. He forced himself to focus on that need, concentrating within its boundaries to banish the exhaustion and the despair. He turned over in the snow, sat up and brushed at his visor. The storm howled around him. Everything was white, but he knew that Ann was somewhere behind him. He had to find her. She would not die. She would not be another Lia.

Jacob forced himself to bury his fears and listen for the rumble of the engine. The possibility that it might have stalled he pushed away.

There! His heart pounded as he recognized the sound. Thanking the spirits, he stumbled toward the barely audible rumble. Plunging his arms deep into the snow, he grasped the handlebars and pushed himself fully upright, jerking the machine out of the snowy grave.

"Ann!"

He listened, but heard no reply. The storm was worsening. He had to find her quickly.

Intent, he turned the snowmobile around, using the headlight to search the immediate vicinity. On his second pass, he saw it, a sharp refraction of light that could only be something metal. Leaving the vehicle pointed in that direction, he raced up the mini-avalanche, his head bowed low against the wind. When he reached the spot, he dropped to his knees. Grasping what looked like a silver buckle, he pulled. Ann's jacket came into view.

Ann sputtered, brushing snow from her visor. She felt Jacob before she saw him, felt him clearing the snow from around her body. The chore was endless for the wind was blowing so fiercely that no sooner did he remove a pile of snow than another took its place.

Finally he bent down over her and carefully pulled her out of the pile of snow. "Are you all right?" he shouted close to her ear. She nodded. Reaching out, he tugged her upright and together they stumbled down the snowbank to the waiting snowmobile. Shaky and disoriented, Ann mounted, putting her arms around Jacob's waist. She had no idea where he was taking them, but just having him with her, she realized, allayed the fear freezing her throat. She pressed her face against his back and clung to him.

The snowmobile pushed on through the storm. Jacob could barely see, but he knew the fishing camp he'd been heading for wasn't far away. When it suddenly came into the headlight's view, he roared up alongside and cut the engine before sliding off to the side and flipping up his seat to reach inside for his survival gear. The snowmobile would likely be buried, but he could always dig it up. Right then it hardly mattered. Getting inside, did. Capturing Ann's hand, he raced for the shelter.

Jacob shouldered in the door and together they collapsed, both inhaling huge gasps of air. With his foot he closed the door, plunging them into total silence. Everything was dark, midnight black and icy cold. After a moment or two, Jacob twisted around and pulled off Ann's helmet, before discarding his own. Both helmets banged loudly as they hit the floor. Then his arms closed tightly about her, forcing her head to his chest.

Ann listened to the heavy pounding of Jacob's heart, oddly secure in the comfort of his arms. She lost track of time, but eventually their breathing leveled and they both calmed down enough to gaze around. Releasing the tight hold she'd had on his jacket, she mouthed a question, but her lips were so stiff she had to try again.

"How long will it last?" she asked hesitantly, her voice a hoarse whisper of fear.

A freak blizzard like this could end swiftly, or it could go on for days, but Jacob didn't want to alarm Ann, so instead he didn't answer her.

"Give it to me straight, Jacob," she demanded shakily.

Jacob focused inward, calming his mind, refusing to even entertain the possibility that once again he was at the mercy of the elements.

"Jacob?"

"We'll make it" was all he said, making no move to release her.

Ann Elliot had shown herself to be both brave and courageous, but now that they had found shelter, he felt the shivers of reaction take hold of her body. He held her tighter, the need to protect her overwhelming. She felt so small and helpless. He remembered the way she had looked in the green qiviut sweater that had so softly molded her womanly figure, and the way her eyes had widened when he'd told her she was beautiful. She hadn't believed him. He would have to prove it to—

Abruptly he released her. He had to think. He had to find out what supplies were available. *He had to get away from her.*

"Don't move," he ordered, then stretched out his arms until his fingers nudged against his gear. Grasping the small duffel bag, he pulled it toward him and sat up, discarding his gloves.

"What's that sound?"

"My bag." Zipping it open, he felt inside and extracted a flare. "Cover your eyes."

"Why? It's pitch dark. I can't see anything, anyway."

"Just do it, Ann."

She did as he'd requested, swallowing her desire to tell him to quit ordering her around. She wasn't, she realized, in any position to argue. "Okay, ready."

Jacob ignited the flare, bathing the room in a deep red glow.

Ann dropped her hands, noting absently that they were shaking. "Why didn't you just say you had a flare?"

Jacob shrugged and continued rummaging in his bag. He pulled out a shallow-surfaced ceramic bowl, a small animal skin pouch and a dried plant that looked to Ann like moss of some type.

"How many flares do you have?"

"Just one." He placed a section of moss in the bowl, then carefully opened the pouch and poured some of the fluid over the moss.

"*One?* What kind of a survival kit has one flare? We need light. That flare's not going to last forever."

Jacob paused and looked up. "You need to understand something, Ann. This is my land, and I'm the only one who knows it and has survival training. So, until we're out of this, you follow my rules."

Bending down, he set the flare across the moss. It ignited, emitting a steady light and a familiar odor. "You're alive because I saved you. You've got shelter because I found it. And you've got this Naniq lamp because I have provided it." He wiped angrily at the blood trickling down his forehead. "The reality is—we're stuck here and we don't know for how long. Whether you like it or not, whether *I* like it or not, you're dependent on me."

A chilled black silence followed Jacob's words. Ann didn't move from her spot by the lamp. She also didn't take her eyes off him. They both knew the discussion was ended.

Chapter Seven

Leaving her the seal oil lamp he'd fashioned, Jacob hefted the flare and began investigating the shelter. The plywood walls were aged and rotting, the dirt floor hard-packed and frozen. Jacob paused at the far wall to examine some articles on a driftwood shelf. An old grass basket contained dried tea and a ceramic cup. In another he found a small length of moose hide. When he uncovered the stockpile of driftwood, he nodded in satisfaction. They had light and now warmth. They would survive.

"Find anything?"

Ann had to reach deep down to come up with that mundane question. She didn't want him knowing how thoroughly he'd rattled her. And though she hated admitting it, everything he'd said was right. This was the land of his people and she didn't know what she was doing. It just didn't sit well, after years of Richard's overbearing attitude, to be told so bluntly that she was all but useless.

Carefully picking up the miniature seal oil lamp, she moved to investigate the cabin. She didn't find much: a rotting bench, an empty shelf, a few odd-shaped carvings. But no food. She glanced back at Jacob. He hadn't answered her question.

"Find anything?" she repeated.

"Driftwood. And some dried herbs. After I start a fire, I'll make tea."

"Tea?" Surprise laced her voice. "Really? What'll we use for water?"

"Melted snow."

"Oh, yeah," she replied, feeling a bit foolish.

She watched the effortlessness with which he hefted two of the larger driftwood pieces. It disturbed her that she could be so incensed with him yet still notice the broad expanse of his shoulders. He returned to the center of the single room, where a circular depression was dug into the frozen dirt floor. Within minutes, the shelter's aged walls reflected the autumn-colored glow of a warming fire.

"Please, come sit down."

Removing his gloves, Jacob extended his hand. Would she accept the peace offering? Her face looked pale in the flickering light. There were blue circles beneath her eyes. She was exhausted and she had a right to be.

He studied her thoughtfully. Her eyes were too large and too defensive, yet she stood poised and ready to fight him. Against his will, his spirit responded. He silently applauded her courage while berating his own actions of the past few minutes.

What was it about this woman? When they were together, she made him feel, bringing out emotions he'd deliberately buried on the frozen ocean floor with Lia. Once he'd been happy alone. But her arrival had somehow changed all that.

When he looked at her, he thought of forbidden actions, things that involved the heart and the soul of a man. He wanted to taste the lips that seemed forever to be closed against him. He wanted to feel the body that she kept shrouded beneath layers of shirts and sweaters and jackets and boots. He wanted her smiling and naked. He wanted her to look at him with other than resentment. He wanted her open and willing. But above all, he didn't want her afraid of him.

Ann looked down at the hand Jacob offered her, then up into his face. The firelight illuminated his eyes. She recognized regret and gentleness there, but there was also something deeper, something she couldn't quite decipher. Inwardly she reminded herself that she could not allow her defenses to fall. Men were all the same. Richard had also shown remorse and though she'd forgiven him time and time again for the games he'd played with her self-esteem, he had never changed. Tightening her lips, she ignored the hand but sat down beside him. Her entire body ached. She was wet and tired and cold.

For a while the cabin was silent as each gazed into the flames of the fire.

"How is Patrick doing in his classes?"

Ann gazed at Jacob suspiciously, but his expression was guileless. Against her will, his interest warmed her insides.

"Great, all things considered. Last night, he came home full of enthusiasm about these odd-sounding games he'd been introduced to during gym class. He told me you were there yesterday, as a matter of fact. And then he told me he wants to be the W—E—Something-or-other champion, like you were."

"W.E.I.O." Jacob replied, watching the tension ease from her face. He felt himself relax. "Patrick was talking about the World Eskimo Indian Olympics."

"Olympics? Like the International Olympics every four years?"

"Almost. Same principal of sportsmanship and cooperation, but different competitions," he replied. "And it's held annually. Thousands of Eskimos, Indians and Aleuts compete. It's actually more a way to preserve our culture than anything else. We even conduct our own mini-competitions in the gym during the Christmas holidays. The winners are honored to represent the village in Fairbanks."

"So that's why he wants to be the junior champ. He wants a free trip." Ann's tentative smile invited him to join in. Jacob did. Ann's breath caught at the seductive yet boyish effect on his usually somber features. She continued, loathe to break the easy atmosphere developing between them. "He was trying to show me what to do. But once I realized he actually expected me to put a string around my ear and suspend this weighted ball off the floor, I gave up. It didn't seem particularly safe to me. Or fun, for that matter."

Jacob shrugged. "The boys like it."

"No kidding," Ann replied, borrowing one of Patrick's expressions. She couldn't believe how easily they were talking. "But is it safe?"

Jacob remembered the ten-pound weight Mark had suspended from a string looped around his ear last year and how, after he'd lost the competition to an Aleut man lifting sixteen pounds, his ear had swollen to twice its normal size. He decided not to tell Ann about that.

"At Patrick's age, I wouldn't worry. The younger kids can't lift that much and wind up having more fun than anything else. But the competitions teach endurance and discipline, two traits the Yup'ik children need to develop to thrive in a subsistence life-style."

With a long narrow section of driftwood, Jacob stirred the fire. The cabin was becoming warmer but it still had a way to go before he could consider removing his parka.

"He was certainly impressed." Ann smiled, recalling Patrick's excitement. She watched Jacob's gestures, her memory recalling the strength of his hands, the powerful strokes he'd used to push the snow away from her buried body. She shivered, thinking what might have happened if he hadn't backtracked and found her. "I think my son's developing a serious case of hero worship."

Jacob's smile abruptly vanished. "I'm no hero." *Heroes don't let innocent people die.*

His eyes captured hers. They were angry like the storm, pitch dark, his thick, sooty black lashes blocking intrusions on his privacy. It was hard for Ann to look into his eyes and not be put off by the emotional barrier he'd so obviously built around himself. He *had* acted heroically. Why wouldn't he acknowledge it? The distinctive odor of the seal-oil lamp drew her attention to the miniature lamp.

"What did you call this?" She lightly touched the ceramic pot.

"A Naniq. Our Siberian cousins used it for heating, cooking and as a source of light. Its use dates back to 300 B.C."

Ann couldn't think of anything she used on a daily basis that had such a long history. Its presence in Jacob's bag seemed to point to the very real differences in their backgrounds.

Her gaze rose to the cut on his forehead.

"You want me to take care of that?" Reflexively, she reached toward his forehead, but Jacob's hand snaked out and captured her wrist.

"Don't."

Again their eyes met. Ann became very conscious of how close their bodies were to one another, how near his lips were to hers. His scent was distinct, alluring. A flickering yellow light surrounded them, releasing the pungent odor of the seal oil lamp. It was like being caught in a time warp—only she didn't know the Yup'ik equivalent of Adam and Eve.

And they weren't naked.

When Jacob's gaze fell to her lips, she wriggled nervously, but he wouldn't release her.

"There's something you need to do," he said, his voice oddly hoarse.

"I know. I need to have my head examined for being here in the first place. But as you so eloquently put it, although not in so many words, I can't leave without you." She looked pointedly at her wrist, hoping to distract him enough that he wouldn't notice her galloping pulse.

He released her, never taking his eyes off her face. "I didn't mean it the way it sounded."

"Didn't you? It's been my experience that men like you usually say exactly what they mean."

Jacob frowned. "Men like me?"

"Yes. They're called chauvinists."

"Your ex-husband is a chauvinist?"

"Was. Richard *was* a chauvinist. He's dead now."

Jacob's stomach knotted. His eyes narrowed. "You're a widow."

She nodded.

"What happened?" The question passed his lips before he could pull it back.

"That's none of your business."

"But he's why you won't admit to being dependent on me, isn't he?"

Ann compressed her lips to keep from really letting loose. "Why don't you stay out of my personal life? You don't see me satisfying my curiosity, do you?" Jacob's expression closed. "See, there you go."

"What?"

"The way you pull back into yourself. Do you think I'm blind that I don't notice? Every time I come near you, you do it."

His lips tightened. "My reactions have nothing to do with you."

"You're lying."

His expression was thunderous. *"What?"*

"I said, you're lying. You must be. You've spent the last two-plus weeks making darn sure I know exactly what you feel about me. And when I see you pull back and that dark cloud settles over your face, believe me, I know." She unzipped her jacket with quick, agitated strokes. "You just can't stand the fact that I'm adapting, can you? What are you afraid of? That I'll decide I like it enough to stay beyond spring?"

"I need more driftwood. The fire must not burn out."

Jacob stood up, even though it meant Ann would know for certain that he was retreating. Before he could take so much as a step, she scrambled to her feet, her hand reaching out to bring him around.

"You started this conversation, Jacob, and I am tired of having it over and over again. Let's finish it now."

"I repeat, my reactions have nothing to do with you."

"And I repeat. You're lying."

"It's none of your business, Ann."

"At least that's honest. And at least now we're getting somewhere."

"Leave it alone, Ann."

"No. I told you, I want this finished. Done. Why do you hate me so much? And don't tell me it's my imagination because I won't believe you. Even Ben's noticed it."

"I don't hate you. I don't feel anything for you."

"Could have fooled me," she said roughly, noting his burning eyes and tense features.

Extremely annoyed, he held his breath for a moment before releasing it with a grunt of resignation. "You strike me as the least dependent woman I have ever met."

Diverted, Ann smiled. "That's the first nice thing you've said to me."

He shook his head. "No. I told you that you were beautiful, remember?"

She colored but didn't look away. "Don't ruin it. We were just making progress."

"That's a matter of opinion. But if you're looking for some indication that I don't hate you, I'm willing to acknowledge that you're a good teacher. The students are lucky to have you."

"Damn you, Jacob! Stop trying to change the subject! I'm cold, I'm wet, and I'm not in the mood to spar with you anymore. Why won't you open up?"

With an abrupt twist, Jacob stalked angrily to the driftwood pile, hefted a few more pieces, then stalked back and laid them in the fire. Sparks and hisses sounded in the room.

Startled, Ann stepped back. Then he stopped and removed his parka, his boots and his down overalls. When he started in on his sweater, Ann exclaimed, "What are you doing?"

"Opening up. That's what you wanted, isn't it?" He whipped off his sweater and started in on his turtleneck.

"Yes, but . . . you're undressing?" Her voice rose an octave or two.

His eyes darkened. "So should you."

Ann's mouth worked, but no sound came out.

"Did you hear me? I want you to take off your clothes."

Alarmed, Ann backed up, putting several feet of distance between them. "Are you crazy? I'll grant you that I might have come on a bit too strong, but that's no reason to. . ." Her voice faltered when his chest appeared from beneath his top. It was smooth and strong and well-defined. Suddenly she found it difficult to breathe. "Jacob, I . . ."

"Get undressed," he ordered again, starting in on his pants. He didn't seem to notice her preoccupation or her fear.

Ann took refuge in anger. "What happened—the storm freeze dry your brain? Forget it, Jacob. I'll take my clothes off when hell takes over."

"Then look outside and start undressing." Jacob's mouth was tight and grim. "You're cold and you're wet. You just admitted it. And you've been pulling at the collar of your sweater for a half hour now."

"So what?" Ann responded defensively. "I'm wet. I've been wet before. That doesn't mean I'm prepared to strip. Or to let you. . ." She gulped.

Something in her tone of voice made him look up. He paused, his hands motionless on the zipper of his jeans. "Let me what?"

"Have your way with me," she rushed out quickly.

"Is that why you think I'm taking off my clothes? To take your body?"

She blushed but nodded.

He muttered a Yup'ik word she didn't understand. "Listen, I don't want your body. And if there were some other way we could keep warm, I wouldn't even suggest this. But we're in a survival situation here. Neither of us has a change of clothing—"

"Exactly," Ann broke in, humiliated that she'd misunderstood. How could she have been so wrong? Of course he wouldn't want her body. "What do you expect me to do? Prance around with nothing on?" She paled at the thought, completely missing the sudden stiffness in Jacob's body. She'd endured enough ridicule over the years from Richard. Just the thought that Jacob might see her plump thighs and not-too-pert breasts caused her acute embarrassment. Heat stole into her face. "Forget it, Jacob. I won't do it."

"Then I'll have to do it for you."

She backed a step farther. "We're on to that again, are we? Don't come near me, Jacob. Do you hear me? Another step and I'll—"

"You'll what? There's nowhere to run, Ann. You've given me no choice. Either take off your clothes or I'll do it for you."

She breathed in shallow quick gasps. "You'd like that, wouldn't you? Humiliating me?"

He regarded her soberly. "I promise not to touch you."

"I've been promised lots of things in my life, Jacob."

"Not from me."

She clenched her hands as the silence between them lengthened. She examined his expression, noting the straightforward way he kept her gaze. He'd meant what he'd said. Ann swallowed.

"I'll freeze."

"It's already too warm for that. Soon the room will turn into a virtual sauna. This shelter is built into the side of a hill. The earth and snow will keep the heat in and provide all the insulation we need against the storm."

He sounded so damn reasonable. She thought about him removing her clothes and panicked. Then she thought about removing them herself and panicked. She was in a no-win situation here. Tears started in her eyes.

Seeing them, Jacob sighed.

"We need dry clothes before going back outside, Ann," he reasoned, hoping to ease her discomfort. "Any moisture, even sweat, turns to ice under these conditions, and your body will be hypothermic in no time. It is only logical—"

"Logical!"

He flinched at the increased volume and held up his hand. "I won't let you leave here if you're wet, and we can only remain here so long before we run out of wood."

He was right about that. Ann felt herself lose ground. Her heart jumped. "But what makes you think my clothes can't dry on my body if I sit close to the fire?"

He shrugged. "They might, but in the meantime you might also catch a chill. Chills can turn quickly into fevers. And we only have a small first-aid kit."

She could see that Jacob was serious. He really wanted her to strip. A blush began to spread itself over her body. No, she thought with an unconscious shake of her head. She couldn't do it. Other women might be blasé about such things, but she'd never undressed in front of anyone but Richard. And he'd long ago lost interest in her body, reminding her on many an occasion just how unexciting he found her.

"What'll we sit on?"

He walked over to where his survival blanket lay on the ground and brought it back to her.

"But what about you?" Ann asked, taking the blanket. Somehow, it seemed too small and flimsy to provide her adequate cover.

"There's a scrap of moose hide over there in the corner. I'll use it."

"That's not enough!" Ann said, and immediately regretted the outburst. Another blush stained her cheeks.

"No choice," he said, his hands returning to the zipper on his jeans.

Ann stood transfixed. The survival blanket slipped unheeded to the floor. His pants fell, revealing the smooth glow of olive-toned skin. Her eyes feasted on a body tough and sinewy from a life-style that demanded physical expression. The powerful thighs bore not an ounce of fat, the calves rounded and firm in their wide-footed stance. She thought it odd he didn't remove his socks, but it didn't detract from his appeal. He was breathtaking.

"Ann?"

Her head snapped up from where she'd become fixated on his ripple-hard stomach. She heard Jacob's rasp and immediately dropped her eyes.

"Ann?"

She heard his soft footfall and quickly turned her back on him. "I can't, Jacob. Don't ask me to."

Stunned, Jacob stood frozen, his eyes glued to the graceful curve of her neck peeking out from beneath the straggly wet curls. What he'd seen in her eyes just then had been both thrilling and terrifying. She'd wanted him. Despite the arguments, the threats, the outright disapproval, she'd wanted him.

The shocking revelations sparked a windstorm of confusing thoughts and emotions within him, the foremost of which was a sudden soul-shattering rush of desire. He reached out, intent on bringing her around. Then, abruptly, he dropped his hand. What was he thinking? A union between them would lead nowhere. She was not of his world. His language was unknown to her. Though her desire spurred his own, he couldn't risk involvement. Not again. The pain of her leaving would only add to that which he now carried. She'd been right to say he was afraid. He was. Afraid of involvement, afraid of more pain, afraid of adding to his guilt.

Bending down, he picked up the covering, taking care not to touch her when he draped it around her shoulders. She tensed at the contact. Anticipation perhaps? The thought reeked havoc with his control. Fists clenched at his side, he stepped back and away, purposely making his words and voice hard and unflinching.

"You want to get sick? Dehydrated from the heat in here or hypothermic from the ride back to Twilight? Fine. Then stay dressed. We'll get another teacher for the children. I'm going to get some sleep."

And he did just that. Within minutes the cabin was silent save for Jacob's rhythmic breaths.

Ann turned. Jacob was sprawled near the fire. Except for his parka, which he'd used to lie down on, his clothes were neatly laid out in a semi-circular fashion halfway around the circumference of the fire. He looked so compelling, even in sleep. Firelight played over his muscled body, creating interesting shadows in the valleys and creases of his shoulders and

legs. His forehead bore a bandage, no doubt from the first-aid
kit lying open next to his duffel bag. He'd fashioned a skimpy
loincloth around his middle, but Ann blushed to see how little it covered. He was powerfully male and that maleness both
seduced and frightened her.

Tentatively, she tiptoed nearer the fire. Mesmerized by his
face and form, her fingers curled inward, crushing the silvery blanket. The urge to touch him was strong, shocking in
its intensity. Never had she felt such a desire, not even when
she and Richard had first met. Firelight caressed his hair, reflecting red-gold in the blue-black strands. Ann wondered
what it felt like, what he felt like. She blushed and hid her hot
cheeks in the cool blanket.

She was so attracted to him. How could she have allowed
this to happen? Come spring, her contract ended. She and her
children would leave Twilight and likely never return. Why
then did her heart persist in this one-sided desire? He argued
with her at every opportunity, yet risked his own life to save
hers. Two weeks she'd known him and still Jacob Toovak remained virtually a stranger. She sighed, exhausted, and let her
eyes roam his sleeping form. For an hour she sat beside him,
aware of the heat in the cabin and the sweat drenching her
clothes. Watching him warily, she lifted the blanket and shook
it out. Once again, he was right. Slowly she began removing
her clothes.

Ann started awake suddenly, wondering what had disturbed her. From where she lay on the floor wrapped in the
blanket, she had to arch her back and cock her head sideways to see Jacob. When she did, her eyes widened. He was
tossing and turning on his parka, obviously in the grip of a
nightmare.

She sat up. The blanket slid down her bare shoulders to her
waist. Alarmed, she reached out and pulled it back up her
body, securing it sarong-style across her naked breasts before
standing and approaching Jacob. Should she wake him? His
breathing was harsh, ragged, and every so often he let out a
low, painful moan. Looking down at him, she wondered what
to do.

He was sweating. She could tell because the firelight reflected the sheen of moisture on his chest and stomach. The

skimpy moose hide covering his lower abdomen was also soaked from perspiration. His face was damp, his eyes clenched tight in pain, and his straight black hair lay flat against his forehead. It, too, gleamed darkly from moisture. She couldn't understand what he was saying, so she knelt carefully down close beside him and lay her ear next to his mouth. The gruff words were Yup'ik and as she sat back on her knees, he gripped the sealskin parka, flexing and relaxing his fingers repeatedly.

Ann leaned forward again, unwilling to watch his pain. She had to wake him, had to stop the nightmare. Hesitantly she reached out, gently shaking his shoulder. She shuddered at the contact with the smooth, wet skin, but he didn't awaken. She tried again, only harder this time. He tensed, aware of something, then turned roughly on his side away from her touch.

Now what? Ann wondered, her glance drawn helplessly down to a bared buttock, exposed by his agitated twist to the side. He was so beautiful, she thought. Beautiful and strong. Waking him from his nightmare could be dangerous. But what choice did she have? She'd suffered enough with her own demons to know that wakefulness was infinitely better than the helplessness of sleep.

Balancing herself on her knees, she leaned forward once again and grasped his one exposed shoulder, shaking him hard twice.

"Jacob," she called calmly, evenly. "Wake up. You're having a nightmare."

He twisted around, pulling her down beside him with such force that her head hit the floor. She cried out and his eyes opened, but the torment there told Ann he was still asleep.

"Don't give in, Lia!" he cried out. "We can make it. Just don't give in!"

He started shaking her and muttering Yup'ik words that Ann couldn't understand. The blanket loosened and twisted around her waist, hampering her efforts to free herself. She struggled against him, becoming frightened by his overpowering strength and his intense urgency. Again and again he shook her, calling out the unknown woman's name. Finally, in desperation, she answered back, clinging to his shoulders and holding on tight.

"It's me, Jacob. It's Lia. I'm all right. Wake up. I'm all right."

She knew precisely when he woke up. His hands, which tightly gripped her shoulders, loosened abruptly. With a startled cry she fell backward onto the floor, while he, too, reared back, stunned disbelief sweeping over his features.

"What are you doing?" he demanded hoarsely, his eyes drawn to her heaving breasts.

"Don't, oh please, don't look at me," Ann said, trying to move away. He wouldn't let her.

"What are you doing?" he repeated.

Ann turned her head away and squeezed shut her eyes. Shame flushed her body and she groaned. She couldn't bear seeing his indifference to her, not when his body was so perfect. "You were having a nightmare," she whispered. "I wanted to help . . . I tried to wake you up."

He groaned. Gently he reached out and grasped her chin, bringing her around to face him. A single tear spilled down her cheek. "Open your eyes, Ann," he murmured soothingly, blatantly taking advantage of her weakness to indulge his own by running his hand across her reddened cheek, then up into her hair. He let it slide silkily through his fingers. She was so beautiful. "Ann, did I hurt you?"

She shook her head, unconsciously arching to give him greater access. Jacob's eyes darkened at the innate sensuality even her restraint couldn't control.

"Thank God," he muttered, hanging his head. "Sometimes it's so bad, I don't know what I'm doing . . ." His voice failed him.

Hearing his pain made Ann open her eyes, intent on soothing the hurt. "It's all right, Jacob. It's over now."

He nodded, though he knew it to be a lie. With his forefinger, he traced the track of a tear. "You're so perfect," he murmured, leaning forward across her body. Nothing could have stopped him from settling himself on top of her so that her breasts flattened against his naked chest. Sweet fire enveloped him at the contact. He felt her trembling reaction and groaned, any last shreds of control gone.

"Don't stop me," he whispered, dipping his head to hers.

Ann couldn't have stopped him even if she had wanted to. Shock over his description of her yielded to intense pleasure as his mouth settled hungrily over hers. She hadn't been kissed in so long. She felt herself arch up to meet his passionate lips, deeply satisfied by the depth of his hunger and her eager response. His mouth scorched her cheek, then plundered her throat before returning to feast greedily on her lips once again. Ann responded joyfully, gladly, greedily, wanting this as much, even more than he.

Jacob wrapped his arms tightly about her, rolling them both so that he lay beneath her. He needed her body surrounding him, needed her hair fanning out to create a pocket of darkness around him. His hands caressed her body, pushing at the blanket with agitated strokes until she was free, groaning in satisfaction and gathering her close to him. Then he kissed her with a wild, passionate abandonment that carried her along, emotions long ago buried erupting to the surface.

But with the passion came fear. As Jacob's fingers skimmed the generous curve of her thighs, tension and insecurity resurfaced. She felt his readiness, knew that if she didn't do something soon, there would be no turning back. And she wasn't ready for this. Not yet, not now. Though he could command her passions, he was still a mystery. She pulled back and stared down into his desire-sharpened features.

"I can't do this, Jacob."

He stared up at her, shocked. "What?" he rasped.

Ann looked down at her breasts lying softly against his chest. She blushed a brilliant red.

"I can't do this, Jacob," she repeated.

"What game is this?" he said, tormented, lifting her off him with such force that her upper arms ached.

"It's no game! I just...I just don't know you well enough, Jacob. Since I arrived you've been at my throat, and now..." She scrambled to her feet, hefting the blanket and gathering it with trembling fingers securely around her body. Jacob remained seated on the floor. For a moment his shoulders seemed to sag and Ann fought an urge to cross the small space separating them and soothe the agony so obvious in his posture. But she didn't. Instead she asked a question.

"Who is Lia?"

Jacob stiffened but didn't look up. He didn't want to talk about the cold finality of Lia's death. Not while his body still pulsed with life-giving desire for Ann. Somehow it was wrong. "She has nothing to do with you."

"Doesn't she?"

Now he did glance up. "No."

"Why were you calling out her name?"

He stood and walked over to where his clothes lay. Picking up his jeans, he pulled them on over the moose-hide wrapping. Then he tugged on the rest of his clothing.

"What are you doing?" Ann hadn't moved from her position opposite him and across the fire pit.

"Listen."

"I don't hear anything."

"Exactly. The storm's passed. It's time to go." Having said his piece, he donned his parka and boots, pulled on his gloves and strode purposefully to the door. Before going outside, he turned around, barely containing his reaction at the vision she made silhouetted in a silver-red glow. "I'm going to dig out the snowmobile. When you're dressed, we'll leave."

The door slammed shut behind him.

Chapter Eight

Ann ran a tired hand through her curls as she headed toward her office Thursday afternoon. They'd motored into the village early Sunday morning and it had been a tough five days since. Jacob had reverted to his silent brooding self. Only now she sensed an added emotion—resentment. He thought she'd played him for a fool; that she'd deliberately led him on. The villagers sensed the tension between them and their speculation that something had happened between them during their time in the cabin would be comic if it weren't so distressing.

How could things have gotten so out of hand? All she'd wanted to do was wake him from a nightmare, for goodness' sake! She couldn't even look at him now without remembering the smooth feel of his skin, the power in his arms as he'd held her. Mostly she lay awake nights, remembering the way she'd felt when he'd kissed her. Her heart pounded at the mere recollection.

Spotting Siksik in her blue jeans and colorful native *kuspuk* pause at Jacob's office, she called out, "Your brother's in Juneau, Siksik."

"In Juneau?"

"He's giving testimony on subsistence rights."

"Oh, that's right." She crossed the hall and leaned against Ann's office door. "He was preparing for that before you two went to Tununak. I hope he remembers to buy me a Big Mac before he comes home tonight."

"A Big Mac? From Juneau?"

"Uh-huh. Mark took me to a McDonald's three years ago when we were in Fairbanks visiting Jacob in the hospital. It was great. Even with the pickles. Kind of expensive, though. We never told Dad, so it's sort of a secret, okay? Mark said it was a special treat just between us."

"I promise I won't tell," she replied, curious about Jacob's being in the hospital. Did it have something to do with his limp? she wondered.

"Is Sharon planning to play bingo tonight?" asked Siksik.

Wednesday night bingo was a village custom. Held in the gym, practically all the villagers attended. "I don't know. Maybe you could drop by after we eat dinner and ask her. It would do her good to get out of the house," Ann replied with a smile. She really liked Siksik. "She hasn't been feeling very good lately. I just hope she hasn't caught a cold or something."

"If you want, I could bring you some special tea leaves my mother and I dried last summer. It doesn't taste very good, but if it's only an upset stomach, one cup of this will cure it real quick."

If only every problem were that easily solved, Ann thought. "That's right, you want to be a nurse, don't you?"

"Yes." She smiled softly. "Jacob says it's good having old Milak here to provide the traditional medicines for minor problems, but the villagers need someone who knows the old ways and has *kass'aq* training, too. Last month, when Hanna had her heart attack, it took forever to get help."

Siksik sounded so mature for her age. Ann couldn't imagine Sharon, or any of the kids she'd taught in Anchorage for that matter, concerned about such serious subjects. For them an emergency was solved with a phone call to 911. Here in Twilight, though, such social services didn't exist. There were no police or fire departments. And other than the radio, medical emergencies were handled by anyone and everyone. It wasn't surprising that Yup'ik children seemed more capable and more mature than their city peers.

"I don't think that Sharon's ready for any tea just now," she gently refused Siksik's offer. "But if it gets worse, I'll let you know. By the way, who is Milak? I don't think I've met anyone by that name."

"That's because she doesn't leave home now except when the village elders meet," Siksik answered. "She says it's too cold in the winter and her bones ache. She's ninety." Siksik smiled, her black eyes soft with affection. "Milak's a good healer and has taught me many things. Would you like to meet her? She doesn't speak English, but I could go along and translate. When I was visiting her last week for a sleeping tea for Jacob, I mentioned we had a new teacher."

A sleeping tea? Ann was just about to question Siksik when Patrick rushed down the hallway.

"Hi, Mom!" Patrick hollered, and braked to a squealing stop in front of her office door. He smiled at Siksik. "Where's Jacob?"

Ann sighed. She could have guessed where Patrick's thoughts lay. His admiration for Jacob was growing so fast that Ann didn't really know how to stop it without hurting her son. Tuesday evening Jacob had taken him snowmobiling. Patrick had been on top of the world ever since. She ruffled his hair. "He's not here. Remember I told you he had to fly to Juneau today?"

Patrick's slender shoulders slumped. Then he brightened. "Can I go play bingo with Paul tonight?"

"Only if you've finished all your homework by then," she replied. She got up, reached for her boots and grabbed her hooded jacket and gloves. "I've got to run to the store, wanna come along?"

"All right!" Patrick rushed out of the office, his "Bye, Siksik" a clear afterthought.

"Anything to get out of doing homework," Ann said, but her smile at Siksik was affectionate. "Want to come along? Billy will probably be there."

The girl blushed and dropped her eyes, allowing Ann a moment to sigh nostalgically over the peculiarities of young love. Despite Billy's star athlete status, to Ann he was just a tall and slightly too skinny teenager. His height made him stick out among his classmates, a fact that made him that much more the center of attention. But though he tended to swagger a bit, he did have a very engaging personality. That was why she'd picked on him last week. With all the other kids looking up to him, it made sense to let him set the example of what discipline and education could provide. Besides, Ann knew he took his dream very seriously.

"No thanks, Mrs. Elliot. I've got to go to the gym and practice."

"Oh, that's right. Mary told me during lunch that she'd chosen you to perform the solo in the Woman of the Sea Dance. Congratulations!"

Siksik's shy brown eyes sparkled with excitement. "It's really an honor. I only hope I don't mess up."

"You won't," Ann assured her warmly.

"Mom!" Patrick's voice echoed down the hallway. "Are you coming or what?"

She sighed and rolled her eyes. "Coming!"

"Learn anything interesting today, Patrick?" Ann asked her son as they trudged together through the cold and rapidly darkening afternoon. Already the sun was down and Twilight was truly living up to its namesake.

"We watched these two really old guys working on some dead walrus teeth. Big ol' monster teeth! Long and sharp and sort of curved like real fangs. Man, they were rad!"

"They were tusks," Ann automatically supplied the right word.

"Yeah, I guess that's what they called them. Anyway, these two really old guys said they're going to sell them for lots and lots of money. I asked why anyone would pay for old yellow teeth and everybody laughed."

Ann was having difficulty not laughing herself. She reached out and gave her son's shoulder a quick squeeze. "Those old yellow walrus teeth are pretty valuable, Patrick. They're ivory, and Eskimos, like those two really old guys you were talking about, are the only people allowed to carve walrus ivory."

"You mean on the whole planet?"

Ann laughed. "Yes, I guess so."

Patrick thought about that a moment, then continued. "My teacher showed us how the tusks were registered with this silver tag and everything. Then we got to do some carving, only we didn't use real big pieces, just little chunks they didn't need for anything anymore."

"And did you enjoy it?"

Patrick shrugged. "So-so. For old teeth, they sure were hard. Gym class is a lot more funner."

"More fun," she corrected automatically.

"What time do you suppose Jacob will be back? I've been practicing for the ear weight competition and I'm getting real good! Almost better than Paul."

"You're being careful aren't you?" Ann asked, avoiding a direct reply. She still wasn't certain she wanted Patrick honing that particular skill. Something about the way Jacob's eyes had skirted hers when she'd questioned him about it.

"Aw, *Aanaq*," Patrick mumbled.

"*Aanaq?* What's that mean?"

"That's Mom in Yup'ik. Paul taught me. Hey, there's the store!" he yelled, and promptly raced off ahead.

Ann shook her head, wishing she were as carefree and untroubled. As her boots crunched along the well-worn trails connecting the scattered homes to the school, the church and Billy's father's store, Ann realized that of the three of them, Patrick was the only one really adapting to the life-style within the village. Though she'd bragged to Jacob about her adaptability, try as she might, there were just so many new customs to absorb that she was feeling a bit overloaded.

Their house was a major problem. Sharon and Patrick just weren't used to sharing a room like other Yup'ik families and the tension and lack of privacy were getting to both of them. And then there was the bathroom and the strange foods, and a thousand other things that just kept piling up until Ann wondered if she'd carted her family into another age. Living without a phone was an adjustment she'd made with surprising ease, but there were others that hadn't been easy on any of them.

Like having to haul driftwood because propane heating was so expensive. And preparing meals on that antiquated cook stove was an ordeal Ann dreaded. She only hoped she learned how to properly use the thing soon. So far Patrick hadn't complained, but then he had a way of sensing when things were hard for her. Sharon, on the other hand, was a completely different story. Her moodiness had been affecting her appetite, but when it returned, Ann was certain she'd hear about the quality of the dinners.

John Muktoyuk's store was filled with the scent of brewed coffee and stale tobacco smoke when Ann entered the spacious front room, lined wall-to-wall with shelves of foodstuffs. Several young children were running around unleashing after school energy, Patrick among them, their cheeks red and their snow suits unzipped as they munched on after school snacks. In the background, Ann heard the blare of a television set as several elderly neighbors chatted and watched "The Price is Right." She set about gathering the few items she absolutely needed, absorbing the atmosphere and the idle relaxed comfort of the people as they passed away the afternoon.

"Is that it?" John Muktoyuk asked when she paused by his register. He was a tall, lanky man in his mid-fifties with a weather-aged face full of wisdom and quiet strength. He was also a man very serious about his work—and his money apparently, Ann thought, swallowing a smile at his brand new cash register. Compared with the makeshift shelves and inadequate lighting in the store, the machine stood out with glaring modernity, its keypad functions and LED display blinking green neon.

"I see you have a new toy," Ann said as she paid for her purchases.

"Good, huh? Came in this morning's mail drop." His work-roughened fingers patted it proudly. "Billy set it up for me real quick and now everyone wants to try it. I told them they could if they bought something." He laughed heartily. "This thing'll do everything! Keep track of how much I got and tell me when I need more. Come summer, when Billy and I sign on with the fisheries at Clarks Point, my father will have it made. Even makes our receipts in duplicate." He promptly ripped off the paper and handed her a copy.

Though Ann didn't need it, she took the receipt anyway. "Billy's very good with his hands," she complemented his son. "We were talking just yesterday about his maybe studying to be a doctor while he's away at college. That way, if basketball doesn't work out, he'll have something solid to fall back on, something he can use here in the village, like Jacob."

Ann could feel the villagers' abrupt switch in interest. The store grew silent, except for the false brightness of the television program. Even the kids had stopped running around, their eyes huge in their faces as they stared at the two of them. Now what? Ann wondered. Had she said something wrong?

"Billy isn't going to no college."

John's low spoken pronouncement floated heavily upon the smoke-filled air. Ann stared. "Not go to college? But why? Even if he can't play at U.C.L.A., there are state programs specifically for people of Native heritage. Money for college education—all four years—room and board, books and, in some cases, a daily allowance. If I could—"

"Billy isn't going to no college," John repeated, his expression closed.

Ann's confusion must have shown on her face. He sighed. "Look, Mrs. Elliot. I know education's important to you because you're a teacher. And I'm not saying Billy isn't good and everything, but around here playing basketball don't feed a growing family. Every May, me and him go to Clarks Point and sign on with the fisheries. After that, we come home and take the family to fish camp. I need him. He's the oldest boy I got and he's not married. That means he's got to help feed the rest of the family. And I got six other kids. We don't fish in summer, we don't eat during winter. It's as simple as that. And Billy knows it."

Ann stared at him in consternation, certain that Billy did know it. Unfortunately she was equally certain Billy was being torn two ways. His dream was so important to him. Playing pro-basketball was all he ever talked about. It distressed her to think his hopes might be smashed before they even had a chance to succeed. And she'd learned enough about village politics to know that once Billy's father had taken a stand on tradition, he wasn't about to change it for a nontraditional reason like basketball. Not without a damn good reason anyway.

So you better find a damn good reason, Ann told herself. Picking up her bag of groceries, she smiled at John, avoiding a direct reply. She quickly said her goodbyes to everyone else in the store, called Patrick and headed for the house.

"Money certainly does make the world go around," she mumbled under her breath. Patrick skipped along beside her.

"Billy won't be going to college, will he?"

"Yes, he will," Ann answered. "But don't tell anyone I said that, okay, honey? I need some time to figure out what to do."

"Sure, but maybe if you talked to Jacob, he'd come up with something. Especially since he's gone to college and everything."

Her heart took an extra beat. She smiled down at her son. "That's a good idea, Patrick. I might just do that."

Sharon was at home when they arrived and Ann promptly set both children to doing their homework. She and Sharon would talk later, after Patrick had gone to bed. Removing the hamburger from the refrigerator, Ann set about shaping patties, her mind mulling over the pros and cons of discussing John Muktoyuk's attitude with Jacob. He would, she acknowledged, be her best ally, since he'd benefitted from a western education himself. But would he listen to her? Maybe. The children *were* important to him. But Jacob was also a very traditional Yup'ik male. He might not approve of her plan.

As always, whenever she thought about those hours in the cabin, her heart raced. What was it he'd rumbled after waking from the nightmare? "You're so perfect." She blushed. Yes, that's exactly what he'd said. And then he'd kissed her. A kiss that had torn at her heart and mind. Would she ever forget it? Not likely. He'd made her feel more feminine than she'd ever felt before. He'd made her feel beautiful. And yes, perfect. His kiss had stirred so much more than her heart. She was afraid that it had stirred her soul.

And that frightened her.

For thirteen years she'd been dependent on Richard. She'd come to Twilight hoping to reawaken her family's value systems, values Richard had systematically destroyed with his drinking and carousing and high-roller spending sprees. She hadn't come to Twilight to reawaken her heart. Only that's just what she was afraid was happening.

Ann sighed worriedly and flipped the burgers. "Time to clear the table for dinner," she announced. Immediately Patrick jumped up with an enthusiastic "All-ll right!" and slapped closed his schoolbooks. Ann laid down the spatula and approached her daughter.

"Hey, sweetheart," she said lightly, gently shaking her daughter's shoulder. "Dinner."

Sharon looked up, her usually pretty face pale. "I'm not really hungry, Mom."

At fifteen, Sharon was as tall as her mother and had always been very healthy. Ann noted now that she seemed to have lost some weight. "You don't want a hamburger? I thought they were your favorite."

"They are," Sharon replied. "But I guess I'm not very hungry right now. Maybe later."

"I think you should try eating a little something now," Ann insisted, reaching out to place her hand across her daughter's forehead. "No fever. And you're not near your period are you?"

"Jeez, Mom! Tell the whole world why don't you."

Ann frowned. "I think you should try to eat something."

"But—"

"Just try, okay? If it doesn't work out, you can stop." She delivered the words with an encouraging smile. The last thing she wanted was to get her daughter so riled up that she couldn't eat at all. Thankfully, when the hamburgers were done, Sharon did eat something, but not much. Just as they were finishing dessert, a knock sounded on their front door.

"That must be Paul," Patrick said, leaving the table and racing for the door. He flung it open. "I'm almost finished with din—" He broke off. "Oh, hi, Mark."

"Expecting someone else, huh, sport?"

Patrick nodded and stepped aside, letting Mark's broad frame in through the narrow doorway. "My friend Paul's coming over. We're going to bingo together."

Wiping her hands on a dishrag, Ann's gray eyes smiled her welcome. "What brings you here?"

"Three things," he replied, his broad face lighting up with a huge grin. In his hands he held a wonderfully wrought straw basket. "Tradition, good tidings and mail. Hi, Sharon. There's a letter for you."

"There is?"

Sharon's voice showed its excitement as she grabbed the letter from Mark. Seeing the return address, she squealed and ripped it open, running to the couch, where she flung herself down to read.

Ann smiled, happy that one of Sharon's friends had written. She turned to Mark. Ever since their first meeting at Ben's home, the two of them talked often at village functions. Ann enjoyed his relaxed, casual attitude. In comparison to his brother's solemn demeanor, Mark seemed happy and worry-free.

"Good tidings?" Ann gazed at him warily. If she'd learned one thing about Mark, it was that he never seemed to take life all that seriously; and he loved poking fun at her because she did. "This isn't another unknown custom I have yet to learn about, is it?"

"Would I do that to you?"

Ann's eyebrow raised.

"What's that?" asked Patrick, looking at the basket in Mark's hands.

"This is Eskimo food, sport," Mark answered Patrick, though his eyes laughed at Ann's suspicious glance. "A belated housewarming gift, which, I believe, is one of your own customs, isn't it?"

"Better not show Sharon any," Patrick was quick to advise. "She'll just throw up."

"Patrick!"

Mark laughed, his gaze settling on Sharon's pale features. Apparently she'd finished reading. "Don't like black seal ribs and dried ptarmigan?"

Sharon put one hand over her mouth and rushed from the room.

"See?" said Patrick with a smug little nod. "I *tooooold* you so."

Mark shot Ann a quick concerned glance, then shrugged. "Guess you did, sport. Well, hope you two like it. Sorry it couldn't be a more traditional bottle of wine."

"Jacob told us it's against the law to have alcohol here," Patrick informed Mark importantly. "So if you had wine, you'd just get into real bad trouble."

"Good point." Mark crouched, bringing himself to eye level with Patrick, who was already lifting the lid and reaching into the container. "Now be careful with that basket. You can use it for lots of different things once you're finished with the food inside. Siksik made it."

Ann walked over and took the basket from Patrick. "It's really beautiful," she said, examining it carefully. Mary had told her that several of the girls made baskets using tundra grasses gathered and dried during the long days of summer. They sold them at Native arts and crafts fairs in the bigger cities, and some sold for hundreds of dollars, depending on the detail of the design, the size of the basket and the skill of the craftsperson. "I'll have to thank Siksik for this when she comes by later," Ann remarked. "And thank you for the meat. Believe me, it's really appreciated, even if Sharon can't eat it at the moment."

"If you want to eat it like we do, you need to dunk it in seal oil."

"Isn't seal oil used in a *Naniq?*"

Mark's eyes widened in appreciation. "I see you've been studying. How did you hear about the *Naniq?*"

From Jacob, but Ann couldn't bring up how without inviting questions. So she just said, "Mary told me. She said that's how you used to light things around here before there was electricity. With seal oil and *Naniq* clay pots."

"We use it for lots of other things, too. But it does make the meat taste better. Less dried out."

She decided to take him at his word. "We'll try it tomorrow night. Sharon didn't eat much of her hamburger, so she can have leftovers while Patrick and I try the ptarmigan."

"And the black seal ribs and seal oil syrup?"

Ann laughed. "One new dish at a time, okay? As you can see, we were just having common variety strawberry Jell-O for dessert. You're welcome to join us if you want." She invited him into the dining area and set about clearing the dishes off the table. "Siksik told me today you'd taken her to a McDonald's in Fairbanks when Jacob was in the hospital," she ventured in what she hoped was a suitably casual manner.

"She did, huh?" Mark laughed, failing to catch on. "That was supposed to be a secret. Things were pretty tense for all of us during those first few days and I thought she'd get a kick out of eating at a place like that."

"Don't worry, I won't tell," Ann promised, consumed with curiosity. She already knew Jacob had been hospitalized. But what for? She was so busy mulling over the possibilities that she almost missed Mark's question.

"So how do you like living in Jacob's old house?"

She almost dropped the plate she was holding. "What are you talking about?"

"This is Jacob's house?" Patrick cried out excitedly. "Wow! totally cool! Why didn't he say something?"

Mark shrugged nonchalantly, though his black eyes focused closely on Ann's sudden pallor. "He probably thought you already knew, Patrick. Everyone else knows, so I guess he just sort of forgot."

Patrick accepted Mark's explanation. "Then why doesn't he live here anymore?"

Ann's gaze moved abruptly to her son. "Patrick, are you done?" Since he'd just popped the last spoonful into his mouth, he didn't have much choice but to agree. "Then why don't you get ready for bingo." She looked down at her watch. "Paul ought to be here anytime now."

"But, *Aanaq!*"

"Please, Patrick. I want to talk to Mark privately for a minute."

Mumbling that he never got to hear the good stuff, Patrick left the room. Ann turned to Mark.

"He's really learning our language quickly, isn't he?"

"Yes, he is," she replied, not about to be sidetracked. "Much more quickly than either Sharon or I. I guess it has something to do with his being so young. He's not as afraid to make mistakes, and the kids all like him, so it's easier to try." A silence fell between them. She sat down facing Mark. "What's this about our house belonging to Jacob?"

Mark shrugged, observing her curiously. "I thought by now someone would have told you."

"Mark, no jokes for a moment, okay? If this is Jacob's old house, did the three of us force him out because there wasn't enough room elsewhere in the village? Now that I think of it, when I told Mary where we were staying, she seemed surprised. Told me the teacher that was here before lived somewhere else."

"You're really upset, aren't you?"

Ann was remembering how preoccupied Jacob had seemed the morning they'd first met. Now she was afraid she knew why. If this was his house—his *home* for God's sake!—he'd obviously resented giving it over to some unknown teacher that he wasn't even sure would stay. A horrible thought occurred to her.

She was sleeping in his bed!

Her face flushed bright red. "Of course, I'm upset! I don't relish the idea that I forced Jacob out of his home."

"Well, don't worry, you didn't. No one forces Jacob to do anything. You ought to know that much about him by now."

He was right. Jacob wasn't a person one forced to do anything. "So, what's going on? Why are we living here and he isn't?"

"Do we have to talk about Jacob?" Mark complained. "I came bringing good tidings. And I thought you invited me to dessert. Talking about Jacob isn't exactly what I had in mind."

"All right," she gave in graciously, standing and returning to the sink. There was more than one way to skin a cat. "If that's the way you want it, I guess I'll just ask Jacob himself when he gets back tonight."

Mark shook his head soberly, as if he'd just been pushed into a corner. "Did you know you can be as stubborn as he is? Don't smile, it's irritating," he mumbled, then took a deep breath. "Okay, here goes. Listen good, because I'm not repeating myself."

Ann nodded.

"I wouldn't advise asking Jacob about anything regarding this house," Mark said quietly. "He hasn't lived here for three years. Voluntarily."

"Why?" Ann asked softly.

"Because this is where Jacob used to live with his wife, Lia."

Chapter Nine

The words echoed loudly in her brain, but they didn't make sense. *This is where Jacob used to live with his wife, Lia.*

For the second time in so many minutes, Ann almost dropped a plate. *Lia.* The woman he'd called out for. . . .

She sat down abruptly. "Jacob's been married?"

"Didn't you know? I figured someone would have told you by now."

"No, I—I didn't know. No one told me anything. Where is Lia? Where does she live now? She's Yup'ik isn't she?"

Mark clearly didn't want to talk about his brother's wife, but Ann insisted. Jacob's nightmare had been so frightening, and he *had* called out for her. Ann had to know more.

"Yes, she's Yup'ik, but she doesn't live here. She doesn't live anywhere. She's dead, Ann."

"Dead?" The word dropped with harsh finality into the silence. Ann slumped in her seat. "Jacob's a widower? What happened?"

Mark's sigh was impatient. "You really want to hear this? It's not a happy story, you know. Besides, I thought you were going to bingo."

"I am going, but Mark, you can't drop that big a bomb-shell and leave me hanging. What happened?"

"Don't you think Jacob would have said something if he'd wanted you to know? Why's it so important?"

Her troubled eyes met his. "It just is, okay?"

Something odd flickered in the back of Mark's eyes. "All right, short version. Jacob and Lia and his best friend, Jonathan, went out hunting one day about three springs ago. Only Jacob came back."

Only Jacob came back. Again Mark's words echoed hollowly in Ann's brain.

"Mom, it's been hours! Can I come out now?"

Ann jumped, startled out of her daze by Patrick's voice. "Of course, honey, come on out."

Mark was clearly relieved at Patrick's interruption. He accepted the strawberry dessert Ann spooned into a plastic bowl and conversed with her son while he ate.

"What's wrong with your sister? She sick?"

"She's always sick," Patrick complained as he pulled on his snow boots. "Only lately, it's been lots worse. Mom says it's not her dumb old you-know-what, so I guess maybe it could be stomach flu. Just so long as she doesn't give it to me," he grumbled.

"Sisters can be a pain, can't they?" he chuckled sympathetically. "You know, I never noticed it before, but you look a lot like your mother."

"Lots of people say that," Patrick answered proudly, slipping into his ski bib. "Sharon takes after Dad more."

"That right?" Mark addressed Ann, who was staring off into space. She hadn't yet moved from her seat.

"Ann?"

"Hmm?"

"You okay? You look sort of pale."

Ann blinked and pulled herself together. "No, no I'm fine, really, Mark. What was it you asked?"

His black eyes focused speculatively on her pallid features. "I asked you if Sharon takes after her father."

"Pretty much. She inherited Richard's dark brown eyes and hair. But the curls she gets from me."

"He must be a good-looking man."

Mark was still watching her closely. Ann dropped her gaze. "Sharon adored him. They were very close."

"My Dad's dead," Patrick supplied innocently.

Surprise and then sympathetic understanding showed in Mark's eyes. "I'm sorry, Ann. No wonder Jacob's story—"

"That's okay, Mark," Ann interrupted with a quick nod toward Patrick. Mark intercepted the message and nodded.

A knock sounded and Patrick rushed to the door. Apparently Paul had arrived. "Bye Mom. Bye Mark," he yelled and was gone.

As the two boys' excited chatter faded into the night, a silence descended in the small house. Perhaps her expression telegraphed her unease, because Mark rose from the table and crossed the room to peer out the window.

"Listen, I think the plane's coming."

Ann followed, noticing how many of the villagers were heading out to the landing strip. *Jacob's back,* was her first thought. She glanced curiously at Mark, wanting to talk about what he'd revealed. But she sensed Mark's reluctance and wondered what stood so firmly between the two brothers.

"Do people always do that? Go out to meet the plane?"

"Uh-huh. It's our connection with the outside world. It brings in all of our nonsubsistence foodstuffs, our mail and the occasional visitor. Hanna's coming back today, so lots of people will be on hand for that."

"Hanna's the lady who had the heart attack, right?"

He nodded. "It was hard on her. I could tell she was in a lot of pain. We used the radio to talk to the medi-link doctor and he helped us make her as comfortable as we could. But in the end, we had no choice but to wait for the plane."

Ann shivered, suddenly reminded of Twilight's remoteness. "Living without a phone is one thing, but living without a doctor or even an emergency medical technician?" She gazed at him. "Don't you feel unprotected?"

His face clouded over. "We have the radio. The hospital in Bethel has a doctor on call."

"But what about immediate emergencies?"

"That's why Siksik wants to be a nurse, I guess. So that we'll have real live help around here."

"And a plane? What about transportation? Like you said, in the end you still had to wait to fly her out of here."

A cold, shuttered expression settled on his face. "We're survivors, Ann. Ask Jacob."

Ann frowned, perplexed. "What is it between you two?"

The softly voiced question filled the air between them as they watched the villagers hurrying toward the landing strip. Ann thought he wasn't going to answer, but then he turned, as if brushing off the unusual bout of seriousness, and smiled engagingly.

"Any more of that Jell-O?"

Ann accepted the change in topic. She sensed, from Mark's tightly held posture, that his problem with Jacob was something that went too deep for casual discussion. She returned his smile and moved away from the window. "I'm waiting for your sister, want to come to bingo with us?"

He brightened, visibly relieved she hadn't pursued their conversation. "Sure."

In the tiny bathroom, Sharon sat cramped and bent over on the toilet. Her eyes were glued feverishly to the floor, where she'd dropped the plain white envelope she'd ripped open in such haste. But for the moment she wasn't thinking about the contents of the letter Jimmy had written. At the moment her thoughts were centered solely on her upset stomach.

Testing the nausea, she sat slowly upright. Nothing happened. But that didn't mean it wouldn't, she reminded herself. If only she hadn't eaten that stupid hamburger! She'd told Mom she hadn't wanted it. Why hadn't she just refused to eat? It was her stomach after all. No one else was feeling sick and retching. No one else was pregnant.

Sharon glanced at her reflection in the small square mirror over the sink. Her makeup was washed out and her hair a mess. And in a few minutes Siksik was coming by and the three of them were supposed to go play bingo! How was she going to get through it?

Abruptly she stood and leaned over the sink, her eyes squeezed tightly shut. If only there was some way to get to Anchorage. Her eyes dropped to the letter and she bent to pick it up, careful to move slowly.

Sharon no longer believed that they would be going home anytime soon—not after seeing how much Patrick liked living here. Mom was always doing what Patrick wanted—just like Dad had always let her do what she wanted. Only Dad wasn't around anymore. He was dead. And now Jimmy was as good as dead, too. Tears burned her eyes and she brushed at them feebly, feeling depressed. She just knew he'd cut it off with her because they lived so far away!

Oh, if only she could get to Anchorage! Then she could show him how much she loved him; show him how much they belonged together forever, just like they'd vowed.

Tears of desperation streamed painfully down her face, streaking her mascara. There was no way out of this frozen prison! She couldn't fly, couldn't drive, couldn't even walk. She was stuck here.

Why did you do it? Jacob fumed inwardly as he mashed in the recline button and his seat back rose for landing. *You should never have touched her!*

For four days he'd raged at himself. For four days he'd watched her bowed head across the hall, helpless to suppress the sensual memories. There was no getting away from it. He'd lost control of himself, of the situation, of her. His emotions had run clear away with him.

Jacob slapped one sealskin glove against his suit-clad knee. How could he have let it happen? Since Lia's death, control had been his middle name. Ann Elliot's arrival had changed all that.

He didn't notice the loud drumming of the Twin Otter's engine. He sat there, uptight and upright, his booted feet extended, not even bothering to pick up the conference papers strewn around him as Twilight grew larger and the plane landed.

He was back. Back home with Ann. Excitement and anticipation hit him like an avalanche. Then he realized that he was the last person she'd want to see. With another burst of inner disgust, he stuffed pages into his briefcase. How could he have let it happen? Nightmare or not, he should have been stronger, should have been able to push her away.

But he hadn't and for that split second of weakness he now had to live with the memories. Memories of how, for an instant, she had made him feel whole, made him forget the past and look to the future. She had made him feel needed.

Groaning, he snapped closed the briefcase and hefted his parka. As he strode down the narrow aisle, the image of Ann's wide gray eyes and soft kissable mouth became brighter and more focused. Against his will, his pulse raced.

He would never forget the feel of her skin. Smooth and delicate and flushed with a rosy hue, it felt like the softest, lightest down. And her hair. For weeks now he'd subdued the desire to know its texture, to touch those wild springy curls. They, too, were soft, but a different kind of soft. Feminine soft. Woman soft. Drowningly soft.

Like her breasts. And he'd drowned all right. The instant her startled gaze had connected with his, the instant his mind had registered her nakedness, a surge of emotion had welled up inside him and he'd lost his own will to resist the urges tempting him to reach out. She'd wanted him to touch her and nothing at that moment could have stopped him from giving her exactly what she wanted.

Even now he could see the blush that dusted her cheeks, the blush that swept aside his reason and opened the door to insanity. It was crazy. *He* was crazy. But frightening though the realization was, when she'd pulled back, he hadn't wanted to let go. Angry, he'd lashed out when she'd tried to move away, when it was himself he was disgusted with.

How would he survive the loneliness if she left? he wondered. How would he withstand the temptation if she didn't?

When Jacob finally disembarked, it was to find his father and Siksik waiting for him.

"Hanna looks really good, doesn't she?" Siksik asked in Yup'ik after accepting Jacob's warm hug of greeting and taking two small bags to carry for him. "She said the doctor wants her to relax and take it easy, so I told her I'd help out after my classes if she needs anything."

Ben smiled at his daughter. "That was kind, Siksik. Twice in one week you've made your mother and I proud. What next?"

Siksik glowed under Ben's approval and the tension Jacob was feeling about seeing Ann again temporarily vanished as the three set about unloading the Twin Otter of his purchases for the high school.

"You look tired," Ben commented as Jacob handed him a box. He loaded it onto his snowmobile. "Did the testimony go as planned?"

"It went fine, only it didn't accomplish anything immediate. I think we underestimated the strength of the sport fishermen's lobby. They were a big group, bigger than our Native representation.''

Ben frowned. ''Should we call a meeting of village elders?''

''No, I think everyone should hear what happened in Juneau today. It's time we decided to fight for our way of life. All of us need to be united. After what I saw and heard today, there's no other choice. We can't afford to stand on middle ground anymore.''

Jacob knew the philosophy didn't apply to his turbulent feelings for Ann. To remain sane, he *had* to walk the middle ground, had to balance what he wanted against what he couldn't have. He might ache to explore the soft willingness of Ann's consent, but he'd never forgive himself if he did. She was not Yup'ik. She would leave Twilight come spring. Though temptation was a powerful motivator, so was pain. And he had a feeling the pain of her departure would be harder than anything he'd ever experienced if he lost any more of his control.

''I think maybe you should talk to everyone tonight, before bingo,'' Ben suggested as he positioned the last box, then mounted the snowmobile. It sputtered to life and the headlight cut the darkness. ''I'll drive these to the school and get Billy and the other boys started unloading. Then I'll pass the word about the meeting. What time?''

Jacob brushed back the sleeve of his parka and squinted at his watch. ''Twenty-five, thirty minutes.''

Ben nodded and drove off.

Jacob started walking toward town, his sister silently trudging beside him. His eyes followed his father's fading silhouette. Isolated rays of light burst from scattered homes, creeping along well-worn pathways and illuminating scattered debris of all sizes and shapes. Nature's windstorm had again shifted the face of the land, covering some things in high mounds of white while uncovering others. But despite the white carpet, the poverty of his people was plainly evident. And soon, it could become worse, Jacob knew.

''Want to come with me to Mrs. Elliot's? I'm supposed to pick up Sharon for bingo.''

Coming out of his reverie, Jacob shot his sister an assessing look, startled by the unexpected invitation. Siksik avoided meeting his gaze. "What's wrong? Did Mrs. Elliot ask you to come for Sharon and you were too polite to say no?"

"No, I asked her if Sharon could go with me," she answered truthfully. "It's just that I'm not sure Sharon will. She doesn't seem to like me much."

He'd noticed Sharon's less than social behavior, too, but he didn't think it wise to comment on it. Instead he looked down at his sister. She was so warm, so giving. He only hoped the troubled teen didn't hurt his sister. Siksik's heart was too soft to withstand much hurt. "I'll go with you," he said before he could change his mind. Siksik smiled softly and slipped her hand into his.

"What's in the bags?" she asked, swinging one of the ones he'd given her.

"Some S.A.T. study books Mrs. Elliot asked for and handouts from the meeting," Jacob replied as they headed toward his old house. *Ann's* house now, he admonished himself. Since their return from Tununak, he'd decided that if he was going to succeed at maintaining control of his emotions, now more than ever, he needed to start thinking of the house as hers and not his. Yet as they approached the familiar structure, Jacob could feel tension mounting within him.

The comfortable sound of friendly laughter drifted to his ears as he and Siksik climbed the few steps to the front door.

"Oh, good, Mark's here!" Siksik said, her slender shoulders relaxing as she recognized her brother's voice.

Jacob stiffened. At Siksik's knock, the laughter abruptly stopped. It suddenly occurred to him that while he couldn't have Ann, someone else certainly could. And from the easy sound of their laughter, Jacob concluded Mark had figured out the same thing.

Needing action, Jacob relieved Siksik of the packages. No more than a few minutes earlier he'd told himself that Ann was off-limits, but the reactions he was now experiencing made the rationalization seem crazy. He felt angry, jealous. Illogically he found himself wanting to smash down the door and demand that Mark leave his house.

"It's about time you got here. The three of us were about to go to the gym without you." Mark's laughing eyes welcomed Siksik, until he noticed Jacob's hulking presence and dark angry glare. "Bad day in Juneau?" Mark drawled, amusement clear in the tone of his voice. That he suspected why Jacob was angry was obvious in the insolent tilt of his eyebrows. Jacob said something in Yup'ik that made Mark bark out a sharp laugh. Siksik gasped. "I had no idea you loved me that much," Mark replied, not in the least disturbed. Stepping away from the door, he let the duo enter.

Mark's proprietary behavior irritated Jacob. He was certain his brother had deliberately phrased his not-so-casual comment to sound like he and Ann were going to bingo together. Unreasonably upset at the possibility, Jacob stepped intently into the room, filling it with the power of his presence. Ignoring Mark, his gaze searched out and zeroed in on Ann.

She was bent over and just pulling on her boot. Jacob stood still, his eyes meeting Ann's as she looked up, recognized him, and blushed a brilliant red. Her hands, still holding the boot, clenched tightly around the insulated fabric.

Jacob fought to keep his eyes from the pale slope of her breasts, visible from the V-neck of her blue sweater. Softness and light. Warmth and comfort. Before him stood temptation personified, sweet and enticing and infinitely desirable. He had to forcibly remind himself that this would not change. She would tempt him often in the coming months and it was something he had to learn to deal with. Now was as good a time as any.

"Take Siksik and Sharon and go on ahead," he addressed Mark, though his gaze never wavered from Ann. "I need to talk to Ann."

"Don't forget the meeting," Siksik said, her soft voice puzzled.

There was a long pause before Mark finally moved, herding Sharon and Siksik out of the house. Only then did Ann realize she'd been holding her breath. As casually as she could, she finished pulling on her boot and stood.

"Where's Patrick?" Jacob asked, forcing his mind away from the generous curves beneath the sweater.

After his abrupt dismissal of everyone, his ordinary question left her nonplussed. "He left a while ago, with Paul. He was looking for you earlier today. I had to remind him you'd flown to Juneau. He had something he wanted to show you, I think."

Her sentences were short and jerky but she couldn't help it. Now that he was here, in front of her, a thousand questions crowded her brain. How long had he been married? Did he have nightmares often? Did what happened have anything to do with his limp? And why wasn't he yelling, or at the very least raging about how she'd pulled away from him back in the cabin? But most of all, she just wanted to know why he was here with her now. The days since the cabin incident had been long. Had he missed her as much as she'd missed him?

Moments passed in silent contemplation, moments filled with uncertainty and indecision and the memory of a stormy night that stood like a visible link between them.

Jacob remembered the desire in her eyes.

Ann recalled the harsh words he'd spoken.

"I shouldn't have—"

"Did you mean what you—?" she asked at the same time.

Both stopped talking, aware that the same instant was on both their minds. Then Jacob set the bags on the coffee table, thrusting his hood off his head. In one smooth move, he removed his gloves, unzipped his parka and sat down heavily in the armchair.

Ann swung her gaze from the caribou and sealskin mukluks to the white shirt and gray pin-striped suit before sliding up to his dark expressive eyes. The man was a meld of old and new, tradition and progress. Her heart pounded crazily. Following his lead, she sat on the couch.

"I'm sorry," he began, his forearms resting heavily on his thighs, his eyes on the floor. It was hard enough saying something he didn't believe in, but looking her in the eye while he said it was impossible. "Sorry about what happened ... about kissing you. It shouldn't have happened."

Acute embarrassment flooded Ann's body. He hadn't meant it. Hadn't meant anything he'd done or said. Abruptly she stood. Shame coursed hotly through her veins as she headed for the hook on the wall beside the door. Reaching up, she pulled down her jacket, swinging into the garment with the swift efficiency of someone needing to get out of a bad situation quick.

"Shall we go? Siksik mentioned something about a meeting, and I don't want to miss it."

"You've got time. I'm running it, so they can't start without me." Jacob stood, his eyes narrowed, watchful. She'd deliberately turned away so he couldn't see her face.

"I need to make sure Sharon's all right and that Patrick's not getting into trouble." She jerked on her gloves, then reached for the doorknob.

"Ann, wait."

She paused but didn't turn around. Puzzled, Jacob strode toward her and it wasn't until he stood inches from her taut body that he noted the deep red blush suffusing her face. "What is it?"

"Just leave it alone, Jacob," she whispered. Her voice wasn't up to anything more substantial. "You've said your piece and I listened. Now shall we go?"

Jacob reached out, only vaguely aware that he was doing exactly what he'd told himself he wouldn't do. Gently he turned her to face him, then released her. She still wouldn't look up.

Ann swallowed.

Jacob spoke, compelled by the stiffness in her shoulders, the burn in her cheeks to explain, to tell the truth. "I know you were only trying to wake me up. Believe me, I'm more angry at myself than you could ever be. I shouldn't have kissed you, shouldn't have said what I did. I meant it . . . but I shouldn't have said it. You were right to pull back."

Ann heard his words but only three sank in.

I meant it.

She looked up. "You meant it? Then what— Why? I don't understand. . . ."

Her words, like an Arctic breeze in winter, sliced deeply at Jacob's resolve. They were so shy and vulnerable. He knew what he should do. He should step back from temptation, retreat from the soft entreaty in her voice. But he couldn't. Time seemed somehow suspended in feeling. Renewed feeling. And awakened desire. His gaze dropped to the curve of her neck.

A sudden breeze caught the door and shook the house. Ann shivered.

And Jacob reacted. To protect, to comfort, to hold. His arms reached out and he enfolded her easily despite the down jacket, tilting her chin and taking her mouth much as a hunter takes his prey: swiftly and without hesitation. Even as he felt the first contact, however, he also felt the pain, felt the "see" of his reason slide to the "saw" of insanity. He hadn't realized until that moment just how beautiful insanity could be.

Her lips were like the rest of her: softness and light, sweetness and comfort. Her breath feathered into his mouth, filling his lungs with her scent, her taste, her essence. Gently he trailed his tongue over her bottom lip, testing its fullness, nibbling at its Arctic Rose-petal texture. He couldn't get enough and had to restrain the urge to force her back against the wall so he could gain deeper access. The last thing he wanted to do was frighten her.

As the rigid control of Jacob's broad shoulders communicated itself to Ann, the last remnants of her doubt dissolved. He tasted of things she didn't know, things she wanted to learn, to understand. He was familiar yet a stranger, an overwhelming power that was everywhere at once. She'd always felt guilty with Richard because she'd performed her occasional wifely duties without any real enthusiasm. But with Jacob there was no guilt, only a burning desire so intense that nothing could withstand its heat. The blood in her veins pounded with renewed life, a surge so deeply moving that tears burned her eyes. Tears of happiness. Tears of relief. Tears of sweet, painful longing.

For thirteen years she'd been married, and in all that time, nothing in her experience had come close to the wonder she felt at the possessive intent of Jacob's questing lips. He seemed to be everywhere at once, nibbling at the corner or her mouth, then moving to the other side to repeat the erotic gesture. He rubbed and licked and teased and claimed and she returned the motions, learning his likes and dislikes, repeating the gestures with the same fevered urgency. She groaned when he seemed to lose an inner battle and, murmuring endearments in Yup'ik, pressed her back against the wall, for as much as he wanted to increase the contact of their bodies, so did she. She felt herself open to him freely, willingly and without restraint. Her breasts were crushed against his chest and she only wished she didn't have her jacket on. Wished they were both bare, for she could now admit to herself how much she wanted to run her hands across the massive expanse of his rock-solid chest.

Jacob pressed into Ann's softness, groaning as her hands slipped inside his parka and around his chest to splay against his back, pulling him deeper in to her. He spread his legs until he fit flush against her body, until the thickness of her jacket couldn't hide the soft pressure of her breasts or the inviting cradle of her pelvis. She was small and he had to spread out wide, but it didn't matter. Nothing mattered except this feeling of release, of sweet willingness on her part that was driving him crazy. He could feel her desire! He could feel . . . need. Hot, aching need.

He opened his eyes and froze. Hanging on the wall above Ann's head was an old dance fan. Lia's dance fan. Jacob jerked his mouth from hers.

"I—I can't," he said on a broken whisper, pushing back and away from her.

That was when he saw the disbelief, the confusion and the return of doubt in Ann's eyes.

"It's because of Lia, isn't it?"

Chapter Ten

In the electric silence that followed her question, Jacob's harsh intake of breath was clear and loud.

"Who told you about Lia?"

"Your brother. He didn't mean to, but he thought I knew that this house was yours and then, well, one thing led to another..." Ann's voice faded as she searched Jacob's frighteningly bleak, emotionless expression. She reached out, but he flinched, stepping back beyond her reach.

"We can move, Jacob, if that's what's bothering you. Mary told me the other teacher lived somewhere else. Maybe on the weekend, the kids and I—"

"No," Jacob interrupted, the words coming from between clenched teeth. "You can't move. This is Twilight, not Anchorage. There's nowhere else to go."

"But if it hurts you to have us here—"

"It doesn't!" he all but shouted the lie. Abruptly he zipped up his parka and jerked open the door. "Let's go. I've got a meeting to run."

Ann walked alongside Jacob, sensing he was more likely running away from something than he was hurrying toward the high school gym and the waiting villagers. When she slipped, his arm shot out to steady her and their eyes met in a brief blazing look that told her more than his words had revealed: Jacob wanted her, but he didn't like it.

He swung open one of the gym doors. Ann ducked beneath his arm, stepping from the silence and near pitch darkness of the night into the loud ricochet of voices amid the bright lights of the auditorium. Though the high school itself was the most modern building in the village, the gym was nothing more than a rectangle lined on two sides with metal bleachers for seating, and a wooden floor painted with the outlines of a variety of sport courts.

Ann paused, letting her eyes adjust, automatically scanning the jam-packed room for Sharon and Patrick. She found Patrick first, off in a cluster of his peers, shouting and yelling and apparently practicing for the W.E.I.O. competitions. People were seated everywhere, mostly on the gym floor itself, and mostly grouped into families. Grandmothers sat rocking little babies, their daughters working diligently on handicrafts, some baskets, some beadwork. The men drank soda pops and smoked, swapping tales as they arranged their bingo cards in readiness for the evening's play.

The villagers were an intriguing combination of the old and the modern, with mukluks and *kvspuks* right alongside tennis shoes and floppy T-shirts. Most of the teenagers were crammed along the walls, clustering together in boy and girl groups. She spotted Billy in the midst of the boys and followed his gaze to Sharon off by herself, her wild curly hair and overly made-up face standing out like a beacon. Siksik she located on Sharon's other side and Ann was disturbed to realize the young girl was watching Billy watch Sharon.

It was hot inside the gym. With quick movements she shed her jacket and gloves, aware that Jacob hadn't yet moved from behind her. She turned and their eyes met.

"I'm a big girl, Jacob," she spoke softly, her voice resigned. "So don't worry about me. I can take care of myself." He paused, searching her face, reading the truth of her words and the caution, too, Ann imagined, but she couldn't very well do anything about that. Self-protection she'd learned the hard way and she donned the cloak with bitter but familiar ease.

She watched him stride toward the makeshift podium, where his father sat among other village elders and where she assumed the bingo numbers would later be called out. She spotted Mary who waved her over. When she'd settled down beside her friend, Ben opened the meeting, signaling for Jacob to speak.

"In ancient times we were a fierce people. Some of you still tell grandchildren the old stories and treasure the blades and spears of our warrior ancestors. We had strong leaders then, and brave fighters. We were a victorious people, proud of our history and proud of our culture."

Murmurs rebounded around Ann at the seriousness of his words. Children stopped their games, teens stopped their roughhousing, even the babies somehow sensed their parents' mood and stopped crying to listen to the deep rumbling voice.

"It is time to resurrect the pride of our ancestors and stand together in a modern day battle. Only this time all Natives must join together—Yup'ik and Athabascans and Inupiats. We must band together as one, for the preservation of our land and our future is threatened. No longer can we be 'the invisible people'. No longer can we let wrongs go unrighted. I've just returned from a meeting in Juneau where the battle is already under way. The enemy is clever and powerful. It uses our own weaknesses as its strengths. We must stop it. We must stand up. We must defend our rights and our land."

"What is this battle we must fight? Who is our enemy?"

Ann recognized the voice: Billy's father, John. Several adults around her had the same question, concern and worry filtering audibly through the group. Ann herself was concerned for she didn't know where Jacob's speech was headed. What was he trying to do? Start a war?

"Our enemy is ourselves as much as it is the laws of the *kass'aqs*. When you use a snow machine instead of a dogsled, what do you gain?"

"Speed," a teenager shouted out. His friends cracked smiles and punched the youth in mock reprimand.

"Comfort," someone else added.

"Convenience," a young mother said.

"But at what cost? Gas is expensive; so are repair parts. While the white man's technology is often convenient, it's an advantage that is slowly draining our peoples' strengths. Look around you. There are more broken-down snowmobiles than there are dogsleds and dogs. Have you never wondered why this is?''

No one had an answer for his question.

"Dogs don't break down when the weather gets cold. So long as they have food, they will serve. Our grandfathers and great-grandfathers knew this. Why have we chosen to forget?''

Again, no one answered.

"Listen to me. Comfort is dangerous. Convenience is dangerous. Even speed is dangerous when it propels us toward an age where the old ways die out, carelessly discarded along with aluminum cans and plastic wrappers. The *kass'aq* technology creates dependence. A dependence all the more dangerous because we have reprogrammed ourselves and voluntarily changed our way of life to see this quiet invasion as progress.''

Ann had no idea how other villagers were taking Jacob's speech, but she was worried. His words pulled them apart. Had he done it deliberately? Well, if he'd wanted a reason to push her away, he'd found one. She couldn't combat something she couldn't change. She would never be Yup'ik. In time she might adapt, might learn the language and customs, but she'd never be Native. Question was, if she could be, if being Yup'ik allowed her a chance to deepen whatever was growing between them, would she?

Ann snapped out of her reverie when Mark abruptly stood and addressed the group.

"Don't you think you're exaggerating? How many of you really want to return to the old days, without snowmobiles and motorized boats and rifles? How many of you want to give up electricity for seal oil lamps and fancy new cash registers for paper receipts?''

Ann watched the younger Toovak scan the gym floor, his eyes as fired as his brother's. "You see? Nothing has been taken that we haven't gladly given up. If our culture is to survive, then I say we must join with the white man, not fight against him. Progress isn't dangerous. We have benefited from the *kass'aq*. For the first time we have an opportunity to be put on equal ground with urban Alaskans. I don't think we should fight against the sports fishermen's lobby but be willing to compromise our rural priority that sets us apart. Equal footing gives us leverage. Power that we'll need if we're ever to succeed in our own attempts to lobby for improved social services, educational opportunities and legislative representation for our people. And, if we think hard enough, we might even come up with some ways to make money from the new opportunity.''

For the briefest of instants Ann sensed Jacob's scrutiny, but when she looked his way, he quickly averted his glance to John Muktoyuk, who had stood to speak.

''My store sells *kass'aq* goods. But that don't make me rich. I got six kids, Mark. You don't got any. Try feeding six kids and then tell me what you think. Even with the store, I couldn't afford a limit on how much I fish and hunt. We don't fish, we don't eat.'' He sat down.

Then an old woman, her face deeply etched with time and wisdom held up her hand. Ann quickly leaned toward Mary. ''Who's that?''

''Milak Nayakik, our healer. The only woman on the council of elders. She's ninety years old.''

Ann felt an air of expectancy shiver through the audience, apparently this woman was very powerful. When she spoke, her words were surprisingly strong. But they were also in Yup'ik. Many people murmured after she was through. Dying of curiosity, Ann again turned to her friend.

''What did she say?''

''She said we must think carefully about our future and remember that good and evil are often hard to tell apart. She reminded us that alcohol was a *kass'aq* benefit that practically destroyed us until we banned it from the village.''

Again Ann sensed Jacob's scrutiny. Their eyes met and held, both recalling the two bottles of wine she'd brought in her suitcases. The discussion continued for a while, with several villagers telling how the change in subsistence rules would affect them. Finally, Jacob spoke again.

''You all know I've just returned from Juneau. The sport fishermen's lobby is gaining support. One of their proposals is to treat Natives like sport hunters and sport fishermen. That would mean we could catch only a few salmon per person per day during the peak fishing season. It would mean we could hunt only a few caribou. And it would mean we couldn't gather some of the traditional foods we now take for granted.'' An uncomfortable murmur reverberated through the villagers. ''In short, that proposal would mean we wouldn't have enough to eat. So, if we're going to win this battle, we need to begin fighting now.''

Apparently Jacob's words ended the discussion, for Ben suggested they all think about it and give their input to the council members.

Then Ben moved on to other lighter topics. Siksik's shy announcement that Billy had received two letters from college basketball scouts was received with surprising good cheer considering the seriousness of the discussion just completed. Ann glanced from John Muktoyuk's frown back to Mary, who was smilingly arranging her bingo cards. Children started talking again as families readied themselves for the evening of fun.

But Ann couldn't so easily switch streams. "Mary, how do you feel about this? Is the danger really that serious?''

She shrugged, the lightweight cotton *kuspuk* falling easily on her broad frame. "It's really hard to know what to think, Ann. Mark's got a point, but then, so do Jacob and Milak. Before we banned alcohol, the men would drink too much and lots of the women and children were beaten by their husbands. We didn't advertise the fact, but that's the way it was around here for a long time. Maybe we should be monitoring what we accept more closely. I don't know.'' She eyed Ann curiously. "I noticed you and Jacob came in together. Did something happen?''

They'd kissed. And if there hadn't been a meeting, and if she hadn't mentioned Lia, they would have been making love right now. But there was no way she would reveal any of that, not even to a friend as nice as Mary was.

"He came by the house to give me some S.A.T. study workbooks I ordered.'' Ann averted her eyes, her hands idling with the bingo cards.

"He came by the house, did he? Interesting,'' Mary replied, eyeing her curiously. "You've heard about Lia, then?''

"I know she's dead. Mark told me. I told Jacob we'd move since he seemed so uncomfortable having us there.''

"You did? But there's no other place.''

"I know that now. Jacob said exactly the same thing. Still, I'm uncomfortable knowing he's upset with the situation.''

"Well, don't worry about it. Jacob hasn't set foot in the house since the accident. You've forced him to do something he's been avoiding. And I personally think it's about time.''

But did Jacob? Ann wondered. She knew from her own experience that you couldn't push people into doing or feeling things before they were ready. It had taken some years for her to obtain the necessary emotional strength to separate from her husband. If Jacob hadn't ventured inside that house before her arrival, then he hadn't been prepared to face his past with his lost wife.

But if he was still so entangled, then why had his arms implied possession as his lips captivated hers? He was a man of intense emotional depths. Now she understood the turmoil clouding his eyes so often. What she didn't understand—and what was so temptingly dangerous—was his passion. What if, despite his own objections, he kissed her again? He'd made her feel pride in her femininity, giving her a gift of priceless value. Would he do so again? Could she resist him if he tried?

One thing she did know was that she didn't want to become involved with Jacob while he was mixed up inside. Besides, a relationship with Jacob could never be private. Twilight was too small, and everyone knew everyone else's business. They might not talk about it, but that didn't mean they didn't know.

For a while longer her thoughts stayed on the same track, and she automatically followed the bingo game on the cards Mary pushed her way.

"Guess what?" Mary smiled triumphantly a few minutes later. She held up her card. "Bingo!"

While all around her people groaned with good-hearted cheer, Ann noticed Ben motioning for her to join him and a group of others off to the right of the podium. Telling Mary she'd be back, she quickly checked on her kids, surprised to note Sharon and Siksik were actually having a conversation. Patrick was playing bingo with Paul's family. Zigzagging through the maze of seated bodies, she crossed the room to where Ben stood conversing with his sons and several village elders.

Now what? Ann thought as she pinned a smile on her face.

Three nights later, a windy and cold Saturday evening, Jacob sat at his dinette, surrounded by carvings in various stages of completion. The statue of the Eskimo hunter was done, broken foot concealed within a solid base of petrified whale bone. The silence was absolute save for the wind outside and the scraping sound of the tiny sharp-edged knife as he carefully etched into the hard ivory. A knock sounded on the door.

"Come in!"

Jacob looked up, his gaze locking with his brother's as Mark entered and purposefully unzipped his snowsuit to the waist, slipping out of the arms. He had just come from the gym and he was wearing a T-shirt and gray sweats underneath. Around his neck dangled an old pair of tennis shoes tied at the shoelaces. He dropped them to the floor.

"Missed you at practice," Mark began, his expression a fluctuating combination of uneasiness and determination.

"Did you?" Jacob raised an eyebrow, though his gaze remained fixed on the carving. "Or did you set a new height record at the one-foot high kick and decide to come tell the old champ all about it? Well, I'm not interested."

"Lay off the heavy guilt, will you? If you wanted to compete in the W.E.I.O. games you could and you damn well know it." His gaze dropped to Jacob's bare right foot. His toeless right foot. "It's not my fault you're lame. And it's not my fault you got stuck out on that ice floe. I'll tell you something, Jacob, I'm getting pretty tired of having you take it out on me."

"I don't."

"The hell you don't."

"You know what the problem is, Mark. And you also know it has nothing to do with what happened to me."

A tense silence enveloped the room. Finally Mark grunted and settled down in one of the dinette chairs. Reaching out, he picked up the Eskimo hunter. "Good piece," he spoke into the quiet. "I like what you did with the whalebone. Sort of makes him look tied to the past the way his feet are bound up in the bone like that." Startled by his brother's unexpected insight, Jacob stiffened. "You'll probably get eight or nine hundred for it in Bethel. More if you sell it in Anchorage."

At that, Jacob looked up. "Do you think of everything in terms of the money it will bring?"

Clearly offended, Mark replied, "What do you expect? Someone's got to look forward with an eye to our future. Besides, look who's talking. You're the one with the fancy degrees. You're our damned business manager, remember?

That's all you do everyday is think about money. Hell, you probably dream about it, too."

If only he could. But there was already one dream—nightmare—that haunted his soul. Lately, though, the familiar visions were blurring, changing in subtle ways he sensed but couldn't yet grasp.

"The carving is not for sale."

Mark shrugged and set it down. "Suit yourself, but while this one's on display, you could be carving yourself another."

"It's not for sale," Jacob repeated. The Eskimo hunter had become a symbol to him. A symbol of his own prison, where he remained locked within himself, unable to move forward.

Mark's eyes flared, though Jacob didn't notice. He picked up a smaller carving. "What about this? *Kegluneq,* the wolf, right? Your *inua.* You keeping that, too?"

Jacob had given it serious thought. He'd carved the image of his spirit guide shortly after his return to the village, hoping the strength implied within the image would support his troubled soul. And it had, though if pressed he knew he couldn't describe the unusual sense of reassurance it afforded. As if something out there was watching over him, protecting him.

"Yours is there, too."

Mark scanned the priceless collection. "I don't see it."

"Look for the money clip. It's got *Tuntu* on it."

"Money clip?" Mark picked up the shiny brass-plated object. On top Jacob had glued an oval ivory carving of a caribou. "You put my *inua* on a *money clip?*"

"A buck on a buck holder." Jacob chuckled, the sound more bitter than merry. "It fits you, brother. You can't escape your nature. Like the caribou, you're a wanderer."

"And like the wolf, you're a hunter," Mark shot back, clearly angry at the implication.

Jacob nodded, aware he had little right to hand out advice when he wasn't willing to accept any. As he inched the sharp blade along an emerging curve in the ivory he was working on, he thought back to when Mark and he had been close. They'd always discussed their heritage and how best to preserve it, but since Lia's death, discussions had been harsher, more hurtful and vindictive. Was Mark right to imply that Jacob's feelings were souring their relationship?

"Jacob?"

With a start, he realized his brother had spoken. "I'm sorry, Mark. What was that you were saying?"

"I said, we really need to talk."

Jacob glanced down at the money clip in Mark's hands. "You can have it if you want."

The gesture was clearly a peace offering. Jacob withstood Mark's probing glance, letting his brother see his uncertainty. For a long while, neither spoke. Finally Mark said, "It wasn't your fault, you know. No one can predict the weather, even us. You did everything humanly possible and then some. You survived."

Jacob nodded, more to get his sibling to drop the subject than because he believed what Mark had said. He went back to carving. "So, what's important enough to make you miss the Saturday night movie?"

"Ann Elliot," Mark replied, standing and crossing to the refrigerator. Opening the door, he peered inside, then reached for a soda. "Want one?"

Jacob shook his head, his eyes once again wary as they watched Mark flip the ring top and take a long swallow.

"Look, Jacob, I know she's a sore subject with you. I mean, she's living in your house and everything... and I couldn't help but notice the tension between the two of you the other night... Anyway..."

Jacob had a feeling he wasn't going to like this. "Anyway what?"

Mark sighed and wandered over to the window. He leaned against the wolf pelt curtain. "I think she's a courageous lady. I like her."

Jacob's stomach knotted.

"Come on, Jacob. Admit it. She's done a great job so far. And I think she can do a lot more for Twilight. I've been thinking about your speech Wednesday night. Maybe we can work together on this subsistence thing. There's got to be a compromise somewhere, right? I think Ann might be the bridge. When Dad called her over and asked her all those questions about people we don't even know..." He shrugged. "I was as surprised as you were to find out her ex was this big real estate wheeler-dealer in Anchorage. But the fact is, she's got contacts. Contacts that we need." He took another swallow, observing his brother closely. "You know the guy's dead, right? That she's a widow?"

Jacob nodded. He didn't look up, afraid that if he did, Mark would see the wanting in his eyes.

"Anyway," Mark continued, and Jacob could hear the frustration in his voice, "you're the most qualified to work with her from that end."

The pounding in Jacob's head increased. The thought of being alone with Ann set his mind to spinning with excitement and denial. Too often he forcibly had to remind himself that she wasn't Yup'ik and that even if she were to adapt, she'd be gone come spring. It was the only way he could maintain a distance between them. Only the arguments had become a litany that were fast growing weak, repeated whenever he saw her and remembered the taste and feel of her lips.

"Jacob?" When Mark sensed he once again had his brother's full attention, he continued. "You can work with Ann, then report back to us and the council. I think it's a good approach, *if* you can control yourself. It'll protect both our interests. What's especially perfect is that Ann knows how to contact legislators leaning toward Native concerns. Do you? Can you get in to see the governor?"

"Can she?"

"Her chances are better than yours, probably better than Dad's. I don't know, Jacob. I don't know how this thing will turn out if we don't have more power on our side. More *kass'aq* power, I mean. You said so yourself. They're very influential."

"I know," Jacob said, but the words were flat, lifeless. He didn't relish the idea of deepening his contact with Ann. She was too tempting. He was too weak. "So you want me to talk to her," Jacob said, resignation in his voice.

"Yes. And I want you to stop making her feel so uncomfortable. She's got enough to deal with without your overbearing personality." Jacob eyed him but Mark kept talking. "I know she's in your house, hell, she's sleeping in your bed—" The carving knife clattered to the table. Mark's eyes narrowed intently. "Look, all I'm asking is that you lighten up. There's a lot at stake here."

Jacob knew that only too well. Since their night in the fishcamp shelter, he'd thought of little else but just how much was at stake. He glanced at his brother. "And what about you?"

"What about me?"

"You said you liked her."

Mark's forehead crinkled, then widened in comprehension. "I do like her, but she warned me off that first night over at Dad's." He shrugged. "We're friends. Which is what you two should be."

Which was exactly what Jacob feared they could never be. He sighed, suddenly bone-tired. Tired of the nightmares, tired of walking that narrow road. Why had he allowed her troubled gray eyes to lure him across the line? Now he couldn't forget the sweet taste of oblivion, for that's exactly what she'd offered and what he'd discovered during those brief mad moments when their lips and bodies had met and melded. Heavenly oblivion.

But life couldn't be pushed away forever. And now it seemed it couldn't even be put off until next week. Ann was forcing him into dealing with life, with the emotions he'd tried to bury.

"I'll talk to her Monday," he promised. "We'll see what we can come up with."

Monday afternoon Jacob sat at his desk, his fingers idle on the keypad of his personal computer. He needed to speak with Ann. Mark's suggestion nagged at his conscience. Making up his mind, he crossed the hall to her office.

"We need to talk."

"Good afternoon to you, too, Jacob," Ann grumbled, not bothering to look up.

She felt battered and frustrated. Sunday had been a particularly long day. Sharon had refused to be drawn out and Patrick had all but climbed the walls, cooped up inside because of another cold front. She hadn't slept well, either. Her dreams of Jacob had been so sensual she'd seriously considered sneaking outside to cool down her active imagination.

"If you need the letter we drafted on the revamp of the statewide test, I'm not finished with it yet. I know I said I'd have something by today, but—"

"That's not why I'm here," Jacob interrupted, his temperature rising at the mere sight of her. She was wearing the green qiviut sweater again. He had to restrain the urge to lean across her desk and stroke the curve of her breast through the downy soft weave. "You told my father last Wednesday night that you could arrange a meeting with the governor. Can you?"

Ann glanced up and almost gasped aloud. Gone were Jacob's clothes. For an instant, he stood before her in nothing but the scrap of moose hide he'd worn back in the cabin. Her gaze traveled across his shoulders, then down his muscular stomach to the thighs she remembered as being so rock-solid. To think that she'd pulled away from his lovemaking! No one had ever looked more riveting than he had silhouetted by the light of a seal oil lamp. She stared at him.

"Ann?"

"Hmm?"

"Can you?"

"Can I what?"

"Arrange a meeting with the governor."

"The governor? Yes, I—I suppose so." She blinked, dispelling the sensually disturbing images. "At least, I know people who could. Why?"

"Mark suggested we combine our resources. Your knowledge of *kass'aq's* with mine of the issue."

"I see," she murmured, covering her dismay beneath a false calm. There was no way she could agree. A project like this would require days to complete. Maybe weeks. No, he'd just have to find someone else. Someone who wasn't fantasizing about making love every time he walked in the door!

"Close the door will you, Jacob?" Once he had, she cleared her throat before saying nervously, "I don't think it would be a good idea for us to spend that much time together."

"Why?"

The word was flung like a gauntlet. Ann's lips tightened. "Come on, Jacob. You know why. And frankly, I'm shocked you're even objecting. We aren't together two minutes before we're arguing. We're doing it now, for goodness' sake."

Placing his palms flat on her desktop, Jacob leaned forward. "We've been arguing since the day you arrived, Ann," he said softly. "What's really bothering you?"

"I just told you. It's a legitimate concern, Jacob."

"Is it? Then how come we still managed to compile enough information to draft that letter you haven't finished?"

"I didn't say we *couldn't* work together, I said I didn't think it was a good idea."

"Why?"

"Damn it, Jacob. Leave it, alone."

"Not until you're honest with me."

"I am!"

"Partly, yes," he conceded. "But shall I tell you what's really bothering you? You're embarrassed. You can't stand the fact that I've seen you naked. Just what do you think I'm going to do? Lose control? Maybe do exactly what you've been thinking about since I walked over here?"

Ann choked. "How dare—!"

"I dare a lot when my people's future is at stake," he breathed softly, his face inches from hers. "If this bill goes through, we could be forced into a quota scheme that limits our seasonal yields. That's the bottom line as far as I'm concerned. The land's important. It's our birthright. It's who we were, who we are today, what we believe in. I'd do anything necessary to ensure we maintain free access to its resources."

Tension filled the room. "I see," Ann eventually murmured. "And that includes spending time with me though it's the last thing on earth you want to do."

"Don't put words into my mouth. Retaining the subsistence priority is critical to my people. I won't let my personal concerns interfere with something that will help our cause. And I won't let your unfounded paranoia interfere, either."

Ann swallowed hard against the heat burning her cheeks. "Why don't I just give you a list of the people. You and Mark can work out the details."

He scowled. "Forget it. Mark and I don't get along."

"And we do?"

He curled his right hand under her chin, lifting her mouth to his. "On occasion, yes." Ducking his head, he brushed his lips across hers.

As before, it was tantalizing and instantly arousing. The soft touch made her feverish, light-headed. She curled both hands around his wrist, feeling the hard, fast beat of his pulse beneath her fingers. She tugged, trying to push him away, but he wouldn't release her. His strength made a mockery of her attempt. She whimpered.

"Stop this, Jacob," she pleaded against his roving lips. "I won't be a substitute for Lia."

He reared back. "What did you say?"

"I said, I won't be a replacement for your wife. She's dead."

His anger was as visible as the silence was loud. It erupted through his body and into hers. He looked as if he would like to strangle her, he was so incensed. Ann's heartbeat tripled.

Jacob turned and strode to the door. With his hand on the doorknob, he paused but didn't turn around. "Are you going to help or not?"

Ann felt terrible. How could she have said something so hurtful? All right, so he'd gotten out of hand with his macho tactics, but was that any reason to be cruel? She gazed at the tense outline of his shoulders.

"Jacob, I'm sorry—" she began but he cut her off.

"Are you or aren't you? That's all I need to know."

Ann sighed. "Sure. I'll clear my schedule."

Chapter Eleven

Ann sat on the aging couch in her home, surrounded by long and short pieces of sealskin and caribou hide. She was making mukluks for Sharon and Patrick. With Mary's instructions the sewing was coming along fine, but the caribou hide sinew wasn't the easiest string to sew with. Stretching to relieve a cramped neck, Ann sighed deeply, laying aside the heavy needle to gaze contentedly out of the window. Outside, gray dawn carpeted the snowy November midmorning. The almost continuous snowfall of the previous weeks had stopped today and the sky had cleared, a sign Ann knew particularly pleased Patrick because he and Jacob and Siksik were going ice fishing.

They had been in Twilight a month. During that time, she'd administered the statewide exam, organized the S.A.T. study group, and had begun developing some lasting friendships. Patrick was doing fine and even Sharon had befriended Siksik finally. Life in Twilight challenged her daily. She'd become more self-sufficient.

Surprisingly a large part of that confidence was due to Jacob and his attitude throughout their meetings. He kept the meetings strictly professional and allowed her ample opportunity to express her opinions. They never argued and, con- sequently, Jacob's visits to their home had increased in frequency, until it seemed strange not to have him around discussing one thing or another. Occasionally she'd find him observing her oddly. That was when she'd remember their last kiss and the nasty accusation she'd flung in his face. And though she wanted to, the opportunity to apologize never arose.

Again she picked up the caribou hide, telling herself to be patient. The time would come.

"He's here!" Patrick yelled, already geared up. He flung open the door. "Hi, Jacob! I'm all ready. Let's go!"

Ann laid aside her sewing and got to her feet. "Hi, Siksik, Jacob."

This Saturday his broad shoulders were laden with a heavy- looking net and pickaxes. She turned to her daughter.

"You sure you don't want to go, honey?"

"It'll be fun," Siksik added, with a hopeful smile at her friend. "You and I can dig one hole while Jacob and Patrick dig the other. Ice fishing's great. We'll make it a contest."

"No, but thanks for the invite." Sharon paused and looked up from the teen magazine she'd been reading.

Jacob listened to the girls as they talked, his eyes automat- ically cataloguing the touches Ann had used to make the house more comfortable. He'd learned in the last few weeks that she was a natural homemaker. Whether it was cookies or brownies or snack cakes, there was always something for him to munch on when he arrived.

The familiar heat pulsed through him as he absorbed the hesitant smile of welcome she gave him. Sometimes, espe- cially when she looked at him with those wide gray eyes, he knew she wanted to apologize, but he didn't want to hear it. She'd been wrong to accuse him of using her as a substitute for Lia. But to admit it meant entering into a personal dis- cussion, and he knew he couldn't handle that, the emotions far too deep and painful. Not to mention the fact that every time he got close enough for a serious discussion he wound up kissing her. A very bad sign, since the next time he was fairly certain he wouldn't stop at just kisses.

"Ready?" he asked Patrick and Siksik.

"Maybe we can get together later on," Sharon added.

Siksik smiled. "I'll pick you up for the movie."

"That's cool. See ya."

After they left, Ann turned to her daughter. "Siksik's nice, isn't she?"

"She's okay, I guess," Sharon mumbled from behind the magazine. Then suddenly she laid it aside and looked at her mother. Her brown eyes were wary. "You really like it here, don't you?"

"It's different," Ann answered carefully. Was Sharon finally ready to open up? "I wouldn't say that life's easy or anything, but it's definitely a challenge. Why?"

Sharon shrugged. "Life in Anchorage wasn't such a breeze, you know."

"I know, honey, but all things considered, we're better off here." Ann recalled their tiny apartment and shuddered. She was glad they'd moved. Jacob or no Jacob. "What about you?"

"Definitely Anchorage."

"In that little place we lived!"

"It was bigger than here, Mom," Sharon complained. "And at least there I had some privacy. With that brat always in and out of my stuff I don't get any now. God, he's such a little snit."

"Your brother's not a snit."

"Dwebe, then."

"And he's not a dwebe, either. If he gets into your stuff, it's probably because he forgets which drawers are yours. What's with you two anyway? You used to be so close."

Sharon hid behind the magazine again. Ann had to stifle the urge not to rip it out of her fingers. "Honey, what's really the matter? Do you mind sharing with Patrick so much or is it something else? Like your Dad maybe?" The silence continued, but Ann saw Sharon stiffen. "That's it, isn't it? What you really want is for everything to be the same as it used to be."

Silence.

"Talk to me, Sharon."

Silence.

Finally, frustrated with the blank wall she was coming up against, she shoved the magazine aside, meeting her daughter's startled gaze. "Sweetheart, I know how close you two were but, accidents do happen. At least we know he didn't suffer. The best we can do now is to try putting it behind us.

To move on. I'm sure he'd say the same if he were here instead of me."

"Dad would never have brought us here."

"No, he wouldn't, would he? He was definitely a brass-and-glass kind of guy." Ann hoped to lighten the atmosphere. It didn't work.

"Why did you have to leave him, Mom? He'd probably be alive now if you hadn't."

Ann swallowed against the pain. She'd suspected Sharon blamed her for the separation. Sharon had idolized her father.

"You don't really believe that, do you?" she began softly. How could she defend herself without destroying her daughter's fantasy image of a father who could do no wrong?

Sharon dropped her gaze. "No," she mumbled unconvincingly.

"Honey, please understand. Your father and I—well, we had problems and there came a point when we just stopped getting along. Do you really believe life was better with your father and I arguing all the time? And with Patrick so tense he hardly ever talked when your dad was around? And don't tell me you were very comfortable, either."

Sharon sank farther into the armchair. She stared down at the magazine. Inside the oversized yellow sweatshirt she wore her slim shoulders drooped.

"But *why* did you have to argue with him?"

"It wasn't only the arguing, there were other problems, too."

"You mean his partying and coming in late and stuff, don't you?" Sharon defended her father. "He had to do that. Entertaining clients is how deals are made. Daddy told me himself that selling real estate wasn't like a regular job and that in order to make it in the big time he couldn't punch a time clock or be home as often as other dads who did boring everyday jobs."

Ann listened to her daughter's arguments and wished she could scream. Instead she took a deep calming breath, inwardly railing at the way her ex-husband had taken advantage of his daughter's unconditional love for him.

"Sweetheart, I think it's time you understood a few things," she began, choosing her words carefully. "Your father may have been exciting and full of plans and energy, but beneath it all, he was running scared."

"Scared? What are you talking about? Why would Daddy be scared?"

Ann sighed. This was so difficult! "Sharon, did you ever stop to think about why people sometimes think we're sisters when they see us out shopping together?"

"No, it was just sorta something cool," she answered.

"I think it's cool, too, but the fact is, we're only eighteen years apart." She waited for it to sink in, waited for some response from her daughter, but none was forthcoming. "Sharon, the reason we're so close in age, is because I had you when I was eighteen."

Sharon's eyes widened as the implication set in. "You and Dad..."

"That's right," Ann quickly broke in. "And we got married and tried making it work. Only it didn't. Not really."

"Because of me?"

Sharon's tiny voice squeezed Ann's heart. "No," she lied. "Because we were just too young. And we didn't know ourselves well enough. When you're eighteen, it's hard figuring out what you want to do with your life after high school. Add a marriage and a baby on top of that..."

She reached out and took her daughter's hand. "Life wasn't easy for us. Grandma and Grandpa Elliot were upset. So were my folks. There was lots of responsibility all at once and not a lot of money. Unfortunately, your Dad didn't handle it very well."

Sharon looked puzzled. "Then why did we live in such a nice place? He must have been successful. Why was he always buying me things?"

"Once or twice, yes, he really did make a big profit, on his real estate deals. That's when I insisted he buy our condo outright and put some of the money away in CDs. He was smart enough to realize it was a good idea." She sat back. Would her daughter understand? Would she accept her explanation?

"So you had to get married."

"We didn't have to, but you know grandma and grandpa. They insisted."

"And you guys argued about his spending too much time away."

And about his drug habit. And about his lack of fidelity. Two things Ann was certain her daughter wasn't yet prepared to hear much less discuss.

"Your Dad and I had some long-time adult problems that we just couldn't resolve. You're right, I wanted him to spend more time at home, so we could be a real family, only he didn't want that. Sometimes these things happen, Sharon. Not every story has a happy ending."

"I know," Sharon's eyes filled with tears. "I guess I just don't understand why ours couldn't. It seemed like we used to be so happy and now he's dead and we're here . . ." She didn't finish the remark. Her lips trembled.

"Oh, sweetheart!" Ann dropped down beside her and put her arms around the young girl's shoulders. "Someday you'll understand, believe me. Just you wait until you've got a boyfriend. You'll see that sometimes no matter how hard you work at it, things just don't work out." The increased tension in Sharon's shoulders wasn't lost on Ann and she could have kicked herself for making her think of Jimmy. She released her. "You'll adjust—really you will. I know you don't mind it here so much, right?"

"It's not that bad, I guess. I just never get to see my friends in Anchorage."

Tears filled Sharon's eyes and spilled over onto her cheeks. "Oh, Mom, everything's so different here. None of the kids like me. They all look at me weird."

"Sharon!"

"Well, they do!"

"Siksik likes you, right?"

"Oh, great. One person. You're so busy playing teacher that you can't see it, that's all."

"Oh, honey!" Once again Ann wrapped her arms around her daughter's stiff shoulders and hugged her warmly. "Believe me, I've noticed. But it's not that they think you're weird. It's that they're as put off by how different you are from them as you are by how different they are from you."

"Yeah, sure. What's so strange about me?"

Ann smiled. "Your hair, your makeup, some of your clothes. Probably the same things that you think are unusual about them." She hugged her again. "I love you, Sharon. And because of that love, I thought I might smother you if I interfered. I didn't want you to think I was one of those meddling mothers.''

"I don't," Sharon mumbled, then sniffed. "I just wish we could go to Anchorage for a visit."

"We can't afford it, honey. I'm sorry."

Sharon's stricken gaze pierced Ann's heart. Determined to lighten the mood, she smiled down at her daughter. ''What do you want for dinner tonight? You can invite Siksik if you like."

Sharon groaned but managed a watery smile. "Something bland," she replied, an odd look coming over her features. "And maybe we could bake some of those butter cookies?"

By the time the trio returned from their ice fishing it was not only dark but also snowing heavily. Worried, Ann hustled them into the welcoming warmth of the house.

"Boy, Mom, what a day!" Patrick shouted, his enthusiasm still at a high pitch. He shed his clothes, dropping them in a growing pile. "We had a blast! You really should have come with us, huh, Jacob? You, too, sis."

Ann smiled, for the moment, genuinely happy. Sharon was coming along and Patrick was even responding in a more brotherly way. Now if she could only find the right opportunity to apologize to Jacob.

"Sharon and I baked cookies, *which,*" Ann stressed, smiling across at her daughter and at the same time capturing Patrick's collar just as he was readying to spring into the kitchen, "you can have after dinner, Patrick."

"Aw, Mom, I'm hungry now."

"Then why don't you help your sister set the table? The faster it's done, the sooner we'll eat and the quicker you'll get to the cookies."

Laughing at his disgruntled expression, she turned to Siksik and Jacob, who were both chuckling. Her eyes absorbed Jacob's earthy magnetism with pleasure. "You'll stay for dinner, won't you? It's not fancy, but you're welcome."

Ann could tell Siksik wanted to, but the young girl waited politely, allowing Jacob the final word. Ann was relieved when, after shooting her a curiously intent look that had her blushing, he nodded. Then he headed over to her sink, where he began cleaning the catch.

The evening was unaccountably festive, with both Patrick and Siksik keeping them entertained with a running commentary on their day.

"Sounds like you had a good time," Ann remarked to her son as she cleared away the dishes and brought out the longed-for plate of cookies. Patrick immediately grabbed the plate. "Patrick! We have guests, remember?"

Sharon swallowed a laugh that earned her a black look from Patrick. Embarrassed, he picked up the plate and offered first Siksik then Jacob a cookie. Deliberately bypassing his sister, he grabbed three for himself, then set the plate back down on the tabletop.

"You want one, too, Sharon?" Ann asked her daughter, shooting Patrick a pointed look.

"No thanks, Mom," Sharon answered, shooting Patrick a smug look. "I've had enough already." She excused herself from the table and resettled on the couch.

While they munched cookies and sipped on the tea she'd brewed, Ann learned about ice fishing. Siksik explained that they walked out past the shoreline about two hundred feet, then started chiseling two holes into the sea ice sixty or so feet apart. The net was then strung between the two holes, using long poles and ropes as pulleys. Once properly set, anything caught in the net would get pulled through the hole. Ann asked what kind of fish they usually caught in the net and was informed that anything from seal to tomcod was possible. By the end of the mini lecture, Ann felt as though she had a pretty good idea of how it was accomplished.

She also had a pretty good idea that Jacob approved of her sweater, not to mention what was inside it. Several times she felt the brush of his eyes upon her and a quick glance in his direction as she offered him the plate of cookies confirmed her suspicions. Rather than looking down at the plate, his eyes looked down at the scooped cowl of her sweater, tracing the upper slope of her breasts, which were made visible by the slight gap created as she leaned forward.

She straightened, aware of the heat flushing her cheeks. He wanted to touch her, Ann realized. Did that mean he'd forgiven her comment about Lia? The plate shook and their eyes met. But while the desire was there, so was the denial. Ann turned away, shaken.

"The storm's worse, Jacob," Siksik remarked worriedly. She'd left the table to go to the window. When she turned, the lights suddenly flickered, then faded completely, plunging the room into darkness. For an unsettling moment, no one said anything. The storm's ferocity shook the house.

Jacob's deep voice broke the silence. "Ann, where are your lamps?"

"They—they're in the bedrooms, Jacob. One for each room, in case of emergency." She stood. "I'll go get them."

"I'll get mine," Patrick immediately offered.

"Patrick, no, it's too dark. If you fall, the glass—" Suddenly realizing that she was overreacting, she broke off, continuing in a calmer voice. "Okay, but please, be careful. Sharon?"

"Yeah?"

"Stay put."

"Don't worry," she mumbled, jokingly. "It's not like I was thinking of going to a movie or anything."

Ann followed closely behind her son until they reached the narrow hallway. It seemed impossible, but the darkness deepened. Arms outstretched, Ann felt her way into her room, moving cautiously across the floor to the nightstand where she kept the lamp.

It wasn't there.

Frowning, Ann searched the countertop, her arms slowly traversing its length, ready for the slightest contact with the tall glass kerosene lamp. Nothing. Backing away, she bumped her shin on a corner of the bed. "Ouch!"

"You all right?"

"Jacob?" She sensed him enter her room, knew he was moving toward her, using her voice as a homing device.

"Are you all right?" he repeated softly.

He stopped so close that Ann was certain if she reached out, she could touch him. She trembled. "I'm fine, really. Just banged my shin on the corner of the bed."

Silence fell between them. A tense, expectant silence filled with unspoken words and unfulfilled desires.

Jacob didn't need light to feel Ann's desire. He didn't need light to hear the abruptly ragged intake of her breath. Or to smell the sweet clean scent of her hair as it lay softly on her shoulders like a wild halo. He reached out, but almost as if she'd sensed his intention, she backed away. His hand dropped, accidentally brushing the aroused tip of her breast.

Both gasped audibly. Both stilled intentionally. Both groaned unwillingly. Again the silence enveloped them. Ann could almost see Jacob's chest expand as his breath dragged in the heated shimmering air around them. Then Jacob spoke, his voice low and husky with suppressed emotion.

"Patrick has both lamps. He said you must have put it in his room when you were cleaning."

For Ann it was still much too soon to speak. His touching her breast had summoned a response for which she'd been totally unprepared. But when he turned to leave, she reached out, realizing now was her opportunity to apologize.

"Jacob, wait," she whispered. Her hand closed tightly around his upper arm. She felt the biceps flex and dropped her hand. "I know you don't want to hear this, but I need to apologize. What I said about you using me as a substitute for Lia was way out of line. Worse, it wasn't any of my business. I'm sorry. Sorry I said it, sorry I hurt you."

Ann paused, waiting for some response. There was none, and the tension she thought would be relieved once she'd apologized, remained. "Jacob. Aren't you going to say anything?"

"You didn't hurt me. To hurt, you have to feel, and I don't."

Who was he trying to convince? Ann wondered as she followed the sound of Jacob's footfall back into the now lighted living area. She'd never met a man who felt so deeply.

"What took you so long, Mom?" Patrick asked. "I got in and out with two lamps before you even found out I had yours."

Black eyes met gray as Jacob's glance fell to the generous swell of her breasts, clearly still aroused and wanting.

Ann blushed and stifled the urge to cover herself. Shaken, she gave Patrick a vague reply and crossed the room, sitting down on the couch next to her daughter and Siksik, who were deep in a whispered conversation about boys. Jacob settled into the lounger.

Within seconds Patrick had Jacob occupied, leaving her free to think. Richard had been her only lover. But after her experience with Jacob she knew, without a shadow of a doubt, that Richard's sloppy manipulations paled in significance to even Jacob's brief brush against her breast. And to think Richard had blamed *her* for the blandness of their occasional intimacy!

Stunned, Ann gazed at the man who had so unintentionally changed her life. She didn't understand how he could claim to be unfeeling. He was so passionate in defense of his people and so considerately attentive with Patrick. He'd even befriended Sharon—no mean feat, considering how moody she'd been of late.

As if he sensed her thoughts, Jacob looked up. What he saw in her eyes made his own narrow with a burning heat that threatened to flame out of control.

"Siksik, I think we should go home now," Jacob said tersely, abruptly rising to his feet.

"Aw, can't you stay the night?" Patrick rushed to the window and looked out. "It's really bad out there. Worse than the first time back in October." He turned from the storm, his hopeful features illuminated in the lamplight. "Mom, don't you think they ought to stay here?"

Ann crossed to the window. The wind and blowing snow *were* fierce, from her vantage point coming together in a way that made them appear almost horizontal. None of the usual village lights were visible through the dense blizzard. Dampening the unexpected thrill of the possibilities such a situation created, she turned her mind to practicalities. She addressed Siksik.

"Won't your parents be worried? Although I think it would be a good idea if you stayed, I'd hate for them to be up all night."

"They won't get upset," she answered with certainty.

Patrick whooped in delight. "Oh, boy! You're staying!"

"Patrick," Ann warned. "Hold on a minute, okay?" She turned again to the young girl.

"Actually he's right, Mrs. Elliot," Siksik answered softly, her own enthusiasm evident at the prospect of spending the night. "We stopped off at my house to give my mother some of the fish we caught before we came to you. They know where we are. So it's okay, if it's okay with you."

Ann nodded, then looked at Jacob. Compelling black eyes prolonged the moment until she voiced the carefully polite question. "Would you like to spend the night?"

Chapter Twelve

Intense desire flashed across Jacob's hardened features. Seeing it, Ann unconsciously stepped toward him, unaware how much she revealed by the movement.

Jacob's eyes burned hotly. He glanced out at the storm, then across the dimly lit room at Siksik's coaxing smile and down to where Patrick had seated himself on the braided rug, his face bright with excitement. Only Sharon's expression was subdued as the girl's glance shifted uncertainly back and forth between himself and Ann. Abruptly he nodded. Patrick let out a shout of happiness. Even Siksik hugged a surprised Sharon.

Ann, on the other hand, didn't know what to feel. She took an unsteady breath. "Sharon, will you help me get things situated? Patrick, bring one of the lamps, please. You and I will share the double bed tonight."

"Aw, Mom—" he began as he scrambled up to do as she'd asked.

"No buts," Ann cut in tersely. "We're all going to have to compromise, okay? Siksik will take your bed and Jacob will use the couch." Ann turned to her guests, just managing a smile. "We'll only be a minute."

The available light dimmed even further when the trio left the living area. Standing by the window with his eyes on the storm, his ears tuned in to the faint but audible tension in Ann's voice, Jacob missed Siksik's soft footfall as she left her position on the couch and came to stand beside him.

"You don't want to stay here tonight, do you? Maybe Patrick's idea wasn't so great. Maybe we should try going home."

"Through that? Do you really want to?" He could tell she didn't. Jacob glanced at the small hand resting delicately on his forearm. He covered it with his own. "No, Siksik. If I really minded I could probably make it home on my own, but then you'd worry wouldn't you?" She nodded. He briefly wondered if Ann would worry and decided she would. Caring for others was her nature. He stretched, attempting to relieve the tension knotting his neck muscles. "It's all right, Siksik. The storm really is bad. If this were Billy's house we wouldn't even think twice."

Her lashes lowered. "But it's not Billy's house, is it? It's yours."

"Ann's," he corrected gently, observing Siksik's embarrassed confusion. He recalled both Ann and Mary commenting that Siksik had a crush on Billy. Apparently it was true, if one went by the reaction the mere mention of his name caused. "It's Ann's house now. Though I wasn't here when the village council made their decision, I agree with it. The other place is too small. Besides, I can handle it." Even as he said it, he realized it was the truth. Somewhere along the line the pain associated with the house being occupied again had vanished. It was Ann's home now.

Siksik nodded. "Jacob, you...like Mrs. Elliot, don't you?"

Again he looked at her sharply, but only open concern shined from her trusting features. "Yes. She's a good teacher. And a good mother."

Was she also a good lover? The unbidden question rose unexpectedly in his thoughts and Jacob stifled a groan. Recalling the sweetness of her kisses, the responsive tightness to her breast, he instinctively knew the answer.

"I like her, too. But I wish she could stay longer. Spring is so near. Do you think maybe if we ask her to stay longer she would?"

The possibility didn't bear thinking about. He was only so strong. "That's a decision for the council," he reminded her, then deliberately changed the subject. "How are you and Sharon getting along?"

Patrick returned just then, with Sharon and Ann close behind.

"This is almost like the camping out I did with the Boy Scouts last summer, only we had a real fire instead of lamps." He grabbed the last cookie from the oval platter and stuffed half of it into his mouth before plopping down on the rug. "Hey, I know! We should tell ghost stories!"

"Ghost stories?" Siksik asked, moving to the couch and sitting beside Sharon.

Jacob waited for Ann to choose a seat, settling into the lounger only after she sat down beside her daughter and Siksik.

"Ghost stories!" Sharon groaned at her brother's suggestion. "What for? So you can get all scared and hide under the covers again?" She dodged a wadded up piece of paper Patrick threw in her direction. "Chill out, dwebe! It's not my fault you're a wimp when it comes to scary movies." She leaned toward Siksik and stage-whispered, "He can't take the blood and guts and stuff. About croaked when he saw *The Fly*."

"Did not!"

"Did, too! Screamed bloody murder he did. Woke up the whole damned neighborhood almost."

"Sharon," Ann warned. "I told you about swearing, didn't I?"

"Sorry, Mom," Sharon apologized quickly, then grimaced across at her brother. "Forget it, bat breath. You might not need sleep, but the rest of us sure as he—" she swallowed the word with a quick look at her mother "—heck do."

"Jacob's a good storyteller," Siksik volunteered, eager to avoid her friends' arguing. "He used to tell us the old stories sometimes when our father was too tired after a long day of hunting walrus."

"But there aren't any ghosts in those stories are there?"

"No ghosts, Patrick," Siksik replied. "But there are spirits. And they're much more interesting."

"They are?" Patrick looked doubtful. He turned to Jacob. "Can you tell us a story with spirits in it?"

"All Yup'ik legends involve the spirits," Jacob answered slowly. "It is the spirit that teaches, the spirit that protects. It is the spirit that gives you your strength. To us, everything has an *inua*. The earth, the sky, the sea. Everything.''

"But what is it? Some sort of power?''

"*Inua* is our word for the spirit that dwells within,'' Siksik informed him quietly, though her eyes remained trained on Jacob. "I am the raven. What do you think Jacob's *inua* is?''

"Something big and mean, no doubt,'' Sharon mumbled.

Jacob heard the comment. So did Ann, but for once she didn't discipline her daughter. Instead she concentrated on Jacob's shadow-carved features. He *did* remind her of something. Some animal she'd read about in one of the books Mary had loaned her on the Yup'ik and their culture. But which animal was it? She watched him stare into the lamplight, her own mind focused inward, aware the answer was just beyond her grasp. Unpredictable. Alone. Intense. A fierce protector. The images described any number of wild animals revered by the Yup'ik. A gust of wind shook the house, diverting Jacob's attention. As their gazes crossed, Ann's impressions suddenly coalesced.

"Your *inua* is the wolf,'' she said, not knowing how, but certain she was right.

"Yes,'' replied Siksik, when Jacob didn't answer. "*Kegluneq* guards my brother. It is a powerful spirit. Hunter and protector both.''

Hunter and protector both. Ann heard the words and knew them to be true. Her eyes never wavered from Jacob's. She knew one other aspect of *Kegluneq*. The wolf mated for life. A cold knot formed in her stomach.

"What's my *inua*?'' Patrick asked curiously.

Startled, Ann broke away from Jacob's gaze. She had no idea how long she'd been staring at him, but she sensed his surprise, his wariness at the accuracy of her guess.

"You are yet too young to know your true *inua*,'' Jacob replied. "When the time is right, there will be no doubt and you will learn it's identity.''

Patrick pondered this for all of two seconds, then returned to his original question. "How did you find out about your *kel*...*keg*—''

"*Kegluneq*,'' Jacob answered, though his voice sounded tight and guarded even to his own ears.

"Jacob, don't...''

The concern in Siksik's voice alerted Ann to the sudden heightened tension in Jacob. Even as her words trailed off at a look from Jacob, Ann wondered what Siksik had been about to say. Jacob don't what? But she couldn't ask. The bleakness in Jacob's eyes, if not good manners, forbade any questions.

"Have you learned yet of the *noonavaliks?*" Jacob asked Patrick.

The boy shook his head. Jacob leaned back in the lounger, his eyes closed, his voice as colorless as he could make it. He realized he wanted to tell his story and was grateful for Patrick's curiosity. He wanted Ann to hear about the forces that drove him to deny her sweetness. He wanted her to know, *needed* her to understand, for knowledge and understanding bred strength. And he'd need her strength to combat his own growing desire for her. A desire that could only bring them both pain.

"One spring three years ago, three of us set out onto the ice of the Bering Sea, hoping to bag a seal. The hours of daylight are short in February and we expected to be home before dark, so we had only our hunting gear with us. The day was warm and, unknown to us, the pack ice broke away from shore, blocking our return. Floating pans of ice can stretch for miles and are called *noonavaliks.*"

"We walked for days, searching for land, but the fierce underground currents carried us away from shore and safety. Once we could even see the coast of Siberia and thought to walk there, but again the ice turned and we lost sight of land. We managed to bag a seal, eating what we could, carrying the rest until it was all gone."

"How did you know it was *Kegluneq* protecting you?"

"Shut up, Patrick, and you'll find out," Sharon said, her eyes riveted on Jacob.

Jacob gazed into their faces. He didn't look at Ann, for in the telling of his ordeal, a part of him would be forever distanced from her.

"The nights were long. Without food and water, the body starves. One still night an image appeared before me during sleep. The image was clear in the moonlit sky and it instructed me to awaken or I would freeze. It told me to lead the others west and to do so quickly. It was *Kegluneq*. I did not question the image, only performed the task and followed the stars. On the morning of the eighteenth day, I was found."

A chilled silence enveloped the room after Jacob's voice faded. Ann looked around and realized all of them, even Siksik, were deeply affected by Jacob's story.

"*You* were found?" Sharon's question was hesitant. "What happened to your friends?"

For a moment Ann thought Jacob wouldn't answer. Along with the others, she stared across at him, waiting, wondering. Then all at once, his head lifted off the backrest of the lounger. Ann winced at the torment she glimpsed in his eyes. That was when she knew. One of the three had been Lia. She went very still, knowing what was coming, not really wanting to hear.

"I alone survived."

There was a long, brittle silence. Then Sharon asked hesitantly, "Only you?"

"Yes." His lips scarcely moved.

"Awesome," Patrick murmured reverently. "And all because of your *inua.*"

Jacob nodded and closed his eyes. When he opened them again, he felt tired, resigned. The weight on his shoulders had increased, not lessened as he'd hoped.

"Enough storytelling." Ann purposely lightened her voice, attempting to dispel the tension. "It's ten o'clock. Definitely past your bedtime, Patrick."

"Aw, couldn't we stay up a little longer? Jacob's—"

"Tired, Patrick," Ann interrupted firmly, rising off the couch. She picked up one of the lamps. "I imagine he could use some rest after all of that ice fishing. You, too, girls."

"Mom!" Sharon complained. "Why do we have to go now? It's Saturday night, remember? No school tomorrow."

"I guess you can talk once you're in bed, but not too long, okay? If the storm's gone by morning, there's church tomorrow, don't forget." Ann headed into the hallway. Siksik joined her, throwing Jacob a good-night smile.

Amid more groans and moans, Ann herded her children and Siksik to their rooms. When she returned a few minutes later, the living area was empty. Had Jacob left? Immediately her trepidation about being alone with Jacob vanished, replaced by concern. She crossed the dimly lighted room to the window. Why had he left? Did she make him so uncomfortable that he'd rather chance a storm than talk with her?

She couldn't imagine surviving an ordeal such as his. Eighteen days! And every moment he'd lived with hunger and thirst and the frightening possibility that the next hour, the next minute, would be his last. His best friend, gone. His wife, gone. Tears formed in her eyes; she could hardly bear the thought of what he'd survived. He'd had to leave them both, alone on the frozen Bering Sea. Could she have walked away from her children in similar circumstances? Could she even have left, say Patrick, if it meant saving Sharon? Would she have had the strength of will to save herself after losing them both?

Absorbed in her thoughts, she didn't see the slight movement way back in the shadows of the kitchen by the refrigerator. Jacob stood still, his gaze fixed on Ann. Her expression was laid bare, the concern for his safety plainly evident. Jacob found he couldn't speak. She stood there, her right hand extended, fingertips touching the frosted glass pane as if she could somehow call him back.

She'd known his *inua*. A guess? Or something more? He watched tears form in her eyes. Tears of pain, of sorrow, of need?

Ann moved away from the window, finally catching sight of Jacob. She started. "Jacob! I—I thought for a minute there... Was there something you needed? A soda pop? Milk? Cookies? I hid a few away. Patrick didn't eat all of them."

The spurt of questions hung between them while Jacob grappled with his emotions. His gaze traced the tears on her cheeks. "You said your husband died. When was that?"

Tense, Ann stared at him for several moments, then her shoulders relaxed. He'd told her about Lia, after all, and that couldn't have been easy. "Richard died two years ago when he ran his car into a retaining wall on the Seward Highway."

"Deliberately?" he asked gently, though inside he was shocked.

"Who knows? He was... a coke addict. He said it was the 'in' thing and that all the moneymakers were 'doing' it. He said he could handle it."

"You tried getting him to stop?"

"Oh, yes," she replied. A shiver traveled up her arms. Now that she'd opened up, she found she couldn't stop the flow of words. "I tried everything I could, but he wouldn't. And of course, he *couldn't* handle it. His moods would swing wildly. I never knew what to expect when he came home. That is, *if* he came home. The kids didn't know. At least, I never told them, but I think Patrick sensed something wrong with his father."

Jacob's stomach knotted. He waited for her to look up and away from the floor she was studying, waited for her to add something, but she didn't. It was as though the wound she carried inside was too deep to risk being exposed. Jacob knew the feeling. Three years of dealing with Lia's death had made him an expert on pain.

"You loved him." It was a statement, not a question.

Had she? Ann shifted, uncomfortable with the question because her memories of being eighteen were not particularly pleasant. She'd regularly baby-sat Richard's little sister and had, therefore, seen the wild, popular college freshman often. Now Ann could look back and see that Richard had enjoyed her wide-eyed awe, had enjoyed it and had taken advantage of it. Only she'd become pregnant. She looked up.

"The drugs changed him. He wasn't the father I'd hoped he'd be."

"And your children? How did they take his death?"

"Not good. Especially Sharon—she was closer to him than Patrick." In her mind's eye, she relived those first few days after the accident. "It was probably the toughest thing I've ever done, telling them he'd died. Despite the divorce and everything else, he *was* their father, even if he wasn't a good one." Abruptly, emotions surged within Ann's chest. "Sometimes I feel so guilty! Maybe if I hadn't separated from him in the first place, Sharon might not have fixated on it, or me, as the reason for what happened. As it is, she's just now starting to come to terms with it all."

"Sharon believes you caused her father's death?"

"Not directly, no. But she's fifteen, Jacob. To her, it's all very clear. I left him and a year later Richard was dead." Drained, she moved to the couch and sat down. She'd never told anyone about Richard's drug abuse. "Sometimes . . . especially at night when I can't sleep . . . I wonder if she isn't right. If I should have tried again."

Jacob hesitated, wondering how to soothe her torment. Platitudes were useless, no matter how well meant, they did little to alter conviction.

"You did the right thing, Ann. What happened wasn't your fault. Sharon may be upset with you now, but she'll understand someday. Perhaps when she has her own children."

Ann looked up into Jacob's eyes. Like hers, they were filled with the harsh lessons of life. "You did the right thing, too," she said gently, concerned when she saw darkness cloud his face. "Tell me about Lia. What was she like?"

His eyes narrowed. Ann sensed the rigid control he was exerting over his emotions. If he could, she knew Jacob would just as soon run out into the storm than face answering her question. But he couldn't run outside, and he couldn't leave. As the seconds ticked by, Ann found herself holding her breath. Would he respond or would he withdraw?

She rose from the couch, going to him. Her right hand closed around his muscular forearm. Jacob flinched but didn't pull himself from her grasp.

"Please," she said softly.

He stared down at her, his eyes focused inward. "She was beautiful. Gentle and kind. She didn't deserve to die."

Ann nodded encouragingly, letting her hand drop to her side. He stood apart from her, hands shoved deeply into his pants pockets. "How long were you married?"

"Six years."

His voice was flat, emotionless, but she wasn't fooled. She saw the nearly imperceptible shudder that swept through him. "And since she's been gone, no one else?"

Again she thought he wouldn't answer. Then all at once, Ann felt him give in, as if having waged and lost a battle from within.

"You." The terse but succinct word was nonetheless filled with strong emotion.

Ann suddenly realized that the wind had temporarily ceased rattling the house. Jacob's reply weighed heavily between them. She hesitated, her gaze dropping to his lips, recalling the passion of his kiss.

"You're very brave," he said solemnly, aware of her thoughts. "Perhaps *Kegluneq* claims you, too."

Ann's eyes widened, the implication that her *inua* was also that of a wolf's startling her. "I'm not strong like you."

"Are you not? You protect your children. You lead and teach others to know themselves. You risk my rejection. To me, you're very brave."

Ann blushed. "But I'm not Yup'ik."

"No, you're not," he commented softly. "And I'm not *kass'aq.*"

Her heart caught at the way he'd phrased his reply. "That bothers you, doesn't it? That we're not of the same culture."

"The spirit of the Yup'ik is close to the land. We gain our strength from the sky and the sea, from the seasons and from our past. I understand the *kass'aq* ways, work within the *kass'aq* rules, but I can never live a *kass'aq* life. Deep in my heart, my soul is Yup'ik."

Her eyes filled with tears. She was afraid of what he was trying to tell her. "You want to hear something funny? I didn't come here looking for anything but peace. Peace and a chance for my family to heal. I never thought...never thought I would even care for a man again."

Jacob reached out and touched her cheek. "Ann, I do care, only—"

"But caring's not enough, Jacob," she interrupted, stepping back and away. She felt deep sorrow and not a little anger, certain this had been a roundabout way of saying he wanted her, but that there was no future for them. "I need more. And I'm not willing to start something that will only end in spring. I couldn't handle an affair. Not here in Twilight. Not anywhere."

"I didn't ask you to."

"No, you didn't. But just for the record, I'm through compromising my feelings. I did that for thirteen years and look where it's gotten me. I'm thirty-three years old, Jacob. I've got two children who desperately need stability in their lives." Her eyes filled with helpless tears and she held up her hands, pleading for understanding. "Patrick's a perfect example. The way he's attached himself to you, he's bound to be hurt when we leave. With Richard, I was weak. Not anymore. My children have a right to a loving attentive father. Someone who's there for them all of the time. They deserve that. And you know what? For the first time in my life—so do I."

She sat down and swallowed hard against the dryness in her throat, striving desperately to keep her body from trembling.

Jacob stood a breath's length away, strangely quiet, contemplative.

"What you're asking for is a commitment."

"Yes, I guess so."

"Because of the children?" She nodded. "Do you realize you're using Patrick and Sharon as a shield?"

Stung by the accusation, she replied, "I could say the same for you, Jacob. Are my western ways and your Yup'ik traditions so far apart? Are they truly the reason you won't even consider a commitment?"

His eyes blazed. "We hardly know each other."

"That's your *kass'aq* mind speaking." She spoke with quiet certainty, for in revealing her own demons, she'd stumbled across the root of Jacob's anguish: guilt over Lia's death. "What does your Yup'ik soul tell you?"

Jacob already knew. In the space of four weeks he'd come to know her mind as well as he'd known Lia's. Instinct had warned him that her presence would change his life. She wanted a relationship, a commitment. What frightened him was the possibility that his heart had already made the decision and his mind no longer had anything to do with it.

His eyes searched her face, reaching into her soul for an answer to the turmoil in his own.

"Help me."

It was odd how two words could say so little yet reveal so much. Ann's heart wrenched at the painful confusion in his eyes. A flood of emotion poured into her heart. What did she tell him? What did she do?

She reached out and pulled him down beside her, gathering him into her arms and pressing his head against her chest. For a long while she just rocked back and forth, holding him against her, her hand caressing the midnight-black hair, soothing him, offering comfort without the pressure of a response. Her hands moved rhythmically over the hard wide shoulders beneath the white cotton *kuspuk* he wore, learning his contours, absorbing his tension, returning only calm and peace. Fresh tears formed in her eyes at his vulnerability. She couldn't answer his questions because they were too closely linked with her own. He'd have to make his own decisions and eventually she'd have to make hers, as well.

Jacob looked up suddenly and saw her tears. As if it was the most natural thing in the world, he reached up and brought her mouth to his. His big hands roamed up from her waist and pulled her down next to him so their lips were on a level with each other. He gathered her hair into his hands, lifting it from her neck, and fanning it out again. Ann shuddered, her mouth ravaged under the intensity of his passion. There was no longer any soothing quality to their embrace; he kissed her hungrily, as a man starved of emotion. His mouth roamed feverishly, leaving her lips to sear her neck, her cheeks, her nape and then her lips again. Ann responded helplessly, gasping, overwhelmed by the release of his desire but willing and even eager to meet it head-on.

Jacob lifted her into his lap, embracing her within the heated circle of his arms. He needed the increased contact, crushing her close, shaping her to him as if she would escape should he loosen his hold. Kisses rained on her neck, her ear, the force of his abandonment as wild and uncontrolled as the storm still raging coldly outside. Only Jacob was hot, so hot Ann was swept along with the molten storm he created within her, unable to resist his heated caresses, not wanting to.

When he switched positions, pressing her back onto the couch, Ann uttered a moan, feeling the strength of his hard body over hers. She tasted him eagerly, her tongue dueling with his as his seeking hands crept beneath her sweater to her breasts, stroking their softness through the lace of her bra, testing their weight, wringing from her small cries of aching, painful delight and yearning. She was burning up, her emotions rolling toward an explosion of feeling as he finally lowered his full weight on top of her, allowing her to feel his readiness. She whimpered when he released her mouth, his own breathing ragged, hot, his hands burning down her thighs with ever-increasing impatience.

"Help me," he repeated his earlier plea, except this time it was more of a command. His fingers grabbed a handful of her sweater, intent on pulling it over her head.

In that instant the past burned an image in Ann's mind. Her hand flew up and covered his.

"Don't," she rasped. Jacob drew back, and even in the dim light she could see his expression switch from raging desire to absolute confusion and disbelief.

"Not again," he spoke hoarsely, almost to himself. "You want me, I know you do." His agonized glance fell to her sweater, bunched up around her neck, her breasts straining against the white lace of her bra. He captured one breast.

"I do," Ann said, remembering the cabin. She'd stopped him then, too.

"Then why? Are you trying to torment me?"

"No! It's just—I can't let this happen Jacob. Not this way," she choked out.

He pulled free of her with one swift motion. Ann scrambled to a sitting position and pulled her sweater down, covering her breasts. Jacob forced himself to stand and cross the room. He ran a hand through his hair. Ann could see he was trembling, could see how hard it was for him to control himself.

"I don't understand," he said eventually.

For a moment Ann's head hung forward in defeat as shame took away the last of her desire. When she looked up, it was to encounter Jacob's stare. Gone was the need for her. In its place was the familiar mask.

"I got pregnant when I was eighteen. Richard gave me some money, but I wouldn't take it, and when our parents found out, they insisted we get married. God knows I love my children, and I've never regretted having them, Jacob, but that one irresponsible act changed my whole life. I'm not going to take that risk again."

Not without love, she added inwardly. Her eyes pleaded with him to understand, to take a step and make some sort of a commitment. But he didn't. She could tell the moment his own reservations surfaced for his expression became even more closed, leaving her in no doubt as to his decision.

"Jacob?"

"It's late. You'd better get some sleep."

Chapter Thirteen

In the bedroom Sharon carefully lowered herself onto the mattress. She shouldn't have eaten so many cookies. Watching Siksik look around curiously, Sharon swallowed and wished for a cigarette. Abruptly her stomach rolled. Maybe not. Taking a shallow breath, she hoped she wasn't going to be sick.

"So you want to be a nurse, huh?"

Siksik nodded, her eyes examining Patrick's poster of Batman. "I can't imagine doing anything else. I've wanted to ever since Jacob was found."

"But what about all that blood and stuff?"

"I'm used to it. Jacob took me on my first hunt when I was ten. And Milak, our healer, has been teaching me the old methods since I started bringing her injured birds and dogs when I was little."

"And it didn't bother you? Killing, I mean?"

"We don't kill for sport, so no. To the Yup'ik, death means life. The animals give their lives so that we can live. In return we honor their sacrifice by using as much of the meat and skin as we can. It's simple. Jacob calls it harmony."

He would, Sharon thought. Tonight she'd noticed for the first time the way her mother and Jacob looked at each other. Was something going on between them? She hoped not. She couldn't bear it if her mother decided she liked Jacob enough to stay in Twilight past spring.

"Is this where you used to live?"

Siksik had picked up a framed photo on the dressertop. "Uh-huh. That's our condo. And that's my brother and me with my dad."

"Jacob told me about your dad being dead," Siksik said softly. "You look a lot like him."

"I know. Pretty radical isn't it? Whenever the four of us used to go out to dinner, people would stop and say how much Patrick looked like Mom and how much I looked like Dad."

Siksik smiled, unaware of Sharon's physical discomfort. "I guess I'm more like my mother. Except for being too tall."

"What's so bad about that?"

"The boys make jokes about it," Siksik murmured, her head hanging dejectedly. "And my girlfriends aren't tall. I'm the only one."

"Tell me about it," Sharon mumbled; she'd learned what it was like to stand out. The look that passed between them was one of understanding. "You're not that tall, you know. A girlfriend of mine back home is taller than you. And she's not even fifteen yet. She says she wants to be a model."

"Then she's probably beautiful like you and has lots of boyfriends."

Beautiful like me? Sharon gazed sharply at Siksik, wondering if the girl was making fun of her. But she wasn't. She could tell Siksik genuinely meant the compliment. She took several shallow breaths, forcing her nerves and her stomach to relax. After a few moments, when she felt better, she gazed pensively over at Jacob's sister. "You should have seen our condo. It was really awesome. All my friends said so. I used to invite them over and we'd go to my room and watch TV and talk on the phone."

Siksik sat on Patrick's bed. "You had a room all to yourself?"

"Sure." Sharon looked around and grimaced. "I can't believe this place. Bad enough she says I can't see Jimmy anymore. Now I don't even have privacy."

"Are you talking about your mom?"

"Who else? Just because he smoked one little joint in the house she says I can't see him anymore. And then she hauls us way out here where nobody in their right—" Sharon halted in mid-word. She shrugged apologetically. "Look, I'm sorry, okay? But it's not like this place is Fantasy Island or anything."

Siksik observed her quietly. "You miss Anchorage, don't you? What's it like?"

"Really outrageous compared to here. You can come visit me when we get back."

"I can! Really?"

Sharon watched as Siksik began unraveling her braids. "Sure. We'll go to the malls and hang out. I'll introduce you 'round. I'll even lend you some of my clothes."

"Maybe I can have my hair done like yours."

"Why? You have great hair," Sharon commented, watching Siksik brush the long tresses until they hung in a sold black sheet almost down to the girl's waist.

"I do?" Siksik paused, then sighed as she squinted in the dim light at her reflection. "Billy seems to like yours though."

"Yeah, well, he can keep his like to himself." Sharon missed the relief in Siksik's eyes.

"Sharon?"

"Hmm?"

"You think Billy will ever notice me?"

"Who knows?" Sharon answered. Impossible things were happening all the time lately.

Like being dumped.

Like getting pregnant.

She looked down at her stomach, then across at the girl.

"You like Billy a lot, don't you?"

"I love him. If he asked me to, I'd give up nursing and leave home to go with him to U.C.L.A."

The quiet certainty with which Siksik uttered the words startled Sharon. Siksik give up nursing? That's all she ever talked about. What would she give up for Jimmy? Sharon wondered, then thought, what would Jimmy give up for her?

"I don't know, Siksik. I'm not saying it's impossible, but even if he does notice you, that's no guarantee he'll love you back." Thankfully Siksik missed the bitter tone Sharon couldn't quite remove from her voice.

"I know."

"Anyway, does it really matter since he's leaving for college soon? He'll be gone for four years, more if he makes it to the pros. He'll forget you ever existed."

"You're probably right, but I'll miss him, when he's gone. You miss Jimmy, don't you?" She peered sadly at her reflection, then blew out the lamp and scrambled into Patrick's bed.

"Jimmy and I are making plans to get together," Sharon lied, her voice taut as she tried hiding the hurt of his rejection. Since his letter had arrived, she'd spent hours planning their reunion. She was convinced he hadn't meant what he'd written. It was just the distance, that's all. Once he saw her again, once they had a chance to talk and she told him about the baby...

Don't panic! Everything will be cool. Once Jimmy knows, everything will be just fine, she told herself, swallowing hard against the fear. She stared wide-eyed into the darkness, her stomach churning with anxiety.

The following week was full of activities as Ann submerged herself in the villagers' preparations for the W.E.I.O. games and Christmas potlatch. She put in extra time with Billy, helping him study for the S.A.T.s. Once or twice she was tempted to discuss his father's attitude toward college, but decided not to for fear of draining the boy's enthusiasm. Yet, watching him struggle, Ann knew she couldn't let him down. He was caught between his family's needs and his own and she renewed her promise to herself that, somehow, she would find a solution.

Patrick was subdued, a behavior Ann put down to his missing Jacob, who was in Juneau for a week of meetings with legislators sympathetic to the Native lobby on subsistence rights. She herself missed Jacob's presence, despite the hurt and disappointment she was feeling over his reluctance to deepen their relationship with a commitment.

His nightly phone call—progress reports—caused Ann a vexing combination of relief and frustration. Relief because he restricted his comments to meeting updates and frustration because the strain in his voice made her aware that had she not been in John's store, where everybody unabashedly listened in, he might have delivered a more private message.

But in all honesty, as Ann entered the crowded gym for the weekly night movie, she knew it made no difference. She wouldn't have known what to say, not after last Saturday, anyway. Jacob's intentions remained unclear.

The highlight of the week was the developing friendship between Sharon and Siksik. Ann was relieved and made no objections when the two wanted to spend time together at Siksik's home or at the gym, where Sharon watched Siksik practice her dance.

As she sat on the gym floor amid other movie-watchers, Ann felt a small measure of peace. She missed Jacob and wanted matters to be resolved between them, but she sensed within herself a newfound confidence that no matter how things turned out she would be fine. Her children were healing. And since their talk, she and Sharon had grown closer.

"Care to share your spot?"

Ann looked up and smiled at Mark. "I didn't expect to see you here tonight. Figured an old love story like *Gone With The Wind* wouldn't be your style."

He grinned and plopped down beside her. "Just goes to show how wrong we can be, now doesn't it?"

Ann laughed, enjoying his company. He reminded her of Jacob. It wasn't the carefree attitude certainly. No, it was his physical resemblance, his bearing. It struck her that the quiet strength both exuded so naturally was a byproduct of the Yup'ik life-style and that, likely, Jacob would always be dependable, solid.

"What's the latest with Jacob in Juneau?" Mark asked. "He told me he was going to try meeting with Harry Koyuk."

"He did." Ann experienced a surge of pride. Arranging a meeting with such a man was an accomplishment. Harry Koyuk was the CEO of the Kuskokwim Native Corporation, one of the largest and most successful of the Native-owned businesses in Alaska. "According to Jacob, he's intrigued by the idea of the people in Twilight officially declaring themselves a tribe."

Mark's eyes lighted up. "But did he think it could work? That the governor himself would go for it?"

"There's precedent. Apparently three villages have been granted similar rights, but Jacob said Mr. Koyuk cautioned him that certain legislators continue to argue against it.

Something about the Alaska Native Claims Settlement Act precluding it."

"They would say that. Because those same legislators know it could solve our subsistence problem. We'd be virtually immune from lawsuits, could pass our own civil laws, even operate a tribal court."

"But I thought Twilight already has a council of elders."

"We do. But mostly, they advise. It's rare that they're called upon to actually enforce village law. With this change, their power to do so would be unquestionable."

"Well, hopefully Jacob will convince the right people. We'll find out when he gets home tomorrow."

"Yeah. A tribal designation could really unite the village." A moment passed in companionable silence. Then Mark looked at Ann curiously. "You and Jacob seem closer."

"Don't make something out of nothing, okay, Mark? Jacob and I worked together. We put in a lot of long hours to get him ready for this trip. But that's all it was, *work.*"

"I see. Jacob had dinner at your place practically every night last week because it was convenient."

"Right."

"And he repaired the kitchen cabinets and the living room furniture because he felt like it."

Ann gazed at him, surprised. "How did you hear about that?"

"Patrick."

"Oh. Well, I just happened to mention one night that the exposed edges on the cabinets had given Sharon a few splinters..."

"And Jacob fixed it. I know."

"Do you?" Ann sighed, wishing just this once that Twilight wasn't quite so small. "Any relationship is a two-way street. I shouldn't have to tell you that. So, please, don't go jumping to the wrong conclusions. Jacob and I are both dealing with past issues. Things we need to resolve on our own."

"You're sure of that?"

"Yes. Whatever friendship there is between your brother and me, I don't intend pushing him into saying or doing something he's not ready to do or say."

"But you're ready?" he persisted.

Was she? What if Jacob offered her the commitment she needed? What then? Was she ready for another relationship? Or had she used Jacob's uncertainty as a smokescreen for her own? Before she could gather her thoughts together, Mark spoke again.

"It may be that because of Lia, you'll have to make the first move." He paused, taking in her suddenly closed expression. "Look, Ann, I know what his problem is, too, you know. Everyone does. Only we haven't been able to do anything to help him heal. You, on the other hand, can do something. In fact, you already have." Mark leaned forward. All trace of levity had left his usually smiling features. "Since you arrived, Jacob's changed. Ask Siksik. They're really close and she'll tell you the truth. Without you, he would never have stepped foot inside that house again. Without you, he never would have considered my suggestion that you and he pool your resources on this subsistence thing."

"Why are you telling me all of this, Mark?"

His lips tightened. "No one should have to live in the dark. Jacob's paying dues for something that wasn't his fault, Ann. No matter how much he gets on my nerves at times, he's still my brother and he deserves more.

"Call him up," Mark urged. "Tell him to stay in Juneau, that you'll join him for a day or two. You can take the plane he was coming in on tomorrow morning. Maybe away from everyone you two can sort out a few things. I'll square it with my father. Your students can have a study hour and I'll tell Mom to watch Patrick and Sharon. They can sleep over, too."

"Do you always plan things so swiftly?" Ann asked breathlessly, overwhelmed by everything he'd said.

Ann thought of the passion she'd shared with Jacob, his admission about how deeply she affected him, and was tempted. But was it fair of her to go rushing off to Juneau when she wasn't even certain that Jacob would welcome her presence? And even if he did, where would that leave them come Monday or Tuesday? No, the signals were all wrong. She looked up and met Mark's knowing gaze.

"No go, huh?" She shook her head. "You're making a mistake," he warned. "Juneau's one hopping city."

Ann smiled, relieved to see him back to normal. "Maybe I'll let you show it to me one day."

Chapter Fourteen

"Jacob! Over here!"

His arms loaded with cargo, Jacob disembarked the Twin Otter, wondering what kind of reception he'd get. His eyes swung toward Patrick's voice and not only found Ann and Sharon, but Siksik, Ben and Mark, as well. Placing the boxes on a nearby snowmobile, he caught Patrick up in his arms and swung the boy around.

"Boy, am I glad you're home!" Patrick said enthusiastically.

"I'm glad to be back," he laughingly agreed, setting Patrick down, then tousling his curly brown hair. His eyes automatically sought Ann's, sensing her delight as well as her reserve. It was to be expected. Turning, he pulled three familiar bags from one of the boxes he'd brought home.

Spotting the golden arches, Siksik squealed. "Oh, Jacob! Thank you."

"Hey! Rad! A Big Mac and fries." Patrick immediately dug in.

When Jacob handed Sharon hers, she thanked him politely, her expression observant as her gaze flicked back and forth between him and Ann.

"Ann tells us the meetings went well," Mark began as they all started the walk toward the village.

"They did. Thanks to her, we now have some powerful voices on our side."

"*Assirtuq,*" Ben said, using the Yup'ik word for good.

Jacob's gaze met Ann's. The morning sun reflecting off the glistening white snow made her eyes sparkle and highlighted the rounded curves of her lips as she gazed solemnly at him. "I'm supposed to say hello from Senator Ross."

"How is Merriam?" Ann asked with interest.

"Busy. They all were. But just as you predicted, they all took the time to listen to our concerns. Offered good suggestions, too."

"Like what?" Mark asked. "Maybe we should call another village meeting."

"I think we should wait on that, son," Ben advised. "At least until the village council has been briefed. You know what happened the last time. I don't want a repeat of that."

Ann watched Mark bite down a comment. She understood the urgency compelling him to find the quickest and most profitable solution to the problem, but in this instant, she couldn't help but agree with Ben. For days after the last meeting, villagers had literally taken sides against one another. She'd heard the teenagers discussing it during class breaks. Even Patrick had come home full of concern about two of his classmates who'd wound up fighting because their fathers held opposing viewpoints.

"How's the dance practice going, Siksik?" Jacob asked, smoothly changing the topic.

"Better, but I still haven't learned all the moves yet," she answered as the group approached the school building. "Sharon and I are going to practice some after we eat."

Jacob found he didn't want to leave Ann just yet. For the entire six days he'd been away, he'd thought about what she'd told him. Their phone conversations had been frustratingly impersonal.

"Let's take a walk," he suggested when the group paused momentarily. "There's something I want to show you."

Drawn to the seriousness in his eyes, Ann quelled the spark of hope that he'd reconsidered his commitment to her. She turned to Patrick. "Honey, Jacob and I shouldn't be too long.

If you're still hungry after that hamburger, fix yourself a snack, okay?''

"Okay," he murmured, a bit disappointed at being left out. Then he brightened. "Can Paul and I play with his three-wheeler?''

"If it's okay with his dad, yes. Just be careful."

Agreeing, Patrick waved and was soon out of sight. Slowly everyone else dispersed, too, with Mark obtaining Jacob's promise of a full rundown later.

Left alone, the natural silence of Twilight surrounded them. Ann inhaled deeply, recalling Mark's friendly yet pointed advice. He'd told her that Jacob had changed, that her presence in their village had been the catalyst to those changes. Well, she had changed, too, and she realized that the reason was standing right in front of her. She felt linked to this man, bound to him in some deeply spiritual way that she couldn't explain or deny. It was time she admitted it. Jacob was important to her peace of mind, important to her future. Telling Mark she had no intention of pushing Jacob into acknowledging his feelings for her had been a lie. When he'd walked off that plane she'd known that for certain. Jacob needed her. And looking up at him now, she vowed to make him realize it, too.

"What is it you want to show me?" she asked, curiosity getting the best of her.

Wordlessly Jacob extended his hand, wondering if she'd take it. Her eyes widened at the unexpected gesture but she placed her gloved hand in his.

For a while they walked along in silence, the Sunday slow and peaceful, the only occasional sound that of children's voices. He was glad to be back home again. A week without Ann had made him face his own needs. His eyes fell to their hands, then up to find her watching him curiously. A tentative smile played at her lips and he returned it in full measure, absorbing the captivating picture she made when she was relaxed and content. Though he hadn't consciously intended bringing her to his home, when they reached the one-room house, he held open the door and stepped back, allowing Ann entry.

He watched her expression as she slowly unzipped her jacket and removed it, absorbing the sparse surroundings. He'd heard about the luxurious condominium she'd left behind. The rich life-style she'd led with her ex-husband. Her friends in Juneau hadn't liked the man, but they had all liked her. "Real people," her friend Merriam had said. "Ann Elliot was real people." He'd been startled, for the direct *kass'aq* translation of Yup'ik was just that, "real people."

"This is beautiful," she murmured softly, stroking her hand along the silver-haired wolf pelt that covered the one window.

Jacob took in the green qiviut sweater that always managed to make his heart rate increase. Then, at the thought of her caressing him the way she was the wolf pelt, he went hot all over. He swallowed. "Mark and I found him trapped in a snare. He'd lost too much blood to save."

She would have guessed that Jacob would try saving the animal first. His natural compassion would have been augmented by his *inua* which in itself made for a special sensitivity to a suffering wolf. Unaware of Jacob's reaction to her sensual stroking, she continued, enjoying the oddly soft-rough feel to the fur, slightly nervous at being alone with him again. When her eyes fell on the tools and carvings, she exclaimed in surprise, "You carved those? They're wonderful!"

Jacob's chest unaccountably swelled with pride. "Most of the men in the village work with ivory. It occupies us during winter and provides an extra source of income."

"Only the men do it? Why? Wasn't there ever a little girl who wanted to learn carving? Or, come to think of it, a little boy who enjoyed beadwork?"

The faint censure in her voice made him smile. Her ways were so western, so modern. Funny, while any signs of her being so different would have bothered him six weeks ago, he found he didn't mind them half so much now. It was, after all, a part of what made her so unique. His grin widened at the thought even as he answered her query. "I'm sure there were."

"Jacob, it may be amusing, but it's serious, too. The Yup'ik children should have a choice as to what they want to do, without traditional role stereotypes getting in the way."

Jacob removed his parka, then walked to the kitchen. "Would you like some tea?" he asked, his tone conversational. "My mother gathered the leaves on the tundra during late summer. Want to try it?"

"Yes, please, but don't think you can change the subject so easily, Jacob Toovak."

He chuckled. "I'm not one of your students, Ann. That stern 'do as I say' tone won't work with me."

"Sometimes . . ." she began in exasperation.

"Sometimes, what? You want to wring my neck?"

"Yes! I mean, no!" she grumbled, containing her own smile with difficulty. She couldn't stay angry. She was simply too happy to have him home. *Home.* She sighed, liking the word. And she had to admit, she also liked seeing this light-hearted, teasing side of him. It was nice to know that she could spark more than just anger and passion from within him.

Curious, she moved closer to Jacob's collection, intrigued by a statue of an Eskimo hunter in particular. She examined the statue, liking the cool, smooth feel of the ivory. "You know the spirit mask in your father's office? I thought it was beautiful, but this...it's really something, Jacob," she praised him softly.

"I carved that spirit mask when I came home last year," Jacob admitted, again feeling a surge of pride at her approval of his work.

"It's yours?" Now Ann was really stunned. The detail he'd achieved pointed to days, maybe weeks, of painstaking work. His carving was fantastic, and she realized that the spirit mask, like the Eskimo hunter, had drawn her as surely as the man himself. Accepting the tea Jacob offered her, she took a tentative sip.

"Hmm, good." Nervous, she looked around, her eyes avoiding the sleep-rumpled double bed.

"You can relax," Jacob spoke, guessing at her thoughts. "As much as I might want to, I won't pounce. I remember what you told me and I'll respect your wishes."

Startled, her eyes flew to his. His expression was rueful but understanding, the deep blaze in his eyes clearly reminding her of the more passionate confidences they'd shared. Looking at him leaning against the counter, his large hands wrapped as tightly around the white ceramic mug as they'd once wrapped around her yearning body, she knew the real meaning of temptation. She took another sip of her tea, feeling a trembling begin in her heart.

They were too alone here. And it was far too silent, though the wind moaned a high-pitched solitary cry that Jacob felt echoed in his heart. He looked at Ann, who'd nervously sat down next to him. She sat but inches away, staring down into her cup. Her cheeks were faintly flushed, her hair seemingly alive with static electricity. She looked dismayed and totally bewildered with the unexpected intensity of her feelings. He knew, because that's how he was feeling himself. He ached to pull her into his arms.

Picking up her tea, Ann left the dinette area and wandered to the floor space in front of Jacob's bed, where his polar bear rug lay. Jacob's eyes blazed even brighter, seeing her there as he'd imagined her on countless nights.

Kneeling down, Ann stroked the fur. It was much denser and coarser than the wolf's had been. "It's strange," she murmured, her voice hesitant. "I've never wanted to go hunting, wasn't even sure I approved of it, but since moving here my perspective has changed."

Jacob drew in a ragged breath, needing to go to her, knowing he couldn't. Unbidden, an image of her passion-drugged eyes and full, flushed breasts came to mind. His body tightened.

The wind continued to moan. The yapping of a dog sounded in the distance. Jacob took a deep breath, forcibly drawing back from an impossible fantasy. Ann wanted—deserved—something more permanent than he could offer her. Desires or no, for her sake he had to remember that. Taking another deep breath, he focused on Ann's remark.

"Maybe it's because we hunt to survive. It's a skill, not a sport. We pit our tools and our minds against nature and the elements. If we're good, we succeed and our village thrives."

"And if you're not?" Ann stopped stroking.

"You pay the price," Jacob said with finality, a trace of cold steel in his voice.

"That's why you don't hunt anymore, isn't it?" Ann's voice fell into the stillness. "Because you believe you paid too high a price?"

Jacob's jaw tightened as her words brought back the pain of that long-ago hunt, one he feared he'd never fully recovered from. His eyes slid over her body, lingering on the thrust of her breasts, the slim curve of her waist. Her gray eyes were hesitant, her gentle fingers curled tightly around her cup, and he wanted her with such an anguish of need that it almost choked him. Instinctively he knew that she could do what no one else had been able to—make him forget. Abruptly he slammed down his cup, his movements jerky and uncoordinated as he crossed to the bed and whipped off his right shoe and sock.

Ann just managed to swallow her gasp at the sight of his toeless right foot.

"This is a very small part of the price I paid," he said bluntly. "And every time I look at it, I remember."

"Oh, Jacob, I'm so sorry. I didn't know."

"Well, now you do," he ground out, purposely using his bitterness as a wedge against the ever-growing need for the comfort he knew he'd find in her arms. "Do you still think I made the wrong choice to stop hunting?"

Ann looked at his foot. Although far from perfect, there was no possible way that she could label it ugly. It was a part of Jacob, and she was fast coming to realize that, to her at least, every part of him was beautiful. But how was she going to make him understand that?

"What, no answer?" he asked sarcastically.

"If you must know, yes. I guess I do think you made the wrong choice, Jacob," she replied calmly.

Clearly he hadn't expected that. His foot jerked back.

"No, wait!"

Her hands reached out. She could feel his entire body stiffening at the unexpected contact, but though she sensed he wanted to, he didn't pull away from her grasp. He'd have to push her to do so and Ann trusted her instincts that he wouldn't use his strength against her.

But without recourse she could see him retreating into himself, and she knew she had to do something fast. Her grip tightened.

"Listen to me, you stubborn Eskimo. There's a reason I said you made the wrong choice. Last Saturday night I told you about my being pregnant at eighteen. It was a very frightening period for me. My family was shocked, my friends rejected me, even Richard wasn't inclined to be supportive after he'd realized what he'd gotten himself into. I went through nine months of hell, Jacob. Nine months of knowing that with each passing day things could only get worse because the proof of my irresponsibility would become more and more noticeable. By the time I had Sharon, my parents had convinced me I didn't deserve her. That I was cheap and dirty."

"You made the right choice," he said tightly, intensely aware of her hand around his foot.

"I kept Sharon, yes. I discovered that I wanted her desperately. She was just a baby, but I knew she'd love me unconditionally," she whispered, her voice unsteady. "But I shouldn't have let my parents force me into marrying Richard. It was my life and I let them run it for me. You see, I believed what they believed. And when they acted like I was dirt, I believed that, too. I thought I didn't deserve Sharon."

Jacob's eyes flickered. He searched her face for the truth and read the suffering she didn't bother to hide. "You're a good mother."

"Perhaps, but I didn't think I would be back then. They're my parents, Jacob. I trusted them."

"What's the point, Ann? At least you had a choice. I didn't." He couldn't believe he was talking about this. Again. What was she doing to him?

"Yes, you did, Jacob. That's what I'm trying to tell you. I had a choice and so did you. There's always a choice. It's how we deal with the results of our decisions that matters more than the choices we make. You're not perfect, and God knows, neither am I. If I were, I would have kept Sharon and raised her without Richard. But I was young and scared."

"Why are you telling me this? I don't have your excuses, Ann." He sat down on the bed, bemused when she followed suit. Still holding his foot, she began to caress it. The sensations she was producing were decidedly distracting.

"Does it matter? You live with your foot just like I lived with my parents' rejection. It's the same thing, Jacob. You said it yourself. Only I had to get over the guilt so that I wouldn't take it out on my daughter. You have to do the same for yourself. Let go of the guilt. Go hunt. You love it, I know you do. It's part of who you are, part of your heritage. Why give it up?"

She moved slightly, and gently, reverently, she leaned forward and kissed his foot.

His head jerked up and he looked at her as if he couldn't believe what she'd just done.

"I'm no more a tramp than you are a murderer," she said with conviction.

Perhaps it was her choice of words, but Jacob seemed to snap out of a daze, his eyes glittering dangerously. He reached down, his steely grip unconsciously harsh about her upper arms as he jerked her up against him on the bed. "It's my fault they're dead," he said roughly. "Can't you see that? Yup'ik women don't hunt the big game. Yet I let her come along anyway, because I wanted her to be with me. If I had been strong, she'd be alive now." His broad frame seemed to vibrate with tension.

Ann recognized the desperate torment in his face. For years she'd lived with her own choices. She reached up to his furrowed brow and stroked it gently. He flinched, but when she moved to withdraw, he captured her hand, pressing her palm to his chest.

"Don't stop." He was suddenly so tired. Exhausted. He searched her face. "I like having you touch me," he admitted huskily.

"I like touching you," she murmured. "All of you."

He stiffened, understanding the message underneath the words. Pulling her against him, he held her gently, his eyes closed as he absorbed the quickened beat of her heart. "I didn't hurt you, did I?"

"No." Ann closed her eyes. It was heaven, this closeness between them. She trembled with the sheer pleasure of it.

Jacob felt the shivers and drew her even closer. He could feel her breathing quicken into rapid little bursts against his throat, an erotic pulsing that made him hard instantly. She felt soft and yielding lying in his arms. The sensations brought back memories of last weekend, when she'd opened her soul to him. He pulled back.

"Ann."

I want you.

Good or bad, Ann understood Jacob's need as if he'd spoken it aloud. She stroked his chest, eyes locked with his, absorbing his strength and his restraint.

She sensed frustration; she sensed guilt. She sensed sorrow, constraint and doubt. But mostly, she sensed a burning desire for her.

Held captive within the blaze of that desire, Ann could feel the heat of his chest sear into her palm, feel his midnight-black eyes reach deeply into her soul and, urged by an inner force she couldn't deny, she leaned forward. Her lungs struggled for air as chest slowly, deliciously, met breasts.

Sweet—Jacob gritted his teeth, straining not to tighten his hold, pull her down and ravage her right then and there. Didn't she know what she was doing to him?

"Ann...?" Her name was both plea and sensual demand.

She looked into Jacob's eyes, willing him not to talk, not to disturb this moment with words. For now all that mattered was the fire between them, the need to drown in each other that increased with every breath they took. When he finally moved to take her back into his arms, she could only moan. His weather-roughened hands slid down her spine, caressing first the curve of her waist, then traveling up to cup her face to meet his hungry lips.

At the touch of his mouth, Ann's whole body tensed, then relaxed with a sweet, hot breath of release. As his fingers wove urgently through her curls, she felt free, floating in the slow warmth of his passion. She opened her mouth, seeking deeper contact. Immediately he entered, his tongue reaching to claim the new territory, to explore its taste, its depths, all while his hands continued to stroke her sensitive back, pulling her ever closer, crushing her breasts against his rock-solid chest. His tongue dueled with hers, a primitive dance of spirit and fire, eternal man and woman locked together in a rhythm of ancient times.

Ann couldn't get close enough. Restlessly she arched her body against his, wanting him more and more, almost frightened by the need, craving his touch, aching for something just beyond her reach.

Jacob sensed the loss of Ann's control. Abruptly he released her, but only long enough to carry her to the rug. The fantasy in his mind was being played out in reality, only the reality was far better, far sweeter than he'd imagined. Reverently he fanned her hair out on the rug, absorbing the picture she made, hair wild, lips soft and wet with the stamp of his kisses. He lay down beside her, pulling her into his arms, marveling at her need of him, humbled at the realization. Tenderly his hand brushed the curve of her thigh, skimming lightly across the heat of her femininity. At her instinctive gasp, he smiled, cupping her breast through the cloud-soft qiviut. She moaned and he throbbed, her pleasure propelling his own.

Ann arched against Jacob's hand as he kneaded the soft fullness of her breast, helpless in her longing for more, over-whelmed by a need to throw out the chains of old inhibi-tions. She cried out when he swept the sweater from her eager body, his hands trembling with the depth of his desire. Gent-ly he lowered his lips to the sweet, rounded curve, inhaling her scent, learning her body.

He sucked the darkened tip of her breast, rapacious tongue alternately flicking back and forth in short, demanding strokes, then pulling the extended, hungry nipple into his mouth. He groaned. She echoed with her own husky sigh.

He caressed her shoulders, her arms, her throat, drawing back only to remove his own sweater, letting her gaze at him with the same fevered excitement with which he had gazed down at her perfection. Then he joined her once again, pull-ing her around and on top of him, accepting her weight, the feel of her body stretched out along the length of his. She made his heart beat triple, his head spin. She made him for-get the world outside. "Ann . . ." he rasped against her warm wet nipple.

She was a teacher. From her, he had learned compassion; and now he was learning need. He was a willing pupil.

Energized with need, her body aching and pulsing with de-sire for him, Ann arched up, resting her weight on her arms to give him full access to her breasts, enjoying the trembling in her arms even though she knew she wouldn't be able to hold herself upright for long. In giving to him, she was receiving a far greater pleasure, satisfying a thirst she hadn't known ex-isted within her.

Looking down, she met his intense black gaze. His parted lips, his deep ragged breaths, his trembling limbs, all pointed to the power she had, a power she'd never before cared to ex-plore. Wonder and awe washed over her as she realized that, with him, she wanted to explore the boundaries of her sexu-ality, craved it. Perhaps because, somewhere down deep, she recognized that this man, unlike her ex-husband, would be with her every step of the way. With Jacob she instinctively knew her pleasure would be boundless. Then he drew her down, surging upward with his hips, and Ann experienced a spear of desire so great she gasped out loud.

Looking deep into her eyes, Jacob only read desire for more. Suddenly he couldn't wait another second. With swift, effortless motions, he removed the remainder of his clothing, purposely giving her time to absorb his nude length, the broad expanse of his chest, the hard, tensed curves of his thighs.

Then he joined her on the rug again, bare chest to bare breasts, his eyes demanding she touch him, kiss him.

Ann reached out, only too willing to comply. Hot, his skin felt so hot beneath her trembling hands. He smelled of tea and lemon and of something else, a surprising mixture of Native and western ways. Parting her lips, she kissed him all over his neck, his shoulders, wherever she could reach. The taste of him was intoxicating. He tasted of sea storms. Mesmerized, she stretched herself alongside his body, attempting to absorb his very essence.

"Jacob..." she murmured, wanting to say more, knowing that she couldn't. "Oh, Jacob..." she murmured again.

He drew back, his eyes smoldering, glazed with a need that went deeper than passion. "I want you, Ann," he rasped. "So much... so very much." Then his mouth bore down on hers again and communication became a silent exchange of tongues and caresses. His hands swept down the heated hollows of her body, following the womanly curve of her waist to the band on her slacks. With a harsh, ragged breath, his fingers skimmed down and reached for the zipper, opening it with a deft movement. Then he gently removed her pants, pausing to gaze at what he'd revealed, aroused by the feminine triangle that was barely hidden by the lightweight cotton covering. Reaching out, he removed the last barrier, then softly, tenderly, swept his hands down along her thigh to the heat of her.

Ann arched helplessly, gasping at Jacob's gently intimate caress. She moved to touch him, too, enjoying the freedom of seeing him naked, watching the afternoon light play across his body. She stretched out her hand and stroked the hard muscled curve of his thigh, gazing in awe and delight at the hardened evidence of his desire for her. Touching him, she felt him throb, felt a primitive need to give him release with the warm moist recesses of her body and soul.

Jacob sensed her readiness in the urgency of her eyes, in the way she restlessly moved against him. When he parted her thighs, his eyes met hers, telling her without words that their joining was more than an act, it was a bond, a connection of two hearts and two souls. He was *Kegluneq* and she was his mate.

Slowly he joined them.

She felt his entry, his slow measured glide to the very depths of her soul. Her hands moved without conscious volition, sliding down the tensed powerful thighs and pulling him in, urging him deeper into her body. Her fingertips dug into the sinewed muscle of his buttocks, absorbing the potent thrust and meeting it with an equal urgency of her own. She cried out as she fully sheathed his length, shuddering as the sensations rose and ebbed like a massive wave on an endless sea of passion. Again and again they surged together, learning each other's needs, fulfilling each other's deepest desires. He was man and she was woman, locked together in a ritual of basic need and fulfillment, performing the steps of a universal dance destined to take them to the stars and beyond.

She had never felt more vulnerable. She had never felt more invincible.

A storm began building deep within her, a storm so strong and wildly compelling that Ann felt helpless in its grasp, helpless to control its fevered rise. Where a moment earlier she'd aggressively mirrored Jacob's movements, now she followed his lead, eagerly pulled along into a turbulent tidal wave of dizzying madness and flickering lights. She called out and he answered, her hips rising up off the rug, higher and higher, asking him, pleading with him for something just beyond her reach, something only he could give her.

And then he did. The fevered flick of his tongue at her breast sparked an explosion of sensation and love, sending vibrations trembling through her body to surround his, forcing her to cling to Jacob, her anchor in this brand new world of passion and sweet release. She held him tight, even as she heard him cry out and felt him follow her up to the stars. Afterward, as they floated down together, free yet connected, Jacob suckled gently at her breast.

Slowly his body relaxed, his hands lightly caressing the passion-moist softness of her shoulder as he repositioned himself beside her, pulling her close against the curve of his body. "You're more beautiful than I imagined," he murmured against her hair.

"So are you," she whispered back, brushing her lips against the forearm supporting her head. The soft caress made him shudder lightly, a reaction Ann absorbed with smug satisfaction.

They lay there for a while, silent, relaxed, thinking of what had happened, and trying not to speculate on what would happen now, afraid to test the fragility of their new relationship. Jacob wanted to tell her that she was everything he'd ever wanted; that from now on, they would be together; that he wanted her to be his wife. But even as the thoughts danced across his mind, so did others, thoughts that reminded him of the world outside, of the past and of the differences between them.

"Ann—"

"I know," she forestalled him, preferring to be the one to say it first. She'd sensed the direction of his thoughts, had felt the tension reenter his body. Defensive, she crossed her arms over her breasts. He wanted her, but not enough. Not enough to set aside the past or work through their differences. Her face flamed and she sat up, pain striking her heart. His rejection hurt more than she'd thought possible. How could she have believed that it wouldn't matter? Head angled so that her hair covered her face, she murmured, "I should get back. The kids will be wondering what happened to me."

Painfully aware of her nudity, Ann could feel her insecurities surging to the surface. She bit her lip. How was she going to get out of here without him seeing her?

Jacob observed the protective way she was shielding herself. Frowning, he sat up. But when he reached out, she pulled back from him, alarmed. Thinking back to the night at the cabin, he put two and two together. "Ann, please, don't turn away. You're beautiful."

She shuddered. "You don't have to say that, Jacob. I'm a big girl now. I can handle it."

"But it's the truth."

"Please, just leave it alone," she whispered, totally embarrassed.

But Jacob wouldn't leave it alone. He didn't want her hiding from him. Reaching out, he grasped her arms and brought them down to her sides. "It's the truth," he repeated solemnly, his heart wrenching at the bleakness he'd heard in her voice. "Don't be ashamed of your body, Ann. You're perfect."

When she still refused to look up, he released her, transferring one hand to her breast.

"Jacob!" Shocked, despite what they'd shared only moments ago, Ann did look up.

"It's the truth," he repeated gently for the third time. Leaning forward, his mouth captured hers and he kissed her softly, just once, before pulling back. He searched her face, seeing her dawning belief in her own attractiveness. Then it came to him what he'd done by giving in to temptation. He'd awakened her sexuality, but he'd also hurt her. "Why did you do it?"

Because I love you, Ann's heart cried out, finally admitting to what she'd known for some time now. *Because I couldn't bear to see you in pain. Because all the objections in the world aren't as important as what I feel for you.*

"You were hurting," she whispered the lie, her eyes shadowed.

Jacob experienced a sharp stab of regret and something deeper that he couldn't identify. Trying to be casual, he helped her get dressed, telling her before they left that he would consider what she'd said about his getting back to hunting. If only everything else could be resolved so easily.

As it turned out, Jacob wound up spending the afternoon with them. And although Sharon seemed unusually withdrawn and preoccupied, Patrick perked up considerably at having Jacob's undivided attention. They were piecing together a puzzle at the dinette table. As always when the two were together, Jacob's moodiness disappeared and a smile replaced the frown. Inwardly bowing to the inevitable, Ann walked over to where her daughter lay on the couch staring up at the ceiling. She frowned down at her.

"You've been lying there for thirty minutes. Why not come over and work on the puzzle with us?"

"I'm not in the mood for a puzzle, Mom."

"Then what are you in the mood for? Scoot over, sweetheart." Sharon grumbled but did as she'd been asked. Ann sat down. "Now, what's the matter? Did you and Siksik have a fight? You two *have* been spending a lot of time together lately."

"No, Mom, everything's fine, okay? I've just kinda got a headache."

"Just kinda, huh?" Ann ruffled her fingers gently through her daughter's hair. "Well, I don't think you need an aspirin then. How about a walk? We can leave Patrick with Jacob and just the two of us go. Dinner won't be ready for a few minutes anyway and sometimes a walk clears up a fuzzy head."

Sharon closed her eyes and turned away. "No thanks, Mom. If it's all right with you, I'll just stay here."

Ann hesitated. "I don't like seeing you like this, honey. You're not still thinking about what we talked about a couple of weeks ago, are you?"

"About not being able to visit my friends in Anchorage, you mean?"

"No, I was referring to what I told you about your Dad and me. But since you mentioned it, is that the problem? Sweetheart, I told you, we can't afford it."

Sharon faced her mother. "Why not, Mom? We used to be able to go out to dinner a lot before Dad died. We haven't done that in ages. You must have saved some money from all the dinners and movies and stuff we haven't gone to this year. Couldn't I go just for a couple of days even? *Please?*"

Young teenagers tended to see things so simplistically. They hadn't dined out in more than a year, so the money just *had* to be saved somewhere, right? Ann turned, encountering Jacob's concerned gaze. That he wished he could help was obvious from his expression. Ann smiled but knew only she could handle this one.

"Sharon, there wasn't much money left after your dad's accident. I had to sell the condo to pay for the emergency medical bills. There was barely enough to move into that apartment I rented and pay down on some of our other bills." Bills like Richard's restaurant and bar tabs all over town. Like his ten thousand dollar loan from a local pawn shop. By the time she'd paid off his debts, she'd been frantic to find a job.

"What about if you give me a ticket as a Christmas present? I won't ask for anything else, I promise. And I'll call Katie. I'm sure she'll let me stay with her."

"Have you written to Katie since you've been here?"

"Every week."

"And has she answered?" Ann already knew the answer to that one, but wanted to make Sharon say it.

"No, but she's probably really busy with school and... stuff," Sharon mumbled without meeting her mother's eyes.

"Too busy to write her best friend a letter?"

Tears filled Sharon's eyes and she jumped up off the couch. "No matter what I say, you always shoot it down, Mom! What's so bad about wanting to see my friends? It's not like I have any here!" she shouted, then ran to her room and slammed the door.

Ann moved to follow but Jacob said softly, "Give her a few minutes to calm down. You won't solve anything if she's still upset."

Ann paused, then nodded. "Patrick, go wash your hands, would you? It's almost dinnertime."

Jacob watched Patrick get up from his chair and quietly leave the room. The boy was so easy to love. He'd adapted to the village and the villagers with surprising ease. Their friendship had been swift and immediate. Already he'd caught himself thinking of skills he could teach him and things the two of them could do together, like mushing and more ice fishing.

But Sharon was a different story. From the beginning, she'd been wary of him, and Jacob admitted reluctantly that the feelings had been mutual. He'd disapproved of her heavy use of makeup, despite the fact that he knew it was "in" for to-day's girls, and he couldn't blame her for sensing his uneasiness and reacting to it. The girl was confused and he knew what that was all about. His first year in Fairbanks had been rough. Strange food, strange customs, and even stranger people, or so he'd thought at the time. So while he didn't know Sharon as well as he knew Patrick, he did respect her feelings and even acknowledged that she had a perfect right to feeling out of sorts. What she *didn't* have, though, was a right to take those feelings out on everyone around her, especially her mother. Ann was already troubled enough.

Ann crossed to the dinette and pitched in with putting the puzzle away. They worked silently for a few moments, Jacob glancing at Ann every few minutes to gauge her mood. Finally, when he'd watched her stare at a single puzzle piece for several moments, he gently took it out of her hand and drew her into his arms.

"She'll adjust to Twilight," he remarked. "It just takes time."

Ann sighed and burrowed into the warm comfort of his chest. "I know. And I also know that she doesn't dislike it here," she murmured. "It's just that she misses Anchorage and her friends so much." She sighed and drew back. "I really don't know what to do, Jacob. It's so hard when you want to give your children the best of everything and you can't."

"I could lend you the money—"

"No. That's definitely not the answer. Sharon's just going to have to learn that she can't have everything exactly when she wants it anymore. That's one of the reasons I took this job. Richard used to give her anything she wanted, whenever she wanted it. I don't know if he even realized he was buying her affection. But I did. We used to argue about it a lot, only it never stopped him." Ann moved away into the kitchen. Pulling plates and glasses from the shelf, she began setting the table.

"As much as I want her to be happy, she'll have to learn the hard way that money doesn't grow on trees. And if she winds up resenting me for it, well, I'll have to live with that, I guess." She positioned the last glass, then smiled up at Jacob. She was grateful for his support. "But thanks for the offer," she said, her eyes full of what they'd shared that afternoon. She leaned over and kissed him. "I really appreciate it."

Neither saw Patrick reenter and then quickly exit the room.

Chapter Fifteen

A week later, Ann seated herself in the bleachers and prepared to watch the day's events unfold. Already, youngsters
were practicing for their competitions. Ann waved at Patrick.

"I see you got here a little early, too."

Ann swung around, then smiled. "Oh, hi, Mary," she said,
her grin widening. "What are you doing in the stands? I figured you'd be down there on the gym floor practicing with the
girls."

"If they don't know the dances by now, an extra few minutes with me sure won't change anything." With an audible
grunt, Mary lowered her short, broad body onto the hard
bleacher seat. "Besides, I'll be here all afternoon. Figured I'd
better take a break while I can. Want some company?"

Ann laughed. "Do I have a choice?"

Mary sighed. "In a few minutes, this gym is going to be
packed and already I'm tired. So, how is the family?"

"Fine. Patrick's with his friends doing some last-minute
practicing and Sharon's over there by Siksik."

"And Jacob? Where's he?"

Ann didn't even blink at Mary's automatic inclusion of Jacob in her "family." With all the time he spent with them, what else could she expect? "He's probably at home resting up. Which is what you should have done, Mary. Don't you want to win a ribbon?"

"Sure, but I doubt I will," she replied modestly.

"The way you handle that *ulu*? Are you kidding? I don't think I've ever seen anyone cut up a fish faster than you."

"And just what makes you such an expert?" Mary replied, though her cheeks flushed at the compliment. Ann laughed, caught out. "We'll see. Siksik's mother is really good, too. And she won it last year."

The gym was rapidly filling up now. Ann watched as men carrying drums and different lengths of poles streamed in alongside their wives and children, who were carrying food dishes for the annual Christmas potlatch held after the dances. Some of the men immediately veered off and began partitioning the gym into sections for specific competitions.

"I think Billy really wants to win the one-foot high kick this year," remarked Ann, watching the teenager practice. During their S.A.T. study sessions last week, he'd boasted of his intent, hoping, Ann guessed, to impress Sharon. He'd been disappointed. Sharon hadn't cared at all, while Siksik's eyes had lighted up like bright, shining stars.

Mary's gaze followed hers. "I don't know Ann, Mark won the one-foot last year and he's pretty good. Consistent, too, which is important since you only get three chances. Billy might have to settle for the two-foot high kick. It's not as prestigious, but then in some ways it's harder."

"Because both feet have to kick the ball?"

Mary nodded. "It hangs about six feet off the floor, remember. I'm too old now, but even when I was young and thin like your daughter, the two-foot always seemed to require more coordination."

Ann fell silent, watching the teenagers hang around, venting nervous energy and razzing one another as they limbered up. She could literally feel everyone's excitement. Her gaze fell on Patrick's face as he readied himself to practice for the knee jump competition. Earlier he'd patiently explained that the object was to start by sitting on your knees, then jumping to your feet, gaining as much horizontal distance during the jump as possible.

"Did I hear you say that Jacob's at home resting up for the games?"

"Yes." Ann's gaze didn't waver as her son took a deep breath and jumped. Afterward, he turned in her direction and waved, obviously pleased with his jumping. Ann smiled and gave him a thumbs-up sign. Then she turned to Mary. "He ought to arrive any minute now."

A companionable silence followed, both watching the crowd.

"Looks like we're starting up," Mary said brightly. "What are you going to compete in?"

"Me?" Ann asked, her voice squeaking in surprise.

"Sure, why not?" Mary replied.

"Oh, no. I don't think so. I wouldn't know how—" Ann began.

Mary cut her short. "You don't need to know how. The blanket toss, you just get on and people throw you up in the air. You just do it. Same with the pole walk."

"Pole walk?"

Mary stood and grabbed her hand. "Come on. I'll show you. They're ready over there, anyway."

Ann had little choice but to follow Mary down the stand steps to the gym floor. Together they headed directly for a vivacious young mother, seemingly in charge of a birch pole that was approximately twenty feet long. Mary halted and the two women exchanged greetings in Yup'ik. Then Mary turned to Ann.

"Ready?"

"No, Mary, wait—" Ann said hastily. "I really don't think—"

"Just watch, okay? Once you see some of the others do it, you'll realize it's not that hard. All it requires is a little balance and coordination."

Ann eyed first her and then the pole's peeled, bumpy surface. It was lathered with some sort of oil and set on concrete blocks that suspended it about six inches off the floor. One of Siksik's friends, a small girl with a full engaging smile, jumped up to try her luck. Mary provided commentary.

"The purpose is to start at one end and walk as far along the pole as you can," she instructed, bending down and removing her tennis shoes and socks. Feeling awkward and uncomfortable, Ann did the same. The bystanders, many of whom were her female students and their mothers, had cheered upon seeing her cross the gym floor. Though Ann didn't particularly want to compete, she knew she couldn't back out now. She considered these people her friends and had no wish to insult them or their customs by refusing.

"You go first," she ordered Mary, who chuckled at her nervousness and nodded acceptance.

Spotting her, both Patrick and Sharon came over to watch. Siksik wasn't far behind.

"You really gonna try it, Mom? Totally rad!" Patrick jumped up and down, excited. "Way to go, Mom!"

Ann managed a self-conscious smile. Several women were lined up ahead of her and Mary. "Like most of the competitions, this one predates our written history," Mary informed her. "Back then the pole was a log leading from a fish-catching wheel in midriver to the shore. The log was slippery with fish slime and the river waters below it were usually icy."

"Are you telling me I should be glad we're not outside?"

Mary chuckled again. "Don't worry so much. It will be fun. You'll see."

And to her surprise, it was. Gaining her balance wasn't easy, but with sheer nerve and a good deal of copying the others' sideways sliding movements, Ann's bare feet inched along the pole bit by bit. Most everyone in the vicinity shouted and whistled encouragement. Ann's forehead beaded with perspiration as she concentrated hard on finding a firm footing on the round slick pole. Her daughter's excited cheers spurred her on. She'd made it almost six feet before she felt her balance shift. Crying out, she tipped off the pole. Familiar arms caught and lifted her clear.

"Jacob!"

Black eyes twinkled down into her flushed face. "Congratulations! I think you might just have won the ladies pole walk."

"Hey Mom, that was neat! Do you really think you won?"

"Yeah, Mom, that was great," added Sharon with a smile.

Ann turned imploring eyes to Mary, who avidly took in the picture she made in Jacob's arms. "I told you you'd have fun."

Ann blushed. "Please, put me down, Jacob." He did, but he kept one arm casually flung around her shoulders. The public display both surprised and discomfited her. Their business relationship must be common knowledge, but she wasn't comfortable with public displays that suggested more personal ties. There were several issues yet unresolved between them, not the least of which was commitment. Disturbed, she turned to her daughter. "You want to try, Sharon? It's not as hard as I thought."

"Aw, she's not coordinated enough—" Patrick began.

"Sharon's going to help me practice—" Siksik said at the same time.

Ann paused, sensing something amiss. Then she shrugged off the peculiar feeling. No doubt it was due to Jacob's body being pressed against hers. The heat he emitted reminded her far too vividly of their lovemaking and how ardent he'd been then.

"Well, sweetheart, what about it?"

Sharon looked from her mother's heated cheeks to Jacob. "No thanks, Mom. I think I'll pass."

Though Ann was disappointed, she didn't press her daughter and the afternoon passed quickly after that. When Siksik finally took her turn, the teenager managed to slither just two inches farther than Ann had, thus claiming the title and the blue ribbon.

Jacob remained by her side, the deep tones of his voice stirring her heartstrings as he told her about the various events and their histories. Ann was impressed, particularly with the genuine feeling of fun and camaraderie that never ceased to exist among the various competitors. Most everyone—except for the few serious athletes, like Billy—cared more about encouraging their friends to do their best than about winning. Together she and Jacob watched Mary in the seal skinning and fish cutting competitions. Her friend's speed and skill with the U-shaped *ulu* were indeed considerable.

"What's Ben getting ready to do?" They'd seated themselves high up in the stands to get the best view.

Jacob's gaze followed Ann's across the gym to where several men were gathered. "That's the four-man carry. A long time ago, we didn't have the guns, three-wheelers and aluminum boats that we have today. Once killed, the hunter carried on his back as much of the moose or walrus as he could. The stronger the hunter, the less kill lost to predators on the way back to the village. The stronger the hunter, the better were the chances of his family's and his village's survival."

"You mean he's going to carry *four men on his back?* Isn't he too old?"

Jacob choked on a laugh and sputtered, "Don't let him hear you say that. He prides himself on the fact that last year he came in tenth."

"But—" Ann broke off, mentally estimating the probable weight. "That must be almost six hundred pounds!"

Jacob nodded, still chuckling. "Just watch, he'll do okay."

And to Ann's astonishment he did, carrying the four men almost seven feet. The crowd cheered wildly for their mayor. So did Ann.

"I can't believe he did it!" She turned to Jacob, her eyes sparkling with amazement. Jacob laughed, but soon stopped, staring at her. She was so beautiful. His eyes lingered on her lips before dropping to her breasts. They were so engrossed in one another that it took a moment for the calls around them to sink in. Some of Jacob's friends were urging him to try the four-man carry.

Immediately Ann felt tension invade his body. He didn't want to do it. Sympathetic, she placed her hand gently on his knee. "It's your choice," she reminded him pointedly.

Jacob's eyes narrowed on hers for several long moments. Then, as if suddenly making up his mind, he stood and descended the steps to the gym floor.

Ann watched him go, her heart tripping nervously. And she'd thought the pole walk was bad! What if he couldn't balance such a heavy weight? For that matter, what if he injured himself? Just because Ben's back managed it didn't mean Jacob's was up to the strain. And from what she'd gathered, Jacob hadn't competed in any of the events since his accident. What if his right foot couldn't handle the awkwardness of the load? As Jacob settled the four men on his shoulders, the villagers' enthusiastic applause and loud whistles of encouragement reached new heights. Even Ann found herself chanting "Go, Jacob, go!" and jumping to her feet along with everyone else as they counted out the distance markers taped on the gym floor. At the one hundred and sixty-foot mark Jacob and his friends plunged to the floor. But they were up in seconds, all laughing, the men patting Jacob on the back. Jacob looked her way and winked, a triumphant sparkle in his eyes.

Ann laughed and waved, her pulse rate skyrocketing with the adrenaline of his success. They both knew what it meant. It was a shared moment, both private and public.

Mark sauntered over, his grin as wide as everyone else's. "Don't pin that ribbon on just yet, big brother," he warned, jabbing Jacob's shoulder with a playful punch. "A real expert's about to take his turn."

"Oh, really?" Jacob grinned, enjoying himself. He hadn't felt this good in years. And the reason was sitting up in the stands.

"Yeah, really," Mark shot back, intertwining his fingers, then stretching his arms above his head. "Clear the way, please. Winner on the floor. Clear the way, please."

Jacob chuckled and retreated, not surprised when Mark did beat his distance and win. But inside, he knew he'd won a battle of his own. Again his eyes sought Ann's and found them trained on him. She knew it, too.

After the games came the dances. Patrick hadn't won anything, but he'd placed in the knee jump and seemed happy with that. Sharon, too, was enjoying herself. Ann scanned the gym, taking in the eight men who had changed into ceremonial mukluks and *kuspuks* both lined, with colorful stitching, fur and beads. On their heads they wore headdresses made of caribou hide, beads and polar bear hairs stitched on in an elaborate semi-circular fan. Ben was one of the men and he was wearing the headdress fashioned by his wife. Sitting cross-legged on the gym floor, each man held a drum made of walrus bladder stretched tight over a driftwood frame. For the occasion, the gym's lights were cut the moment Ben lit the thirty or so *Naniq* lamps. Smoke from the smoldering sea oil permeated the air, signifying the start of the Woman of the Sea Dance.

"Is Siksik okay?" Ann whispered. A single drum began a low level beat.

Sharon rolled her eyes to the ceiling. "Her hands were sweating so much she kept dropping the dance fans. And I couldn't get her to hold still for the makeup, either."

"Makeup?" Ann repeated warily.

Sharon squinted down to where Jacob sat frowning on the other side of Ann. "A little. She really looks pretty. Just wait."

"Here she comes!" hissed Patrick.

All eyes turned to a side door as Siksik, dressed in her finest parka and mukluks, her hair oiled and swinging in a shining loose curtain to her waist, her face nervous yet oddly composed, made her way silently to the center circle of lights.

"Good job, honey. She does look great," Ann whispered, noting the very subtle shading around the girl's eyes and the hint of blush on her cheeks.

"Thanks, Mom."

Burning their welcome, the lamps gave off the smoke of ancient fires and bygone days. The air was thick with anticipation and the smells of reindeer stew, Eskimo fry bread, smoked salmon and the distinctive scent of seal oil.

A single drum beat with heavy solemnity, its lone pulse reaching out and capturing all who watched. Slowly, one by one, the other drummers joined the song, until all were beating and the gym was filled with sound. Ann watched Jacob's sister perform the movements to the beautiful Woman of the Sea Dance, her tall, slender body gliding about the floor as she pretended to be searching for fish. As if seeing one, she disappeared into a circular opening, then emerged with an imaginary fish held in her small delicate hands. She proceeded to eat it, all the while swimming about in the sea. Again and again she circled, the sea abundant, her movements speeding up in tune to the drums.

Ann's eyes automatically glanced sideways and found Jacob, his face reflecting joy and pride, watching not Siksik, but her. His dark eyes, made darker by the lamplight and shadows, looked meaningfully into hers. The message was clear. *This is who I am,* he was saying. *This is where I belong.* Though he walked the path between both cultures, his roots, his soul, were in Twilight.

She knew that he was asking if she understood and she did. But she didn't know where that left her come spring. Since coming to Nelson Island, so many things had changed. The independence she'd wished for was now a fact. She controlled her life and knew she could do so in the future. But thanks to Jacob, she'd also explored her inner self. He'd taught her to trust again and to believe in herself and her attractiveness.

But what would happen come spring? Should he overcome his guilt regarding Lia's death and ask her to stay, would she? Until now, she'd survived here knowing that her stay, after all, wasn't permanent. But if he wanted her to stay on, could she endure the isolation over the long term? And what was more important, could she ask it of her children?

Her eyes blurred and she turned her head away, unwilling to have Jacob see her distress. Billy was in her line of sight, and as she blinked fiercely against the tears, she watched the young man's face transform with something close to awe. Ann smiled inwardly, happy for Siksik. It appeared that at least Siksik's performance had finally alerted Billy to the beauty of Siksik herself.

The sudden thunderous applause penetrated Ann's thoughts. She turned in time to see Siksik bow shyly, then take her place as her classmates lined up to perform another dance.

Ann was stuffed. She'd sampled everything the potlatch offered, including *Akutaq,* the Eskimo ice cream. Made of salmon or whitefish and any of eight different berries harvested on the tundra during early autumn, the mixture was combined with oil and hand-whipped to a consistency as fine and light as that of western ice cream. The taste was decidedly different, though, and one that would take considerable getting used to Ann decided as she exited the gym in search of the drinking fountain. Unfortunately she'd discovered, in the past half hour, that there were as many variations of the dish as there were women in the village. And each had insisted she try their version. Bending down, she depressed the water dispenser button, not entirely certain she wasn't going to be sick. She drank steadily, concentrating on soothing the queasiness in her stomach.

"Too much *Akutaq,* huh?"

Ann's breath caught and water went down the wrong way. Immediately, Jacob pulled her back and away from the fountain, pounding her lightly on the back until the coughing fit passed. "Okay now?"

Ann peered at him through a mist of tears. How could such a big man move so quietly? ''I'm fine, Jacob. At least, I will be in a second. You just surprised me, I guess.''

She coughed one last time, then turned to retrace her steps. Jacob reached out, his hand cupping her elbow. ''While we've got some privacy, there's something I need to explain about us.''

Ann's eyes found his. ''We're friends, Jacob. I know that.''

The words hit Jacob like a dead weight. ''Friends? That's all? Didn't you feel what I felt back there in the gym?''

Denying it would be pointless, so she didn't even try. ''I felt it.''

''Then how can you say we're just friends? We made love,'' he emphasized.

She looked at him in amazement and not a little anger. He, after all, had been the one to set the boundaries on their ''relationship.'' ''We didn't get married, Jacob. You're not responsible for me. You're not responsible *to* me, either.''

For seconds they simply stared at each other. Then Jacob said roughly, ''I held you in my arms . . . within my body. You're saying it meant nothing special?''

Ann sighed. ''Of course not, Jacob. It meant everything to me, but I've been pushed into making decisions and saying things I don't feel all my life. First my parents, then Richard. Which means that I'm not going to use what we've had together as a means of emotional blackmail to force you into saying or doing something you don't feel ready to say or do. Do you understand?''

Oddly enough, he did. He understood she was pushing him away; understood she was hurting because he hadn't offered the commitment she needed.

''I'm not talking about pushing. I'm talking about telling,'' he said seriously.

''And all I'm saying is that you don't *have* to. We're friends, Jacob, and friends understand.'' She swallowed, wondering if her voice sounded as strained to Jacob as it did to her. ''You need to do what's best for you. Just like I do.''

''And what is best for you?'' he asked intensely.

The question hung between them. Jacob watched her closely, noting the way she shifted from one foot to the other. Knowing what he did about her marriage, he could see why she had a need to give him the freedom to choose. But he suddenly realized that he didn't want freedom. He wanted her. That much, at least, he was sure of.

"That's an unfair question, Jacob. You know what I need. Intimacy's not enough. Coming over to dinner and going to the movies and church with us is great, the kids love it, but it's not enough, either. And it's not fair. Not to you, not to me, and not to my children."

She'd wound her arms tightly around her waist, as if protecting herself from blows. Jacob had the impression she was fighting the impulse to run.

"You love Lia," she continued, her voice so soft he could barely hear her. "And you feel responsible for her death. Why in the world would you choose to saddle yourself with more problems? I'm a poor widow with two growing kids. Hardly the ideal mate, under the best of circumstances."

She looked up at him, her somber gaze telling him in ways much deeper than words that she truly believed what she'd said.

"I don't love Lia."

Ann turned away, despair in her heart. He hadn't understood a thing she'd said.

"I don't still love Lia," Jacob repeated loudly, though it was obvious she didn't believe him. Reaching out, his fingers tangled themselves in the wild curls of her hair. He guided her back against the wall, using his body to keep her there. "I don't still love Lia," he repeated for the third time. "I couldn't and still feel like this."

"Jacob," she gasped, the plea fainter than the fierce pounding of her heart. Her hands splayed across his chest as he pinned her between the cold, unforgiving wall and the heated warmth of his muscled body against her breasts. "Please, let me go. This won't prove anything."

Jacob knew he'd done enough talking for now. Though afraid of the feelings building up inside him, he couldn't step back. Letting go was out of the question.

"I can't, not now," he said thickly, his lips closing over hers, his hands seeking and finding her breasts.

Heat exploded within Jacob. He moaned. "I've thought of nothing but this since we made love." He pressed against her, his forehead flush with the wall, his legs spread wide apart, needing to feel her response, needing to hold her close. With his mouth, he worshiped her lips. With his hands, he caressed the soft, aching fullness of her breasts.

Ann could taste his need. Or was it her own? Unconsciously she sighed, feeling too weak to combat his potent masculinity. She remembered the silky feel of his straight black hair and her arms inched up to curl tightly around his nape. The shoulders that had carried six hundred pounds were now closing in around her. She felt exposed, yet protected at the same time. Only once before had she felt this longing, this desire to be closer than close. And that time, too, had been with Jacob. Her senses spun at the intensity of the flame devouring him and searing into her.

"Do you believe me now?" he whispered, his lips moist against hers. He knew he couldn't bear it if she continued denying what they felt for each other. He wanted to hear her say it, wanted to hear her acknowledge the bond burning so fiercely between them.

"Tell me," he heard himself command in a voice low with need. At some point he'd pulled up her sweater and now his hands smoothed over the satiny skin of her back.

Jacob's order caused a war of conflicts in her, one side urging her to give in to what she knew was inevitable, the other side insisting on caution, using experience as a weapon. But with each touch of his lips, with each stroke of his hands, caution weakened and inevitability grew stronger. When he finally raised his mouth from hers, her eyes fluttered open. For a stunned moment they stared at one another.

"I need you," he whispered. "Only you."

Ann leaned against him. "I need you, too," she said, unable to lie. "But—"

"Not without commitment," he finished for her. His gaze skimmed the vulnerable curve of her neck, recalling the Arctic Rose-petal scent of her skin.

"Mrs. Elliot?"

Siksik's soft voice echoed down the hallway. Swallowing an oath, Jacob turned aside, releasing Ann. He didn't look back at Ann, who was hurriedly straightening her sweater, knowing what he'd read in those clear gray eyes of hers. Wanting to give her time to pull herself together, he walked to the corner of the hallway and signaled his sister.

"What is it, Siksik?"

"Do you know where Sharon is?" she asked worriedly.

Knowing what she must look like, Ann brushed a hand through the tangle of her hair, then joined Jacob alongside his sister. "I assumed she was with you."

Siksik shook her head, the black curtain of her hair shivering with the sideways movement. "I haven't seen her for thirty minutes or so. I haven't seen Billy, either."

"What do you mean you haven't seen her in thirty minutes? Where could she be?" Ann said, a note of rising panic in her voice.

"No need to get upset," Jacob interjected, his arm automatically encircling Ann's shoulders. "She's probably just in one of the upstairs bathrooms."

Siksik shook her head. "I checked. Empty."

"The classrooms?"

"I didn't hear anything in the halls, Jacob."

He turned to Ann, feeling her soft trembling. "Why don't you go back to the gym? I'll go look upstairs again."

"No, I'll go with you."

Jacob shook his head. "One of us needs to be here in case she comes back."

With obvious reluctance Ann conceded to the wisdom of his plan. Giving her a quick kiss, Jacob watched them leave, concern overriding passion. Frowning, he hurried for the stairs.

"Holy —" The minute Sharon glimpsed Jacob, she turned to Billy. "What are you, slow? Can the stash!"

"What's going on here?" Jacob asked, an icy edge in his voice.

For ten minutes he'd scoured every room in the building. Concern for Sharon had been uppermost in his mind. He hadn't expected a party.

Four people stared at him. Jacob sniffed. *Beer.* His eyes darkened dangerously as they fixed first on Billy and then on Sharon. "I said, what's going on here?"

No one answered. Jacob strode over to where Billy stood quaking and reached behind him for the can Billy hadn't had time to hide properly. Jacob shoved it in the boy's face. "Explain this."

Billy blanched. The two older youths, both past troublemakers, laughed drunkenly and sauntered by Jacob, apparently unconcerned by the rage in his eyes. He let them go. The council would deal with them. But they would also deal with Billy and with Sharon. His expression darkened.

"Jacob," Sharon began tentatively.

"I didn't ask you." He glanced at her once, taking in her flushed cheeks, her wide wary eyes. He turned back to Billy. "I asked you. Explain."

"We were just . . . celebrating our wins . . ." the boy began haltingly. "Mike and John said they had some and asked Sharon if she wanted any. I tried—" Billy swallowed, clearly terrified at being caught out. "I tried telling her not to but—"

"He told me it was stupid but I wouldn't listen, okay? It's not his fault," Sharon interjected nervously.

Jacob's glance didn't waver or acknowledge he'd even heard her speak. He waited for Billy to finish.

"When she wouldn't listen to me, I decided I better go along."

"Why didn't you just let her go and come tell somebody? You know what this means, don't you?" Jacob demanded, barely stifling the urge to strangle the boy. *"Don't you?"*

Billy looked really frightened now. He had obviously expected some praise for what he'd tried doing but wasn't getting it. "I thought maybe if I was here I could, you know, protect her—" He broke off, shrugging his shoulders.

"How? By drinking yourself? That's supposed to keep her out of trouble?" Jacob's voice rose to a roar for his head was pounding with the enormity of Billy's and Sharon's actions. "Go home, Billy," he commanded curtly, turning away from the tears welling in the boy's frightened eyes. "And if you know what's good for you, you'll stay there."

With one last furtive look at Sharon, Billy left. Jacob turned to Sharon. The day had been so wonderful, Ann so happy and carefree. Now he faced Ann's daughter, realizing that he was going to have to be the one to ruin Ann's day. But first he had to deal with Sharon.

"Didn't I tell you the first day you got here that possession of alcohol was a crime in Twilight?"

"Sure, but beer isn't really—"

"There aren't any buts!" Seizing the empty can she'd hidden behind her, he threw it violently across the room. It smashed against the far wall with a loud empty clang. "You always do exactly what you please, don't you? Well, does it please you to know that sneaking off worried your mother? That dragging Billy into this mess may well ruin any hopes he has of a basketball career?'' Jacob's inner despair fueled his anger. "Do you have any idea what's going to happen now? To you? To your mother? To Billy? Damn it, do you even care?''

"My father's dead!" Sharon cried out suddenly. "I don't have to mind you!"

Her words hit Jacob like a blow. The lump in his throat grew bigger, heavier. He forced himself to back off, striving to regain some measure of control.

"I know I'm not your father, Sharon. But whether you believe it or not, I care about you very much. Just like I care about Patrick. And because I care, I get upset when bad things happen."

The way her eyes challenged him reminded him of Ann. His head pounded. God! What was he going to tell Ann?

"We don't have many laws here, Sharon, but those we have, we enforce. Do you understand what I'm saying?"

He could tell when it sank in.

"Bu-but I'm not Yup'ik," Sharon muttered, shifting from one leg to the other, her lower lip beginning to tremble.

"Doesn't matter. Everyone who lives in Twilight is bound by its laws."

He looked at her for long, silent seconds, unsure how to proceed. When the pounding in his head lessened, he sighed. "I want to be your friend, Sharon, but I guess I've gone about it all wrong," he whispered, his heart aching.

She blanched, then seemed to pull herself together. "I only had one can. I'm not drunk."

Her head hung dejectedly. Jacob longed to comfort her, but in all honesty, he didn't know what he could possibly say to ease her fears. He still felt she had no idea what she'd done; no idea what was ahead of her, or ahead for her family.

"What happens now?" Sharon asked quietly.

"You explain it to your mother," he replied evenly.

"Forget it," she said, her eyes enormous in her white, blanched face. "She'll kill me."

She was frightened and confused and hurting. He could see all those emotions on her face and suddenly he wished he hadn't been so harsh with her. Drawing her into his arms, he was surprised when she didn't immediately draw back. Silence fell between them, and after a few minutes, he could feel the shudders wrack her slender body.

"Shh, shh," he soothed, running his hand down her hair. "Everything will be all right."

Jacob knew he was making promises he couldn't keep, but Sharon's pain, her trust, sank beneath his own defenses. He hugged her tighter.

She sniffed. "Mom will never understand," she whispered fearfully. "Couldn't you just forget this happened?"

"It's too late for that, Sharon. Even if I wanted to, I couldn't. You and Billy are young, but those other two—they knew exactly what they were doing. Smuggling beer into Twilight was their first mistake. Giving it to you two minors, their last."

Her trembling increased. Clearly he'd frightened her again. "You're fifteen, Sharon. If you're old enough to deliberately break a law, you're old enough to face the consequences."

"But—"

"No buts, Sharon. Not this time, anyway. The sooner you realize that, the easier it'll be on you." Jacob released her and walked to the door. "Let's go."

She looked up, her brown eyes wet with tears. "Go? Go where?"

"Back to the gym for your things," he advised, watching the panic sweep over her features. He was feeling slightly panicked himself. He didn't want to tell Billy's father. He didn't want to tell Ann. But he had no choice.

Jacob and Sharon entered the gym together. He kept an arm around her shoulders, sensing she needed the extra support. Wordlessly they crossed the gym floor, weaving their way in and around the sea of dark heads. Spotting Ann, he headed toward her.

Ann turned in time to see them both. "Oh, Jacob, you did fi—" Her stomach clenched. Something was wrong. She could see it in his eyes and in her daughter's. "What's wrong? Has something happened?"

He nodded. "I think you'd better go home. Now."

A wave of apprehension swept through her. "Go home? Why? What's going on?" Her gaze swung to her daughter, noting with concern Jacob's arm slung protectively about her slender shoulders. "Sharon, what is it, sweetheart?"

Pallid, Sharon didn't respond. Clearly her daughter was too upset to say anything. More worried than ever, Ann's gaze swung back to Jacob, waiting for an explanation.

"I found her drinking a couple of minutes ago," he said flatly, knowing there was no use in prevarications or window-dressing.

"Drinking!" She stared at him, completely shocked. The full import of what Sharon had done hit her. Her eyes swung to her daughter, whose head was slumped forward. "Oh, sweetheart," she whispered sadly.

"I think you should go home," Jacob said. "Sharon can explain it to you there."

"Yes, of course...." Ann started across the gym, her thoughts jumbled, confused. Then she stopped, asked Sharon to wait here and turned back to where Jacob was standing where she'd left him, his eyes bleak. She retraced her steps, her hands reaching out. Jacob clasped them tightly within his. "You'll bring Patrick home?" she asked.

He nodded. "But I need to talk with John first."

"John?"

"Billy's father."

"Oh, Billy was there, too?" Her voice wavered. "Jacob, what's going to happen?"

"I don't know," he said truthfully, stifling the urge to draw her into his arms. Now wasn't the time or the place. "But I do know it's in the hands of the council. There will be a trial—"

"Trial!" Fear filled her eyes.

"Go home," he said gently. "I'll bring Patrick as soon as I can."

Chapter Sixteen

As promised, Jacob brought Patrick home, but one look into Jacob's dark shuttered eyes told Ann his meeting with Billy's father hadn't gone well. Briefly he glanced at Sharon's tear-stained face, then turned and looked at Ann for a long moment. His gaze told her nothing of what was on his mind. Ann waited for him to pull her into his arms, waited for him to ease the fears gripping her heart. He did neither. Instead, he left, leaving her alone and confused and frightened.

She questioned Sharon, trying to determine why she'd done something so irresponsible when she'd known drinking alcohol was against village law. But her daughter revealed no more than Ann had already heard from Jacob. Except for the trial. Apparently Sharon didn't know about that. Seeing how upset she already was, Ann decided not to discuss it until she had more information. She knew Sharon would have to be punished, but how was unclear. She couldn't cut off phone privileges she no longer had, or even stop the allowance she no longer received. They lived so frugally that the normal disciplinary channels just weren't available. Disturbed, she prepared a dinner only Patrick ate. Afterward she rose numbly from the sofa and retired to her bedroom, her own thoughts too tension-filled and confused to obtain but snatches of sleep.

Sunday morning arrived with a windstorm. Perfect, Ann thought as she emerged from her bedroom and padded automatically into the kitchen, intent on making herself a cup of tea before church. It was an hour before Patrick and Sharon needed to get up and get ready. This morning, however, they were already awake. The sounds of their subdued voices penetrated Ann's worried thoughts. Their whispered exchanges didn't surprise Ann. She wasn't feeling particularly lively herself.

A knock on the door captured her attention. Picking up her mug Ann crossed the living area, the morning greeting swallowed by the tense angry look on Jacob's stark features as he gazed at her through a swirl of heavy snowflakes.

She stepped back, allowing him entrance. His brooding intensity immediately invaded the room, much like the storm hanging over Twilight. His presence charged the air, playing on Ann's already frayed nerves.

She tried ignoring it with a quiet remark. "I haven't fixed breakfast yet, but would you like some tea?"

Jacob's dark eyes flickered briefly. Ann took that as an affirmative and retraced her steps, awareness of Jacob's anger throbbing within her.

"The kids aren't up yet," she said when, after enduring his silence as long as she could, she knew she had to say something. Anything to start the ball rolling. "But it's early yet for church. Hours."

It didn't really work. Jacob simply slipped his arms from his jacket, hanging the garment on the peg by the door, then sitting down. Perplexed, Ann watched him for a moment. His anger she could understand; after all, Sharon had done something extremely irresponsible, but this, this wasn't the kind of anger she'd been expecting. This anger was somehow imbued with another quality Ann found hard to identify.

Pouring a second cup of tea, Ann carried it to the recliner where Jacob sat, then returned to the kitchen to prepare breakfast. Her own appetite was nonexistent. Patrick, however, would be hungry. And Sharon would likely pick at something. Ann listened as the shower turned on. They'd be dressed soon.

"More tea?" Ann asked, noting how quickly he'd drunk the hot beverage.

"No thanks," Jacob answered, then again fell silent. Although he hadn't yet moved, Ann felt his impatience as surely as if he were pacing back and forth. His silence bothered her; his fixed concentration disturbed her own. She had the distinct feeling that inside him a brutal storm was raging.

If only he'd let it out, or at the very least, say something, Ann rationalized. She studied him as she prepared oatmeal and toast. His sharp profile seemed to be carved in ice. The squinted, tightly engrossed expression belied understanding.

Ann stifled an urge to scream, the continuing silence becoming unbearable when there were so many things she wanted to ask, needed to know. "Jacob, what's the matter?" she asked finally. "Why are you being like this? All right, Sharon made a mistake. And I realize the seriousness, particularly in Twilight, of this kind of a mistake. But children do make mistakes occasionally, you know. It's a part of growing up."

"I know that," he answered tersely.

"Then what?" A disturbing thought occurred to her. "You think this is my fault, don't you? That if I had been watching her more, we wouldn't be in this mess." She watched Jacob's shoulders tense. "Well, maybe so. But I'm not one of Patrick's super-heroes with eyes in the back of my head. I couldn't watch him and you and her all at the same time yesterday."

"I know that," he repeated. "And I don't blame you."

"Then what is it?" She turned off the stove, impatience warring with concern. She crossed to stand in front of him. "What's made you so uptight and angry?"

The question echoed in his mind. With the strictest of controls he maintained a semblance of calm, but he wasn't at all sure he'd be able to keep it up much longer. He was scared. Last night, the nightmare had returned, only it hadn't been Lia he'd been forced to leave behind, it had been Ann. He'd woken up, agonizingly aware that he was more afraid of her leaving than of his past guilt.

"Damn it, Jacob, stop it! You're frightening me! Now, I know what Sharon did. What I don't know—what you don't seem to want to tell me—is what's going to happen!'' she nearly shouted, but remembered Sharon and Patrick just in time. Whispering, she said, ''What's this trial you mentioned yesterday?''

A muscle twitched in his jaw. ''The council of elders. They decide all matters regarding laws that are broken.''

''Decide all matters...? But we're not Yup'ik!'' Ann said. ''You said so yourself, remember?''

He did remember. He remembered too many things he'd said, and too many things he hadn't. Suddenly the tension and guilt exploded within him and he stood, venting his rage.

''Don't you think I know that? But when you moved here— you and Patrick and Sharon—all of you became subject to those laws.''

''I can work this out on my own,'' Ann flashed defensively. ''Sharon made a mistake. A big one. And she'll be disciplined. I've been too wrapped up thinking about the trial to come up with something suitable. But I assure you, I will. And she won't do it again.''

''That's right she won't,'' Jacob replied. ''Because, just like in Anchorage, when laws are broken, you get punished.''

''Oh, for heaven's sake, Jacob. She's fifteen years ol—'' The heated angry words were stolen from her throat as the full implication of his statement suddenly hit her.

Punished. Ann paled.

''Wh-what sort of punishment? You can't honestly believe that I'll let Sharon—'' Her head moved from side to side, trying to shake away the thought, as if she hadn't heard the words he'd spoken. But the echo—the terrible frightening echo—lingered. ''You won't let them punish my baby...will you?''

Jacob stood in front of her, his fingers encircling the soft flesh of her upper arms.

''If I could stop the trial, I would, Ann. But I can't.'' He saw fear, stark and vivid, glittering in her eyes. Despair engulfed him. ''The elders are wise. They'll understand that Sharon's new to our ways.''

''I said I'd punish her. Isn't that enough?'' She tried pulling away from his grip.

He wouldn't let go. ''I expect you to do what's right. If she'd broken a law in Anchorage would you run away?''

''No! But it's not the same—''

"Yes, it is," Jacob cut her off. "Our laws aren't just for us. They're for everyone who lives here. For everyone's protection. Including hers."

He released her arms, drawing her close against his chest. Fear raged within him as he felt her body's trembling. She clung to him and he to her. The familiar fragrance of her hair filled his lungs as she burrowed into his arms, oblivious to the agony her despair made him feel. He wished he could protect Sharon. He wished he could protect Ann. But he couldn't.

"I can't stop the trial," he repeated raggedly. "But I can speak to the elders before they render a decision."

She shuddered.

Automatically Jacob tightened his embrace, trying to give her comfort, absorb her pain. He didn't understand her willingness to be held by him, but like a starving man in need of food, he accepted the morsel she offered.

Ann's eyes closed, a feeling of dread building in her body. "When?" she asked.

Jacob knew what she meant. "Before church. That's why I'm early," he answered, his voice unsteady. Ann flinched. His arms tightened briefly, then he stepped back. "You'd better tell Sharon. We need to go."

The small council chamber, located in one of the two tiny anterooms of the village church, was packed. A stack of folding chairs and two long tables were collapsed and stacked against plain walls. The electrical light was dark, allowing two large Naniq lamps to flicker with somber intent. The odor of seal oil drifted in the air.

When they entered, a hush fell over the villagers. Ann gazed at the sea of faces, dazedly absorbing the presence of two older youths she didn't know. Also present were Billy and his father, Siksik and Mark, Ben, Milak and the three other elders who made up the council of five. The atmosphere was solemn and grave. Those not council members stood, occasionally whispering among themselves. The elders, garbed in ceremonial headdress and robes, sat on caribou hides in a semicircle in the center of the chamber, their seated shadows silhouetted against the walls. They were silent and watchful like the judge and jury they were.

Billy came to their side, his usually cocky smile gone. "Mrs. Elliot, I'm really sorry, I—"

Ann's heart ached for him. Billy stood to lose as much, if not more, than Sharon. She reached out, gathering him into her arms for a brief hug. "It'll be all right, Billy," she whispered softly, praying that she wasn't lying. Desperately her eyes sought Jacob's.

He was standing next to Patrick leaning down, explaining something to him. He looked up and met her eyes. His blazed with a possessive determination that imbued Ann with hope, and she felt such a wave of love for him that she almost did believe everything would turn out all right.

Almost.

When she looked away, her gaze encountered Ben.

"We will begin." His usually kind weathered face was remote. Ann shivered as the room became still.

Billy glanced briefly into Sharon's ashen features. He seemed about to say something, but apparently decided against it. Quietly, he returned to his father's side.

Ben solemnly stated the reason for their gathering. He turned toward the two older youths Ann didn't know and asked them to state their case. They did, each in turn spelling out his part in the fiasco. When they were done, silence reined. Ann watched the council but their faces gave nothing away. Ben turned toward her.

"You will speak for your daughter?" His gaze flicked briefly at Sharon, noting her fear, her obvious inability to do no more than stand upright. Ann's gaze flew to Jacob; she knew instinctively that she wouldn't do much better than Sharon. Having a Native—especially one as well-respected as Jacob—speak on her daughter's behalf would also undoubtedly help Sharon's case.

"I will speak for Sharon," he spoke out gravely.

Ben nodded once. "Proceed."

As Jacob stepped forward, Ann's anxiety increased. She was startled when he spoke in Yup'ik, but immediately sensed that the low, emotional tones of his voice as it spilled into the room were somehow more compelling than the *kass'aq* language would have been. Again she watched their faces—especially Milak's, whose wise old eyes seemed particularly alert and watchful. Ann permitted herself some hope when she saw how attentively they listened, how deeply Jacob's words seemed to affect those not on the council.

There were tears in Siksik's eyes and Billy shifted, uncomfortable. Ann gathered Sharon close into her arms, and Patrick, too, for she could tell both of them were extremely anxious. Her gaze slid to Mark, who was squinting and pressing thumb and forefinger across the bridge of his nose to relieve the pressure. When he looked up again, Ann caught his glance and held it.

"What's Jacob saying?" she mouthed.

He crossed to her side, taking care to walk well behind Jacob, who stood directly in front of the council. "He's telling them you're a widow, how Sharon misses her father and how she's had trouble adjusting to the many changes in her life. He related his own fear and confusion when having to leave his home for the hospital in Fairbanks, reminding them that it's not only the young that can be frightened by changes, but that it is the young who know least well how to deal with it."

When Jacob stopped talking, Ann felt her heart begin beating frantically again. No one seemed to move. Finally Ben turned to John, asking him if he would speak for his son. But Billy stepped forward. Jacob returned to her side, a drained look in his eyes.

Her heart expanded with love for him. Only now was not the time for thanks. Billy had yet to speak, and then there was the ruling. Ann shuddered and gathered Sharon closer. Patrick had moved to Jacob's embrace.

Billy chose to speak in English, the tone of his plea accepting of his responsibility. He urged them to be lenient with Sharon, and tears gathered in Ann's eyes at his broken, faltering speech. Once he even stopped completely, too overcome to continue, but Ann watched him forcibly control his emotions, watched as he seemed to grow and mature before her eyes. When he finally finished, his father's face was shining with a sad but eloquent pride.

"We will consider all that has been said here," Ben said.

A tremor quivered through Ann's hands. Now what? She glanced at Jacob.

"We wait," he replied, anticipating her question.

* * *

It didn't take long. After the regular church ceremony—which Ann barely heard, her mind was so occupied with her fears—Jacob led them back to the small council chambers. Ben sat with the other elders.

"We have decided."

Ann felt her stomach knot. This was it. Unconsciously she reached out. Jacob clasped her hand.

"In the matter of Mike Adams and John Ross, both are banned from the village."

Ann gasped. Jacob's face remained fixed, but a muscle twitched in his jaw. A shudder ripped through her. If they ruled so harshly for them, what would they decide for Sharon?

I can't! I can't let this happen. With every passing second, the certainty gained firmer ground. Almost wild with fright, Ann turned desperate eyes on Jacob. "Jacob, I can't . . . this is—"

"Wait."

Jacob saw the fear in her eyes and used the last remaining dregs of his own willpower to bolster her faith. In a low voice, he repeated his earlier statement. "Wait. Mike and John were troublemakers. Sharon and Billy aren't. The council will be wise. Trust me."

Trust me. Dazed, Ann stared up at Jacob, cold dread a lead weight in her stomach. She looked deeply into his eyes, seeing his belief that all would be well, his need to have her believe in him. She saw all of this and gained from it the necessary strength to control her own emotions. She nodded.

When the two youths had left, Ben signaled for the readings to continue. "In the matter of Sharon Elliot, the council confines her to her home and the classroom until spring. Billy Muktoyuk is banned from the high school basketball team."

Ann didn't get a chance to feel any relief or even to fully grasp the extent of the council's decision regarding Billy before a gasping cry of pain ripped from her daughter's throat. Twisting out of her arms, Sharon rushed forward, facing the council.

"It's not fair! It wasn't even Billy's fault!"

Tears raced down Sharon's cheeks as she raced for the door. Ann made to follow her, but Jacob's arms stopped her.

"Give her a few minutes," he said gravely.

"No, Jacob, she's hurting. I need to be there. I have to—"

"What? Upset her even more? You're not in any condition to be helpful." He looked down at Patrick, whose gray eyes were huge and fearful, then across at his own sister. "Let Siksik go. That way you'll have a few minutes at least to calm yourself."

He was right. Until just then she hadn't been aware of the tears spilling down her own cheeks. All she could think of was Sharon and what she must be going through. She nodded. With one sorrowful look at Billy, Siksik raced after Sharon.

The house was cold when Jacob, Patrick and Ann arrived. Ann flicked a switch. The room flooded with light.

"Sharon? Honey, we're home."

Nothing.

Ann's hard-won calm vanished in an instant. Frightened, she turned to Jacob. "She's not here."

Patrick, who had gone on into the bedroom they shared, returned. "Nobody in there. Everything's just like it was before we left." His eyes were wide, frightened. "Maybe they went to Siksik's house."

Sudden fear clutched at Jacob's heart. Without a word he turned and exited the house, the windstorm pulling at his parka, whipping the hood down off his head. Going around to the back of the house, it took him only a second to discover what he sought.

"She's gone," he reported, his breathing ragged as he reentered the house.

Ann swayed.

"Mom!" Patrick cried out in alarm.

Jacob raced across the room, his arms enfolding Ann, steadying her. Gently he guided her to the couch. "She'll be all right, Patrick." He took his eyes off Ann just long enough to take in Patrick's frightened features. "Can you make your mom some tea?"

"Sure, but—"

"She'll be okay," he repeated, in what he hoped was a reassuring manner. "It's just the shock. Make some tea. I'm sure she could use some."

Patrick left and Jacob's gaze settled back on Ann. She was shaking her head slowly, her curls spilled in a frenzied mass across her shoulders.

"Where could she be?"

He pulled off her gloves, then bent to pull off her boots, all the while considering how much he should tell her.

"The snowmobile's gone. That's what I went outside to check. I think . . . I think she might have run away."

Ann gasped, attempting to stand. "Run away?"

He forced her to remain seated. "I also think Siksik is right behind her, because there were two sets of snowmobile tracks." He reached up to unzip her parka. Immediately the subtle fragrance of her assaulted him and for a half crazy glitch out of time, his thoughts raced back to that Sunday afternoon when they'd made love.

"But . . . run away to where?" Ann's face, so close to his own, held a look of aching vulnerability.

He recognized that look. Had seen it countless times, only not on Ann's tear-stained face. On Lia's. First when she'd cried for help. And then just before he'd failed her.

"The tracks lead out to sea," he said, standing and making for the door.

"Jacob, wait!" Ann rose, watching him warily. A dreadful premonition filled her heart. "What are you going to do?"

"Find her," he said flatly. He wouldn't allow what had happened to Jonathan and Lia to happen again. No matter what it took, this time he would not fail.

The enormity of what he was thinking of undertaking made Ann doubly fearful. She wished she could tell him not to go, but she couldn't. Sharon and Siksik were lost out there somewhere in a storm that was steadily worsening.

He stopped at the door and turned. Images swirled in his mind: his hunt on the Bering Sea; the recent nightmare of being lost and having to leave Ann behind.

"Can I go, too? Please, Jacob?"

Patrick. In the tension of the moment, they'd all but forgotten his presence. Jacob knelt down in front of the boy. "I need you to stay here and take care of your mother," he said.

"But—"

"Patrick," he interrupted. "I need you to do this. Your mother's upset and you're really the only one I can count on to take good care of her, okay?"

Ann, standing silently behind her son, was suddenly struck by a sense of longing so acute she almost cried out. The love in Jacob's eyes and the way Patrick seemed to grow taller, stronger, more mature now that he'd been given such an important responsibility, gripped her soul with shattering intensity. That was when she realized she'd never be able to confine the emotion burning within her; would never be able to hide the love she felt for this man who was about to venture out into his own personal nightmare.

For her.

A moment of silence fell over the room. Then Patrick looked at Jacob through anxious eyes. "You'll be careful, won't you?"

Jacob expelled a long breath. He gave the boy a hug. "Yes, Patrick, I'll be careful. And I'll have your sister home as soon as I can."

He looked up and into Ann's eyes, the words a comfort as much as a vow. He sealed it with a quick, hard kiss. He would find Sharon and Siksik. And he would bring them home.

Or die trying.

Chapter Seventeen

The storm raged all around him. Despite the beam of the headlamp secured on his helmet beneath the hood of his parka, Jacob could barely see the leader of the dog team. His grip tightened on the sled; his legs tensed on the runners, knees slightly bent to absorb the shock of the ragged terrain. He remembered it all too well: the razor-edged bite of the wind; the deafening noise accompanying it that threatened sanity; the roll of the ground, which was at once solid, yet not solid. He remembered and felt fear strike his heart. He remembered and wished to be anywhere but inching along an ice-blurred trail, out toward the sea and an unknown destination.

But as it was then, so it was now. He had no choice.

The dogs were his only chance of finding them. While he was all but useless in the face of the swirling snow, they sensed the windswept trail, using their paws as they ran, testing the snow and following the hard-packed trail. He only hoped they followed it swiftly, for while Siksik could survive in such conditions, Jacob knew Sharon could not.

Jacob fought back a wave of fear, concentrating instead on Ann's parting kiss. It had held all the warmth and promise the

Bering Sea did not. Though fear had stolen her speech, he'd seen the emotion in her eyes. She believed in him. She believed he would find her daughter and his sister, and return as he had done before. He didn't share her faith, but he clung to it now as he peered into the ever-darkening blizzard.

He was insane for heading into a storm like this one when instinct demanded he seek shelter. But Ann was depending on him, and Jacob knew he had no choice but to once again face the Bering Sea, to once again fight it for the lives of two people he loved.

Rolling clouds swept inland as he and his dogs traveled seaward. He calculated he was perhaps an hour behind Siksik what with gathering the dogs and the necessary survival equipment. Several of the men in the village had ridden out as well, only inland, not seaward.

Jacob focused on his goal, concentrating on maintaining his footing and his sanity. After a while, he ceased to be aware of the burning, stinging claws of ice whipping against his face and his body. He burrowed into himself and cleared his mind of all but the need to find them, his heart of all but Ann's trust and belief.

He called on his *inua,* inwardly chanting for guidance in Yup'ik, projecting his soul, his being into the storm's swirling currents. Slowly the wind's brutal effect lessened, the fog before him clearing. His focus narrowed, his breathing slowed. It was as if he traveled down a long dark passageway, a trail that he knew ended in light and calm. Within his soul, this dream that wasn't a dream created within Jacob a sense of safety and security. With softness and light surrounding him from within, he heard wind rushing but it didn't touch him. He heard ice sheets splitting away from the shore nearby, but the ground beneath him remained firm, instinct leading him away from trouble spots. Eyes nearly closed, he searched the lighted clearing within himself, seeing his *inua,* seeing the image of his soul and his protector.

Yet his *inua* was not alone as it had always been. Beside him waited another, smaller, lighter figure. Jacob did not understand the presence of this other, sensed only its purpose was similar to his own.

Down the passageway they traveled together, to where the strong-willed Raven sat waiting for the passing of the storm, sat caring for one yet unnamed. Jacob knew the Raven. It was his sister, Siksik, and he guessed the one yet unnamed was Sharon. The two sat huddled in a snow cave, protected from the elements, waiting.

Jacob felt his heart contract. Once before, two others had waited for him to save them, to show them the way. Two had waited, and two had died. Jacob shied away from the unbidden thought, fearing a repeat of the past. Only his *inua* would not let him turn away. He peered into the vision, seeing lost love and lost friendship. And for the first time, seeing their weakness instead of his own.

As the vision blurred and the seconds passed, Jacob understood the message of his *inua* and was both shocked and angered. Jonathan and Lia had decided to die. He had led them, but they had not followed. They had given in and given up, through no fault of his own. He had done his best, but the choice had been theirs to make. They had chosen their own paths.

Jacob blinked. The vision disappeared, leaving him alone on the Bering Sea. But that was okay, because now he understood. Now he felt free. Heat suffused the nearly frozen limbs of his body, giving him strength and renewed purpose. Suddenly, out of the hazy swirling snow, a faint beam of light reflected back at him.

He'd found them.

Ann knew she'd never forget the sight of Jacob heading out toward the sea. She'd braved the icy wind and blowing snow, going outside to watch until he was no longer visible, aching to be with him, yet knowing she could not. She'd returned to the house and let Patrick fuss over her, responding to her son's considerate attentions though her mind never strayed far from Jacob and his search. Mentally she sent her love, warmth and strength to help him. She imagined she could see him, surrounded by softness and light, imagined she was there beside him in some indefinable way. And where he traveled, she followed, eventually somehow sensing when he found them, experiencing a calm in her soul that she couldn't explain. Anxiety fled, to be replaced by an urgency to see her daughter, Siksik, and the man that she loved once again.

The moment Patrick spotted the headlight on Jacob's helmet from the window, relief flooded her veins in a deluge so intense that it weakened her legs and brought a choked cry to her lips. Racing across the living area, she grabbed her jacket from the peg and stumbled outside. The wind was so icily powerful that the torrent of snow it pushed felt like millions of tiny hail pellets slapping her face. Frantic, she fought to remain upright while pulling her jacket close around her body. The storm swallowed the sounds of Ben and his wife, Mark, Billy and Patrick emerging right behind her. Eyes fixed on the sled in the distance, Ann waited as Jacob mushed to a stop in front of the house.

Sharon lay pale and unresponsive beneath a mountain of furs. Siksik immediately jumped off the snowmobile she'd guided in behind Jacob and flew into her father's open arms. Ann dropped to the ground beside the sled.

"Is she all right?" she gasped in renewed fear.

Jacob squinted through the dark at the small snow-encrusted figure kneeling beside the sled. He hadn't heard her question, but he could guess what it was. Dragging his eyes away, he switched off his headlamp and then hand-signaled to his brother and Billy. Together they unloaded the sled and carried Sharon inside.

The abrupt absence of sound was tremendous. Jacob slumped against a wall, torso bent over, one hand propped on each thigh. His eyes closed.

He'd made it! With the help of his *inua*, he'd once again battled the Bering and won. Breathing hard, Jacob's dazed mind slowly absorbed the warmth of the house, the softness of the light and the overwhelming sense of relief. Though anxious voices drifted around him, their very existence spelled success.

"Jacob, are you all right?" Ben asked, concern deepening his voice.

Jacob raised his head. Father and son exchanged a long look, words unnecessary. Ben nodded and stepped back. He smiled. "You have done well, my son."

Jacob straightened, aware his father referred to more than just this latest ordeal. "I'm fine, Father." Slowly he shed his parka, gloves and boots, then crossed to where Sharon lay covered on the couch. Ann sat crouched beside her.

"Is my sister going to die like your friends did that time you got lost, Jacob?" Patrick asked, fearing the answer.

Jacob heard Ann's tiny terrified cry. Her eyes were enormous as they focused on him. "No, Patrick," Jacob said quickly, kneeling down in front of him. "She's not going to die. She's very sick, but she'll make it." He gave the boy a hug.

Patrick's worried glance moved from the couch, where his sister lay so still, to his mother. "Jacob saved her life, didn't he, Mom?"

"That's right, honey," Ann replied, blinking fiercely against the tears that threatened to overwhelm her. Her eyes gazed deeply into Jacob's, the love and gratitude she felt there for him to see. "He brought her back just like we knew he would."

Struggling for a note of normalcy, Ann asked Patrick to make them all some tea. Reassured by the simple task, he went off to do as she'd asked. Billy looked at Siksik for a long moment, then pulled her unexpectedly into his arms for a brief hug before leaving to tend the dogs and inform the rest of the villagers. Ann turned from the brightness in Siksik's eyes to the lifelessness in her daughter's. Her breath caught.

"What's . . . what's wrong with her?" she asked haltingly.

Sharon was lying beneath such a mound of blankets, Ann could barely make out her face. But the deathly pallor her skin held told its own story. She fought back tears as she studied her daughter. She looked so alone, so delicate, so far away...

She uttered a distressed sound.

Jacob pulled her into his arms so that her back was cradled in the curve of his chest. Just then he didn't care what impression he was leaving on his family. All that mattered was easing Ann's pain.

"She's in shock," he explained softly, tightening his hold when she tensed. "And she's hypothermic. Siksik told me that about ten minutes after leaving Twilight, she found Sharon huddled beside her snowmobile. Siksik built the snow cave that sheltered them as quickly as she could, but it wasn't fast enough for Sharon. By the time she'd finished, Sharon was unconscious and Siksik could do nothing but pull her inside and wait for one of us to rescue them. So right now, we'll need to keep her warm and we'll need to get her to a doctor as soon as possible.''

Twisting around, Ann looked up into black eyes that were rimmed with exhaustion. ''Oh, Jacob,'' she whispered, as if she'd just come to her senses. ''All that you've been through...'' Her eyes glistened and she shook her head. ''I've been so scared, so wrapped up with Sharon, I didn't think. Thank you. Thank you for everything.''

Jacob controlled the urge to kiss her, his gaze breaking from Ann's and locking with his brother's. ''What's the forecast?''

''Bad. No idea when the storm will break,'' Mark answered, his own eyes suspiciously moist.

''You called the Air Rescue Squadron?''

''They're on standby,'' Ben replied, moving purposefully toward the door. ''Now that you're back, they can come get her.''

''Oh, thank goodness. I was so afraid no one could make it through in this kind of weather.'' Ann sniffed and wiped the tears from her eyes. ''When?''

''They're coming from Anchorage,'' Ben replied. ''They'll give me an ETA when I radio in.''

''Then I'd better get our stuff ready.''

Going from Sharon and Patrick's room to her own, Ann quickly grabbed clothes for both herself and Sharon, stuffing them into two suitcases. She had no idea what she'd taken, but that wasn't important. What was important was Sharon and her need of a doctor. Relieved when Ben assured her he would watch Patrick while she was in Anchorage, Ann sat down on the floor by the couch, her eyes trained on Sharon. Praying for her daughter's life, Ann waited for the A.R.S.

Two hours later, she followed Jacob and Mark as they carried Sharon out the door. The flight was a nightmare. For once Ann was glad Sharon wasn't conscious. Winds tossed them about with such force and so unexpectedly at times that Ann wondered if they would make it to Anchorage.

Once they crossed the South Central mountains, the storm dispersed and the pilot of the MH-60 Pavehawk helicopter made excellent time. A few hours later, Ann sat looking down at her daughter's pale features as she rested on the safety and security of a hospital bed.

"There's nothing more you can do here, Mrs. Elliot," Sharon's doctor, a middle-aged and kindly woman by the name of Betty Cobb, said sympathetically. "The warming process will take some time. It's nothing we can rush, I'm afraid. And until we run some tests and determine how quickly she's responding, we won't have anything to report. I suggest you and your husband get some sleep."

Ann didn't even acknowledge the doctor's comment, missing entirely her assumption that Jacob, who hadn't left her side once, was her husband. Though exhaustion weighed heavily on her body, she had no intention of leaving until Sharon at least regained consciousness.

"Ann." Jacob had to repeat himself twice before she responded. "Ann, look at me." The fear and fatigue in the gray eyes blinking solemnly across at him made Jacob ache with the need to protect. Standing, he held out his hand. "Dr. Cobb's right. You won't do Sharon any good by making yourself sick. You need sleep and so do I. I've booked us into the Sheraton and Dr. Cobb has the number. If there's any change, she'll call."

For the longest seconds, Jacob waited patiently for Ann to digest what he'd said, but her gaze remained blank and he began to wonder if she'd heard him at all. Then suddenly she placed her hand in his. It trembled slightly.

Before she could change her mind, Jacob led her out of the hospital and into a waiting cab.

They arrived and were checked in within minutes. Jacob led Ann to the elevators. He'd booked them a single room, determined that nothing on earth—not even Ann herself— would separate him from Ann this night.

The card key unlatched the lock. Ann walked in ahead of Jacob. While he flicked on the light and deposited their cases, she examined the room. Or more precisely, the single king-size bed.

"You're not angry, are you?"

Ann turned. Jacob's eyes, like his question, were filled with uncharacteristic uncertainty. Ann found she couldn't summon even the smallest spurt of disapproval, for deep inside, she'd wanted this herself. She knew she needed to sleep, had understood Jacob's advice back at the hospital, but she also knew that she wouldn't get any sleep without his arms around her.

She needed him.

She shook her head. "No, I don't mind."

His eyes, red-rimmed and exhausted though they were, never left hers. "You're sure?"

She nodded. Jacob handed her her suitcase. "You take the bathroom first. I'll go in after you're done."

Again, Ann nodded. Quickly she brushed her teeth, deliberately averting her gaze from the mirror. She didn't want to see her face, didn't want to see how tired she looked, how worry over Sharon had lined her features. And most of all, she didn't want to see how very much she wanted to snuggle down next to Jacob. Rummaging in the suitcase, she realized she'd forgotten a nightgown. Sighing, she slipped on one of Sharon's T-shirts, which she'd mistakenly placed in her bag. Again, her eyes avoided the mirror, only this time for different reasons altogether.

Mercifully, the lights were off when she emerged. Feeling her way, she inched along until her outstretched hands encountered the side of the bed. Then she crawled in and pulled the covers to her chin, aware of Jacob's seated silhouette, outlined by the hallway light streaming in through the crack at the bottom of the door. Had he fallen asleep in the chair? Troubled, she was debating getting up again when suddenly he stood, stretched and padded silently by the bed to the bathroom. With a sigh she turned over and burrowed down into the sheets to wait.

She didn't have to wait long. Within minutes Jacob slid in beside her. He seemed to hesitate, then gently reached out and fitted her into the curve of his body, enfolding his arms about her waist.

His sigh ruffled the hairs on her head.
Her sigh disturbed the hairs on his arms.
They slept.

Jacob awoke in stages the next morning, aware of a deep
sense of well-being that warmed his soul and filled him with
an unusual sense of contentment. In a hazy half dream he
watched himself trek through a windstorm that for some reason wasn't cold, saw himself guiding a sled that required little effort. Everything was easy for him, everything was
smooth, as if he'd been granted a new lease on life, maybe
even a new lease on love...

It took several minutes for the half dream to melt away, but
when it did, Jacob became aware of the sleep-warm thighs
that curved flush against his own. He stiffened. Then his arm
loosened from around Ann's waist and settled on that thigh,
a possessive sort of action that increased the feeling of satisfaction warming his soul.

And it was then that it came to him. He loved this woman.
He didn't understand it, didn't know how it had happened or
even when, but he knew with the same instinctive certainty
that had led him home through the storm, that he loved her.
He loved her soft vulnerability, her unexpected strengths and
the way she stood up for herself. He loved the way she looked
to him at times for support and advice, making him feel
strong and needed. He loved the way she talked, the shapely
womanly curves that even now were hidden beneath a neon-
pink T-shirt. He decided, with a silly grin on his face, that he
loved everything about her.

Ann yawned and turned to face Jacob, still half asleep, her
hair a wild tangle, her chin nestling into the hollow of his
throat. Gently Jacob smoothed the hair from her forehead,
enjoying the sensation of her warm breath against his neck.
She blinked and the brush of her lashes tickled his skin. He
chuckled.

The low rumbling awakened Ann fully. Slowly she raised
her head...and found herself staring directly into Jacob's
twinkling eyes.

"You remind me of a husky pup," he murmured softly.

Ann's eyes widened and her heart began pounding. The air was suddenly filled with the closeness of their bodies, the heated awareness that they were alone and in bed together. She searched for something to break the tension, but the broad expanse of his chest as he sucked in air scattered her thoughts. All she managed was a weak, "I do?"

He nodded, aware of her struggle and inwardly pleased by it. "Only I don't have any milk to feed you."

Ann blinked. She felt bemused, caught in the spell of his eyes, the hardening warmth of his body. "I'm not...I'm not really hungry anyway," she managed finally.

Jacob's gaze fell to her lips. The bright intensity of his expression filled her limbs with a surge of heat. His head lowered to within an inch of her lips.

"You're sure?" he breathed.

Ann couldn't have answered if her life depended on it. The immediacy of her arousal astounded her. Reaching up, she fitted her mouth to his, telling him without words just how hungry she was.

Jacob's lips were demanding, as if he, not she, were starving. His almost desperate need made Ann's heart beat triple time with pain and hurt and love. So much had happened to him . . . to her. She sensed he needed their closeness as much as she did.

Jacob, she cried out silently. *Oh, Jacob, I love you so much.*

With one all-encompassing movement, Jacob pulled her T-shirt up and off her body, nuzzling the soft, full curves of her breasts before zeroing in on the tight, hard buds of her nipples. She cried out, her arms sliding down his back and beneath the fabric of his briefs to clench tightly the muscles of his buttocks. He surged forward, then pulled back, his movements jerky as he removed his briefs, then joined her again.

She was shaking. So was he. As their lips met, so did their bodies, merging with the instinctive seeking of two lost souls. This time there was no build up, no tantalizing love play, the need in them demanding instant gratification. He filled her with one quick hard thrust and she cried out in satisfaction, her hands clenched tight in his hair, her legs wrapped about his thighs. Together they rocked through a universe of colors, bright with stars and the promise of heaven.

Afterward they lay, still joined, content and replete.

"I feel so lucky to be alive this morning," Ann ventured on a languorous sigh.

Jacob curled an arm around her shoulders. "I know what you mean. Last night, at least for a time anyway, I wasn't sure where I was."

Ann realized then that she hadn't asked him for any of the details to his ordeal in the snowstorm. Misgivings clouded her euphoria. He'd endured so much for her, for her family. Propping herself up on one elbow, she gazed down into his eyes. "You got lost?"

Jacob, who was lying back looking up at the ceiling, hesitated and then said, "No, not lost. I had another visit from my *inua*."

"From *Kegluneq*," she repeated softly, her eyes widening slightly. "But how? You didn't sleep out there, did you?"

He knew she was recalling the story he'd told that night so many weeks ago. Still, he looked at her swiftly, surprised at her ready acceptance of so non-western a concept. Her belief filled him with a strange contentment.

"No, but the visit seemed dreamlike anyway. I knew the dogs were running and could see the storm, yet the cold wasn't there. And it was very bright."

"Bright? As in sunny?"

He nodded. "My *inua* showed me the Raven and another body yet unnamed."

"Your sister," she breathed. Siksik had told them her *inua* was the Raven. "And Sharon."

Ann smiled, truly overwhelmed by the events that had transpired in the past twenty-four hours. Jacob had risked his life to save her daughter. A lump formed in her throat and she felt her eyes burn. She had to say it, had to tell him.

"I love you," she whispered softly, her eyes searching his. What they'd experienced together was more than she'd ever even dreamed possible. No matter what happened come spring, Ann knew that for her at least, the decision had been made. She loved him. And because she loved him, she wanted him to know.

She stared at him. His expression was guarded, the slight flinch in the muscles of his legs telegraphing his reaction to her announcement.

Disappointment flooded her heart and she looked quickly away lest he see the tears gathering in her eyes. She should have expected it. Nevertheless the reality hurt. Purposefully she moved away from his embrace. That he let her go was just another pinprick. Reaching for the T-shirt he'd so feverishly discarded mere moments ago, she pulled it on, then scooted to her side of the bed and stood, forcing her mind to where it should have been all along.

"I need to call the hospital and check on Sharon."

"Ann." Jacob watched her warily as she crossed the beige carpet to the phone by the dresser. She'd rolled away so abruptly he felt cold, alone. He remained where he was, his heart heavy with dread. "Ann . . . I don't know what to say."

"Then don't. I didn't ask you to say anything," Ann replied evenly.

Jacob caught a glimpse of her face, strained and pale, as she cradled the receiver to her ear and punched in the numbers that would connect her with the hospital. Her expression was controlled, remote, as if she'd somehow shut him out. He knew his failure to return her declaration of love had hurt her, but he honestly didn't know what else he could have done. He *did* love Ann, but would never tell her. Knew that if he did, he'd only cause her more pain.

And that was something he couldn't bear.

This way there would be no choice. Without his declaration, Ann was free to tend Sharon, free to leave in the spring. He wouldn't stop her; refused to even think of binding her love. She'd said she wouldn't use emotional blackmail on him. Well, he wouldn't use it on her, either. Sharon hadn't adapted to Twilight and his peoples' customs as Patrick had. Likely, Ann wouldn't want to stay if Sharon was truly unhappy, nor would he want her to. There would be no happiness in Ann's having to choose between her daughter and him. He shivered a little with cold, realizing that once again he walked a narrow middle ground, only now Ann's needs were on one side, his on the other.

"Fine, Dr. Cobb. I'll be there as soon as I can." Instead of replacing the receiver, Ann quickly punched in another number. She kept her eyes averted from Jacob's still form as she waited for a reply. "Billy? Ann. We made it safely to Anchorage and everyone's fine." She paused, listening. "Yes. I just talked with her doctor. Sharon's going to be all right. I'll be going to the hospital to see her in a few minutes. Tell everyone, okay? And give Patrick a hug."

Jacob's eyes narrowed at Ann's choice of words. *She'll* be there? Did she intend going alone?

"Billy, it's all right. Now stop worrying about it." Again, she paused. "No, I don't know when we'll be back, but I'll call when I get a better idea . . . Sure, I'll tell him. Bye."

Ann slowly replaced the receiver. She briefly thought about passing Jacob by on her way to the bathroom, but she couldn't. It wasn't his fault he couldn't love her. She'd accepted the risk involved, knew he cared for her in his own way. Only it wasn't enough. Still, she hadn't the heart to be so deliberately cruel. Not after what he'd risked last night.

"Billy says hello. He apologized again for everything that's happened."

Jacob nodded, though he knew Ann wouldn't see it. She was still avoiding looking directly at him. "And the doctor? Sharon's all right?"

"Yes. At least, she's been conscious for some time now and is responding to treatment. The doctor said we can go in anytime we want."

Jacob watched her closely. After a moment, when it seemed she wasn't going to add anything else, he snapped back the covers and moved to the edge of the bed, totally forgetting his state of undress until Ann's startled gasp made him pull up short. He remained seated, though he followed the direction of her gaze.

Jacob sat very still, experiencing a flow of hot need at the unwilling desire in her eyes that couldn't be denied or hidden. Ann's high color told him she'd also recognized the fact.

"Go take your shower," he ordered roughly. The pain of his arousal forestalled softening the request.

She didn't move. Ann knew he hadn't expressed his feelings out loud, but the fever in his eyes as they burned into hers spelled out more than like. At least that was what she wanted to believe, needed to belive.

"Ann, please. If you're going to shower, go now."

The air between them crackled with electricity. Indecisive, Ann still didn't move. She wanted to go to him and yet . . .

Jacob observed the confusion in her eyes. He'd done exactly what he'd just decided he wouldn't do: place her in a position of having to decide between him and Sharon. Damn. He gazed at her, wanting to get up and enfold her in his arms, knowing that she'd want that, too. Only it wouldn't be right.

"I'll be fine, Ann," he spoke softly, pained by the raw ache in her eyes. "Go take your shower. Sharon's waiting."

Chapter Eighteen

"Dr. Cobb!" Ann recognized Sharon's physician. Picking up her pace, she hurried to the kiosk, where the doctor stood conferring with a nurse. "How is Sharon?"

"She's going to be all right, Mrs. Elliot. There's no longer any need to be anxious." The doctor's glance shifted between Ann and Jacob. "Why don't we go into the lounge and I'll fill you in."

They walked down a wide hallway to a small U-shaped alcove, lined with brown plastic seats and a large rectangular table strewn with magazines. "Sit down, please. And stop looking so upset. She's fine, really she is. In fact, I'd say that right now she looks better than you two do."

"So there's no problem if we go in and see her?" Ann asked, sitting down. "She's awake?"

"Yes, by all means, go in and cheer her up. We've thoroughly examined her. She's weak, but that's expected, given what she's been through."

"And the blackout?" Ann pressed, needing to make sure everything really was all right. "Is that normal, too?"

"In some cases, yes," the doctor answered. "Depending on the length of exposure, of course. In Sharon's case, we've given her some shots—"

"Shots? What for?"

"Food supplements, mostly. The lab reports showed her very low on some of the essentials, especially vitamin B." She paused, looking at each of them in turn. "Has she been under any undue stress lately?"

Ann felt Jacob's hand engulf hers. As before, it gave her the strength she needed. "Sharon's been through a lot of changes. Especially this past year. I've tried making her eat balanced meals, but . . ."

"But she's a teenager, right?" Dr. Cobb smiled sympathetically, noting Ann's dejection. "Don't be too rough on yourself, Mrs. Elliot. Teenagers are a species unto themselves. Believe me, I know. I have one of my own, and sometimes I'm not sure where he gets the energy to do the things he does given the food he puts in his mouth when I'm not around."

When it looked as if Ann wasn't going to say anything, Jacob took over. "What should we do?"

"I'd say that for the next few months at least, you need to watch her diet more closely. One of the reasons she didn't respond as quickly as we'd hoped to our treatments last night was the fact that her little body is just worn out. She didn't have the necessary energy reserves to help us speed her recovery."

"But she's fine?" Jacob persisted.

"Almost as good as new, I'd say. However, when we release her—which will hopefully be tomorrow sometime—I'll write you a prescription for some intense vitamin supplements. Those ought to balance out her system and give her body a chance to recover fully." She stood. So did they. "Were there any other questions? No? Then why not go on in and visit her? I'm sure she's looking forward to it."

"Thank you, Doctor." Ann smiled sincerely. "You've been a great help."

"All in a day's work," Dr. Cobb remarked jokingly as she left them.

They strode silently down the hallway toward Sharon's room, Ann worried about the next few minutes. Now that Sharon was safe, what should she say to her? How should she react? Running away had been a crazy thing to do. Not only had she risked her life, but also Siksik's and Jacob's, and the ten or so others who had searched for her. At the very least, Ann knew, Sharon would need to apologize.

But that was only the half of it. What about the trial? And the fact that she'd been caught drinking? Ann chewed on her lower lip, distressed. She missed Jacob's concerned glance. As he held the door for her to pass through, his arm forestalled her.

"Before you go in..." His voice trailed off uncertainly. Ann waited. Jacob eyed her with resignation. "Look, I know it's none of my business, but...well, now wouldn't be a good time to discipline Sharon about everything that's been happening. She's probably sick to her stomach, scared about what you'll say."

It didn't surprise her that Jacob had discerned her thoughts. Since the storm, she'd felt particularly attuned to him. Apparently, so did he to her.

"I know. I'll wait until I get her home again." Decided, she ducked under Jacob's arm. "Good morning, sweetheart." Ann forced a smile into her voice as she entered the semiprivate room and walked to Sharon's bedside. Leaning over, she kissed her daughter's forehead. "Jacob and I were just with Dr. Cobb. The results are in and you'll be just fine, thank God."

Sharon turned her face toward the wall.

Unnerved, Ann's glance switched anxiously back to Jacob.

"You want some privacy?" He motioned with his head. "I can wait outside."

Ann nodded, unaware her eyes conversely begged him to stay. He paused, his indecision equally obvious, but then he looked over at Sharon's tense shoulders and quietly left. When the door whooshed closed behind him, Ann paused, uncertain how to begin. Reaching out, she gently stroked her daughter's hair. Sharon flinched and drew away.

"It's not the end of the world, you know, Sharon," Ann began tentatively, her mind on the trial and the council's decree. "You'll see, the months will go by faster than you think. We'll get you on a diet of good food and exercise and before you know it, you'll feel a lot better."

"You know then." Sharon swung back. Her cheeks were tracked with tears, but her eyes were relieved. "And you don't mind?"

"Of course I mind," Ann replied, unaware Sharon referred to her pregnancy. "Drinking that beer was foolish. You know the law. If it hadn't been for Jacob and the way he defended you, we might not even be returning to Twilight. And running away like that was dangerous. But right now, what's most important to me is your health. And the doctor says you're recovering just fine."

"And the baby? What did she say about the baby?"

Ann felt the room tilt. Abruptly she sat down on the bed. "Baby?" She looked at her daughter. "What baby? Are you saying you think you're pregnant?"

Sharon's eyes filled with tears at her mother's obvious shock. "You said you knew."

It was several moments before Sharon's sobs penetrated Ann's daze.

"Sharon, honey, you've got to calm down. Remember what the doctor said." Automatically Ann scooted forward on the bedside and enfolded her daughter in her arms. They rocked together, holding each other tightly until the sobs lessened to occasional hiccups. "Better?" She reached toward the table beside Sharon's bed and plucked a tissue from a box on the bed stand. "Here, mop up."

Sharon accepted the tissue. Ann took the time to control her own rolling emotions. My God, what more was she going to have to withstand? First the alcohol, then the storm and now this. Sharon thought she was pregnant? By whom? Billy? Jimmy? Ann groaned. She hadn't even known her daughter was . . . she swallowed and forced herself to mentally verbalize the thought. She hadn't known her daughter was sexually active. Just thinking about what could have happened struck fear in her heart.

"Is that what's been bothering you for so long? You thought you were pregnant?"

Sharon nodded.

"Well, you aren't. The doctor said nothing about your being pregnant. Understand, Sharon? You're not going to have a baby."

"I'm not?"

Mother and daughter eyed each other. Then Ann shook her head.

"Then why have I been throwing up all the time? I couldn't eat anything and I've been losing weight. I even missed two periods."

Ann sighed tremulously. Her heart was still beating hard. "Honey, why didn't you come to me?"

Sharon's eyes squeezed shut. A tear tracked down her cheek. "Because I figured you'd hate me," she said in a small weak voice.

"Hate you!" Ann reached for her daughter's hands. They were cold and trembling slightly. "I could never hate you, sweetheart. I love you. I love you so much it hurts."

Sharon hung her head. "I should have told you that time we talked about you and Dad," she mumbled.

"Then why didn't you?" Ann asked gently.

"Scared, I guess. Every time I even mentioned Jimmy, you hit the roof."

"I did not!"

"See!" Sharon's eyes filled with tears again.

Immediately Ann backed off. "Well, okay, maybe I did get upset, but it's just that I was afraid of him." The words surprised Ann as much as they did Sharon. "Remember how I told you your Dad was in high school?"

Sharon sniffed. "Yeah, sort of wild, a real stud muffin. So?"

"Well, that's what Jimmy reminded me of. How your Dad was when he was Jimmy's age. I was terrified you'd get carried away and make a mistake."

Ann watched her daughter for a moment, then forced the most important question out of her mouth. "Did Jim use any kind of birth control. Did you?"

"No." Sharon's face flamed. "We did some heavy... but we didn't... he didn't really... you know."

Ann blinked. "He didn't? You mean you're still a virgin?"

"Mom!"

"Sharon, listen to me," Ann replied, her heart fairly skipping with relief. She'd been given a second chance. "If you're old enough to do it, you're old enough to discuss it." She eyed her daughter sternly. "When we get home, we're going to sit down and have a long talk about this stuff. I should have done it a long time ago, but I guess time got away from me."

"I'm sorry, Mom."

"So am I, Sharon, but sometimes, sorry isn't good enough. You need to make sure you're protected, too."

"Believe me, I'm not ready to go through this again."

"I don't want you to ever go through this again. From now on, you're going to be responsible. And I'm not just talking about sex, young lady."

Sharon hung her head. "I know," she mumbled, then looked up. "What I don't understand is why I felt like I was pregnant. And why I missed my periods."

"It's got to do with stress. It's not abnormal for some women to miss a month or two when they're under a lot of pressure."

"Boy, can I relate to that."

"You're not planning on writing or seeing Jimmy anymore are you?" Opening the clasp of her purse, she pulled out a letter. "I found this last night," she began hesitantly. "It must have been stuffed in one of your drawers back home. When I packed, I just sort of crammed anything I could lay my hands on into two suitcases." She handed it over.

Tears welled again in Sharon's eyes. "Did you...read it?"

"Yes. I'm sorry, sweetheart. I know it must hurt."

"Why doesn't he want me? Why?" Sharon's gaze was anguished.

"Honey, boys like that aren't much for long distance relationships," she began. "But is it really so bad living in Twilight?"

"No, not really. I just thought...you know...with a baby and all ..."

Ann hugged her again. "I'd never, ever send you away. Do you understand me, Sharon?" She pulled back and looked straight into her daughter's eyes. "What happens to you, happens to me. I love you."

They looked into each other's eyes, really communicating for the first time in months. Then Sharon's lashes dropped.

"What about Jacob? Do you love him, too?"

Ann sat back, wondering what to say. "You know he's the one who found you and Siksik, don't you?"

"Yeah."

"Why do you think he did that?"

"I don't know. Siksik was out there," she mumbled, dropping her eyes again.

"Only because she's your friend, and she was afraid for you. So was Jacob."

She remembered the fear in his eyes. Fear for Sharon. Fear for Siksik. Fear for himself. Yet despite it all, he'd ventured out, facing his own personal nightmare. Tears gathered in her eyes.

Forget it. He doesn't love you, remember? If he did, he would have told you so this morning.

"Sharon, he went out there knowing he could get lost again just like he did three years ago. I'd say he must care for you a lot to go through something like that again."

Forty minutes later, when she finally left Sharon's room, Jacob was still waiting. His gaze traveled over her face, seeing her pain. Ann turned away, too drained to protest when his arm encircled her waist and he led her out to a waiting cab that drove them directly to the hotel. As he keyed open the door, she moved quietly into the room. She and her daughter had come a long way in the past hour, but they still had a long way to go. Once back in Twilight they would have to face Sharon's punishment, and she intended making time during those at-home hours to have a serious discussion about sex. Sharon had come too close to making a mistake that would have been tragic.

"Ann? Why don't you get some more sleep? You look about ready to drop. I think I'll go out awhile," Jacob said suddenly.

Ann nodded, aware he'd been as silent and preoccupied as she had been.

"We'll talk later."

Not until she heard the click in the door did she lie down on the bed and cry.

When Ann woke, it was dark. She padded into the bathroom, intent on making herself presentable before she returned to the hospital for evening visiting hours. Just as she was brushing her hair, she heard the lock click.

Jacob.

Immediately her eyes flew to the mirror. Disgusted with herself, she slapped off the light and followed his stiff form into the main room. When he turned, Ann swallowed a gasp. He looked miserable. Yet there was an icy determination about him, as if he'd made some decisions.

"You look better," he said as he unzipped his parka and laid it across a table. "I called the hospital. Sharon will be released tomorrow morning."

"Thank goodness." Ann sagged down onto the bed.

Jacob sat on a chair. "I've been talking with Dr. Cobb. She indicated that the best thing for Sharon would be plenty of rest and then a gradual program of exercise."

"Exercise?" Ann got up, pacing the small area of carpet in front of the bed. "What's she supposed to do? Run around the house a hundred times?"

Frowning, Jacob studied her worried features. "Sharon's confinement is to the school and her home. But given her health, I feel the council would agree that school means all of the facilities available there, not just the classrooms."

"You're talking about the gym," she said as she continued pacing. She realized she was feeling nervous and on edge with Jacob, but not nearly as crushed as she had felt only hours earlier. The sleep had restored some sense of balance; her mind was working more clearly. She shot a guilty look at Jacob. Despite her behavior, he'd continued to concern himself in her family's affairs. The knowledge of his support dimmed the pain of his rejection. Maybe it was time they talked. She sat down.

"Ann. I love you."

Floored, Ann forgot what she'd been about to say. Her hands flew to her throat. "But this morning you didn't say anything when I told you that I loved you."

"I know and believe me, if I could have, I would."

"Jacob...I don't understand," she said, her voice all but gone. She gazed at him, stunned. "You *love* me?"

Jacob rose from the chair and sat down beside her on the bed, capturing her hands within his. "Ann, I never told you this, but on the day you arrived, I had a premonition."

"What?"

"I had a feeling that something would happen that day, something that would change my life. Oh, Ann," he murmured before drawing her into his arms. "*You* were that something. You and your family have changed my life. Your love has changed me. I do love you."

Tenderly placing his lips on hers, Jacob held her tightly, feeling the fierce pounding of her heart. Slowly but surely, as the shock of his revelation faded, her own lips began to move beneath his. Her light, tentative caresses warmed his heart, the softness of her hands as they entangled in the hair at his nape making him groan with delight.

"I was so afraid," Jacob whispered against her lips.

"But why, when you knew I loved you?"

"But how much?" He shook his head. "Enough to live beside me day in and day out in Twilight? Patrick likes it, but what about Sharon? They're your children, your life. I didn't want to put you in a position where you'd have to choose between us."

Tears gathered in her eyes. "Then why have you told me this now?"

"Because I realized last night that all the arguments in the world wouldn't change how I feel about you. I understand that you're *kass'aq* and it doesn't matter. I hope you can adapt to a life in Twilight, but if you can't, if Sharon can't, then I'll move. Regardless of what happens, I want you to be my wife."

Ann drew in a sharp breath. "Oh, Jacob!"

Hungrily they kissed, falling back on the bed as their caresses increased in intensity. After a while Ann drew back, staring down at him in wonder.

"I feel so awful," she whispered, brushing back a lock of his hair. "When I think of all you've done for me..." She kissed the hand that reached up to caress her cheek. "Jacob...tell me. What about Lia's death? Have you come to terms with it?"

His hand slipped under her chin. "*Kegluneq* showed me the answer," he replied solemnly. "I did my best, Ann. What happened wasn't my fault. He helped me to see that they chose their own paths just as I chose mine." He pulled her over on top of him. "You haven't answered. Will you be my wife?"

"I want to...but I think you were right. We should wait. You want a united family and so do I. If we rush into this and it winds up making you unhappy, I couldn't bear it. And I also don't want to force you to live away from your home and your people. Give me some time. Give Sharon some time." Her gaze searched his. "Okay?"

Swallowing his disappointment, he nodded. "We'll work it out."

Chapter Nineteen

Jacob leaned against the door frame of Ann's office. "How long do you think you'll be?"

"At least a couple of hours. Three, tops," Ann replied with a quick glance at her watch. She turned and flipped open the S.A.T. preparation book she'd had Jacob purchase last October. So much had happened since then. It was February now, and Billy and two other students would fly to Anchorage to take the test the following day. "Billy is so nervous! I couldn't say no when he asked me to help him cram in a few more hours."

"Are you sure he's the nervous one?" Moving forward, Jacob settled himself on the edge of her desk, drawing her gently into his arms. "Ann, relax. You've done a great job. More than anyone could ask of a teacher."

"Maybe, but you know what's at stake. He wants this so much." She sighed, accepting Jacob's kiss. Immediately the tensions of the day eased and she relaxed. When Jacob kissed her or just held her close, everything faded into insignificance. It was always this way, she reflected. Which was why, after all they'd come through together—the trip to Tununak, the trial and the storm—Ann didn't want to think about spring. Spring meant the end of her contract.

"I just hope he's not disappointed."

"There's no guarantee he won't be. But after what he's been through these last few months, I bet he's just grateful his father didn't refuse to let him take the test at all." He hugged her. "And he's got you to thank for that."

Ann shrugged. "Billy's only seventeen. So he made a mistake. At least he owned up to it. All I did was make John realize that his son shouldn't have to spend the rest of his life paying for one admittedly irresponsible action. Besides, I just hated to see all his effort wasted. He studied so hard."

"I know. And I'm sure John knows it, too. Otherwise he'd never have agreed to let Billy attend college if he receives a scholarship."

"That is exciting, isn't it?" Ann smiled happily. "When Billy gets to U.C.L.A., he can try out for the basketball team."

"You're that positive he'll score well?"

She nodded. "It's his dream. I doubt he's willing to ruin what may be his last option."

"Well, whatever happens, at least Billy will know he gave it his best shot."

He gave her a hug. "I got a call from the lieutenant governor this afternoon."

"You did?" she asked, anger creeping into her voice. "I hope you told him you'll go to court if necessary," Ann muttered. "That man can be so irritating! You've been lobbying for months now. If he hasn't gotten the message that the villagers are united—"

"He did," Jacob broke in. "He called to appoint me to his subsistence committee." He planted a quick kiss on her lips.

"He what?" She squealed with excitement, jumping up from her chair and smothering Jacob with kisses. "You know what that means don't you? You'll be representing the interests of the Yup'ik. You'll be in on formulating the state's future policy regarding subsistence! Have you told Ben and Mark?"

"Yes. They're both happy. The legislators may not let us become a tribe, but now that we're represented on the committee, our concerns will be heard. I'll make sure of it."

"I know you will, Jacob," Ann murmured. "We all have a lot of faith in you."

As Jacob's lips once again settled on Ann's, he couldn't help wondering what the next few months would bring. Though he'd told Ann he'd leave Twilight if necessary, he knew if given a choice, he'd rather remain. He lifted his mouth. "Forget studying, come over to my place for a while and help me celebrate," he coaxed, dropping quick little kisses along her nape. Beneath his lips, he felt the increased surge of her pulse.

"Jacob, much as I'd like to join you, I did promise Billy."

With Sharon almost always being at home, arranging private time was difficult. She loved Jacob and wanted him desperately, but she had to admit that it was a bit embarrassing to be seen coming from his house in the middle of the day, or late at night. She sighed, knowing that although he hadn't pressed her, Jacob was waiting for her to make a move.

"There isn't a whole lot you're going to accomplish between now and tomorrow anyway," he persisted, running his hands down her spine to the rounded curve of her buttocks. "Besides, I thought Siksik was helping him study."

"Depends on what you call help." Ever since Siksik had performed the Woman Of The Sea Dance, Billy's eyes had indeed been opened. They were constantly together and Siksik was understandably on top of the world. "I got the distinct impression he really wanted to work tonight."

"Is there a message for me in there somewhere?" Chuckling, he released her and stood, a resigned expression on his face. "Just so he doesn't burn himself out. And the same goes for you, too," he growled a soft warning. "Hurry home." With another quick kiss, he turned and exited the school building.

Jacob knew that it was almost evening, yet the Arctic sun was already staking claim to the land. It shone for longer periods of time now, its increasing strength a testament to the fact that soon it would be spring.

Before Ann's arrival in Twilight, he'd always looked forward to the season of rebirth. This spring, however, he felt no joy and the sight of the golden sunset glinting off the Bering Sea as it churned and broke from its long winter sleep didn't quite lift his heart. To him the season meant an end, not a beginning. Ann's contract expired next month and, just yesterday, Patrick had told him she'd received a letter offering her a full-time job in Anchorage come fall.

Ann hadn't mentioned it and he hadn't asked. Since returning home from the hospital with Sharon, they hadn't discussed "the future." He'd thought about it, dreamt about it, but he hadn't actually asked her about her plans.

He entered the house. Sharon looked up from her homework.

"Hi. Mom's not home yet."

"I know," Jacob remarked, removing his parka and boots. "Billy asked her to help him study a few more hours before the test tomorrow."

"I thought Siksik was doing that."

Jacob smiled and eased into the recliner he'd repaired and reupholstered. "So did I. Too distracting, I guess."

"No kidding," she drawled, nibbling absently on the eraser at the end of her pencil. "You hungry? Patrick said he was going to eat at Paul's tonight. I could fix you something if you want."

The last few months had changed her, Jacob acknowledged. The heavy makeup and wild hairstyles were gone. She'd grown up, matured. In fact, in the time they'd been back, he'd witnessed an overall improvement. Her reserve toward him had vanished. She and Patrick didn't fight anymore. She'd also made her peace with Billy, was eating well and exercising regularly. Siksik had even coaxed her into joining Mary's dance class. All in all, and except for her confinement, of course, she seemed to enjoy her life in Twilight.

"I'm not really hungry right now, but thanks for asking."

"You're thinking of Mom, aren't you?"

Jacob shoved one hand through his hair. "Among other things," he confessed, shifting his gaze to the half completed straw basket on the end table. He picked it up. "Yours?"

"Siksik's teaching me." She left the dinette, coming to sit on the couch, curling both feet beneath her. "It's all right, you know."

"What?"

"You and Mom," she began gruffly, absently twirling a stray curl around her finger. "Patrick and I talked it over last night, and it's kickin' with us, if it's kickin' with you guys."

His heart pounded. Had he heard right? Was she telling him she approved of their relationship? He sat forward. "Just what are you saying?"

"You love Mom, don't you?"

He didn't hesitate. "Yes. I love your mother very much."

She shrugged. "Then what's the problem. Why don't you two get married? She loves you, too, you know. Anyone can see that."

Jacob was stunned. "You don't mind my loving your mother?"

"At first I did," she confessed, embarrassed. Leaning forward, she picked up the basket and started weaving the grass stems into the coil. "But that was because I wanted to go back to Anchorage again."

Jacob kept his expression open. "And now?"

She shrugged. "Things are different. I'm different." A moment passed, then she looked across at him curiously. "You know Mom got a new job offer don't you?"

"Patrick told me," he answered, and then, even though he really didn't want to know, he asked anyway. "What do you think?"

"It would be nice, but Siksik's been telling me all the neat stuff you guys do during spring and summer. I was sort of looking forward to that."

For the second time in so many minutes, Jacob gazed at her, completely stunned. "But what about your friends, and movies and shopping? Don't you miss all that?"

"Sure, but not as much as I thought. And we get movies here, too. And I have friends."

Jacob couldn't believe it. Joy flooded into his veins. He looked down at his watch, then up at Sharon. "I'm going to my house. When your mom gets back, will you tell her to come over?"

Sharon looked at him and grinned. He didn't bother hiding the excitement in his eyes. "Are there any special Yup'ik wedding dances?"

Later that evening Ann knocked tentatively on Jacob's door.

"Come in."

Ann entered. "Sharon said you wanted to see . . . me." Her voice trailed off as she stepped into the now familiar room. Jacob had turned off the electricity and a single *Naniq* lamp gave off a soft, muted light. The distinctive scent of burning seal oil filled the air. "Jacob? What's going on?"

He motioned her over to where he sat cross-legged on his polar bear rug. Beside him lay his tools and carvings.

"Something wonderful happened tonight," he began when she'd removed her jacket and boots and had made herself comfortable, mimicking his position. "Something surprising. Want to know what it is?"

His eyes smiled and seeing that, Ann relaxed. "Yes," she said.

Jacob's face grew serious, thoughtful. "Sharon gave me a present."

Ann was silent, waiting for Jacob to elaborate. She had something to tell him, too, but it could wait.

"She asked me if I loved you."

"She asked what?"

Jacob nodded, his eyes twinkling. "I said yes, of course. Then she asked me why we didn't get married since it was so obvious you loved me. When I asked her if she'd mind, she said no, that, in fact, she and Patrick discussed it between themselves and decided that our loving each other was 'kickin'' with them, so long as it was 'kickin'' with us."

"'Kickin',' huh?" Amazement filled Ann's voice and the look she gave Jacob was soft with love. How far Sharon had come. How far they all had.

She said, bemused, "Did they set a date for the wedding, too? I can hardly believe it. Sharon really didn't mind?"

Jacob chuckled and maneuvered so that he was lying on his side on the rug. Gently he patted the space next to him. She immediately cuddled down beside him, for a moment pressing her face against his chest and hugging him tightly.

"You're right, it was a beautiful present," she whispered softly, raising her hand and placing it over his heart. Tears filled her eyes. Tears of relief, of happiness. "After all we've gone through . . . she didn't mind."

"That's right. I asked whether she'd miss Anchorage, too, and you know what she said?"

Ann laughed. "If you'd asked me that last October I could have told you, but now . . . ? No way."

He laughed, too. "She said she didn't want to leave, that she was looking forward to spring." His eyes focused on her inviting mouth as he realized that he was talking too much. Leaning forward, he slowly covered her lips with his, drinking in their sweetness.

Silence filled the room as the kiss went on. They held each other tightly, murmuring endearments and assurances, touching and sighing as they caressed and explored each other and the wonder and freedom of their love.

And when passion's call became more urgent, they moved as one, removing each other's clothing with a reverence and a solemnity that spelled out how truly special this occasion was for them. It marked the start of a new life together.

"I know I've said it lots of times," Jacob whispered much later when their union was complete and they lay side by side in the lamplight. "But I'll say it again. I love you, Ann, and I want to share my life with yours. I want to love you and care for you and share your problems and your joys. Will you marry me?"

"Yes," she whispered back. Later she'd tell him about the offer she'd received, the offer that she'd turned down.

Reaching around behind him, Jacob grabbed a small black box. Silently he handed it to her.

"What's this?"

"Open it," he said softly. Ann did as he'd asked. "Oh, Jacob!" she exclaimed. "What a beautiful pin!" She held the intricate carving up against the lamplight. "It's exquisite. When in the world did you make this?"

"After the first time I told you I loved you."

She looked at him searchingly. "In Anchorage," she declared, running her finger along the thousands of tiny etchings making up the fur of the two wolf heads, one larger and behind the other, smaller one.

"You know that *Kegluneq* is my *inua*." His gaze searched hers. She nodded. "He's yours, too."

Ann drew in a sharp breath. "Mine?"

"That night out in the storm, when *Kegluneq* came and showed me the way, with him was another."

Ann abruptly recalled the clarity with which she'd seen him in her mind's eye, the certainty with which she'd known that Jacob had found Siksik and Sharon and was coming home. In a strange, mysterious way, it made sense. He was her mate and she was his.

Jacob leaned over and gave Ann a lingering kiss. As her lips met his and he tasted her amazement, he also felt her calm acceptance. Soon they would be married. Soon they would build a new home, a larger place for a growing family. This spring would indeed be a time of renewal and rebirth. And though he would continue to walk the middle ground, now he had a companion, a woman whose needs met his and whose needs he wanted to meet. Together they would face the challenges of the future, melding the traditional with the modern, the past with the present.

"Let's go tell the kids." He stood up, extending his hand. His body stood proud and steady and erect as he enjoyed the sweet promise of her glance. He smiled mischievously, drawing her into his arms.

"We'll tell the kids later," he murmured huskily.

"Much later," she echoed.

* * * * *

TAKE A WALK ON THE DARK SIDE OF LOVE

October is the shivery season, when chill winds blow and shadows walk the night. Come along with us into a haunting world where love and danger go hand in hand, where passions will thrill you and dangers will chill you. Come with us to

In this newest short story collection from Silhouette Books, three of your favorite authors tell tales just perfect for a spooky autumn night. Let Anne Stuart introduce you to "The Monster in the Closet," Helen R. Myers bewitch you with "Seawitch," and Heather Graham Pozzessere entice you with "Wilde Imaginings."

Silhouette Shadows™
Haunting a store near you this October.

Silhouette
SPECIAL EDITION™

VOWS
A series celebrating marriage
by Sherryl Woods

To Love, Honor and Cherish—these were the words that three generations of Halloran men promised their women they'd live by. But these vows made in love are each challenged by the tests of time....

In October—Jason Halloran meets his match in *Love* #769;

In November—Kevin Halloran rediscovers love—with his wife—in *Honor* #775;

In December—Brandon Halloran rekindles an old flame in *Cherish* #781.

These three stirring tales are coming down the aisle toward you—only from Silhouette Special Edition!

SESW-1

It's Opening Night in October—
and you're invited!
Take a look at romance with a
brand-new twist, as the stars
of tomorrow make their
debut today!
It's LOVE:
an age-old story—
now, with
*WORLD PREMIERE
APPEARANCES* by:

Patricia Thayer—Silhouette Romance #895
JUST MAGGIE—Meet the Texas rancher who wins this pretty
teacher's heart…and lose your own heart, too!

Anne Marie Winston—Silhouette Desire #742
BEST KEPT SECRETS—Join old lovers reunited and see what
secret wonders have been hiding…beneath the flames!

Sierra Rydell—Silhouette Special Edition #772
ON MIDDLE GROUND—Drift toward Twilight, Alaska, with this
widowed mother and collide—heart first—into body heat
enough to melt the frozen tundra!

Kate Carlton—Silhouette Intimate Moments #454
KIDNAPPED!—Dare to look on as a timid wallflower blos-
soms and falls in fearless love—with her gruff, mysterious
kidnapper!

Don't miss the classics of tomorrow—
premiering today—only from

PREM

In the spirit of Christmas, Silhouette invites
you to share the joy of the holiday season.

Experience the beauty of Yuletide romance with Silhouette
Christmas Stories 1992—a collection of heartwarming stories by
favorite Silhouette authors.

JONI'S MAGIC by Mary Lynn Baxter
HEARTS OF HOPE by Sondra Stanford
THE NIGHT SANTA CLAUS RETURNED by Marie Ferrarella
BASKET OF LOVE by Jeanne Stephens

This Christmas you can also receive a FREE keepsake Christmas
ornament. Look for details in all November and December
Silhouette books.

Also available this year are three popular early editions of
Silhouette Christmas Stories—1986, 1987 and 1988. Look for these
and you'll be well on your way to a complete collection of the
best in holiday romance.

Share in the celebration—with Silhouette's
Christmas gift of love.

SX92